FATE'S
RANSOM

ALSO BY JEFF WHEELER

Nonfiction

Your First Million Words

The First Argentines Series

Knight's Ransom
Warrior's Ransom
Lady's Ransom
Fate's Ransom

The Grave Kingdom Series

The Killing Fog
The Buried World
The Immortal Words

The Harbinger Series

Storm Glass
Mirror Gate
Iron Garland
Prism Cloud
Broken Veil

The Kingfountain Series

The Poisoner's Enemy (prequel)
The Maid's War (prequel)
The Poisoner's Revenge (prequel)

FATE'S
RANSOM

THE FIRST ARGENTINES

JEFF
WHEELER

47NORTH

Text copyright © 2022 by Jeff Wheeler
All rights reserved.

No part of this book may be reproduced, or stored in a retrieval system, or transmitted in any form or by any means, electronic, mechanical, photocopying, recording, or otherwise, without express written permission of the publisher.

Published by 47North, Seattle

www.apub.com

Amazon, the Amazon logo, and 47North are trademarks of Amazon.com, Inc., or its affiliates.

ISBN-13: 9781542027427
ISBN-10: 154202742X

Cover design by Shasti O'Leary Soudant

Printed in the United States of America

In memory of
Travis Ashcraft

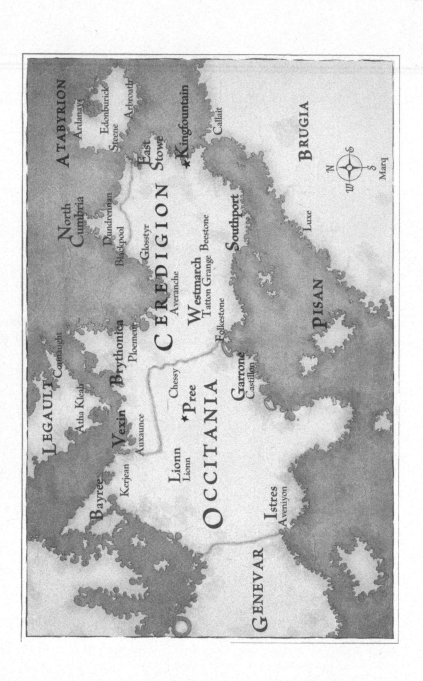

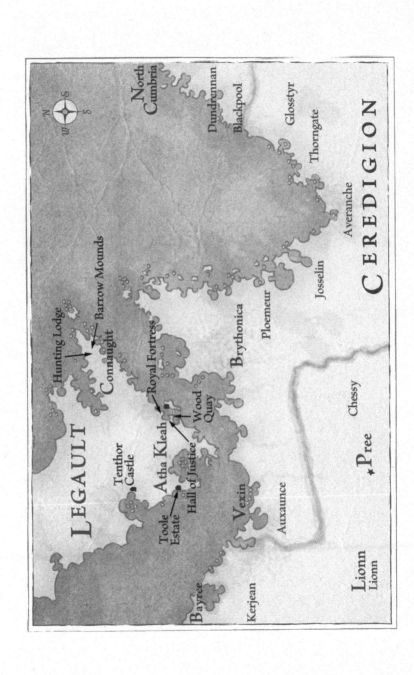

There's a saying in the Fair Isle—"May the dreams you hold dearest be those that come true." Yet it's my nightmares that haunt me and fill me with dread. I slept poorly last night, for in my sleep I was again a prisoner in the queen's tower in Kingfountain. And Jon-Landon, the prince, kept coming and trying to woo me. In the strange way of dreams, I knew I was married to Ransom, only I was not. Jon-Landon kept pressing me to accept him, to make him lord of Legault. And when I refused, he became angrier and more demanding, until I hurled myself from the tower window. I woke before hitting the stones.

It was a loathsome dream, and the dread of it worried in my stomach all day long. Now, at dusk, I gaze out the window of Connaught castle, wondering when Ransom will be home again. He's fighting a war with King Benedict, trying to reclaim the lands we have lost to the Occitanians, whose hunger for broadening their empire has brought so much pain to our people. Benedict is laying siege to Tatton Grange, and Ransom is trying to retake Josselin castle. Duke Kiskaddon is playing the scourge, ravaging the Occitanians' fields and lands.

I'm grateful it was only a dream. I'm grateful that Benedict became king and not the youngest Argentine. It would be a disaster if Jon-Landon ever wore the hollow crown.

—Claire de Murrow, Queen of Legault
Connaught Castle
A Midsummer's Eve

PROLOGUE

The Wizr Board

The stench of smoke choked the air, and the hiss of crossbow bolts came like the drone of angry bees. Ransom Barton gazed at the walls of Josselin castle—*his* castle—and felt anger burn inside him. The Occitanians' garrison was formidable, and each attack that day had been repulsed. It was a strategic castle, along the western border shared by Ceredigion, Occitania, and Brythonica. Seeing a banner with the Fleur-de-Lis hanging from the castle made him want to rip it down and burn it.

He stood solemnly, sweating beneath his armor on the hot summer day, watching as his men continued to lash together another siege ladder in preparation for the next assault. Crossbowmen lined the walls, taking aim and loosing arrows down on Ransom's soldiers, who had built pickets to protect themselves. Occasionally a shaft made it through and injured one of the men.

A rider came into the camp carrying a shield with the emblem of Prince Jon-Landon: three lions atop each other, the tallest on the top of the shield and the smallest on the bottom. It was a variation of King Benedict's standard of a single lion. Ransom had heard it said, in jest, that Jon-Landon had chosen three lions to represent himself and his two elder brothers. Privately, he suspected Jon-Landon had chosen three because Benedict had only chosen one.

"Where is Lord Ransom?" asked the newcomer with the shield.

"Over there," answered one of Ransom's men, pointing. "And get off your charger before you get shot at, you fool!"

Even as the words were spoken, a bolt whooshed past them and struck a nearby tree with a resounding thud. The knight dismounted without any haste, seemingly unaware or unaffected by the danger, and then walked over to where Ransom stood observing the castle from within the shelter of the trees.

"My lord duke," said the knight. "My name is Captain Faulkes."

Ransom had heard of the man. He was Jon-Landon's battle captain, the knight Benedict had assigned to keep Jon-Landon from getting himself killed in battle. A royal bodyguard. He looked too young for the job, for he was surely younger than Ransom, but then, age was not always a quantifier of ability.

"Why aren't you at the siege of Averanche?" Ransom asked the knight.

"It's all smoke and fire. They're keeping us within the walls. I'd rather be here where the real fighting is," said Faulkes, putting his gauntleted hands on his hips. "The prince asks you to send a hundred men to join him in retaking the castle."

"I don't have a hundred men to spare," Ransom said with a snort. "Did he ask the king for more men?"

"He did not," Faulkes said with a tired look. "For he knew the answer would be no. The king needs all he has to retake Tatton Grange."

"Just as I need all I have," Ransom said. "We don't have the funds Estian does. We can't hire mercenaries to join our ranks."

"Pity the ransom we paid was so high," Faulkes said, giving Ransom an accusatory look.

Ransom had negotiated the release of the king from his imprisonment in the Wartburg in Brugia. The amount was higher than any ransom that had previously been paid by any king. A hundred and fifty thousand livres. Some of the money had come to them as a windfall, but the rest had come directly from their coffers and put them sorely in debt.

"I don't have a hundred men to spare," Ransom said, ignoring the jab. "If the king bid me, I would find a way to do it, but I have a hard enough task as it is. We're about to make another run at the castle."

"Can I help?" Faulkes asked, gazing at the castle. "I'm in no hurry to go back. Especially knowing the answer will displease the prince."

Dawson, part of Ransom's mesnie, came up to him. "The ladders are all ready, my lord."

"Looks like I came at the right time," Faulkes said. "I'll tie up my horse and join the fight."

"As you will," Ransom said, although the man's attitude didn't impress him. If Ransom had been serving Jon-Landon, he would have returned with the news as soon as possible.

Ransom gave the order to prepare for the assault. Knights with broad shields prepared to lead the way, followed by those bearing long ladders with smaller shields perched atop. They'd be under a torrent of crossbow fire as they arranged them at the base of the wall.

On the cusp of the attack, Ransom found himself thinking of his wife, Claire, and his family in Legault. He felt a throb of longing to be with them instead of fighting the king's wars, but it was Benedict who'd allowed him to marry Claire, and he owed him everything, including his rank as Duke of Glosstyr. Loyalty bound him to do his king's bidding.

When the men were ready, Ransom gave the order to attack, and the three crews hastened out of the cover of the woods. The soldiers guarding the pickets had been alerted and quickly removed sections of the fencing so the crews could charge past them and throw the ladders up in three different places. Cries of alarm rose from the castle walls, and the defenders began to rally. Ransom watched in consternation as black shafts began to rain down on his men, clattering against shields and armor. But some found weak spots, the vulnerable gaps in the armor.

Ransom observed fitfully as his men charged toward the wall, the advance led by Dawson and others he trusted. He had deliberately resisted using trebuchets, both because he didn't want to reduce his own castle to rubble and because the king needed them at Averanche and Tatton Grange. Cries of pain and shouted curses came from Ransom's men as they jogged ahead under the onslaught.

He saw the first ladder clack against the wall as the knights began to position it. Once it was set, some began to scrabble up the length to reach the defenders atop the wall. He knew Dawson would be in the forefront, even though it was the most dangerous part of the charge. The young man was occasionally too brash for his own good, but Ransom admired his pluck and courage.

The second ladder went up and then the third. As Ransom watched, clenching his fist and tapping it against the tree trunk, he saw several Occitanians appear with long spears and hooks. One of them managed to snag the edge of a ladder and then shoved it backward, the weight it supported dragging it down. Ransom's mind went black with rage as he heard the groans from the impact. The soldiers at the pickets rose to get a better look, the anguish they felt obvious at any distance.

Ransom backed away from the tree and then whistled to get Captain Baldwin's attention.

"That was unlucky," Baldwin said, his head protected by a chain hood. "I'm going to send in another score of men to get that ladder back up."

"I'm going to lead the charge. Tell them to follow me."

"That's too risky," Baldwin said. "The king would—"

"I'm going!" Ransom barked. He lowered his visor and started to jog toward the wall. He heard Baldwin cry out for men to follow him, and a quick backward glance revealed there were more than a score coming up behind him. Ransom felt a crossbow bolt deflect off his armored arm, but it didn't even slow his pace. More shafts rained down on him, but he was too angry to care about the danger. When he reached the fallen ladder, he saw the knights pinned beneath it, twisting and groaning to free themselves from the weight. Ransom signaled to his men to grab it and help the wounded retreat.

Together, they hoisted the ladder up against the wall, and Ransom was the first to begin the climb. He had no shield himself because he fought with a bastard sword, which required two hands. His lungs burned for air, and his legs throbbed from exertion, but he ignored both sensations as he scrabbled up the ladder. One of the other ladder crews had made it onto the wall, and fighting had broken out. He had a glimpse of the shield with the three lions—somehow Faulkes had made it up before him and was already dispatching opponents with skill.

As Ransom reached the top, a man with a hook and pole approached and tried to upend his ladder. But he was high enough to grab the hook, and he pulled hard, sending the defender into the edge of the wall with a grunt of pain. He let go of the weapon before he could be pulled from his perch.

Three knights charged at Ransom as soon as he breached the wall. He drew the bastard sword, and his Fountain magic roared to life as he smashed into his opponents, knocking them back and barreling forward to provide room for those behind him. Down below, he saw more Occitanian knights trampling through his gardens.

"Dex aie! Dex aie!" he shouted. It was the battle cry of the Argentine family.

His sword bit into armor, eliciting a shriek of pain, and Ransom elbowed the second man, pivoted, then withdrew his blade and whirled around to cut down the third knight. He felt something jolt against him and a tingle of pain, but he was too ablaze with fury to sense it, and he knew the Raven scabbard he wore would begin to heal the wound immediately.

More knights of Ceredigion streamed up the ladder. The momentum was shifting. Some of the knights down below had begun to flee to the interior of the castle, which would make the castle harder to take. But if they could claim the outer walls of Josselin, and hold them, then it would only be a matter of time before the defenders were starved into submission.

And it was right then, in the thick of the battle, that he felt a grinding sensation in his soul, as if a boulder were being dragged. With the sensation came the immediate compulsion to go to Tatton Grange. He recognized the feeling instantly. The king's Wizr board had been activated. The board's powerful magic allowed the royal families represented by the pieces—the Argentines of Ceredigion and the Vertuses of Occitania—to summon their loyal supporters where they were most needed . . . and to keep watch on the other side's moves. Estian, the Occitanian king, had possessed it, but Ransom had stolen it from him.

Benedict had summoned him in the middle of the fight—a fight he *knew* he could win.

It made Ransom furious. He was so close to accomplishing his objective, to reclaiming the castle he'd lost to Estian. Part of him wanted to rebel against the order. But the mere thought made his Fountain magic shrivel. His power came through loyalty to the king, and any direct disobedience would strip him of his magic.

Silently cursing, Ransom looked around and then ordered his men to keep pressing onward. They needed to take the gatehouse so that they wouldn't have to scale the walls to get inside. Already his knights, led by Dawson, were fighting down the stairs leading to the interior. Ransom walked back to the wall, still gripping his bloodstained sword, and saw more knights emerging from the woods to join the attack.

Since he couldn't make it down one of the ladders—too many men were still coming up—he went down the stairs, following his rushing men. Dawson and the others had conquered the guards at the gatehouse, and a cheer went up when the iron door was thrust open.

It pained Ransom to walk away from the battle, from the sweetness of a possible victory, but he did. He returned to the camp, and Captain Baldwin approached him with a worried expression. Although Baldwin had once trained Ransom, back when both of them served Lord Kinghorn, Ransom's cousin, the man now served under him. Seeing him always served as a reminder of Ransom's long ties to the Argentine family, for it was Baldwin who had paid for Ransom's release from Lord DeVaux's dungeon at the bidding of Queen Emiloh.

"Are you injured?" Baldwin called out.

"No," Ransom answered. Despite the wound he knew he'd sustained, he couldn't feel any pain. The compulsion to leave was so powerful he found himself gritting his teeth. "I have to go to Tatton Grange."

"Now?" Baldwin asked with confusion.

Few people outside the royal family knew of the Wizr board's existence, so he couldn't explain the summons. Staying as close to the truth as possible, he said, "Yes. I want to take some men with me. I think the king is in trouble."

"Is that what the other captain told you?"

Ransom shouted to one of his squires to have his destrier, Dappled, saddled. "Be quick about it!" Turning back to Baldwin, he said, "No, he came on Jon-Landon's orders, asking for a hundred men. We can't spare them. I'll bring a score with me to go to the king."

"Why not fifty?" Baldwin suggested. "There are Occitanian knights rampaging everywhere in the borderlands. Best to be cautious."

"Fifty, then," Ransom agreed. "I'm going now."

"It's nearly sunset. Wait until morning."

But a feeling of dread pulsed through him, and suddenly he was sure the king *was* in trouble. This was no normal summons.

"I've got to ride now. Get the men ready."

"Aye, my lord."

In the fading light, the knights were assembled to ride for Tatton Grange. Dappled stamped impatiently as the others mounted. One of

Ransom's squires offered him a leather flask, and he accepted it and drank quickly.

Captain Faulkes strode up, his armor dented in a few places and smeared with dust and blood. "You're leaving?" he asked Ransom with a tinge of anger. "I couldn't believe it when I heard."

"I've been summoned to the king," Ransom said.

"What for?" Faulkes asked with a tone of impertinence.

Ransom gave him a hard look and didn't answer. Faulkes rubbed his mouth as he gazed at the company. "And you're taking men with you? Men you couldn't spare?"

"Return to your master," Ransom said curtly. "I'll not suffer your insolence any further."

Faulkes glared at Ransom and then shook his head and stormed off. Through his Fountain magic, Ransom could tell that the knight was highly trained. He'd fought hard during the campaign in the East Kingdoms. But there was a spot of darkness in his soul. It seemed to suck the light from the fading sky.

Dawson approached next, giving Faulkes a dismissive nod as the man passed him, then said to Ransom, "He's a brainless badger, isn't he?"

It was one of the terms that Claire liked to use, and Ransom appreciated its use in that moment. "It's true. Hold the gatehouse gate, Dawson. I'm hoping I won't be gone long. Take your orders from Captain Baldwin."

Dawson nodded, and Ransom could see from his disappointed look that he'd hoped to be placed in command. But he didn't argue. He was maturing. "Of course, my lord. Ride safely."

There was no questioning of Ransom's sudden departure. His men trusted him, and he counted on their obedience and discretion.

They rode all night long, trying to reach Tatton Grange by dawn. Some of the knights' horses went lame from the punishing pace, so they were down a tithe in men by the time they arrived at the king's camp. It was midmorning when they rode in, and the looks on everyone's faces showed grimness and defeat. Some of the knights shook their heads at Ransom with haunted expressions.

"What happened?" muttered one of Ransom's men.

Ransom dismounted Dappled—whose strength had far outlasted the other mounts—outside the king's pavilion. Although he was weary from the fighting the previous day and the all-night ride, he immediately marched to the tent and opened it.

The smell of sickness wafted to him at once.

King Benedict lay on a pallet, sweating profusely, his face pale but for the dark smudges under his eyes. The smudges weren't from lack of sleep. It was dried blood. The sight so viscerally reminded him of the deaths of Benedict's father and brother that his insides clenched with dread. He glanced at the king's barber, who knelt by the pallet, and the man gave him a helpless look. "He took a crossbow bolt in the shoulder yesterday," he said, his voice trembling. "I pulled it out straightaway, but it's infected. The king said . . . the king said he's been poisoned."

Ransom knew it to be true. His stomach shriveled as he knelt by the king's side, his hand falling to his Raven scabbard as the king's feverish eyes opened.

"Is that you, Ransom?"

Ransom gripped his hand. "I came. I felt the summons."

"Sir Gordon? Did he bring you the chest?"

Ransom wrinkled his brow. "I've seen no one. No one came." He looked around the tent and noticed his brother, Marcus, among the few gathered. The look of sadness and agitation on his brother's face showed they all knew the truth.

The king would soon die.

Ransom didn't think he could save him. He'd attempted to use the Raven scabbard to heal the Elder King, and it hadn't worked.

Benedict shut his bloody eyes. "She was here, Ransom," he croaked. "I saw her piece on the board."

Ransom knew what that meant. He referred to Lady Alix, the Fountain-blessed poisoner related to both the Argentines and the Vertuses. She'd killed Benedict's brother and his father, and now she'd given him a death sentence too. A feeling of helplessness and outrage thundered inside Ransom's heart. If she'd been there, he would have twisted her neck and killed her with his bare hands.

"I'm as weak as a pup," Benedict said.

Ransom glanced at Marcus. "Did you send for the queen dowager?"

"Aye," Marcus said. "But it's days to Kingfountain and back."

The king squeezed Ransom's hand, drawing his attention. "I'm dying, Ransom. I'm going to the Deep Fathoms . . . to be with my brother . . . my father." Benedict's fevered eyes bore into him.

Ransom swallowed and maintained a firm grip on the king's hand. "What is your will, my lord?"

Benedict coughed, and there were flecks of blood on his lips. "Estian has my nephew in Pree. He made Constance . . . marry one of his knights. The boy is lost to us, and Brythonica too. My brother is my heir. All of you are witnesses. Jon-Landon will be King of Ceredigion. Swear your loyalty to him. I beg of you. It is my will, my last command as your king."

Ransom squeezed harder, his stomach twisting with resentment. The other men he'd served—he'd believed in them, however flawed they had been. But Jon-Landon? He didn't know if he could serve such a man. He unbuckled the scabbard and laid it on Benedict's chest. The other men gathered wouldn't understand the significance of the gesture, but none questioned it. Ransom watched the raven sigil, hoping it would start glowing. It did not.

There was nothing else he could do to save the king.

Returning the scabbard to his belt, he bowed his head. The Fountain had made his duty known to him. He was meant to protect the Argentine line, to ensure Jon-Landon's unborn son rose to the throne. The boy's descendants would hearken the return of King Andrew's glory.

"I swear it," Ransom said firmly, looking Benedict in the eyes.

"I so swear," said the other knights and lords assembled in the pavilion.

The strength left Benedict's grip, and his head sagged to one side. "Good," he sighed. "Send someone to my brother. Tell him to come claim his crown. I want . . . to go into the river, Ransom. Not the palace. Here. Like my father. His curse won in the end."

Tears filled Ransom's eyes.

"My lord," said one of the knights, putting his hand on Ransom's shoulder. "Who should go tell Jon-Landon? May I?"

Ransom hardly knew the man who'd asked the question. He turned to his brother, Marcus. "Take your knights to Averanche. Tell Jon-Landon his brother is dying and to come at once."

Marcus nodded and left the tent without a word.

It was the last time Ransom saw his brother alive.

One of Ransom's knights arrived today. He didn't bear a written message for fear of it being intercepted by the Occitanians. The king is dead. The Wizr board is lost. It was an ominous message, even more so because ill tidings often come in threes.

—Claire de Murrow, Queen of Legault
Connaught Castle

CHAPTER ONE

Wounds of the Heart

t was the third time Ransom had waited for a king to die. Benedict was moved from his tent to the sanctuary of Our Lady at Fountainvault, where he lingered, suffered, and bled. At least Ransom did not hold the vigil alone this time. But he did take a moment to craft a note to Queen Portia, who had never returned to Kingfountain following the truce with the East Kingdoms. And now she never would.

The king's mother had raced from Kingfountain at breakneck speed and arrived to offer a little comfort. Emiloh sat by his deathbed, gripping his hand and stroking his brow. And then he was gone, his final ragged gasp a whisper of love to his mother before the Deep Fathoms reclaimed him. Ransom did not weep, but his heart weighed heavier than a boulder within his chest. Emiloh wiped her eyes on her velvet sleeve and then lifted the coverlet to cover her son's face. When she rose from the bed and looked at Ransom, her shoulders were hunched with grief and she looked to have aged ten years since the beginning of the ordeal.

"Would you walk with me, Ransom?" she asked.

He offered his arm and felt her frailty as she touched him. The constant pressure of worry and war had taken a toll on her. For a moment, she looked as if she might faint, and he paused. But she closed her eyes, breathed in through her nose, and then left the chamber with him and ventured into the deconeus's garden.

"I feel this moment keenly," Ransom said to her. "I can't imagine what you are enduring."

"Grief is an old friend," she told him. "We've long been companions. I will be all right. I'm glad you are here."

"Where else would I be?" Ransom said. "My duty is here."

She patted his arm. "There is much to discuss before Jon-Landon arrives. Still no word from Sir Gordon?"

Sir Gordon was the knight to whom Benedict had entrusted the Wizr set. He and the knights who rode with him had vanished.

"It's been three days," Ransom sighed. "I thought at first that we might have passed each other in the dark. I sent someone back to Josselin, and he's already returned with word from Captain Baldwin. Sir Gordon never arrived."

Emiloh's lips pursed. "Then we must assume it's been stolen. Alix must have guessed Bennett would send the Wizr set away after he was attacked. There was probably an ambush waiting for Sir Gordon and his knights. Bennett should have kept the board with him."

"He might have feared someone would infiltrate the camp," Ransom said. "Either way, it was the worst possible time for Estian to snatch it back. We're blind to his army now."

"Indeed. It won't be easy to win a war against an opponent who can see our every move." She shook her head ruefully. "We're at war with Occitania, and Brugia is in upheaval with Lord Gotz fighting to become king. Once again the world is in turmoil. It makes me long for gentler times, for when Gervase stepped down and we began our rule. How things have changed for the worse."

Ransom thought back to King Gervase, who had been like a father to him. Things hadn't been simple back then either. The hollow crown had beaten him into the ground.

The sound of riders approached, and they both turned their gazes. Had Jon-Landon come already? They were expecting his arrival imminently.

They walked back through the small orchard they'd been crossing and were soon joined by Duke Kiskaddon, who looked weary from the ride. His army had been menacing the Occitanian countryside, wreaking havoc and burning crops. He strode up to them forcefully and knelt before Emiloh.

"My lady, I bring my deepest sympathies," said the duke. His face was a mixture of emotions, but the predominant one was worry. Close in age to Benedict, he had been a loyal friend to the king and likely feared how the younger brother would treat him.

Ransom understood how he felt.

"Thank you, Hal," Emiloh replied. She touched his shoulder, and he rose.

"I came as soon as I heard the news," he said, his voice strong and full of energy. "I came too late. He's already gone."

"He died not long ago," she answered. "I'm glad you are here. You can help bear his boat into the waters."

"We're not taking the body back to Kingfountain?"

Emiloh shook her head. "This is where he asked to be set free. Near his father."

Kiskaddon nodded, his mouth turned down at the edges. "Bennett was a good man. A good friend."

"He thought highly of you as well. He spoke of you, before the end."

Ransom had always been in awe of the care Emiloh took for others' feelings.

"I am grateful, madam, that you came in time to bid him farewell. He told me many times how much he regretted not doing more to free you from the tower."

Her husband had kept her there, along with Claire, for years following Devon the Younger's attempted rebellion.

Emiloh offered a sad smile. "He suffered that guilt needlessly. Thank you for coming."

After Lord Kiskaddon left, Emiloh sighed again. "Hal and Jon-Landon despise each other. If you remember, he was one who spoke out for harsher treatment after Jon-Landon tried to claim the throne in Benedict's absence. He will need to watch himself, Ransom. All of us will. I've never been close to Jon-Landon, although I have tried. He'll test all of us. I don't think he trusts anyone."

Ransom nodded. "I must admit I'm worried about the future."

"We will do what we must, Ransom. Serve him as you served my other sons. When he wears the hollow crown, he will be our king. Can you give him your loyalty, Ransom? Even if he despises you for taking what he wanted?"

Jon-Landon had wished to marry Claire and, through her, lay claim to Legault and Glosstyr. But Ransom had married her instead. He smiled at the impossible situation. "The Fountain has whispered to me, my lady, that Jon-Landon's son is to be our king."

Emiloh inclined her head. "Lady Léa is going to have a son?"

"I know it," Ransom answered. "And I have no doubt that Estian will try to destroy all of your posterity. It is my duty to prevent it."

Emiloh gave him a fierce look. "Do your duty, then, Ransom." She squeezed his arm firmly. "I'm counting on you."

Her words weighed on him. If he was all that stood between Estian and Jon-Landon, he wasn't sure he was enough.

The king's body was prepared for the funeral rites and lay in a canoe with a sheet draped over him, gripping his sword between stiff fingers. The stink from the corpse permeated the air despite the bouquets of flowers assembled in the vaulted chamber in the sanctuary. The coolness of the marble floor after the hot summer sun was a relief. Ransom leaned against one of the pillars, arms folded, watching as different people descended on Fountainvault to pay respects to the dead. Jon-Landon had not yet arrived.

The clipping noise of boots came from behind Ransom. Hal Kiskaddon leaned on the pillar opposite him. "Can we talk, Lord Ransom?"

"If you wish," he answered. They wandered over to one of the small alcoves, where a fountain splashed noisily. Brightly colored light streamed in from a thick stained-glass window depicting the Lady of the Fountain. Now that he was farther from the source of the flowery stench, he could smell the wet stone. Several stained coins and a few fresh ones lay in the basin of the fountain.

Ransom gazed at the Duke of East Stowe and arched his eyebrows.

"Hear me out before you raise any objections," Kiskaddon said.

Ransom scowled. "I don't like the sound of this already."

Kiskaddon held up his hands placatingly. "Just listen. I've been giving this a great deal of thought. Why not sue for peace with Estian now? His purported purpose for invading us is to give the hollow crown to Goff's son, Andrew. I'm telling you, Ransom, that I think we'd be better off with that boy as king than Jon-Landon Argentine."

Ransom didn't argue straightaway. He stared at the duke with impassive eyes.

Perhaps the silence encouraged the man, for his next words were even bolder. "I don't trust Estian, and neither do you, but this war has been costly for both sides. Maybe he's had enough. If Andrew becomes king, he is too young to rule by himself. He'll need a protector. I would support you in that role, Lord Ransom. I think the duke of the North would as well. Rainor is old and decrepit. Dalian Kinghorn does not have the title, but he is to be the Duke of Westmarch in everything but name. He is young and loyal, and he'd support us too. Think of it! If we could persuade Estian to accept a truce, we could end this bloody conflict. Why not? What would you say against it?"

"The king expressly declared his brother as his heir," Ransom said.

Kiskaddon winced. "I know. Jon-Landon is older . . . in a better position to begin ruling. But you know he's not experienced. He was knighted because his father ordered it, not because he earned it. You and I both know he will be a terrible king."

"That may be true," Ransom said, shifting with discomfort. Kiskaddon's words had made him feel uneasy and sick to his stomach. Although his reasoning was sound, his motives were driven by self-interest. Kiskaddon had been granted East Stowe after Duke Ashel supported Jon-Landon's attempt to usurp the throne. He'd not held it for long, and it was doubtful he'd keep it if the youngest Argentine brother was given the throne.

Ransom heard again the words the Fountain had whispered to him: *The scion of King Andrew will be reborn through an heir of the Argentines. They will try to kill him. You are all that stands in the way.*

"If you let Jon-Landon rule, then watch your back," Kiskaddon pressed. "You are far too powerful. He'll strip away your privileges one by one."

Again, Ransom felt a wrenching sensation in his stomach. He feared the other man was correct, but it didn't matter. It couldn't. "I've heard you. The king didn't ask for my advice on who to declare as his heir. And I know that Devon the Elder always wanted Jon-Landon to rule."

"Even though he betrayed him in the end?"

"Jon-Landon knew his father was dying and couldn't protect him. He wouldn't have been able to defeat Bennett."

"Because he's a knave and a coward."

Ransom gave him a dark look. "And he will be your king. I won't go against my conscience. I won't go against the queen dowager. And you owe your king loyalty no matter who wears the crown."

Some commotion started in the sanctuary hall, and Ransom turned to see a new group come in. There were murmurs of excitement.

"I thought that would be your answer," Kiskaddon said. He sighed. "I fear you will regret your choice, more than any you've ever made or will ever make. May the Lady bless us, for we will all surely need it."

Ransom's sense of dread had faded, however. He felt a peaceful sense of reassurance that he was following the right course whatever came of it. Still, he felt they *would* need the Fountain's blessings, perhaps more so than ever before.

By the time Ransom and Kiskaddon left the anteroom, the prince had entered the sanctuary alongside his mother. Several of his men were there too, their tunics bearing the Triple Lion. Faulkes was among them, and his lip curled up at the sight of Ransom.

Jon-Landon walked up to the canoe and lifted the linen sheet covering it, his nose wrinkling from the smell. A gasp escaped him. "So it's true," he said, the ambition and eagerness naked on his face.

"We've been waiting for you," Emiloh said. "To begin the funeral rites."

"I care nothing for that tradition," Jon-Landon said with a snort. "Throw him in when you're ready. I'm riding to Kingfountain. But I had to see it with my own eyes. How the mighty have fallen!"

The insensitivity of the comment struck Ransom in the stomach. Kiskaddon's hands clenched into fists as he gazed at the prince with undisguised contempt. Ransom nearly put a restraining hand on his shoulder but thought better of it.

"My brother brought you the news?" Ransom said, drawing the prince's eyes away from Kiskaddon's reaction.

Jon-Landon's brow furrowed. "Your brother is dead. He and his knights were ambushed on the way to Averanche. The fool didn't ride with a sufficient guard. One of his knights, Sir . . . Sir Kace . . . made it to me, wounded, and delivered the message before he, too, died. It's unfortunate, of course, but at least he died doing his duty. Can you expect anything less from one who served the house of Barton?"

The news thunderstruck Ransom. He blinked in surprise, trying to understand what the prince had said. Marcus was dead? And Sir Kace? His sister had wished to marry the man, although the match had been forbidden by Marcus. His own anguish was rivaled by the suffering he knew she would feel. He looked to Emiloh and saw a look of compassion in her eyes.

Jon-Landon did not seem to take pleasure in the news, the way he might have had he caused the accident, yet he was completely unmoved by the pain he had caused.

"What are your commands, my lord?" asked Kiskaddon in a tight voice.

"Summon the dukes of the realm to Kingfountain for the coronation," said Jon-Landon. "I want every one of them there. Any who refuses will be branded a traitor."

"Son," Emiloh said coaxingly. "Estian will take advantage of this. He will fortify his positions. Why not do the coronation here at Fountainvault? Summon your lords here so that we might unite against our foe?"

Jon-Landon turned and looked at her in a scoffing way. "You may find this hard to believe, Mother, but I am quite popular in Kingfountain. And that is where Léa is. I'll not have her risk the health of our child by riding this far. No, tradition holds that the coronation should happen at Kingfountain. The kingdom is mine now. Let the past be cast into the waters with the dead. We ride. Now!"

"Aye, my lord!" said Faulkes with vigor.

"Aye!" echoed some of his other henchmen.

Ransom looked at Kiskaddon. He knew that they both wanted to help perform the funeral rites for Benedict, but the future king had given his first command. The duke gave Ransom a look that reminded him of his earlier warning.

Emiloh approached them. "I will see it done," she said softly. "Go back to Kingfountain. I'll join you there."

"Of course you will, Mother," said Jon-Landon with a stony smile. "You're the Duchess of Vexin, after all. You wouldn't want me to name another in your place."

My soul is weighed down with trepidation. Jon-Landon has always been the shadow of the Argentine family. I await news of his coronation. Whom will he keep in the king's council? That decision will be a significant communication of his intentions. He's never wielded any real power before. He might be popular at Kingfountain itself, but the other duchies are wary of him. Surely he will seek to curry favor with Ransom. He needs my husband's prowess and military skill for this war with Occitania. Will he punish James Wigant or reward him? How can we know the heart of one so inscrutable?

—*Claire de Murrow, Queen of Legault*
Connaught Castle

CHAPTER TWO

The Coronation Oath

As Ransom rode Dappled across the bridge spanning the two sides of the river, he saw the decorations were already being put out for the coronation. The people seemed ecstatic about, not wary of, the coming shift in power. Then again, Jon-Landon had always been inclined to put on a show—Benedict had been a different man, more focused on battle than on charming his followers.

Ransom's stomach tightened with dread. He had stayed in Fountainvault to take part in the funeral rites for Benedict, despite Emiloh's suggestion that he leave with the king, and then he'd insisted on personally escorting the dowager queen back to the palace. She'd agreed with a heavy heart, and their escort had hurried back to return on time.

"I remember riding into Kingfountain for the first time," Emiloh said amidst the bustle and noise of the street. She turned and glanced at him. "I had never been so far from the Vexin in my life."

"I remember seeing you," Ransom said. "When you first came to the castle."

Her smile was sad, and strands of hair blew across her face, loosed by the wind and their rapid journey. "That feels like another life.

Another person. This city has always felt bigger than any one person. Its bones will survive long after mine have moldered."

As she spoke, a sudden chill gripped Ransom's heart. He heard the rush of the falls, the relentless churn of waters that came from the mountains in the North. Time would go on, like the river and like the falls. One day he, too, would be put in a canoe and sent as an offering to the Deep Fathoms. The feeling was strange, morbid, and full of dread. He wondered if he would live to be an old man, or if he would meet his end early, like the men he had served.

"Such gloomy thoughts," Emiloh said, shaking off her frown. "Let's hasten to the palace."

When they arrived, they were met by liveried servants displaying the Triple Lion. The men didn't greet them as returning nobles. In fact, the servants' eyes were downcast. After a moment, a man emerged from the castle doors and approached them. Ransom recognized him as Captain Faulkes, Jon-Landon's battle commander.

"You came after all," he said with a disapproving look. "The king is expecting you. Hurry along."

Ransom dismounted first and then helped Emiloh off. She took his arm, her shoulders slumped with weariness.

"Has everyone else arrived?" Ransom asked Faulkes.

"Of course. They obeyed the king's command with alacrity." There, again, was the disapproving look. Had the captain's attitude toward Jon-Landon transformed with the change in kingship? Ambition and opportunity could alter any man who was not wary of them. Ransom's stomach tightened, but he controlled his expression and walked with Emiloh into the palace.

They were brought to the solar first, not the main hall. Jon-Landon was pacing, wearing a sumptuous new tunic fitted with gold thread and crimson ribbons, a jeweled necklace, and rings on his small hands. His wife, Léa, was sitting on a couch, holding her swollen belly. When they entered, a sly smile crossed her mouth.

"They're here," she said to her husband.

Jon-Landon turned abruptly. His cheeks were clean-shaven, but he had a small beard around his mouth. His hair, which had always been darker than his brothers', glistened with oil.

"Greetings, Mother . . . Lord Ransom. I'm glad you both took the *trouble* to come for my coronation."

"Your brother is laid to rest," the queen dowager said. "The rites have been performed."

"Praise the Lady," drawled the king-to-be. He stroked the edges of his jaw with his thumb and forefinger. "I have a question to ask you both. I told Léa about that little stone Wizr set. The one where the pieces move on their own. It is an heirloom of King Andrew's realm." His eyes narrowed suspiciously. "Where is it? I asked Simon, and he said that Benedict had it last. Then I dismissed him. He's no longer the head of the Espion. Bodkin now holds that title. Someone *I* trust."

Ransom nearly grimaced to hear his friend had so unceremoniously been stripped of his position, but he kept his expression calm.

"We don't know where it is, Jon-Landon," Emiloh said.

"You will address me as *Your Highness,* madam. You may have given birth to me, but I am your son no longer. As of this day, I am your king." He said the words with sharpness.

Emiloh's shoulders slumped even more. "I'm sorry, Your Highness. Forgive me."

Jon-Landon nodded, mollified. "How can you not know where it is? Lord Ransom, do you know?"

"Your brother sent it with Sir Gordon to deliver it to me," Ransom replied hesitantly. "He never arrived at Josselin. I've had knights searching the countryside for him and his escort, but he's disappeared."

"A likely story," Jon-Landon growled.

"It's true," Ransom insisted. "I have no reason to lie to you, my lord. That Wizr board gave us an advantage   "

"Which we've now lost!" Jon-Landon shouted. He slammed his fist on a side table. "I want that board!"

"I don't know where it is," Ransom said calmly, though his patience was strained from holding his composure so long.

Jon-Landon shifted his gaze to Emiloh. "It belongs with the hollow crown. If you are keeping it from me, madam, I promise you that your confinement in the tower will be a pleasant memory compared to what I will do."

"In all likelihood"—Ransom stepped forward, inserting himself into the conversation. He was physically larger than Jon-Landon, and he used his presence to cow the younger man—"it was stolen by Lady Alix, the Occitanian poisoner. She was at Tatton Grange when the crossbow was fired. Your brother told me that himself. She counted on Bennett sending it away, and she was rewarded. It's probably back in Pree by now."

Jon-Landon stared at Ransom but didn't back down. There was a small flicker of fear in his eyes, but he kept it in check. "Are you loyal to me, Ransom Barton? Or would you rather have my nephew on the throne?"

"You are my liege lord," Ransom answered. "I've been loyal to your family all along. If I had wanted to oppose you, would I have sent for you immediately? I came back to Kingfountain at your command, even when prudence dictates that it will set us back in our conquest."

"He's telling the truth," Léa said. "Hearken to him, beloved."

Jon-Landon frowned, wrestled his lips into a small smile, then nodded. "I hoped I could depend on you, Lord Ransom. I need your loyalty right now. So does the kingdom. The ceremony is happening at twilight. You are both to be there in proper attire befitting such an occasion. Tomorrow morning, after the revelry, we will hold the first council, and I will make my will known concerning each of you."

Lady Léa rose from the couch and stood next to her husband. Her eyes were full of cunning as she lifted Jon-Landon's hand and kissed his knuckles.

"You may go," he said, nodding to dismiss them.

A knock sounded on Ransom's door while he sat writing a letter to Claire. He looked up, noticing the fading light through his window. The palace was in a frenzy, everyone busily preparing for the coronation, and the commotion and visitors had jangled his nerves. He'd changed for the event, but his temples still throbbed from the earlier confrontation, and he'd hoped for a few stolen moments to write to his wife. Clearly, it was not to be.

Sighing, he pushed the paper away, rose from the chair, and walked to the door. When he opened it, he found his sister, Maeg, on the doorstep. As the king's ward, she lived in the castle, but he hadn't been able to find her earlier. From the look on her face, she'd gotten the message he'd sent ahead from Fountainvault. Although he would have preferred to convey the message in person, he'd thought it best to write ahead for fear she would find out from someone else.

"Maeg," he whispered, holding out his arms, and she came to his embrace.

"Thank you for sending the letter," she said, her voice muffled by the padded tunic he wore. "I still can't believe they're gone."

"Where is Mother?" Ransom asked.

"She's at the Heath. Too sick with grief to travel after the funeral rites for Marcus and Kace and the rest of his knights. May I come in?"

"Of course," Ransom said, shutting the door behind her. He'd wanted to be there for his brother's rites and resented Jon-Landon's order to report directly to the palace. Then again, Jon-Landon hadn't been there for his own father's funeral. Or his brother's. Perhaps he didn't understand.

As Maeg entered, he felt a wave of love and sadness wash through him. They hadn't been given many chances to spend time together. After the Elder King's death, Benedict had taken her as his ward to prove Marcus's loyalty. Now that Marcus was dead, it was Ransom's role to be her guardian. How heartbroken she must be, knowing that her chance had finally arrived to marry Sir Kace . . . but he had perished in the ambush.

"I wish there was something I could say, something I could do to ease your grief," Ransom said, resting his hand on her shoulder. "If you blame me for their deaths, I'll take it fully. I was the one who sent Marcus to give the news to Jon-Landon."

Maeg winced at the name and massaged her temples. "It's not your fault, Ransom. I could never blame you." She turned away from him, beginning to pace, her face pinched with worry and sadness.

"You should go to the Heath. Let Mother comfort you."

"I can't," Maeg said listlessly. "I'm still the king's ward."

"I will speak to the king after the coronation, Maeg. He will restore my rights as your guardian. You need time to heal. Time to grieve."

She looked at him with tear-stricken eyes. "You don't understand, Ransom. That is not going to happen."

Ransom's insides twisted with dread. "What aren't you telling me?"

She retreated from him and put her back against the door.

"Maeg?"

She began to sob quietly. "He threatened me."

"Who?" Ransom asked in a dangerous tone. But he already knew.

"The king, who else?" Maeg whimpered. "He summoned me to a private meeting. I was excited because I thought he was going to free me, that I could finally leave Kingfountain." She paused to catch her breath. "He said . . . he warned me that he was not a patient man. That he had watched some women of court . . . no doubt he meant

Claire . . . defy his father." She looked him in the eyes. "He said it would please him if I accepted Lord James as my husband. He wants to curry favor with the North, and James needs a wife . . . and an heir."

It was the custom of Legault for a woman to choose her husband. That was not the custom in Ceredigion. James had already informed Ransom of his interest in Maeg, and although the man appeared to have changed from the boy Ransom had known in his youth, he would still prefer a different husband for his sister.

"He kept coming closer, driving me back, until I was against the wall. And he kept coming closer. I could feel his breath against my cheek."

Ransom's fury began to ripple with heat. Anger and malice throbbed in his chest.

"He stroked my hair and said if I didn't do as he asked, he would make it so that no man would want me."

Ransom's teeth bit together. The blackness swirling inside him was stronger than a raging river. He took a step forward, determined to confront the king before the coronation.

"No, Ransom," she said, shaking her head, pressing herself against the door. "I've accepted. I told him that I would marry Lord James."

"That is . . . unconscionable!" Ransom hissed.

Maeg closed her eyes. "He did it deliberately, Ransom. Knowing that you'd be outraged." She opened her eyes, staring at him fiercely. "Don't you see? He's looking for reasons to get rid of you. If you slip, even once, he'll arrest you for treason."

"He's a coward at heart."

"And because he's a coward, he's afraid of you. He wants to destroy you. Ransom . . . he would kill you for disloyalty when you are the most loyal man this kingdom has ever known. We need you. Not just your family, but all of us. For the sake of the people, you must put aside your anger. For the sake of the kingdom, you must put aside your pride. For my sake, you must let this go. I've reconciled myself to it already. King

31

Benedict supported the match too, and although I had let myself hope things might be different, Kace is gone. There is no reason for me to balk anymore. So I will marry Lord James, the man who was once your enemy." She swallowed, bringing her hands together and entwining her fingers in supplication. "Please, Ransom. Don't defy Jon-Landon. Not for me."

She was right. Despite his scalding-hot blood, Ransom could see the wisdom in her words. And yet, he was filled with dark emotions that had no release. Grief for his brother. The desire for vengeance on Alix, who'd killed yet another Argentine. His wrath needed a target, but this wasn't a sword fight in the training yard. This was politics, and it required the kind of maneuverings that went against all Ransom's instincts and notions of Virtus.

"I'm disgusted," Ransom said with an ache deep in his chest.

"So am I. I'd hoped that someday Kace and I—" Her voice quivered and caught, and fresh tears spilled from her eyes. "I never saw myself as an attractive heiress. The sister of the Duke of Glosstyr." She came and embraced him again, pressing her cheek against his chest. "I'm proud of you, Ransom. You've always cared for me. I will do this, as hard as it is, for you." She took his hands in hers. "There are worse things in life than becoming a duchess. And in Dundrennan, I will be far, far away from Kingfountain. And the king," she added with a tremulous sigh.

Later on, during the coronation ceremony, held in the sanctuary of Our Lady, Ransom kept glancing at his sister, who stood nearby with James Wigant, their arms locked together in a gesture that revealed to all their coming nuptials. His gaze only shifted to the deconeus of the sanctuary when the man lowered the hollow crown onto Jon-Landon's head. A murmured sigh traveled through the audience of nobles. Then the deconeus set the queen's crown on Lady Léa's brow. She gave a cheerful grin, at odds with the solemnity of the moment, and a little giggle bubbled from her mouth, earning her a few shocked looks from the ladies of court.

Ransom gazed at the assembled body. Lord Kiskaddon was look-ing at him, and when their gazes met, Kiskaddon rolled his eyes and shrugged. Ransom tried not to smirk and failed. Although his heart recognized the significance of the child in Léa's belly—the future king of Ceredigion, chosen by the Fountain—he nonetheless dreaded the decision he'd made to support Jon-Landon. It would have been eas-ier if Drew Argentine had taken the throne. He could imagine seeing Constance there at the sanctuary at that moment, the king's mother. But the image felt wrong somehow. There was another fate in the works.

The deconeus spoke with a strong, resonant voice. "Now is the time for the coronation oath. A king blessed by the Fountain who observes his pact with the Fountain will earn great honor for himself. Mercy will be shown to him, both in this life and also in the Deep Fathoms beyond. If you fail to fulfill that which was promised here before Our Lady, then within a very short time things will grow worse for our people, and for you. Make amends if thou doest wrongly. O beloved sovereign, eagerly protect yourself from the calamities foretold!"

Ransom felt a shiver go down his back as his Fountain magic responded to the deconeus's words of warning. He felt the truth of them prick down to his marrow, but the look on Jon-Landon's profile suggested he wasn't listening. He was bored of the lecture and impatient for the revelry to begin.

"This is the oath. The justice of a consecrated king is that he con-demns no man unjustly. That he holds the good of the kingdom above his personal fortune. That he treats people of all classes and rank with dignity, not disdain. That he protects foreigners and prisoners held for ransom. He must forbid water sprites from deceiving mortals, destroy evil Wizrs, drive murderers and perjurers out of the country, and appoint righteous and honorable men as officers of justice. The king who acts unjustly by means of his might must give a reckoning before the Deep Fathoms for all of it. This is the coronation oath, my lord. Do you so swear it?"

"I do," said Jon-Landon with a graceful bow.

The chamber burst into applause at the proper moment as the king, scepter in hand, and queen turned and faced the gathered ranks of the nobility. A raucous cheer sounded from outside the sanctuary as the people discovered the news that the king had been crowned.

Ransom did not join in the cheers or applause. He stared at Jon-Landon's triumphant face and felt a sickness in his bowels as he wondered which of the oaths just taken would *not* be broken.

⟩X

The years since Jon-Landon assumed the crown have flowed by like a tumultuous river, destroying or damaging those in its path as well as those carried along in its current. I realize, having just read my last entry, that I haven't written since the birth of our fourth child—a girl we named Keeva in memory of my maid who was murdered. There has been so much war and tumult these last years that I feel obliged to write some of the events down for fear that time and chaos will purge them from my mind. But I will not try to describe the hundred ways in which the king has made Ransom's life—and our life together—more miserable. That, I shall never forget.

There is a Gaultic saying that perfectly captures Jon-Landon's reign so far: "He who trusts no one is distrusted by all the world." When he formed his council, he dismissed most of the people who had been loyal to his brother. He sent his mother back to the Vexin and replaced her with Lady Deborah of Thorngate castle. She had served the Elder King well. Lord Longmont, King Benedict's former chancellor and the much-reviled lord protector, was exiled from the realm because of their previous rivalry. He wasn't even allowed to return to the Vexin under pain of death.

The king retained Ransom, of course, but immediately showed his distrust by saying that Legault was not an independent kingdom but one of Ceredigion's duchies. This was argued over a great deal, especially when Jon-Landon sought to reward some of his sycophants with lands that were part of the Fair Isle. Thankfully, the war with Occitania has prevented him from pressing this further, and he was persuaded, begrudgingly, to give up his claims. But it caused much resentment among the nobility here that he would attempt to use the hollow crown to claim authority and overlordship of our lands.

This was not his only blunder. His treatment of Ransom's sister, Maeg, whom he threatened years ago, before she married James, was not an isolated act. Jon-Landon has done the same to other ladies, and we've even heard reports that he's tried to seduce some of the wives of his nobles, including Lady Kiskaddon. Again, it feels like he is deliberately provoking his nobles to revolt so that he can depose them. His indiscretions have no doubt alienated his father-in-law as well. Whether the queen hears of these mischiefs, I cannot say.

One of the ways the king has tried to restore the treasury of the realm is through a practice called scutage. Every knight owes his lord a certain service each year for the king's wars. Instead of sending troops to fulfill this commitment, a lord can pay a fine to the king, allowing him to hire mercenaries instead. Jon-Landon pays the mercenaries less than the amount he raises in scutage, so he profits off each payment. The treasury, which was practically emptied to pay Benedict's ransom, has now been generating consistent revenue because of the war we relentlessly fight.

Before Benedict died, our position was promising, and it appeared we would be victorious against Occitania. No more. We have fought for years, and we are no closer to victory. Neither are they. Tatton Grange was reduced to rubble in the conflict, and there is no fortress to protect the farms and grains. Estian still claims the duchy as his own, but Jon-Landon will not halt his attempts to reclaim it. It seems he is determined to scorch the earth so that neither side will be able to use it. The king's spies, ruled by a wretched man named Bodkin, are everywhere, and the king doesn't even fully trust them. He's created a system of codes so complicated and difficult to remember that not even the king himself understands it anymore. In other words, he's a complete and utter eejit.

Ransom spends most of each year running to and fro throughout Ceredigion, fighting the battles the king has fomented with his own servants while trying to keep our enemies at bay. My husband refuses to pay scutage. But the mercenaries haven't been paid by the king in months and threaten to become a scourge themselves. The latest news I have from my husband is that he's going to Beestone castle, where the king's council has gathered to hear the latest news of the war. I'm glad to be so far away, for if Jon-Landon tried to woo me, I would probably threaten his privates with a dagger.

—Claire de Murrow, "Duchess" of Legault
Atha Kleah

CHAPTER THREE

Oath of Fealty

There was a weariness in Ransom's bones that went deeper than the exhaustion of relentless riding and skirmishes. Never had loyalty to a king cost him so much and paid so little. Still, he had persisted, shutting down the king's constant attempts to incite him into rebellion. Each time he had to visit the king, his stomach seized with dread, and he felt this same weariness sap his strength and dull his wits.

Beestone castle had been fortified during the last several years and represented a stronger hold against Occitanian incursions. The castle was built on a promontory with a thriving town at its base. As Ransom rode Dappled into the boundaries, he saw mercenaries everywhere, some too drunk to walk straight. The lack of discipline was appalling.

Ransom slowed his destrier and looked to Dearley, who rode with him. The other man had started out as his ward, many years ago, but he was now Ransom's most steadfast companion, and he and his wife, Lady Elodie, were dear friends to Ransom and Claire. In this king's reign, Ransom had found it more important than ever to surround himself with people he trusted. He had also brought Sir Simon of Holmberg back to Glosstyr, where he oversaw the training of new knights. Ransom's mesnie had grown over the years, and he no longer knew every man by name. But the cost of supporting so many had taken its toll. His expenses had risen substantially to outfit his host for constant, needless war, yet he received no new income from the king to compensate him for the additional costs. Other lords had given in to the demands to pay scutage, but not Ransom. He refused to resort to the practice, particularly since Simon had told him the king was profiting from it. It rankled Ransom to his core.

"If Estian attacked Beestone, he'd do a lot of damage right now," Dearley said with resentment in his voice. "Do you want me to find their captain and rebuke him?"

"He's probably drunk himself," Ransom said. "Let's get to the castle and see how things are going elsewhere."

"Do you think the king will consider Estian's offer of a two-year truce?"

"I don't know," Ransom answered. The thought of calling off hostilities was a welcome one. But Jon-Landon was too unpredictable for him to judge how the king would react to it.

"I hope he does," Dearley said. "Estian has offered us Josselin castle as a sign of good faith. I should very much like to see it again."

Given that it was Ransom's castle, he suspected this was Estian's attempt to give Ransom motivation to back the peace deal. They'd come so close to reclaiming it years ago, just before Jon-Landon had taken over as king, but the effort had failed without Ransom and his men.

"As would I," Ransom said. "But I don't trust Estian. Nor should you. He doesn't keep his promises."

"Neither does our king," Dearley said under his breath.

Ransom gave him a scolding look, and Dearley looked away, abashed. Still, as unwise as it was to say such a thing aloud, there was no denying it was true. Jon-Landon was not the kind of king who encouraged greatness in his followers—if anything, the opposite was true. Men like Faulkes, who was brave if power hungry, were encouraged to pursue their basest impulses, and loyalty was not rewarded unless it came from a favorite. Favorites were chosen capriciously and changed often.

They took the road up the hillside to the castle, arriving at the gates, where the guards at least looked more alert. Ransom had traveled with fifteen of his knights, and Dearley took command to find them a place to bed down. The courtyard was crowded with baggage carts and horses. A flag bearing the Triple Lion hung listlessly from its pole. Ransom tugged off his gloves and stuffed them in his belt. His tunic was dust-spattered, and the links of metal in his hauberk jangled as he walked into the castle. It was dusk, and the smell of cooking venison made his stomach growl.

When he reached the great hall, he took in the celebratory atmosphere—the sound of lutes and pipes, the sight of a juggler performing feats of acrobatics to entertain everyone. He paused at the entryway to see who else was present. Faulkes, the new duke of Southport, was there, nibbling on a fleshy bit of bone, a serving girl trapped on his lap. Whenever she tried to stand, he kept pulling her down. It made Ransom want to punch him in the face. The ambitious captain had won a seat in the king's council through his flattery and machinations. Ransom still held a seat on the council, but he wasn't the favorite, and the king never lost an opportunity to communicate as much. The constant action in the field also kept him away from the palace for long stretches of time.

Duke Kiskaddon was also there, looking bleary-eyed and disdainful with a goblet in his hand. When one of the king's dogs came snuffling by his feet, he gave it a quick jab with the tip of his boot. His gesture wasn't noticed by the king, whose attention was fixed on a woman with a plunging bodice seated near him. Ransom didn't recognize her, but she looked uncomfortable. The queen was still at Kingfountain, the king's antics likely unknown to her. Then Ransom spied Lady Deborah hastening toward the door to join him.

She was a diminutive woman with graying hair. Although shrewd enough not to gainsay the king too often, she always gave him worthy advice.

"I'm glad you're here, Lord Ransom," she said. "Do you come with news from Estian?"

"I do," Ransom said, looking at her in surprise.

"An Espion arrived this morning with word that an Occitanian herald had been to your camp yesterday. The king wondered if you were dealing treacherously. He was about to order his knights to summon you, but I persuaded him that you'd come on your own. Thank you for proving me right." She gave him a relieved smile.

"I know he's watching me," Ransom said. Indeed, he'd felt Jon-Landon's eyes on his back constantly these last years. "Have you heard any news from the North?"

"Your sister is doing well, and so is your nephew, but the Atabyrions keep menacing the shore. Duke James does the same in retaliation to keep them guessing. A peace accord with Occitania would be timely right now. Is that why you've come?"

"There he is!" boomed the king's voice from across the hall. "The man himself. The most loyal, dutiful, Duke of Glosstyr! Raise a cup to welcome the faithful!" Although the words were flattering, the tone in which they were spoken revealed the king's disdain. Several raised their cups in mock salute. Lady Deborah bowed her head to him, her expression shuttered once more.

Ransom strode into the hall. Kiskaddon perked up, giving him a smile of true welcome, but Faulkes lifted his cup to the insulting toast, malice in his eyes. Using the duke's moment of distraction, the girl managed to escape from his lap, and he frowned in annoyance at having lost her. His expression was anything but welcoming.

"How goes the conflict?" Jon-Landon asked, lowering his cup. His fine clothes matched the decorations of the hall. There were too many torches burning, a wasted expense. Fine behavior from the young man who'd once given a pretty speech about the wastefulness of Lord Longmont when King Benedict was away at war. A stag was roasting on a spit in the hearth and Ransom's stomach grumbled again at the sight and smell.

"I've told you before, my lord," Ransom answered. "No progress can be made in the struggle. We lack the men at arms to drive them out of their castles, and they suffer from the same limitations. We're at an impasse."

"We have sufficient mercenaries," countered the king. "We need bold action, strong leadership."

"Your mercenaries haven't been paid in over a fortnight," Ransom declared. "Many are threatening to sack our sanctuaries and steal what they were promised."

Jon-Landon's face flashed with anger. "Perhaps you are being too lenient with them, my lord duke. Anyone who threatens it should be bound to a canoe and thrown over the falls!"

"They're Brugian, my lord. They don't respect our ways. They're hungry, tired, and want to be paid."

"Then pay them," Jon-Landon said. "Surely you can bridge the gap until the treasury releases the funds. It's none of my doing." The last bit was a total lie. Ransom had heard the king deliberately withheld payment because he was loath to part with his livres.

"Unfortunately, I'm not in a position to do so, my lord. I must pay my own men their wages."

Jon-Landon lifted his jeweled goblet and slurped from it. "Did you come all this way to complain, Lord Ransom? Surely not."

"No, my lord. You asked how the war was going, and I told you honestly and bluntly. But I come bearing news. An offer of a truce from King Estian."

Jon-Landon's eyes flashed with interest. Faulkes scowled, but Kiskaddon leaned forward eagerly. There were lesser nobles gathered as well, the king's barons, and all eyes went to Ransom.

"If he wants to stop the bloodshed, then he must depart Westmarch. I'm not giving up my father's land. Land which belongs, by right and law, to *me*."

Ransom let out a slow breath. "As you know, King Estian says the duchy was part of Occitania originally. Right now, it serves neither of us. The people are suffering. It is the most fertile land—"

"I know this already, Lord Ransom," said the king, cutting him off. "Tell me his offer."

"A two-year truce. Neither kingdom brings their armies into the disputed lands. It is not too late to plant for winter wheat. We share the harvest equally. Each side disbands its mercenaries, which will also save money. After two years, we try to negotiate a permanent peace accord."

Jon-Landon looked skeptical. "I think he's bluffing. Testing us for weakness. If we agree to this, he'll attack us when our guard is down. Maybe it's the right time to press even harder."

Ransom gritted his teeth. "The mercenaries do not want a pitched battle. It's too risky. If they're dead, they cannot collect their wages."

"I know," said the king with a sly smile.

Ignoring his reaction, Ransom pressed on. "As a sign of good faith, King Estian is willing to relinquish one castle in the borderlands to our custody."

"Which one?" asked the king.

This was the part Ransom had dreaded to share. "Josselin, my lord."

Faulkes snorted and shook his head. "One of yours? How convenient for you."

"But it is a key castle," Kiskaddon countered. "He's giving it up? I can hardly believe it."

"Not exactly," Ransom said. He was grateful for Kiskaddon's support, but it would do little to sway the king. Although Jon-Landon had not stripped the duke of his title, he constantly threatened it.

"Say on," said the king.

"He will hand over the castle as a token of good faith, yet he still lays sovereign claim to it. Whoever holds it must swear fealty to King Estian for it."

Jon-Landon rubbed his temple thoughtfully. "Let me see if I understand you correctly, Lord Ransom. You would swear fealty to King Estian?"

"For that castle only," said Ransom. "Clearly the bulk of my revenue and power come from Glosstyr and Legault. Josselin is a trivial amount by comparison."

"You hate Estian, though," said Jon-Landon. "Is he playing you for a fool?"

"I do not trust him," Ransom agreed. "It does not serve my interests in the least to curry favor with him. But Josselin is my castle, so yes, I would be the one to swear fealty for it." He gave the king a bow.

"Interesting." The king rubbed his mouth again. He looked at Faulkes. "What do you think?"

"I think we should take the castle back by force!"

"We've tried," answered the king. "It's too well defended. Which would make it a strategic position for us. We could refuse to give it back. We gain something for nothing."

"My lord," Ransom said, trying to tame his anger. "I am a man of my word. I would never take part in such a ruse."

"Your scruples . . ." said the king with a chuckle. "What if I ordered it?"

"Then I would resign my post," said Ransom firmly.

Faulkes's grin suggested he'd be all for it. They'd taken a disliking to each other all those years ago, at the battle at Josselin, and it had never lifted.

"No, Lord Ransom," said the king. "You're far too valuable to lose. What say you, Lord Kiskaddon?"

"A two-year truce would be a blessing from the Fountain," he answered. "Surely you can see that, my lord. The King of Occitania may dislike Lord Ransom, but he trusts him to be honest. As we all do. Two years could change circumstances substantially. I'm for it."

"Of course you are," sneered Faulkes.

Kiskaddon shot him a warning look.

"Lady Deborah?" asked the king politely.

"Lord Ransom is known for keeping his word. King Estian is not. It could be a trick. However, I don't think Estian would give up such a strategic castle as a trick. It's a sign of good faith. And a shrewd one."

"I agree," said the king. "You have my permission, Lord Ransom, to respond. This conflict has waged on for many years now. I would like my son and daughter to enjoy a season of peace. But I do not relinquish my claims on Westmarch or any of the other lands that have been pried away from us."

Ransom was surprised by the king's response. Up until now, his approach to the war had been much more in line with Faulkes's.

"So I have your permission to swear fealty to Estian?" Ransom pressed.

"Yes, that's what I said," Jon-Landon said impatiently.

"You said I had permission to respond. I just want to confirm your will. I can negotiate a two-year peace and accept Josselin as a token of the agreement?"

"You don't trust me, Lord Ransom? Do you doubt my word?"

"No, I just want to ensure there's no misunderstanding," Ransom said. "I didn't think you would agree to it."

"Ransom, you know me better than that," the king said with a smirk. "Just as I know you to be . . . a loyal man, and I'm very willing for you to pay him homage. You see, the more you *have*, the greater will be your services to me."

The declaration did little to ease Ransom's mind. For it implied the king considered this a favor, one he would use as leverage to demand a return favor from Ransom. Would it be something that Ransom's conscience allowed him to deliver?

"I will negotiate the terms, then," he said. "I'll leave on the morrow."

The king gave him another cunning smile. "You should stay. You look weary. Get some rest."

Ransom had no reason to refuse, so he stayed, and when Dearley and the rest of his escort arrived, they were given an empty table. The meal was hearty, and the music and performances continued into the night.

Dearley leaned forward. "I can't read your expression. What did he say?"

"He said yes," answered Ransom, keeping his eyes fixed on the king's face. Things had not turned out the way he'd expected. Even though the king had done as he wished, he felt uneasy about it. It struck him that Jon-Landon was a few years older than Bennett had been when he died. He'd made it longer than either of his brothers.

"That's good news," said Dearley. He smiled broadly and lifted a cup. "I can't wait to tell Elodie. We're going home."

Ransom raised his cup and struck it against Dearley's.

And yet, the feeling of dread persisted.

Some ill news arrived today from a few ships of Genevese merchants. Estian's fleet barred them from docking in the Vexin. Forbidden to sail to their destination, they came to Atha Kleah instead. Does this new blockade mean Estian is preparing to invade Emiloh's duchy? I've ordered ships to bring supplies to Emiloh's duchy. With Brythonica as its own entity, at least communication can get in and out of the territory by means other than the sea. But it takes longer to send a messenger by horse than by ship.

I've sent Ransom a note of warning, but it will take days before it reaches him. The last message I had from him was that he was going to Beestone to meet the king's council. I shudder to think of what would happen should the Vexin fall to Occitania again. Legault would be vulnerable next. I will summon the lords of Legault to prepare in case this disruption of the Genevese merchants proves to be a foretelling of worse things to come.

—Claire de Murrow, "Duchess" of Legault
Atha Kleah

CHAPTER FOUR

Guardian of the Grove

ansom rode with two hundred knights to Josselin castle. He sent scouts both ahead and behind them to ensure there were no surprise attacks. But they encountered no one and saw no signs of Occitanian forces at any point during the several-day journey. Dearley was perplexed by the overtures of peace. So was Ransom, particularly since he could not yet see the motives behind the offer. As always in the game of Wizr, when a piece was moved, it could mean many things. And the magical Wizr board, which might have helped them understand the meaning of such movements, was, presumably, in the hands of the enemy.

As they traveled, they witnessed the ravages of the constant state of war, from the burnt fields to the stumps left behind after the trees were axed down for firewood, to the looks of fear in villagers' eyes as the knights rode past. Was this what things had been like during the tumult between Devon the Elder and King Gervase? In those days, Ceredigion had nearly been rent apart from within. This time, the damage had mostly been inflicted by foreign enemies.

One evening, as they camped for the night, sitting around a small fire for warmth, Dearley said solemnly, "I hope this leads to a lasting peace. Every year I look forward to the coming of winter because at least the fighting will have to stop for a season."

Ransom nodded in agreement, tossing a fresh stick into the crackling blaze. He, too, enjoyed the long winters in Legault at Connaught. Watching his twin sons wrestle and chase each other through the castle. His daughter Sibyl had taken an interest in fletching arrows instead of needlework. Her hair matched her mother's, a lovely mix of brown and crimson. Then there was the littlest one, Keeva. He'd missed so much of their childhood already, performing his duties to the king. Longing coursed through him at the thought of them, at the image of Claire, her hair unbound. Yes, a large part of him hoped that peace would happen.

"I think we'll reach Josselin tomorrow," Dearley said. "Elodie will be jealous. I wish I could bring her back there. We have so many fond memories of it. We were practically children when we fell in love."

Ransom smiled. "You were afraid that I was going to marry her."

"Why shouldn't I have feared it? We were your wards, and you know the way of things. Besides, you were the famous knight, in favor with the Elder King! I was no one."

"You were my first knight. And you've proven yourself time and again."

Dearley blushed. "I still don't feel adequate, but I try not to disappoint you."

Ransom shook his head. "You've never disappointed me, Dearley."

"Oh? What about that first battle when you got skewered by a lance because you were defending me?"

The Raven scabbard had saved Ransom that day. Dearley still didn't know about it. It was a gift from the Fountain, and he'd kept it secret, telling as few people as possible. "I've had worse."

A knight walked up to their fire. "Sorry to interrupt, my lord," he said. "The patrol just returned. There's no one within a league of us in any direction."

"That's good news," Dearley said, cocking his head.

Ransom believed the report. His Fountain magic usually warned him of danger, but its influence had been more difficult to feel since serving Jon-Landon's interests. The king's wavering moods, distrust, and lack of compassion had created an antipathy within Ransom that strained his connection to the magic. He had respected the previous kings he'd served in different ways. But not Jon-Landon. He always felt unsafe when he was with the king.

"You can rest easy tonight, my lord," said the knight.

Ransom gave him a salute, and the man walked away.

"Perhaps Estian truly does want peace," Dearley said hopefully.

"We'll have a better idea by tomorrow."

They reached Josselin castle by early evening the following day. The sight of the Fleur-de-Lis pennant hanging above the castle made him frown. Did he really wish to treat with Estian? To promise him even a shred of loyalty? The night the castle had been taken, Ransom had very nearly taken it back—only Estian had threatened to hang the prisoners who'd been taken with the castle, one by one, if Ransom didn't withdraw his men. He still begrudged the king that and many other affronts. Estian touted the honorable code of Virtus in his tournament circuits, but his court was rotten on the inside, like a piece of spoiled fruit.

As they advanced, they saw soldiers patrolling the battlement walls. He reached out with his Fountain magic, trying to sense the defenders' intention. Was this a trap?

He felt a ripple in his magic, but it was not a warning. It felt like . . . sympathy. The feelings of unease he'd been brooding on since the meeting with Jon-Landon faded. There was no sense of the poisoner Alix either. He would have known if she were there.

All of his men were wearing armor. It might be a diplomatic mission, but there was little to no trust between the opposing factions.

"Let's go a little closer," Ransom said, nudging Dappled forward. The town looked to be thriving, and he heard the bleating of sheep from across the river. The familiar smell of tallow from large cooking vats lingered in the air. As they passed, he heard the townsfolk speaking Occitanian. Those who had once lived here had fled to Glosstyr.

When they reached the gates, he was surprised to find them open. It was unheard of for a castle to lower its guard in the presence of a strong force.

A man stood in the center of the courtyard, hands clasped behind his back. He wore a tunic with the Raven badge. His dark hair was cut short in the Occitanian fashion, and he had no beard—another sign of his origins. Ransom didn't recognize him, but he did recognize the badge, which matched his own scabbard. It was the symbol of Brythonica. The man wore a chain hauberk beneath his tunic but no further armor. A bastard sword was strapped to his hip.

Ransom reined in before the gate, pausing to look up at the portcullis.

"I am the Duke of Glosstyr," Ransom said. "Are you Estian's emissary?"

"I am Lord Guyaume Montfort," replied the man with a strong accent.

Ransom knew the name, although he'd never met the man. This was Constance's second husband. He felt another subtle ripple from the Fountain as the man looked at him with what appeared to be genuine respect.

"I know you are a man of your word," said Lord Montfort. "My wife assures me that you can be trusted. You've brought a sizable host with you, which I cannot allow inside the castle by order of my king. But you are permitted to bring a guard with you, and the castle gates will remain open during our negotiations. Is that agreeable to you, Lord Ransom?"

"How many defenders do you have at Josselin?"

Lord Montfort scratched his neck. "It would be unwise to tell you in case you decide to attack the castle by force."

"Just as it would be unwise of me to bring in a small guard that could easily be overwhelmed," Ransom countered. There was no belligerence on either side. He felt the knight was sizing him up, so he did the same, using his magic to test the man's abilities. They were formidable. Montfort was a skilled warrior, but he was someone Ransom felt certain he could beat.

"That is true. Do I have your word that you will not provoke an attack?"

"Yes," Ransom said sincerely.

Lord Montfort studied him again, his gray eyes serious and penetrating. "I hold you to it, then. I have only fifty guarding the castle right now. The rest have been withdrawn back to Pree on leave. My king anticipates that we will come to an agreement. I hope he is not mistaken."

"I will bring two dozen with me, then," said Ransom. "The rest will remain in the courtyard."

"That is agreeable. Shall we discuss terms?"

Ransom nodded.

Lord Montfort bowed slightly and gestured for them to enter the castle peaceably. Ransom looked to Dearley to arrange the escort, and his first knight quickly chose twenty-four men to accompany them, fifty more to stand at the gate, and sent the rest off to buy food for the group.

That accomplished, Ransom rode Dappled beneath the portcullis and sighed when he saw the interior grounds had been mended in his absence. The gardens were thriving, and new bushes had been planted to replace those that had been trampled. Ransom had tried to reclaim Josselin multiple times over the years, but it had strong defenses and determined defenders.

They dismounted and followed Lord Montfort into the castle. Dearley had a look of wistfulness as they made their way through the halls, his mind probably steeped in memories of what this place had meant to him and Elodie. Ransom followed Lord Montfort to the solar, a room that had once been one of his favorite places in the castle. The furnishings had changed a little, but it still felt the same.

Lord Montfort walked to the large window overlooking the courtyard down below, and Ransom joined him, looking down at the scene with him. His knights were walking about freely enough, but there was clear tension between them and the castle defenders.

Dearley walked to one of the tables and lifted a figurine that stood there, examining it.

"Does Estian truly want peace?" Ransom asked.

"This war has been costly, my lord," said Montfort. "Many of the dukes have been pressuring him for peace. And so have I." His gray eyes narrowed with determination.

"I notice you do not call yourself a duke," Ransom said.

Lord Montfort shook his head. "I am not. I'm the duchess's consort, just as you are in Legault. From my understanding, your title comes from Glosstyr. We are similar in other ways as well."

Ransom's brow furrowed. "What do you mean?"

"We both seek to do the Fountain's will," said Montfort softly. "After marrying Lady Constance, I see the world through new eyes. The excesses of court offend me now. My lady misses her son. If we can achieve peace through this agreement, then Estian has promised to return him to us."

Ransom turned and looked into the courtyard. Constance's son, Drew, was a scion of the Argentine family, the son of Jon-Landon's brother Goff. He was one of three surviving Argentine heirs, the others being Jon-Landon and the young prince. But the Fountain had whispered to Ransom that Devon, the young prince, was the one who would inherit the kingdom. He was the one the Occitanians would try to kill.

Distrust welled up inside him. Was Montfort, like Kiskaddon, trying to persuade him to make a different kind of deal?

"So your loyalties are conflicted," Ransom said, still gazing out the window.

"As are yours, I believe," Montfort said. "You serve a man unfit to wear the hollow crown. Jon-Landon is inept and mercurial. His efforts to seed spies in Pree is laughable. Do not trust anything his Espion says about our intentions. He's being deliberately misled."

"Because your king seeks to supplant him," Ransom said. He turned his head and gazed into the man's steel eyes.

"That's not our purpose. Both boys are too young to rule Ceredigion, although I'll not deny Drew is better equipped for the job. And with Constance advising him, you know the kingdom would be ruled justly."

A throb of warning flashed in Ransom's heart. "I will not betray my king."

Montfort held up his hands. "I'm not asking you to, nor is it a requirement of this truce. As you know, Estian has promised to return this castle to you so long as you swear fealty to him in all manners related to Josselin. It is a token that his overture of peace is legitimate."

"Then why should I trust you now?" Ransom asked. "After such a confession?"

"You should trust me because Constance trusts me. You were a child during the wars of succession. You were held hostage just as her son is being held prisoner. Four years of peace. Let us stop taking advantage of each other, stop fueling ill will among the nobility. Let us agree to stand down, sheathe our swords, and heal the land, lest the Deep Fathoms lose patience and destroy us both."

"Four years?" Ransom asked. "I was told it was two."

"Four years. Do you not wish to see your children while they are still young? I am soon to be a father myself," he said emphatically. "Constance is with child. You and I want the same thing, Lord Ransom. We both want peace between our realms. Imagine if the four years could become longer. Much can change in four years."

In four years his own sons would be of an age to start looking for where they could train. He'd considered sending one to Dundrennan, under Maeg's care, the other perhaps to Lord Kiskaddon. So much time had been lost already. Their childhoods had been squandered because of the endless war.

"I have come here to broker peace between our realms," Montfort said. "As you have too, if I'm not mistaken. There has been enough bloodshed, has there not?"

Ransom longed for what was being promised, but history bid him proceed with caution. He doubted Estian would keep his word.

"I will not go to Pree to attend to your king," Ransom said, shaking his head. "Estian warned me that if I ever did, I would be executed."

"If I recall, you *did* threaten to decapitate him," said Montfort with a wry smile.

"It was deserved."

"The king would be willing to accept your oath of homage at Chessy instead. You may bring whatever size host you desire. If you are agreeable, if you accept the terms, then I can communicate this to him immediately."

"I have my king's permission," Ransom said. "I don't need to return to Beestone to seek it."

"I trusted that you wouldn't have sent word you were coming otherwise. Am I to hope for a positive outcome, then? The decision seems to hang on you."

Ransom turned away from the window and began to pace. "The decision hangs on whether or not I can trust Estian."

Lord Montfort held up his hands. "He's *giving* you your castle back. I've told you that his dukes don't want to fight anymore. Peace benefits us all. And perhaps, over time, we can negotiate a more lasting truce."

"How so?" Ransom asked, turning to face him.

"Jon-Landon has a daughter. Drew will need a wife. They are cousins, true, but that has not stopped such alliances in the past." He held up his hands. "My point is that we might find new ways to bargain. Our generation has seen enough of war."

Ransom stepped closer to him. He dropped his voice low so that only Montfort could hear it. "Constance has a special talent. Sometimes she knows the future."

Montfort nodded with a knowing smile. Responding in a similarly hushed voice, he said, "I know of the stones, my lord. She's the one who told me that *I* would be the one negotiating with you."

"Has she seen Drew's future?" Ransom whispered.

Montfort shook his head. "She only looks in the stones if the Fountain bids her do so. You know this because she has told you."

Ransom knew that Montfort could not have known about the seering stones unless Constance had told him. And she wouldn't have told him unless she trusted him.

Ransom wanted to say yes. He listened to the surge of feelings in his heart, his ears attuned for a reprimand or warning from the Fountain, but he heard nothing.

"Does Estian truly want Drew to be king?"

Montfort sighed. "Estian only wants himself to be king, but he's wise enough to realize he cannot conquer Ceredigion by war. Not with you standing in his way."

Ransom sighed. That much was true. "So he wants me out of the way?"

"No. A truce is what he wants. He knows there is nothing he could offer that would make you switch sides. Especially not a castle. So no, Lord Ransom, this is no attempt at bribery, no underhanded ruse. What he wants is time to plan his next move, and he's willing to make concessions to get it. Shake my hand and say we have an accord." He extended his hand to Ransom, who stared at it. "As you see, I hold no sword or dagger in it."

No warning came. There were a good many reasons to distrust Estian. But if the Occitanian king reneged on the deal, they would be no worse off than they were now. Indeed, they would have gained a castle from it.

He took the man's hand.

"I will come to Chessy and see for myself," Ransom said. "But if Estian is as good as your promises, then I accept the truce in the name of my king."

Lord Montfort sighed with relief.

"This is tremendous news," Dearley said, rising from the sofa he'd been sitting on, watching the exchange with obvious excitement.

"May we rest here for the night?" Ransom asked, still gripping Montfort's hand.

"Of course. You are protected under the rights of hospitality. And so are your men." They broke the clasp.

Montfort pitched his voice low once again. "Constance said you would say yes. She also bid me give you this." He reached into his tunic and withdrew a sealed note, one with the raven sigil stamped into the wax.

Ransom opened it and turned away from Lord Montfort.

> *Dear Ransom,*
> *You will see my son before I do. Tell him that his mother loves him and thinks of him every day. Guyaume is my husband now. He is loyal and true. I've come to trust him as I have trusted you. Please give him the ring you received from Lord Terencourt. That is one last secret I must share with him. The Fountain bids it, and I have seen a vision that he will need it.*
> > *With charity,*
> > *Constance*

The ships I sent to the Vexin never made it there. Estian's fleet was moored along the coast, making it impossible to reach them. The sailors saw smoke coming from the direction of Auxaunce. My ships returned, and here they'll stay to defend our coasts from attack.

Word came from Ransom of a peace treaty that Estian wants. He's offering Josselin castle as a token of good faith, but there is no good faith in Estian Vertus. The treaty is a ruse, a ploy. I sent Sir Galveson to find Ransom and Sir Trebet to warn the king.

Little Sibyl asked if her papa was going to be all right. I don't know. I fear he's blind to what's really going on.

—Claire de Murrow, "Duchess" of Legault

(the surge of war)

CHAPTER FIVE

Face-to-Face

The countryside of Occitania stretched beautifully before him, full of lush, rolling hills and stands of aspen. As they moved farther from the border, there were fewer signs of the ravages of war. Ransom led his men at a strong pace, and he kept his senses on alert for warnings that they were headed into an ambush. The scouts continued to report that the land ahead was tranquil. They had encountered a few Occitanian knights patrolling the road to Pree, but Ransom's presence was expected, and they were greeted with civility despite the long-standing hostility between the two kingdoms.

The ring's absence was more noticeable than he'd expected. For so many years he'd worn it in secret, prepared to be summoned to the Grove should the need arise, although its summons hadn't come since before Jon-Landon was made king. The Occitanians, once so intent on stealing the treasure in the grove, had put a halt to their efforts, perhaps because Drew had been taken and Constance had married one of Estian's men. He'd given the ring to Montfort, who had departed back to Brythonica per his king's orders instead of joining him on the journey to Chessy.

Ransom knew the road well and marveled at all the new farmsteads that had been built. As they drew near Chessy, located along the road to Pree and adjacent to the Bois de Meridienne, a royal wood used for war games and hunting, his heart panged with memories of his younger days. He recalled walking with Claire through the maze of tents and pavilions when he was nothing but a lowly knight. He missed her deeply. He missed his children. Now, standing on the cusp of possibly ending this war, if only for a few years, he was filled with a fiery surge of longing for his family. He wished to go home. To sit by a hearth and stroke Claire's hair. To listen to the stories of his children and to share his own with them.

Still, the thought of kneeling before Estian and swearing fealty to him for Josselin castle made his stomach churn. It did not require the same depth of loyalty as making Estian his liege lord, but it still meant something, and he had to wonder whether he was making a mistake.

There were only a few Occitanian knights milling about. No tournament was in progress—or at least, Estian had canceled it so the two sides could meet without fanfare. Open fields with tall grass spread out around the encampment and a patch of denser woods could be seen on the farther side. Ransom reached out with his Fountain magic.

And he sensed Lady Alix immediately.

She was Fountain-blessed too, and they'd always had the ability to know when the other was close. Her presence put him on his guard once more, and he frowned as they rode through the main thoroughfare.

One of the tents had been there back in his tournament days. It was adorned with black and white stripes and contained Occitanian confections, his favorite being penuche. He turned to Dearley as they rode.

"Have one of the knights buy some penuche from that tent," he said, gesturing to the one. "I want to take some back to Claire."

"Of course," Dearley answered and pulled back slightly to give the order.

A formidable knight on a massive destrier met them partway down the road. He wore the badge of the Fleur-de-Lis.

"Welcome, Lord Ransom," said the knight, offering the familiar salute. "The king is expecting you."

Ransom returned the salute and replied in Occitanian. "It is my privilege to come. Tell him I come in peace."

All seemed in order. A few of the camp dwellers observed the newcomers with interest. Some with glares of hostility. They reached a huge pavilion set up at the end of the road, a triple-poled tent that was tall and broad and held three sections. He sensed Alix inside the pavilion, and knights wearing the badge of Estian stood guard outside. A dozen, perhaps. He saw others patrolling in the distance.

Ransom gazed at them warily. So far, the promises had been fulfilled. Still, Alix's presence disturbed him. She might only be present because Estian was—the king probably brought her everywhere as his bodyguard—but it left him ill at ease.

When they reached the golden pavilion, Ransom dismounted, and Dearley and Dawson did the same. The latter had his hand on his sword hilt, and he sized up the guards with a look of disdain in his eyes. Dearley looked worried but tried to project strength. He brushed his shoulder against Ransom's arm. "It seems harmless enough," he said in a low voice.

Ransom looked at the guards. "Alix is here," he said softly.

Dearley stiffened. "Do you think she'll attack us?"

Ransom considered it for a moment before shaking his head. "I suspect she's here to protect the king. I doubt he goes anywhere without her. Don't eat anything. Don't drink anything. Warn the men to be wary of her words. She has a way of persuading someone against their better judgment."

"I will," Dearley said and took Dawson aside.

The pavilion opened, and Estian's herald stepped forward. Ransom recognized the man, Moquet, his name was, from previous meetings. He looked older, more gnarled than the last time Ransom had seen him, but it had been some years.

"Welcome, Lord Ransom," said Moquet in his language, bowing in deference to Ransom's office. "The king awaits you within the pavilion.

He has three knights and one lady attending him for protection. You may bring four of your choosing as well. The deconeus of the sanctuary of Our Lady at Rannes is here to witness the agreement and provide his blessing. Is that agreeable?"

Ransom's stomach twisted with nervousness. "It is."

Moquet bowed slightly. "Choose your guardians and follow me."

Ransom nodded to Dearley and Dawson to accompany him. He looked at his other men and nodded to two of the young knights. Grinning at having been chosen, they followed the rest into the pavilion with Moquet.

It was a sumptuous structure with elaborate bronze partitions, designed with the Fleur-de-Lis, at the far end of the pavilion. King Estian sat on the sole chair, an ornate piece similar to a throne, which seemed fitting given the crown nested in his dark hair. He wore a hauberk beneath his royal tunic and had a sword belted to his waist. Behind the bronze works was a display of flowers that filled the pavilion with a pleasant smell.

Even so, he detected the subtle fragrance of lilac. Ransom sensed Lady Alix to the left, and when he looked, she stood in the opening connecting the main area to one of the pavilion's other sections. She wore gold damask and looked at him with a dispassionate gaze. He recognized the strand of pearls wrapped around her wrist and the birthmark on the skin exposed by her bodice. As he looked at her, he felt a stab of desire, but it wasn't as powerful as the flood of magical compulsion he'd experienced when Estian's sister had tried to seduce him. He inclined his head to her, but she stared at him as if he were no more significant than an intruding moth. She was still dangerous—he could sense her skill and the poisons she kept with her.

"Would that we had time for a tournament," King Estian said, rising from the chair. "Even after all these years, I should like to see you riding the lists once more, a lance pointed toward an awaiting shield. You were always a glory to watch, Lord Ransom."

The flattery didn't ease Ransom's feelings. In fact, it made him more suspicious.

Estian was a handsome man who'd hardly aged other than a few streaks of gray in his otherwise dark hair. He'd heard the king had finally taken a wife, the daughter of one of his nobles, who was probably fifteen years younger than himself. He had a son and heir, a boy he'd named Lewis, after his father.

Ransom bowed slightly. "I come to see for myself if you truly seek peace with Ceredigion."

"And it is most appropriate that your king should send his most adept and honorable knight to negotiate the terms. I have word from Lord Montfort that your meeting at Josselin was agreeable?"

"It was, my lord," Ransom said. He noticed the deconeus, a white-haired man with sagging skin and watery blue eyes, dressed in his ceremonial vestments.

"I wish we could have held our meeting in Pree," said Estian with a sly smile. "But unfortunately, the last time you were there, you stole something of great value to me."

More unease rippled inside Ransom. "Is not murder more dishonorable?"

There was a flash of ire in Estian's eyes, but he quickly subdued it and offered a genial smile. "What was lost has now been found. Let us put past grievances—which are many—behind us. Long has this conflict between our realms ended in nothing but bloodshed and ashes. Your king seeks to reclaim land his father once held, such as the duchy of La Marche, without paying homage for it. I seek to reclaim my father's glory too, although all I wish for is for us to get our due—the subservience that is owed to us. Our motives are identical. Shall we not put aside our differences for a season?"

Ransom felt the tingling of Fountain magic begin to swell. It came from Lady Alix. His eyes narrowed with worry and suspicion. Why was she trying to influence the situation with her magic?

"I have come to discuss the terms you offered," Ransom said, giving Alix a warning look to let her know he sensed her interference. She met his gaze without flinching and increased the power of her influence.

"Yes. I will give you Josselin if you will kneel before me and swear fealty to me as your rightful overlord."

Ransom shifted his gaze at once to Estian. "It was my understanding that I would owe fealty to you for the castle alone."

"Serve me, Ransom Barton," said Estian with a coaxing tone.

Alix's magic wove around him, entangling his senses, and he took an involuntary step backward. Although he'd fallen prey to her compulsions before, he understood what she could do now, and his own Fountain magic swelled, helping him resist the compulsion to kneel. Perhaps he was further empowered by his magic's connection to loyalty—they were trying to force him to relinquish his, and he would not do it.

Sweat trickled down from his temple. "What trickery is this?" he answered. "I came to do homage just for the castle."

"I will accept your homage," said Estian. "But with it, you must pledge you will never attack me within my own lands. If your king starts a war and breaks the truce *on this side of the land you call Westmarch*, you will not join in the fighting, or else you forfeit Josselin on your honor."

He narrowed his eyes. Brythonica was west of Westmarch. So was the Vexin. "Your Highness," Ransom demurred, "this was not part of the truce. My king would never agree to such terms."

"Your king was too cowardly to come himself," said Estian flatly. "You are here to negotiate on his behalf. He's authorized you to make this decision. Here are my terms. You are not to interfere if he breaks the truce and attacks anything west of Westmarch. I must insist upon this measure to protect Brythonica, which I have made an independent duchy. If your king attempts to lay claim to the duchess's land, you will not join him. How does this compromise you?"

Perhaps he would have been swayed had he not felt Alix's invading influence pushing him to accept. The argument was not without merit, but it felt dishonest and unreasonable for Estian to change the terms at the last moment. They were on the verge of peace, one that would last for years. Why threaten that?

"If you truly want peace, why change the terms?" Ransom challenged.

"We all want peace, Lord Ransom. Even you. Your knights are exhausted. Your children are without a father. The mercenaries haven't been paid. There is no honor in your king. But I know you, Lord Ransom. I know that honor binds you. If you swear not to get involved, I will trust you to remain true to your word."

He felt the overpowering urge to drop to his knee before Estian, but he knew where the feelings came from and refused to submit to them.

One of his knights, the youngest, went down on one knee. The sound of it rattled Ransom and drew his attention. He looked back and saw Dearley and Dawson were both conflicted. They looked from Ransom to Estian as if their souls were torn by a vicious inner conflict.

"I will accept the previous terms that you offered," Ransom said, turning back to Estian. He glared at Alix once more. A small smile tilted her mouth.

"Unacceptable," Estian said. "You would risk years more war for this? Don't be stubborn, Ransom. Kneel. End this."

"I will not," Ransom said, shaking his head. He took a step backward and felt Alix's grip lessen. Guilt and anguish collided inside him. The war would not halt after all, and they would all remain in its grip. Yet he felt sure he'd done the right thing. In his heart, he knew Jon-Landon would never have forgiven him if he'd knelt before Estian and accepted the new terms. The king would have seen it as a sign of disloyalty.

"Come now," Estian said soothingly. "Be reasonable. Do you want so much blood on your hands? Not even the mighty waterfall at Kingfountain would be able to wash them clean after this."

"If there is any blood spilled," Ransom answered curtly, "it will be your fault. You've reneged on your promise. I'll not stain my honor to kneel before you. Prepare to defend your realm."

Estian looked neither surprised nor disappointed. Indeed, there was a cunning light in his eyes that suggested he'd expected, perhaps even invited, this very outcome. "We shall see. Be gone. Your safe conduct is revoked after sunset."

Ransom glared at him. "It takes longer than a day to travel so far." Especially since the horses all needed rest after being driven so hard.

"Then you'd best hurry," Estian said with contempt.

Ransom shot Alix a withering look and then turned to face his knights. The one who had knelt came back to his feet, his face red with shame. At his nod, they stormed out of the tent as one. The other knights looked at them in consternation, no doubt sensing a shift in mood.

"We ride. Now!" barked Dearley.

Ransom heard Alix's voice back in the tent. As he gripped the saddle and prepared to mount, he tried to listen to what was being said but couldn't make out the words.

He did hear Estian exclaim, "Are you sure?"

There was no way to understand what it meant. Ransom pulled himself up and turned Dappled around. The looks from the Occitanian knights had noticeably altered. They were grim, expectant, as if they'd known all along they'd be giving chase.

"That was . . . that was ominous," Dearley said after mounting and riding closer to Ransom.

A sickening feeling had crept into Ransom's stomach. Estian hadn't wanted a truce after all. Why else would he have changed the terms in such a way that Ransom's loyalty would prevent him from agreeing?

"Let's get out of here," Ransom said to his knights. "Ride hard. We have until sunset before they come after us. If even that long."

I wonder if King Estian thinks my eyes are only painted on? I've called on Lord Tenthor to prepare to defend the coast, but he's fallen ill with gout. He has no sons, more the pity. Lord Toole suggested letting Lord Gambon have a try, which I've agreed to. I want to send more knights to Glosstyr to help in case they are needed, but I must also be prepared to defend the Fair Isle from a possible attack. I think Auxaunce is already under siege. My heart trembles for Emiloh. If anything were to happen to her, I would never forgive myself for not doing more.

The schemes of men and lords. They nearly make me angry enough to eat the cat.

—Claire de Murrow, "Duchess" of Legault
Fortress at Atha Kleah

CHAPTER SIX

The King's Battle

There was more than one road leading away from Occitania. Ransom chose the shortest path, to the crossroads of Brythonica. He sent scouts ahead to look for enemy soldiers blocking the way. He also sent a separate group of knights to Beestone castle to warn the king the peace treaty had failed. All the while, he worried that knights on fresh horses would appear on the horizon behind them.

But when a rider finally did approach them, it was from the road ahead of them, not behind.

The scouts encountered Sir Galveson, one of Claire's personal guards, and swiftly escorted him to Ransom. He was haggard from several days of travel, but he greeted Ransom and Dearley with a knightly salute.

"My lord," he said in his Gaultic accent, "I bear greetings and warnings from your wife."

They'd stopped in the middle of the road, allowing the knights to rest their mounts a bit. The three drew tightly together so that their words could not pass easily to the others.

"What news?" Ransom asked him worriedly. "Is Claire safe?"

"She is, my lord. But we fear for the queen dowager. Genevese ships bound for the Vexin were turned aside by Estian's fleet. They brought their story to Atha Kleah. Lady Claire sent ships to bring relief to the Vexin, but they were outnumbered and turned back. Smoke was seen coming from Auxaunce."

Ransom glanced at Dearley, who shook his head in anger. "That explains the so-called peace."

"You didn't trust those miscreant Occitanians did you?" asked Sir Galveson.

"Almost," Ransom said. "They lured us to Chessy with promises of peace." If he had accepted, it would have compelled him not to defend the Vexin. Except Estian had known he would not accept, hence the threat about chasing them. It had compelled them to seek out the shortest route—to Brythonica—rather than the one that would have led them to the Vexin. "In the end, Estian changed the terms. We left him in Chessy yesterday."

"No doubt he's heading straight to the Vexin," said Galveson.

Dearley let out an angry sigh. "We've been made fools," he growled. "It will take days for our men to reach Beestone and warn the king."

Galveson grinned. "You forget Her Ladyship, the most excellent queen of the Fair Isle. She sent one of our men to Beestone already with the news. The king's army is already on the move. I passed it on my way here to tell you."

"The king's army?" Ransom asked. "Who leads it?"

"The king himself," said Galveson. "Along with the duke of the North and Lord Kiskaddon. They were riding like men being whipped. There were thousands of mercenaries with them, all riding together."

"How many?" Dearley asked.

"At least two thousand by my reckoning," answered Galveson. "When they learned I was going after you, they bid me ride like the devil himself and kill my horse if I needed to. I'm glad I found you before I reached Pree."

Ransom couldn't help but beam with pride. His wife had saved the day, much like she had years before, when she'd shown up with reinforcements just in time to help him defend Glosstyr. "Sir Galveson, you arrived just when we needed you."

"I do my best for the queen," the older man said with a smile of pleasure. "Shall I join you?"

"Every man will make a difference," Ransom said. He swiveled his horse around and addressed the other knights, many of whom were watching him keenly. He lifted his voice to be heard by all. "My brothers in arms! The Black King has deceived us and is laying siege to the duchy of Vexin. The king himself leads an army to the rescue. We must go at once to lend our might to his army. We don't flee from our enemies. We ride straight for them." He lifted his fist into the air. "To the king! *Dex aie!*"

"*Dex aie!*" shouted the knights in response.

No longer in fear of being chased from behind, Ransom and his knights rode over the hills of the Occitanian countryside. They trampled through fields of summer wheat and rode through orchards thick with plums and other fruits. Villagers, startled by their sudden appearance, fled in terror and bolted themselves in their cottages, but Ransom had no desire to harass the people. He knew the road to the Vexin, and when they reached it, the horses thundered toward the fortress of Auxaunce. They passed a few of the king's mercenaries, riding on lamed horses, and the men pointed in the direction the king's army had already passed.

Ransom could tell Dappled was weary from the constant pressure of riding, but he was a desert-bred horse and refused to slacken his pace. Some of Ransom's men fell behind, their destriers unable to match the awesome power of his mount, but Ransom felt a fiery determination to reach his king. Lady Alix was with Estian, and if they had come from Chessy, there was no way Ransom could overtake them. He worried that the king's life was in grave danger.

Estian had played him like a minstrel plucks a lute, using his sense of honor against him. Given what he knew of Lord Montfort, he suspected the duchess and her husband had been deceived as well.

When they were about a league or so from Auxaunce, they reached the spot in the road where Lord Rakestraw, the queen dowager's former constable, had been ambushed by DeVaux's men. Ransom recognized the hedge where he had taken his last stand, after all his companions were slain. His past suddenly reared up in his mind, and he could almost see his younger self, defending himself with Fountain magic he did not yet understand.

A tingle of magic responded to the memory, then reached out and revealed to him the presence of riders headed their way. In the distance, he saw knights approaching them.

Ransom reined in sharply, sweat streaking down his cheeks. He turned and saw his own men in disarray behind him, some still far in the distance. Even Dearley struggled to keep up with him, but now that he'd stopped, his first knight quickly reached him.

"How many do you think there are?" Dearley asked, out of breath.

Ransom didn't feel the sense of danger. "Gather the knights around us. Let's block the road."

"Yes," Dearley agreed. He turned his horse around and gave the orders. Knights began to gather quickly, and those with lances fixed to their stirrups withdrew them and prepared to charge.

Ransom gazed down the road, trying to understand whom the knights belonged to. And then he recognized the decorative armor of the man who led them, once pristine and now dented and thick with dust. It was James Wigant, Duke of North Cumbria.

"It's Lord James," Ransom said. "Follow me."

With the lead knights surrounding him, he started at a slow trot and noticed a long line of warriors following behind the duke of the North. Confusion rippled through Ransom's chest. Were they retreating?

As they closed together, Ransom saw that James had someone riding behind him, a young lad whom he instantly recognized. Although he was quite a bit older than on their last meeting, his identity was unmistakable. This was Drew, Constance's son. Ransom blinked in astonishment. The boy peered around Lord James, his face brightening when he saw Ransom.

"I know that knight," said Drew, giving him a wave and a smile.

"I would hope so," said James. "He's an ugly man but not nearly as ugly as his horse."

Ransom gaped as they stopped in front of each other. "I don't believe my eyes."

"The battle is over," said James with a grin. "When word came of Estian's trickery, I was sure we'd find you already in the Vexin, holding back the Occitanian army all by yourself. Instead, we came on them so fast we caught them by surprise. We won!"

Ransom didn't know what to say. He was relieved but also dumbfounded. "They were unaware?" Estian had the Wizr board. Surely he would have seen Jon-Landon coming.

James looked smug. "They were totally caught off guard, had no idea we were coming. To be honest, I thought the king was half-mad for even trying it. But we came, we saw, we trampled their defenders, and now we have two hundred hostages. Two hundred knights!" He beamed with pride. "I'm escorting them back to Beestone with half of the army. The ransoms alone will be worth a fortune."

Still, the news seemed too good to be true. As much as he wanted to believe it, it felt like part of a larger machination.

Ransom looked at him earnestly. "Was Estian there?"

"He arrived too late, no doubt from your interview with him."

"So Claire's warning came in time?"

"Indeed. When Jon-Landon learned that Auxaunce was under attack, he mustered every horse within the vicinity, and we rode straight through Occitania. I don't think Estian expected such a decisive action.

He probably counted on your meeting at Chessy being a sufficient deception. But no, the king has fought his first battle. And won. He's with Emiloh back at the fortress and has men repairing the damage to the castle. This was a decided victory, Ransom. And for once, you weren't there to save the day."

James had a way of knowing where to hurt a man. They had become allies—*family*—but the smug look on James's face reminded Ransom of the boy he'd been.

"I'm happy for you," Ransom said. "This alone may turn the tide of the war."

"Oh, it will," said James. "Two hundred knights. That is a sizable host, and it will cost Estian a sizable sum. And we have the boy." He glanced back at Drew and gave a friendly smile. "No longer can Estian claim to fight on his behalf."

Ransom couldn't remember the lad's age, but he seemed to be around twelve. Why had Estian sent him into the siege? Was he there to prevent Brythonica from interfering? Surely Constance and Lord Montfort would be discomfited by the part they'd played, however unwilling in Estian's sabotage.

James looked back at the men and steeds who had come to a halt behind him. He raised his hand and prepared to ride onward. "To Beestone! There, to claim our rewards."

Ransom looked into Drew's eyes. "Your mother misses you, lad," he said softly. "She wanted me to tell you that. And how much she loves you."

Drew's face fell. "I miss her, Lord Ransom."

"I know you do, lad."

Ransom had his knights depart from the road so that James and his army and their prisoners could pass. As they did, he watched the defeated eyes, the sullen looks from the Occitanians as they passed. Their helmets were all gone, and none of them were armed. Each man had his hands bound before him, his horse led by Lord James's men. One by one they passed, and Ransom looked at the sea of faces.

To his shock, he saw Guivret among them. Their eyes met, and a jolt of sorrow ripped through Ransom's chest when he saw the look of anger and distrust in Guivret's eyes. It had been years since Guivret had been captured during Ransom's mission to steal the Wizr board from Pree. What had Lady Alix done to him? No one had ever brought a hostage demand to Ransom, and his efforts to find out where Guivret was had all been met with silence.

Another prisoner he recognized was marched past him. It was Sir Chauvigny, Alix's husband and the Duke of Bayree. He had a scar across his eyebrow and eye. He glared at Ransom with undisguised hatred. And he spat on him as his horse passed.

The spittle hit Ransom in the face and trickled down his nose.

"Oy!" snarled one of the knights who'd witnessed the show of disrespect. "I could take your head off for that, duke or no!"

"Let him be," Ransom said, brushing the saliva away with his gauntlet. A sense of satisfaction welled up inside him. Estian wouldn't have allowed such a powerful man to be captured. That suggested Estian's plan really had backfired.

After the knights and their prisoners passed, Ransom and his men rode the final league to Auxaunce. When they arrived, the attackers' camp was still being taken down by Jon-Landon's men. The mercenaries were giddy with excitement, and many of them were drunk on Occitanian wine. Oxen were dragging siege engines up the ramparts to the castle itself. The king's flag with the Triple Lion waved from a banner from the highest spoke of the tower. The wagons had already been stripped of supplies.

A few dead horses littered the field, and dead soldiers had been stacked into heaps.

Ransom rode up to the castle gates. It had been years since he was last there. When he arrived and dismounted, he entered the castle with

Dearley and Dawson, the latter of whom seemed disappointed that they'd missed the fight.

The audience hall was thick with Jon-Landon's knights, who clashed their cups together and drank to one another's success. The king was conversing with his mother, Emiloh, and hadn't noticed his arrival, but Lord Faulkes approached with an arrogant smile.

"You finally made it," he said to Ransom with mocking eyes.

"I congratulate you on the victory."

"It was a devastating victory," said Faulkes. "One that will long be remembered. And where were you when the danger was the greatest? Supping with the enemy?"

Ransom felt his chest tighten with anger. He kept his expression calm. "I was on the king's business."

"Trying to reclaim one of your castles, eh? Did you have to grovel much?"

Ransom wanted to punch the man, and from the way Dearley and Dawson were looking at him, he wasn't alone in that. But he wouldn't stoop to his level.

"I'll speak to the king," he said, walking past Faulkes, who suddenly leaned toward him so that their shoulders jostled. It was a brazen sign of disrespect, the kind that happened between squires in the training yard. Not dukes of the realm.

As Ransom approached the king and the dowager queen, Emiloh noticed him first and smiled in relief. "Ransom!"

Jon-Landon turned slowly and gave Ransom a withering look. "Why are *you* here?"

His coldness shocked Ransom. "I came as soon as I learned about the siege," he said.

"You mean you didn't already know? How convenient."

"My lord," Emiloh said in a calming way.

"He can speak for himself, Duchess," said the king. "Were you not consorting with the enemy in Chessy while my mother's castle was under siege?"

Ransom felt his stomach shrink and twist with discomfort. "I went to Chessy with your permission."

"Oh?" drawled the king. "I find your loyalty suspect. I've asked the Espion to investigate your meeting in Chessy and learn what was said. In the meantime, I order you to return to Beestone castle at once. Wait for me there."

Ransom stared at Jon-Landon in surprise. When he glanced at Emiloh, he saw her look of shock and embarrassment.

Everyone in the hall had fallen silent and turned to watch the scene unfold. Ransom straightened, exhausted from the harrowing ride and little rest. He bowed to the king and then turned and walked out of the audience hall. He dared not look at Faulkes to note his reaction to the public humiliation.

Ransom didn't think he would have been able to restrain his anger if he had.

Where is my badger-brained husband? I've heard accounts that there was a battle fought at Auxaunce, a battle where Ceredigion vanquished the Occitanian army. There is even talk that Drew Argentine was captured during the siege. I've no news of this from Ransom, though. I'm making for Connaught castle by sea, so any word may be delayed further in reaching me. Lord Tenthor's illness is growing worse—I fear he won't survive the coming winter. At least it will be a peaceful winter, without the threat of war looming ahead. If Occitania was defeated, they will need to lick their wounds, pay ransoms for the captured, and hopefully allow us to negotiate for our lands.

It's time to go home. I miss my children. Hopefully, Connaught is still standing. The two boys get into mischief constantly, playing tricks on each other and the castle servants. I have baby Keeva with me still, and I know Sibyl misses her sister. We can be a family again soon. As long as that happens, this will all have been worth the aggravation.

—Claire de Murrow, "Duchess" of Legault
Leaving for Connaught

CHAPTER SEVEN

The Turning

Ransom's knights were beleaguered by the time they reached Beestone castle again. They'd tried camping in yew groves a couple of times, though they mostly rode through the nights, but sleep had been elusive even with their understandable fatigue. Ransom could not help but worry about the change in Jon-Landon's attitude and what it boded for the future. A sickening dread had crept into his chest, tugging and yanking on the strings of his heart. Even though Ransom was the most powerful lord in Ceredigion, he no longer felt protected by his station.

When he was younger, he had lost his place in Lord Kinghorn's mesnie, but that was far from the only thing he'd lost. His favorite horse had been skewered. Years later, he'd nearly lost his leg in an ambush, only to be dragged across Occitania as a hostage for months. He'd become one of Devon the Younger's most trusted companions—and then lost everything again due to unfounded accusations against his honor. He never wanted to feel that helpless again.

When they arrived at the village, there was great rejoicing among the townsfolk, and the mercenaries partook in the ruckus, spending livres so quickly they must have been freshly paid. Ransom saw soldiers trying to ply the maidens of the village for favors, only to be rebuffed.

The lack of discipline was vexing to him, but he rode past the drunkenness and up the hill to the castle proper. He was sore from riding so much and could smell his own reek from being trapped in his armor.

When he passed through the gatehouse, which was heavily guarded by Jon-Landon's men, he saw the inner bailey was full of prisoners in various stages of wretched misery. The knights had not only been stripped of their weapons but also their armor, which they'd need to repurchase after their ransoms were paid. Some had bloodstains on their tunics from injuries that had been left untreated. Some were sick. Mercenaries patrolled the yard and treated the prisoners with obvious contempt. He scowled at the sight, and although he had a mind to intervene, the king had already made his displeasure with him known. From years of working with Jon-Landon, he'd come to realize the king had an uncommon aversion to anything that had even the slightest hint of criticism.

Ransom dismounted Dappled, but a page told him that the castle stables were already full. Every inn was also swollen.

"I'll take the men and make a camp in a meadow outside town," Dearley told Ransom.

"Can I stay with you, my lord?" Dawson asked.

"We'll likely be bedding down on a stone floor," Ransom said.

"It doesn't matter. I have an ill feeling about this. I don't wish to leave you alone."

The request was touching, and Ransom nodded his acceptance. "Very well. Take the others to a meadow, Dearley. Be careful. I don't want any of the knights to start a brawl or be involved in one."

"I'll keep them away from the village," Dearley promised. He ordered the other knights to turn and follow him back down the hill, taking Dappled with him as well as Dawson's destrier.

"Are you worried about the king, Lord Ransom?" Dawson asked in a low voice.

"Aye," he replied simply.

"He treated you with great disrespect."

"Keep your voice down," Ransom warned.

Dawson had always been hotheaded, but he was a formidable knight and an excellent soldier. He was brave and dependable.

All things the king was not.

Ransom stared at the prisoners again and noticed a young man carrying water to them. At first he thought it was a page, but he realized with a start it was Drew Argentine. He dipped a ladle into a bucket and offered each man a drink. The looks the captured knights gave him were full of gratitude. There was a knight wearing the Eagle badge of North Cumbria who shadowed the boy and kept watch over him.

Dawson followed Ransom as he approached the young man. It took Drew a moment to notice him, but then the boy offered an exhausted smile.

"Lord Ransom, it's good to see you again." He dipped the ladle again and handed it to the next man. "Some of these men haven't eaten in two days."

"I'll talk to the castellan," Ransom promised. Pride swelled in his heart as he watched the lad attend to the captured. He had his mother's countenance, and her compassion too.

"Thank you."

Drew had smudges of dirt on his own face and a look of utter weariness, but he kept going, moving from man to man until the bucket had emptied. When the boy walked to the well in the middle of the courtyard, the knight attending to it didn't offer any assistance with the bucket as he lowered it down. Before Ransom could step forward, Dawson took over, retrieving the bucket, sloshing with fresh water, with a few tugs of his strong arms.

"Thank you," Drew said to him.

Dawson shook his head and looked over the scene, his expression brooding. It was obvious what he was thinking. Such a lack of courtesy was dishonorable—it went against the vows Jon-Landon had taken at his coronation, the ones required of him by the Fountain. But Drew was proving his own character, and Ransom was proud of him.

"I wondered, Lord Ransom," Drew said, "if you could send a message to my mother. Tell her where I am. That I'm safe and well."

"Will they not let you send a message?" Ransom asked with concern.

Drew looked at the knight, who wore the sigil of the North, and shook his head. "The king has forbidden *me* to send word to her. But you're on the king's council. Would you do it?"

"I will," Ransom promised. He knelt by the boy as Drew clenched the handle of the bucket. Putting a hand on Drew's shoulder, he offered a nod of encouragement. "Have courage. Your mother will ransom you. I'll make sure she knows where you are."

A relieved sigh came from Drew. "Thank you, Lord Ransom." He looked around the courtyard. "There are many thirsty still. I'd better go."

"Your mother would be proud of you," Ransom said, meaning every word.

"I try to make her proud," Drew said softly, looking down. "I'm grateful to be away from Pree. I liked it even less than here. But I miss Ploemeur. I miss it so much."

Ransom's heart ached for him. "You'll be back soon."

The boy looked into the distance. "I don't know. I don't think the king will ever let me go."

The blunt statement, spoken by a youth, cut Ransom to the bone. Yet he could not deny that he shared the boy's worry. Drew wasn't just Jon-Landon's nephew. He was his rival. The king would make Ploemeur bleed before he released Constance's son.

Ransom stood up and gave the young man a knightly salute. Drew smiled and then hefted the heavy bucket back to where he'd left off. With a jolt, Ransom noticed one of the prisoners was staring at him from across the courtyard. Guivret. The look he gave him was one of loathing.

"Talk to Guivret," Ransom said to Dawson. "See what you can learn from him."

"Aye, my lord," Dawson said.

Ransom left the courtyard and then entered the castle. The daylight was beginning to fail, and he was bone weary. He sought out the castellan and found him speaking with Lord James, who wore a fresh tunic and had a freshly trimmed beard. As he approached, James wrinkled his nose.

"By the Lady, Ransom, you stink!"

"The prisoners haven't been fed," Ransom said, ignoring the taunt.

The castellan's hair and beard were threaded with silver. "I'm trying my best, Lord Ransom, but the soldiers keep stealing from the larders. We're nearly out of food for ourselves."

"Have you posted a guard?" Ransom asked.

The castellan frowned. "I wouldn't go that far, my lord. They wanted to celebrate a remarkable victory. The king said he'd make a feast for everyone when he returns, and I have no idea where the meat will come from! I wasn't expecting to hold a three-day-long celebration."

"I understand, but the prisoners need some bread," James said to the castellan. "I didn't know they'd been deprived so long."

"I'm hoping supply wagons from Kingfountain will be here soon," the castellan grumbled. "As for yourself, Lord Ransom, I have a small room . . . hardly more than a closet. It's the best I can give you, but I can't house your men right now."

"I'm having them camp in the meadow," Ransom said. "I just have one with me."

"Good! I have things to attend to. If you'll pardon me, my lords."

James nodded in dismissal and shifted his attention to Ransom, giving him a wary look. "Are you going to ask the king to take Lady Constance's son as a ward?" he asked. "I know you've been on friendly terms with the duchess . . . in the past."

Was he hoping Ransom would say no?

"I don't think the king looks at me very favorably at the moment," Ransom admitted. "If I did ask, I'm not sure what he'd say."

James nodded and looked over his shoulder. "He wants me to take the boy to Dundrennan. He wants to keep him as a hostage, but he's afraid someone will be sent to rescue him once the truth comes out. I personally agree that he should go with me back to the North, but I didn't want to argue with you about it. Not in front of the king anyway."

Ransom felt a heaviness in his heart. "I don't think he would listen to me anyway."

"Why do you say that?"

"The way he treated me at Auxaunce. He ordered me to return here so he could accuse me of being in league with the Occitanians."

"You?" James said with exaggerated surprise. "Everyone knows you *hate* Estian."

Ransom shrugged. "Estian knows it too. He went to an enormous amount of trouble to trick me."

"Be careful."

"I'm trying to be."

James squinted and shook his head. "I'm more adept at politics than you, Ransom. I think you'd agree. Your integrity has taken you far, and deservedly so, but there are limits to what it can do for you. You're my brother-in-law now, so I'd give you a warning . . . if you'll listen."

"I'm listening."

James lowered his voice further. "I know Jon-Landon. Probably better than anyone except Lady Deborah. He's always been jealous of you, Ransom. And he's told me, in the past, that he wants to humble you. You're just an upstart who should never have been brought into his father's council. You know he's a rake. In my former days . . . I contributed to that defect in his character. I'm faithful to your sister, though! Just so you know!" He sighed, and Ransom swallowed a flare of anger. "He will keep trying to push you into defying him. You cannot give him a single reason to accuse you of disloyalty. If you do, he'll use it to ruin you. He won this battle on his own merits and a thief's luck, and it's emboldened him like I've never seen before. I'm afraid we're all about to discover who Jon-Landon really is."

Ransom licked his lips. "Thank you for your advice."

James gave him a serious look, lacking any humor or teasing. "I'm on your side, Ransom. But the winds have shifted. It won't do me, my son, or your sister any good if I side with you publicly right now. I hope I'm wrong. But I don't think I am."

When the king returned to Beestone, he was greeted by tumultuous cheers from the village below. He rode into the castle bailey with the hollow crown on his head and a royal cape splayed over his armor, his posture emanating arrogance. He gazed at the huddled mass of hungry, miserable men who had been captured in the battle, and the sight of their suffering brought a smile to his lips. There was a fading bruise on his cheekbone from the battle, and from what Ransom had heard, he'd fought in the thickest parts of it with a strength and courage that had startled his own men.

The king was reborn. At least in some eyes.

Jon-Landon's gaze fell on the nobles gathered at the door to the castle, singling out Ransom. There was a look of quiet satisfaction in his eyes. He was drunk on the glory of his victory. Which, to Ransom's way of thinking, had been more a matter of luck than skill. Estian had misjudged his foe—having lured Ransom away, he'd thought it safe to invade the Vexin. He would have been right had Claire not sent her warning. Estian's miscalculation had proven costly for him, but any military leader could have won a battle against a startled foe.

The nobles all gathered together in the great hall, where Jon-Landon resumed his seat on the main chair. Faulkes came to stand at his side, hand on his sword hilt, in an imperious manner. The nobles bowed before their king and were seated on the benches assembled for that purpose.

Jon-Landon spoke with an air of mocking in his voice. "So good of you all to have gathered so quickly. My lady mother is safely ensconced back in Auxaunce . . . if you'll pardon the rhyme. The Vexin is ours still. I've had an embassy from Estian seeking terms of peace. And of course he desires it, after his shameful defeat!"

"Your Grace's courage and fortitude has been proven to exceed his own," Faulkes said lavishly.

Jon-Landon smiled at the praise. "I will make him beg for it. I will make him grovel. As with all kings, it is now time for me to reward those who were faithful and to punish . . . the disobedient." His eyes immediately went to Ransom. "Lord Ransom. Stand."

A sickening bloomed inside Ransom's heart. He felt the strain of loyalty to this man. A man who, because of him, wore the crown. Surely Jon-Landon knew that. And he was about to get his revenge.

Ransom stood and approached the dais. "Yes, my king?"

"I'm doubtful of your loyalty, Lord Ransom," said the king in a taunting way. "It was you who tried to convince me that Estian wanted peace. It was you who stood the most to gain from that peace, was it not?"

How long had Jon-Landon been practicing his little speech?

Instead of answering the question, Ransom looked him in the eye. "I have always been loyal to the kings of Ceredigion. No man can prove otherwise."

"I have it from my trusted Espion that you did not accept the terms offered by Estian at Chessy? Even though I ordered you to accept the terms."

"That is not true," Ransom said. "Estian changed the terms of the deal at the last moment. If I'd accepted, it would have undermined your power and my ability to help protect your holdings."

"Are you calling my Espion liars? Or me?" said the king. He felt the trap creaking, ready to snap.

"I challenge any man who proclaims me disloyal to trial by combat," Ransom answered. As a knight, that was his prerogative. According to the code of Virtus, the Fountain would not let an innocent man lose.

Jon-Landon's eyes narrowed. As the king, he couldn't challenge Ransom directly—nor would he have won. A champion could serve as substitute, but from the silence that hung over the audience hall, no one else was willing to fight Ransom in his place.

The silence weighed heavier. Ransom waited, eyes fixed on the king's.

Jon-Landon's moment was being ruined, and he knew it. With a petulant look at the nobles assembled, he turned back to Ransom.

"You are no longer part of my council, Ransom Barton. I dismiss you. To prove your loyalty to me, you must return to Legault and fetch your sons. And you will bring them to Kingfountain as hostages for your good faith."

Ransom's ears rang as outrage pooled within him, filling every corner of his being. The insult had been deliberately chosen, for Ransom himself had been held as a hostage at Kingfountain. King Gervase had proven to be a kind man, almost a father, but Jon-Landon was not Gervase.

Some in the audience gasped. Murmurs thickened in the room. James's warning echoed in the corridors of his mind. Yes, Jon-Landon was trying to provoke him into rebellion.

Although his heart was torn by consternation, by worry about the boys, about Claire and how she'd react, Ransom bowed before the king. "Of course, my liege. I am obedient to your commands. I have nothing to fear in submitting to your will."

The king looked surprised. He hadn't expected such a mild reaction. "Good. I will be back at the palace soon. You have a fortnight."

"May I depart, then?" Ransom asked.

"I have no further need of you," said Jon-Landon with a dismissive flick of his hand.

Ransom turned and strode out of the audience hall, his cheeks burning. He had never been treated this poorly by any of the other men he'd served, and it galled him. Some of the lords he passed smirked at his fall from grace, but Lord Kiskaddon looked horrified. James gave him a sympathetic glance before subtly shaking his head and averting his gaze. Sir Dawson, who fell in beside Ransom, looked angry enough to rush to the front of the hall and stab the king through with his bastard sword.

When they reached the bailey, Ransom sent Dawson down to the meadow to fetch Dappled. He stood fuming in the courtyard, looking at the distressed prisoners, some of whom had collapsed with hunger. Flies buzzed around them.

What would Claire say when he reached her?

She'd refuse; he knew she would. But what choice did they really have? If the king mustered all Ceredigion's might against them, before the mercenaries were released for winter, then Legault and her dominion over it would be destroyed. They would lose literally everything.

So distraught was he that he didn't hear the approaching boots. He felt a hand on his arm and turned to find Hal Kiskaddon there, a look of outrage on his face.

"That should never have happened," Kiskaddon muttered angrily. "By the Lady, I can't believe my own ears! It makes me sick."

Ransom felt it was only fair to share the warning he'd gotten from James. He said, "Be on your alert with the king from now on. What he did to me, he will do to each and every one of you."

"I pray you're wrong," Kiskaddon said darkly.

"We shall see."

My heart is cold with fear. When we returned to Connaught, a message from Ransom awaited us. It was brief—too brief. He said he is out of favor with the king and has been dismissed from the council. He had to send a rider to Glosstyr and from thence a ship to Connaught to give me news of his coming arrival because he cannot use the king's messengers anymore.

There is more bad news coming. But what it is, he would not say.

What will become of us? I clutch my children close, fearing the day when Ransom's loyalty will be tested to the breaking point. That sniveling, jealous, feckless brat of a king. Ransom is worth ten of him. Maybe it is time to defy him. In a clash of wills, I would think we would prevail.

I am fearful. But I am also full of wrath.

—Claire de Murrow, Queen of the Fair Isle
Connaught Castle

CHAPTER EIGHT

No Good Choices

The ship rocked on the choppy waters, sending a spray into their faces. Ransom leaned against the railing, watching as the cliffs drew nearer. Dearley stood on one side of him, wiping a hand across his mouth, the ends of his hair dripping, and on his other side stood Dawson, gazing at the distant fortress. The land they approached was hauntingly beautiful, with verdant pastures and ageless trees. The stone fortress stood as a formidable defense against the enemies of the Fair Isle. But as he stared up at the walls, he knew they were not strong enough to withstand the full might of Ceredigion.

The Elder King had helped Claire's father tame the island. Even though the Gaultic nobles were more united now than they had been in the past, the memory of the invasion still lingered. They'd balk at defying the man who wore the hollow crown and wielded his power with impunity.

"Claire will be furious," Dearley said, speaking the unspeakable at last.

"She has every right to be," Dawson snarled. His fury at the king had not abated since they'd left Beestone castle.

"The king does this deliberately," Dearley said, wiping his mouth on his forearm. "He's trying to drive us into rebellion."

He'd tried before, over the years, just as he had with all his followers, but never had his efforts been so blatant, so *pointed*. His victory against Estian was behind this.

"And he's an utter pondfoot for daring it," Dawson said. He shook his head. "If you joined forces with Lord James and Lord Kiskaddon, the three of you could stand up to him together."

"Get such thoughts out of your head, Dawson," Ransom said. "The last any of us needs is more war, especially from within. And I won't make any decisions before I get Claire's insights. She has a stake in this as well. And should we lose, we'd lose everything. Including our lives."

Indeed, her counsel meant everything to him, and if they were to rebel, her own lands would likely be forfeit. There was so much at stake, not the least of which was the Fountain's forewarning of who the next king needed to be in order for Ceredigion to survive. If Ransom could not be loyal to the king in his own right, he would *always* be loyal to the Fountain.

The three of them stared glumly as the ship approached the docks. Ransom wanted to be home, but he knew the news he brought would break Claire's heart.

Because the waves were so choppy, a boat from the docks was rowed out to them so they would not have to wait until the winds calmed down. Climbing overboard and into the smaller boat was tricky, but they all managed it, and the two sailors who'd come for them rowed them back with the wind pushing them the whole way.

He looked up and saw Claire and the twins waiting for him at the pier. The boys were whacking at each other with wooden longswords. His heart panged to see them at play. They'd grown so much since he'd last seen them. A sigh escaped him, and Dearley put a comforting hand on Ransom's shoulder.

When they reached the pier, Ransom climbed up the ladder first, and the boys ran to him with exuberant grins and hugged him around the waist.

"Papa! You're back!"

"I saw him first!"

"No, I did!"

He hooked his hand around Willem's neck and dropped down on one knee, clutching both of his boys in his arms. Only then did he look into Claire's eyes, deep wells of worry and fear. Her beautiful hair was streaming in the wind. She approached more calmly, then tousled young Devon's hair.

"Is it so bad as that?" she asked him earnestly.

He nodded, his throat too thick to speak.

It was worse.

Claire paced in their bedchamber, the door bolted, the two of them alone. He'd told her about the trickery by Estian, arriving too late to the battle for Auxaunce, and then the deliberate humiliation back at Beestone. The shock on her face had struck him like a blow. She looked angry enough to take a ship to Kingfountain and challenge the king to a duel, and he had not yet told her about the boys.

"I'm the one who sent him word about the Vexin!" she said with fury. "If not for my warning, he never would have won that battle. And he accuses *you* of intrigue?"

"There is no logic or justice in his words," Ransom said. "I've talked it over with Simon, Dearley, and Dawson, and we all agree. He's using his only victory as a chance to break our power. He does not want to be beholden to us any longer."

"You're the one who gave him the hollow crown!" Claire raged. "Is this how he repays you? No, Ransom, it's not just a desire to be independent of us. He wants to *punish* us both. Me for rejecting him. As if I would ever want such a disgusting eel in my bed. And he hates you because you have character, and he has none."

"I haven't told you the worst yet," Ransom said, dreading the moment.

"How can it be worse than this?"

Ransom looked into her eyes worriedly. "He demanded hostages. The twins. He gave me a fortnight to bring them to Kingfountain."

Her mouth opened, but no words came out. Her hands closed into fists, and her knuckles went bone white. "Our sons?"

Ransom nodded. "He is provoking us into rebellion."

"And what did you tell him? You refused, certainly."

"I did not. I wouldn't have made a decision like that without you."

"But you did make a decision. You told him you'd bring them!"

"What else could I have said that wouldn't have been treated as treason?"

"You could have said no!" she shot at him.

Ransom held up his hands. "If I had, I'd be in a dungeon at the palace right now. As it stands, we are together, and we can make this decision together. If we're going to rebel, we should do it on our terms, not his." He slowed his breathing, trying not to let his emotions rule him. Despite his righteous anger, his protectiveness of his family, he knew down to the marrow of his being that he could not forsake the king without dire consequences. He hoped, through patience, that he could lead Jon-Landon back on a better path, that he might become more like his father and his brothers. But if not, he still had to obey his duty to the Fountain. Ransom himself could not see the larger picture, but he had been shown one piece of it: Jon-Landon's son had to become king. And in order for that to happen, his father must at least temporarily retain that role. If the Argentine dynasty were allowed to fail, Jon-Landon wasn't the only one who would pay the price.

Claire covered her mouth and shook her head. "I was not expecting this, Ransom."

"We won't be the only ones treated thusly. I warned Kiskaddon that whatever happened to us could happen to him next. Hal was Bennett's favorite. Jon-Landon would replace him in a trice."

"Oh, Ransom, what do we do? My mother's heart wants to defy the king, to force him to come here and take my sons away from my stiff corpse. I'm so angry, I could eat his heart like my pagan ancestors used to do." She shook her head again. "But that would just give him what he wants—rebellion and an opportunity to crush it. He'd take everything from us, including our lives. I don't want to see you in a boat heading over the falls, Husband."

"And I don't want to be in one," Ransom said, closing the distance between them. He gripped her shoulders. "The only way we can see this through is to give him what he demands. We refuse him at our peril. I do not trust Jon-Landon with our sons. But I have to. *We* have to. Let him think we're beaten. Wait for the giddiness of his victory to dim. A day will come when he needs us. If we are patient, we can have our boys returned to us."

Tears trickled down Claire's cheeks, but the hot anger had not left her eyes. "We might be able to beat him, Ransom. If he came here."

"Perhaps. It would be costly. But I cannot bring myself to rebel. Every *part* of who I am would be compromised. I'm afraid . . . I'm afraid of who I would become." He stared at her pleadingly, feeling the darkness inside him clamoring to escape.

Claire put her hands on his cheeks. "If anything were to happen to our sons, I would never forgive myself."

"There is more at stake here than just our sons," Ransom said emphatically, with all the sincerity he could muster. "The Fountain has whispered to me that Jon-Landon's son will be our king. I don't know how long it will be before that happens, but I've been told to ensure that it *does* happen."

She studied him for a moment, her eyes widening with surprise and then a hint of skepticism. Although he'd told her before that the

Fountain had spoken to him, he'd never told her what had been said. She didn't believe in the Fountain, and he knew his words were unlikely to sway her. And yet holding the truth back would have felt wrong. She needed to understand the stakes.

Finally, she said, "I believe that you heard a message, Ransom. But how do you know it was truly from the Fountain? Could not the Aos Sí have given you this message? Might they not want all the kingdoms destroyed?" She paused. "Are you quite certain you didn't see Gervase in a dream?"

He sighed. "I don't believe in the Aos Sí, Claire. What I've seen . . . felt . . . witnessed with my own eyes tells me the Fountain is the source of these communications. I've seen the shade of King Gervase, and he spoke to me of the Deep Fathoms. I was awake when I saw him, Claire, as awake as I am now. I cannot deny what happened, or the truths that were shared with me. I don't expect you to believe as I do. But at least I want you to understand why I feel we must endure this."

Claire closed her eyes for a long moment before opening them again. He couldn't tell if she believed in his words or not, but she didn't argue with him.

"It isn't fair of him to take our sons."

He leaned forward until their foreheads were touching. "No, it isn't fair, it isn't right. But he is the king, and he's testing our loyalty. Relenting is the only way we can avoid immediate war." Grief and anger welled up in him. "I don't want to give them up."

"I know you don't, Ransom," she said. She lowered her hands and wrapped her arms around him, laying her cheek against his chest. "His success has blinded him to the possibility of failure. You're right. He will offend others next. Hal should be very wary. And if his son will be king, the boy needs someone he can trust. He needs you."

"Oh, Hal is wary already." He stroked her hair. "Thank you for your faith in me."

"This is not how a king is supposed to act," she said, sighing. "But I agree. We must send them. For the reasons you shared with me, and also because he would surely attack us if we refused. Although I doubt even half of Legault would rise up to defend against him, I don't want to see my home destroyed. I hate to say this, but the twins will probably be thrilled with the news. Maybe they will do so much damage at the castle that Jon-Landon will have to send them home?" She had a smile in her voice, but there were tears in her eyes when she looked up at him. "Oh, Ransom. Why? Why would he be so cruel? What kind of man threatens a child for power?"

Many did. Even Gervase had done so, and the old king had been a good man. Her words put him in mind of Drew Argentine, who would likely be a hostage until he came of age, if not longer. "The practice is far more common than it should be. I saw Drew Argentine after the battle," he said. "Constance hasn't seen him for years. Estian took him away from her."

"I'm sorry for that," Claire said softly, and from the way she said it, he could tell she no longer feared his connection with Constance. Perhaps she sensed, without knowing why, that the magical link between them had been severed with the passing of the ring to Montfort.

"At least Drew will be safe in Dundrennan," Ransom said. Something felt wrong about the words, however, like the prick of a bur against his skin. He felt a little thump in his heart, and then the feeling was gone.

"Do you still know that Espion girl? The one who helped you get Benedict back from Lord Gotz."

"Cecily still works for Jon-Landon."

"Maybe, when you bring the boys to Kingfountain, you can ask her to watch over them. Do you think she would?"

He felt a spark of hope. "I do. For a time. Once Jon-Landon collects all those ransoms, he might be able to afford to send her to Pisan to train as a poisoner. It would be the prudent thing to do. We need our own poisoner to fight Alix."

Claire nodded. "You said Alix's husband was also taken?"

"Yes. I wonder who will be given custody of him? Whoever it is will be in danger. She's not someone you'd want to cross."

"Neither is our king," Claire said. "You have a fortnight to bring the boys to the palace?"

"Yes. I want to spend as much time with them as I can before we go."

"I want us all to spend time together. Sibyl missed you so much, and Keeva hardly knows you."

"Let's gather the family," Ransom said. "They need to hear the news as well."

"May the Aos Sí watch over them," Claire murmured. "Or the Fountain. It might not hurt to pray to both right now."

※

It was a painful farewell. Claire held their youngest in her arms, wiping tears from her eyes as she smiled at the boys and bid them be brave. Devon and Willem were dressed in new tunics, and each had a wooden sword buckled to the scabbard on his belt. They squirmed when she tried to kiss them.

"You must not misbehave," said Sibyl to them in her serious way. Even though she was younger, she acted the part of an older sister to her brothers. Indeed, she had insisted on going with them to keep them out of trouble at the palace. Her request had been denied, but it had touched both Ransom and Claire.

"There's a cistern under the palace!" Devon said excitedly. "We're going to swim in it!"

"People drink that water," Sibyl said with concern. "I don't think you should."

Willem threw up his hands. "Can we go? We should have left already."

Ransom looked at Claire and saw her smiling through her tears.

Claire hooked her arm around Ransom's neck and kissed his cheek. "At least no one can say they dragged the boys away by force."

"Can we go?" Devon said, stamping his foot.

"They'll kiss first," said Willem with a wince of disgust. "Let's get in the boat. Good-bye, Sib!"

Devon shoved Willem and then raced toward the boat, his brother charging after him and crying out that it would be unfair if he beat him.

"Come back to me," Claire whispered in Ransom's ear.

"I will," he answered. But a feeling of foreboding struck him in the chest. Would he be able to keep his promise?

Winter has ended, and the trading ships come and go freely, and still no word has arrived from court. It is strange, truly, to watch Ransom down in the training yard, working with his knights and leading the training of another generation of warriors. I could get used to this. He is more relaxed than he's been in a long time, but I can tell he's anxiously awaiting a summons. There has been little news from Glosstyr, save that the winter was overly mild. One of the Occitanian hostages fell ill at Blackpool and died. That will not look well on us, I think.

I've written to my boys every week during the winter and saved the notes to share with them now that the seas are safe to travel.

Lord Tenthor died. I forgot to mention it. He was a good man, one who was a strong ally to us. He had no sons or daughters, so his niece, a girl of sixteen, will inherit his lands. She's now my ward. Many nobles have been asking for her hand, for Tenthor was a man of great wealth. I have an idea that I need to run past Ransom on that front.

—Claire de Murrow, Queen of the Fair Isle
Connaught Castle
In the spring

CHAPTER NINE

The King's Summons

After spending the morning training the young knights of the castle, Ransom returned to his room to wipe away the sweat and change into a new tunic. Then he strapped the Raven scabbard around his waist again, seeing it glow blue as its magic radiated through him, healing the small cut he'd earned during the training. His reflexes were not as quick as they'd once been, and he needed a bit more rest before catching his breath. He splashed more water on his face, dried off with a towel, and then left the room to find Claire and the girls.

They were in the solar, where little Sibyl was studying a Wizr board, examining each piece carefully before setting it down in its proper place. It was a game that Ransom didn't fancy playing, given all the trouble another Wizr set had caused them, but the set had been brought out during the long winter nights, and he'd played a few rounds with her. She was a smart one, her eyes so serious for one so young.

Claire was writing in her book, which she closed when he arrived. The nurse was changing Keeva from a nightdress to her day attire and speaking to her slowly with a tender Gaultic lilt.

"How was the training yard?" Claire asked, rising from the window seat and leaving her book on the cushion. She came and embraced him, tipping her head up to kiss him.

"They're good lads," Ransom said. "The five eldest are ready to be done with their training, I think. That will give us five more openings this year."

"Is Dawson as strict a sword master as you?" Claire asked in a teasing voice.

"Captain Baldwin is the strict one," Ransom said. "He may be getting on in years, but he's just as surly as I remember him. Dawson trains with the older boys. They love hearing his stories."

"You have stories to tell as well."

Ransom shrugged and settled down in a chair, feeling his lower back ache. The glow of the scabbard dimmed as the magic finished its work.

Claire went to the window seat. She opened a little box that sat there and returned to him with something in her hand. It took him a moment to realize what it was—a piece of penuche, one of the morsels that Dearley had bought in Chessy. The smell of it was tantalizing.

"This is the last one," Claire said, sitting down on his lap. "I thought you should have it."

"I got them for you," he reminded her.

"But I've shared. Here, let me break it in half, and we can both enjoy the last bite. I don't know that either of us will ever venture into Occitania again, so we may as well enjoy it. We prolonged the treat as best we could."

She pinched the morsel in half and then fed one piece to him. The sugary flavor melted on his tongue as he watched her bite into the other piece. The sight of her enjoyment was as delicious as the taste, and the memories of that day with her in Chessy. He'd already loved her then, but there'd been no prospect of marrying her.

"Thank you for the gift, Husband," she said, wrapping her arms around his neck. She leaned in and kissed him again.

He gripped her waist, enjoying the sweetness of the moment, but his thoughts were still muddled at the lack of tidings from court. He was a duke of the realm, and he had no idea what had happened during the winter months or what the king was planning for the future. Or, for that matter, what was happening with his sons. The lack of information troubled him more than he wished to communicate to Claire.

"Have you given any thought to Lord Tenthor's niece?" Claire asked him, remaining on his lap.

He smiled and chuckled. "We've had . . . five requests for her hand already? Who wouldn't want such a wealthy heiress as a wife?" He squeezed her hips.

"So mercenary," she said. "I've an idea."

"I'd welcome it."

"Why don't we introduce her to Sir Dawson?"

Her suggestion came as a shock. "Truly? You don't wish to suggest a husband from Legault?"

"Dawson has been so loyal to you, and it's your duty to reward him for his faithful service. Besides, Dearley already has a wife and so does Simon. Dawson is the obvious choice."

"You don't need to convince me," Ransom said. "It would give him a title. Allow him to inherit lands of his own. Start his own mesnie."

"Then we should invite her to Connaught. Perhaps we could send him to fetch her? It'll be her choice, of course. And his."

"Thank you, Claire. With all the other requests, I'd assumed you'd want to match her with a Legaultan noble."

Claire kissed the tip of his nose and stood again. "I have those letters I'd like to send to the boys."

"Can I write them one, Mama?" Sibyl asked sweetly from her place by the Wizr table.

"Of course, darling. Who should we send to deliver them, Ransom?"

"I should go myself," Ransom said, his heart tugging with longing to see his boys.

"You haven't been summoned to court."

"Do I need a summons to check on my children?" Ransom said.

"One will come," Claire said. "I'm certain of it. It would be best to send someone else, but who?"

"Dearley, of course."

She shook her head. "Elodie is pregnant. He shouldn't leave her now."

"The babe isn't due for a long time still, surely. By boat it wouldn't be a long journey."

Claire wrinkled her nose and shook her head.

"Dawson won't do because you want to send him to fetch Tenthor's niece."

"I like Dawson," Sibyl said, admiring one of the pieces shaped as a knight. "You should let *me* marry him."

Claire grinned at her innocent words. "He's a bit too old for you, darling."

"I'll grow up faster," she said.

Ransom chuckled. "Simon, then. We'll send someone to Glosstyr with the letters. Simon can deliver them to the boys and then come to us in Legault to tell us how he found them."

Claire nodded. "A good choice."

The sound of a horse riding up the cliff road caught their attention. Claire went to the window, and Ransom rose from the comfortable chair, his back groaning again. Sometimes he wished the scabbard healed the aches and pains of his age and rough life. Claire leaned out a little and then pulled back, giving him a worried look. When Ransom poked his head out, he saw their sheriff, Lord Toole, hastening to the gate, which was already open. The horse's hooves clattered on the stones in the courtyard, and then Toole leaped from the saddle and began to hurry toward the castle.

Toole had served Claire faithfully since her return as queen—or "duchess" as Jon-Landon now called her—but why was he here now?

"Did you summon him?" Ransom asked her.

"No," she responded.

"Here's the lass," said the maid, bringing Keeva to her.

"Take her and Sibyl to the nursery," Claire ordered.

"I want to stay here. I like Lord Toole," said Sibyl.

"Mind your mother," said the maid in a scolding tone. Sibyl sighed and obeyed, leaving Ransom and Claire alone.

Her face was drawn.

Ransom had an uneasy feeling too, and it only swelled at the sound of boots thundering down the hall. The door opened, admitting Dearley and Lord Toole, who looked winded and agitated.

"News from Atha Kleah," Dearley said, gesturing to the emissary.

"You've come in a great hurry," Claire told Lord Toole.

"My lady," he gasped.

Ransom fetched him a drink of cider, and he gratefully accepted it and gulped some down. "Thank you, Lord Ransom." He looked at both of them in turn and then sighed. "I hardly know how to begin."

"Tell us," Claire pleaded.

Lord Toole set the cup down and started to pace. "A ship bearing the three lions arrived in Atha Kleah two days ago. It was Lord Faulkes from Kingfountain."

Claire's brow pinched in worry, and she looked quickly to Ransom.

"What did he want?" Ransom asked.

"The castle. He took control of it immediately. Had fifty knights with him, and before we knew what was going on, he'd taken the gate-house in the name of the king."

"Máthair milis," Claire proclaimed under her breath.

"Your knights asked if they should fight, but I told them to stand down," Toole said. "We were outnumbered, and the king's men were already inside."

Dearley gave Ransom a nervous glance, but there was fire behind it.

"He took control of the fortress of Atha Kleah?" Ransom asked. "To what purpose?"

"I asked Lord Faulkes that very question. His answer? That he is the king's envoy in Legault now. Jon-Landon heard of Lord Tenthor's death and has claimed wardship of Lord Tenthor's niece, Orla, whom he's now bestowed on Lord Faulkes."

Claire's mouth opened in shock and then rage. "That's not his right!"

"I know, my lady," Toole said. "Faulkes doesn't care about your rights or our customs. He said Legault is a vassal land to Ceredigion, and that the king's rights triumph."

She looked at Ransom. "The nobles will be furious."

"Some already are, but others see it as an opportunity to win favor with the man who wears the hollow crown," Toole said seriously. He withdrew a letter from his belt and handed it to Ransom. "The king has summoned you to court."

Ransom looked at the message as if it were a snake, but it bore the seal of the Elder King. There was no mistaking it. He took the message and broke the seal. Opening it, he read the formal writing, recognizing the master of the rolls's unique style of penmanship.

> *Greetings,*
> *King Jon-Landon Argentine issues this writ of summons to Lord Marshall Barton, heretofore known as Ransom Barton, to come to Kingfountain in ten days on peril of forfeiting his lands, titles, and the grace of His Royal Majesty. He will bring five thousand livres as scutage in lieu of service of his knights this year and remand said scutage to the king's coffers at the royal palace in person. Signed in the presence of His Royal Majesty, King Jon-Landon Argentine.*

Ransom silently passed the message to Claire, who sucked in her breath.

"What does he want?" Dearley asked somberly.

"Five thousand livres in scutage," Claire said bitterly. "And he's to bring it himself. This is a trick," she added, slapping the message in her hand. "It is no coincidence that Ransom is being summoned just after Lord Faulkes took the fortress at Atha Kleah. Faulkes is here to invade Legault. On the king's orders!"

That was exactly how it looked to Ransom as well. "If I defy him, he will claim the land anyway."

"This is an injustice," Claire said, her voice trembling with rage. "This is my land, my people!"

"If I may," Lord Toole said. "The king is provoking another conflict. First, he demanded hostages from you. Now, he invades your lands. My lord, my lady, tread carefully. Respond to his summons, bring the scutage, but Lord Ransom must not leave Legault until you take hostages of your own."

"What?" Claire demanded.

"Use his own stratagem against him," Toole said. "You know the nobles of the Fair Isle as well as I do, my lady. Some will jump at this moment to switch sides, believing it will open new opportunities to them. With Lord Tenthor dead, you've lost one of your greatest defenders among the nobles. Others will see this as an opportunity to rise up and take a larger piece of the pie. They've only been waiting for a sign of weakness. Show them none. Demand hostages before Lord Ransom leaves, to ensure their loyalty."

Claire looked at Lord Toole in shock and then shifted her gaze to Ransom. "How could we, when we know the pain that will cause?"

Ransom shook his head. "I'll not use children to ensure loyalty."

Lord Toole closed his eyes and bowed his head. "I understand your sensibilities." He opened his eyes again and looked determinedly at Ransom. "Still, I must ask you to reconsider. From what I've heard, Lord Faulkes is a scheming and dishonorable man. He is the king's lackey, sent here to sow discord. If you are gone, Lord Ransom, then he will attack Connaught."

"That would be in direct defiance of my oath of fealty," Ransom said. "If the king breaches the peace first, then I have no remaining obligation of loyalty."

"He's already proven himself incapable of honor," Dearley said. "I agree with Lord Toole. Any hostages we take will be safer than those kept at Kingfountain."

"I will not," Ransom said angrily. "We only train children who are sent here willingly by their parents. I'll have no hostages."

"Nor I," said Claire, meeting his determination with her own. She gripped his hand tightly.

Lord Toole sighed again. "I feared this would be your answer. By doing so you make yourselves and Legault vulnerable. I will not fight the King of Ceredigion, and I will not fight you. I must resign from my post."

"Lord Toole," Claire said with disappointment.

"My lady, I've always given you my faithful service, but I'm growing old. If Lord Ransom goes to Kingfountain, there is every reason to believe the king will delay him from returning. Jon-Landon Argentine is attempting to seize control of Legault. Only a powerful deterrent will stop him from achieving his aims. If you let your personal feelings rule the day, then you're playing into his hands. You *will* lose your power here. I cannot defend the realm if you will not."

Ransom glanced at Dearley, whose emotions were plain on his face. He agreed with Lord Toole. He thought they were making a foolish choice. Turning, Ransom addressed Claire. "I'll go to Atha Kleah and make the nobles swear an oath that they will remain loyal."

Claire swallowed and nodded firmly.

"They won't honor it," Lord Toole predicted.

"Then we will see who is faithful and who is not," Ransom said. "*I* am true to my promises. I will go to Kingfountain." Clenching Claire's hand still, he raised her fingers to his mouth and kissed them.

It was agony watching Ransom leave Connaught castle. He's going to Atha Kleah first to demand oaths of loyalty from the Gaultic lords. Dawson is going with him to Atha Kleah but will return to the castle with news of how it went. Simon will arrange for the scutage to be paid from Glosstyr, and Ransom will travel on the ship that brings the coin to the palace. He left Dearley here and commanded him to defend the castle and our families. Then I kissed him good-bye and watched with an aching heart as he held Sibyl very close. She didn't want to let him go, and it nearly made me blubber. He kissed little Keeva, and then he was gone.

My feelings have been in unrest since he left. He is obeying the king's summons, but I have a dark sense that more is at stake here than we know. There are designs at work for Legault. There are designs against my husband. We have a treacherous man as our king now. I hope Ransom can maneuver what is coming. The other lords of Ceredigion must be watching our situation with worry. If Ransom can be brought so low, then so can any of them.

I pray to the Aos Sí that he'll be protected. But I also put a coin into the courtyard well.

—*Claire de Murrow, Queen of the Fair Isle*
(when vanity is king)

CHAPTER TEN

Broken Virtus

hen Ransom reached Atha Kleah, the town was in an uproar. As he and Dawson and their escort rode down the street toward the fortress, they were besieged by townsfolk, mostly merchants, demanding an audience with him.

"Is it true, Lord Ransom?" one of them asked, a hot-faced merchant with a look of dread. "We must start paying tribute to Kingfountain now?"

Many echoed his concerns. Ransom held up his hand, pressing through the throng with Dappled to get to the open drawbridge. As they drew nearer, Ransom saw the banner flying from the highest spoke—the Triple Lion. It made his stomach sour to see it.

"Lord Ransom! Lord Ransom!"

They continued to shout his name, but he didn't stop. He had no reassurances to offer them. When he and his escort reached the gap, he saw a knight in armor standing on the wall.

"Who goes there!" shouted the guard.

"It's Lord Ransom, you dolt!" Dawson barked back. "Lower the drawbridge."

Ransom wore his hauberk beneath his tunic, along with some arm bracers and leg bracers. It was the first time he'd donned his armor since winter. Although he didn't anticipate a battle, he also didn't want to be caught unprepared in case of trouble. He'd brought a dozen knights with him. Not enough to start trouble but enough to protect him if things turned ugly.

The knight on the bulwark gave a shout, and the winches for the drawbridge began to squeal. The fishy smell of the moat filled Ransom's nostrils as he gazed at the lowering drawbridge. A few gulls made noisy cries as they sailed around the mastheads of the ships in the dock.

With a loud thunk, the drawbridge settled into place, and Ransom and his knights crossed it on their mounts, the hooves thudding against the splintered wood of the bridge. When they reached the bailey, the drawbridge was lifted once again.

The knight from the wall had come down to greet them. "I'm Sir Cole," he said. "Part of Lord Faulkes's mesnie. I recognize you, Lord Ransom."

"Where is he?" Ransom asked, still astride Dappled, looking down at the younger man.

"He's meeting with the nobles of Legault," said Cole.

Dawson grimaced in anger. It was not Faulkes's right to summon the nobles for a meeting. This was another affront. A deliberate provocation.

Ransom dismounted and motioned for his knights to follow him. Cole led them into the great hall of the castle. The knights on patrol all wore the badge of the Triple Lion. One of them gave Ransom a nasty smirk, and he had to quell the temptation to punch the man's teeth in.

When they reached the hall, there was a great deal of murmuring. Faulkes sat in Claire's seat, a goblet in hand and a petulant look on his face. Ransom recognized each and every one of the nobles assembled around him—men and ladies whom he had heard grievances from for years. Many of them appeared upset.

"Ah, Lord Ransom—at last!" shouted Faulkes, raising his cup in salute.

The murmurs grew louder, and all eyes went to Ransom and his knights. Some looked eager, as if anticipating a fight right then and there. He noticed a few of them whispering to each other behind their hands.

"Your visit is a surprise, Lord Faulkes," Ransom said. "I hope you're enjoying your stay."

Faulkes took the greeting with a smug smile. "I must say I'm rather fond of the Fair Isle. The lasses here are quite pretty. I see why you chose to plunge your roots into this soil."

Ransom saw Lord Tenthor's niece, Orla, sitting amongst the nobles. Seeing her brought on another spurt of anger. She would be forced into a marriage she didn't want.

"This is my castle," Ransom said firmly. "By what right do the king's men guard it?"

"By the king's right, of course," Faulkes said, leaning forward. He seemed to relish the opportunity to argue. "Funds to fortify this castle were given to Lord Archer by Jon-Landon's father, the Elder King. That makes it a royal castle, and I have every right to lay claim to it now that the king has bid me do so. I have the writ if you'd like to see it."

"I don't need to see it," Ransom said tightly.

"Good. Now be a good dog, Ransom, and respond to your master's whistle. The king expects to see you at the palace. You'd best hurry."

His manner was provoking enough that Ransom itched to put his hand on his sword. When he was made a knight, he'd been given the last strike he was required to take without fighting back. Faulkes was goading him deliberately. Which made it all the more important for him to resist the provocation. Ransom's sons were hostages still, and their fate hinged on his behavior. Moreover, the Fountain wanted him to support the Argentines.

"I will go," Ransom said, turning to face the assembled nobles. "But I demand oaths of fealty, as is my right, before I leave." He strode to the dais and climbed the steps, standing above Faulkes, who sat in the chair. Whispers began to grow louder as the tension in the room increased. It was Ransom's right to demand their oaths. And any man who lifted arms against Ransom or his kin after taking such an oath would face their due punishment once he returned. Some of the nobles exchanged glances.

"If you wish to waste your time," Faulkes said with a snort. "So be it."

Dawson was the first to drop to his knee and swear loyalty to Ransom and his house. So did his other knights, one by one in quick succession. Lord Dupree came next, without hesitation. But some of those who knelt before him had guilty looks in their eyes. They made their promises—words—but he knew in his heart they wouldn't honor them. None, however, refused.

When the ceremony ended, Ransom turned to Faulkes.

"Satisfied?" asked the lackey.

"I will come back, Faulkes," Ransom said in a low voice. "Remember that."

"Oh, I am sure you will. You may not like the changes instituted during your absence."

"What changes?" Ransom demanded.

Faulkes shrugged, his eyes glittering with animosity. "Ask the king when you see him. Farewell, my lord duke."

Ransom strode out of the hall, accompanied by his knights. When they reached their mounts in the courtyard, Dawson came closer and addressed him in an undertone.

"Let me come with you, my lord," he pleaded. "You will not be treated justly."

Ransom turned and looked at the other man's sincere expression. He sighed. "I need you here to defend my interests. Are you loyal to me?"

"You know I am," Dawson vowed.

"Then defend my family. I have no choice but to go. The vows I've made require it. But your loyalty requires that you stay."

Dawson screwed up his face. "I'll defend your castle. No matter what happens."

"I'm counting on it. I'm counting on you and Dearley and the others."

Dawson nodded resolutely and gave him the knight's salute. Ransom returned it, feeling grateful that he could count on his men.

For he knew that not many in the great hall were as trustworthy.

Ransom stayed in Glosstyr for a few days, reviewing his finances with Simon and handling matters that required his attention. Trade had recommenced after the pause in hostilities with Occitania, and the city was thriving. Ransom arranged for his personal fortune to be sent to Legault, in preparation for the possibility the duchy would be ripped away from him.

"I might not be able to communicate with you after I go to the palace," he warned Simon. "You must *act* as you believe I would. I gave Dawson and Dearley the same instructions before leaving Connaught."

Simon was quick to agree.

On his third day, Ransom awoke before dawn to a familiar feeling in his chest. Another Fountain-blessed was in the castle. Ransom threw off his covers, moving fast as he pulled on his hauberk and strapped his sword to his waist. He went outside his room and barked for the night sentry to sound the alarm. Fear churned inside his stomach, but it struck him that Alix wasn't moving—she was staying put.

As soon as the night watch had assembled, along with a bleary-eyed Simon, he told them to fall in behind him as he followed the rippling sensation of Alix's magic. She still hadn't moved.

As he walked down the corridor, he realized that the presence emanated from one of the decorative fountains near the castle's chapel. The sun was rising now, providing ample light. His throat tight with thirst and worry, he passed the row of arches that overlooked the sea and the harbor farther away from the cliffs.

"Where are we going?" Simon asked him.

"Lady Alix is here," he said. "Estian's poisoner."

Simon's eyes widened. "In the castle?"

"Yes."

Members of the night watch looked at one another in consternation. Was one of them guilty of letting her in? She had a way of convincing others to do her bidding, but that wasn't her only talent. She possessed a magical ability to travel long distances through the fountains. When they reached the end of the corridor, approaching the small alcove adjacent to the chapel doors, Ransom drew a dagger.

There was no disguising the sound of their approach. The march of steps clearly announced they were coming, but Alix still didn't move. She was waiting for him.

He reached out with his magic, trying to sense any other threat.

She was alone.

He paused at the opening of the alcove. There she was, in a luxurious cloak, hood lifted, standing across the fountain from him. The water rippled and burbled between them.

"We need to talk," she told him.

"I have a pretty spot down in my dungeon," he suggested. "Some moldy bread perhaps to break our fast?"

He could not see her face very well, as the sun had not risen very much, but he recognized the pearl bracelet around her wrist. It was, he had long suspected, her relic from the fountain. She carried no weapon, but her very presence was a danger.

"I won't be staying long," she said. "There is something you need to know before you return to Kingfountain. A secret your king is keeping from you."

He wrinkled his brow. She had the power to influence with her words, to make people believe things they might naturally doubt. But she was not using it now.

"How can I trust anything you'd say?" he asked.

"Because I know you'll find out the truth yourself." Her voice was cold, accusing. She seemed angry, although her expression gave nothing away. "I will only tell you. Have the others back away."

"Don't listen to her," Simon warned. "It's another trick."

She stepped partway around the fountain, her cloak swishing against the edge of the stone. "Oh, it is much worse than that," she said. "Estian has given me permission to be here, but I bring nothing but the truth. If you don't want to know what your king has done, then I will return to Pree."

"Ransom," Simon murmured.

Her words did not compel him to listen, but he was deeply curious. He still gripped the dagger in his hand, wondering if he should charge her and try to grab her before she fled through the waters. He didn't think he was fast enough, though.

"Simon must stay," Ransom said.

"Have the others retreat. I won't stay much longer. Just know that you put his life at risk by keeping him here."

"Because you'll kill him?" Ransom said angrily.

"No, because your king will if he finds out that he knows. It's your choice. But make it quickly."

Ransom didn't take his eyes off her for a moment. "Simon . . ."

"I'm staying," he said with conviction.

The other sentries backed away down the corridor.

Ransom glared at her. "If this is another ploy, Alix . . ."

"I would that it *were*!" she said, her voice full of anguish that seemed genuine. She lowered the cowl, and he saw that her emotions were churning. Resentment, disgust, anger, sorrow—all battled and clashed on her face.

"Say what you mean and be done with it!" Ransom demanded.

Alix's eyes burned into his. "The hostages are dead. All of them."

Ransom blinked in surprise. "You don't make any sense."

"The hostages from the siege of Auxaunce!" she spluttered. "They're dead. All of them. Not one was ransomed. They killed them all in cold blood. They even killed the boy—Drew Argentine. He was little more than a child and the king's . . . own . . . *nephew.*" The look of disgust on her face, the twitch of her lips, showed that her horror was real. Then her voice choked. "My husband too. They're all dead."

Ransom was aghast at the news. It couldn't be true. No king would kill prisoners, who might be ransomed for money, in cold blood. Fear and confusion tore inside him.

"How do you know this?"

Her pretty eyebrows softened. "The Wizr board. Their pieces—the important ones—disappeared one by one, starting with Constance's son. The king went to Dundrennan before it happened. He was there. And then . . . the boy's piece disappeared. The others were snatched from the board soon afterward." She took a step toward him but caught herself. "Our own spies confirmed that none survived. Those knights surrendered because they believed they'd be hostages for a price. All of them would have rather been butchered at Auxaunce in battle than to be treated so shamefully by an anointed *king.*" She nearly spat the last word.

Ransom's heart went cold as ice at her words. His sons were at the palace. Had the king murdered them as well? If Jon-Landon had done as she said, then he was capable of anything.

He had no way of knowing whether Alix was speaking the truth, but he could ask his sister in Dundrennan. She wouldn't lie to him.

Alix's expression was full of vengeance. "I wanted you to know that you serve a murderer, so that when I kill your king and his two children and it unleashes a flood of death on your kingdom, you will know why." She glared at him with ferocity. "The game will finally end. Jon-Landon will be the *last* Argentine."

It did not take long. As soon as Ransom was gone, the nobles of Legault began to choose sides. Too many, unfortunately, are brainless badgers who sniff after power, blindly following any changes in the wind. Faulkes and his devils went after Lord Toole first and burned down his manor in Atha Kleah, which caused a sort of riot of glee from the malcontents. I've heard Toole escaped and fled back to his estate in Elkenny, but it's a grim beginning. Faulkes wields the authority of the king with impunity. He is here to subjugate Legault.

I will not be subjugated.

—*Claire de Murrow, Queen of the Fair Isle*
A time of treason

CHAPTER ELEVEN

To Tame a Bear

With that pronouncement on her lips, Ransom lunged for Alix, trying to grab her before she could flee into the fountain. If he could capture Estian's poisoner, it might save the life of the king's son, whom the Fountain had entrusted him to protect.

Alix was quicker. She'd always been quicker. As he reached to grab her arm, she pressed her hand against the edge of the fountain and quickly launched into it. He heard her whisper a word, something that he couldn't make out, and then she was gone, vanished as if the bottom of the fountain had disappeared and she'd plummeted down a well shaft into oblivion. He smelled lilac for an instant, and then it was replaced by the scent of wet stone.

Simon rushed around to the other side of the fountain, a dagger drawn and a ferocious look on his face. "I've never seen her trick before. I thought we'd be able to snatch her before she left."

Ransom bowed his head in frustration. "She can use the fountains as portals somehow, traveling from one to another. She could be back at Pree right now. Or in Kingfountain." He struck his fist against the edge of the railing.

"There is no mention of this in any of the histories. None that I've read," Simon confessed.

"Nor I," he answered, but an image surfaced in his mind of the book Claire had gotten from Lord Dougal's collection, the dangerous tome called *The Hidden Vulgate*. Constance had warned him it had uncanny powers, steeped in darkness. He screwed up his face in disgust.

Simon, correctly interpreting his expression, asked, "Do you believe what she said about the hostages?"

"I do. Why lie when it would be easily refuted?"

"True. But why would she tell you what she was going to do?" Simon asked. "Was she boasting?"

The other knights came to the edge of the alcove, but Ransom waved them back with a shake of his head.

"No, I don't think so." He thought for a moment before a realization struck him. "I think she was trying to provoke me."

Simon gave him a questioning look.

Ransom sighed and sheathed the dagger. "I need to go to Kingfountain immediately. The fastest way is by ship. Walk with me."

The two left the alcove together, and as they passed the sentries, Simon pointed at two of them. "I want that fountain guarded at all times. Have guards stationed at the others, and increase patrols on this side of the castle."

It might not be enough. Claire had once seen Alix disappear into thin air in Legault. The poisoner had uncanny powers. But there was no way of preparing for the incursion of someone who could appear and disappear at will, so he had no choice but to rely on what he knew—that she usually did travel to and from the fountains. The other ability, if she did indeed possess it, seemed to have limitations. If not, she would have dispatched the king and his heirs long ago.

Once they were clear of the men, Simon asked, "What did you mean about it being a provocation?"

"Estian has tried to win me to his side for years," Ransom said as they hurried through the corridors. "I'm wondering if she told me about the murders because she wants *me* to kill Jon-Landon."

There was a part of Ransom prone to violence, to savagery. His training as a knight had taught him to harness that side, something that required a great amount of self-discipline. He wondered where he'd be if he hadn't trained under Lord Kinghorn, who had been a man of principles and keen judgment.

The memory of his relative, of his mentor, brought a pang to his heart. Sir Bryon was dead, at rest in the Deep Fathoms. With each passing year, more people joined him there.

Simon was mindful of Ransom's silence. He didn't press him further, but Ransom could feel his friend's scrutiny.

"I'm not going to do it," he said with a chuckle. "However much I dislike him. He was young when Devon and Emiloh's marriage fell apart. He was the youngest of the sons, the least prepared to rule."

"To be honest, I wish this could be a deception. It's evil news."

Ransom nodded. "I know her. Her anger, her outrage, was real. And they have the Wizr board. If Jon-Landon did kill the hostages, then it would be easy enough for them to find out. You've seen the way she can travel. It would be easy for them to verify what they saw. Which is what I'd like you to do. Discreetly."

"Of course," Simon said. "The one who died here . . . I thought it was an unfortunate turn of health, but he might have been poisoned. There was another hostage sent to Blackpool. I can inquire."

"Do it quickly, but carefully. I don't trust Bodkin."

"I never did," Simon said. "He was a hardened criminal before he joined the Espion. I only used him for unsavory tasks."

"When you go back to Legault, bring the treasury with you and enough men to help Claire defend Connaught. I'll take the scutage to Kingfountain. Make the arrangements."

"I will." He gave Ransom a nervous look. "Be careful. If Jon-Landon truly committed such an outrage, who knows what he's capable of."

"Exactly," Ransom said, walking faster, worrying about his sons.

The ship left immediately and traveled through the night, reaching the palace at the darkest part of dawn, but torches illuminated the palace walls in places. It looked gloomy in the dark, rising up on the wooded hills, a menacing structure instead of the symbol of strength it had always seemed to him. He'd deliberately landed at the merchants' docks, on the other side of the falls. He would go to the castle in the morning, a day earlier than the king had demanded of him. The time would be spent listening, trying to understand the state of things.

He wore no badge on his tunic, though he did wear his hauberk under a large, dark cloak that would help conceal his identity. He gave orders to the captain to bring the scutage tax to the king's dock later that day and then left his ship without an escort and walked down the wooden docks. The sailors he passed were in a jovial mood, having imbibed a bit too much, but he avoided them and began walking the streets of Kingfountain.

He wished he had Dappled, but his destrier was back in Connaught. As he walked the streets, his thoughts turned to home—to Claire, Dearley, and Dawson. To his little girls' sweet kisses.

He stopped first at the home of one of the city guard, a man he'd known for many years. From him, Ransom was able to piece together that most of the sordid gossip about the king was true. The man, whom he trusted, begged him not to mention his name for fear of the king's wrath. Ransom offered his thanks, his assurances, and a few coins. Next, he went to visit a blacksmith who had done work for him in the past. He corroborated that the hostages had been dispersed to different towns. After that, Ransom decided to go to the sanctuary to try to speak to the deconeus.

A warning feeling came into his heart, and he sensed someone walking behind him. Ransom turned, hand on his sword hilt, and saw a skulking figure suddenly flinch and turn the other way. The premonition faded. His Fountain magic had protected him from yet another attack, and he knew it would continue to serve him as long as he stayed loyal to the king. Even if the king didn't deserve his loyalty.

The gate to the sanctuary was still closed for the night, and he thought it unwise to draw further attention to himself by ringing the bell and asking for an audience. Better to find a place to stay until morning.

There were only three inns on the bridge spanning the river and the falls, and he walked to the nearest one. The innkeeper refused to rent a room to a man not wearing a badge, however, so he made his way to the next one and found the management more agreeable. After a generous meal of beef stew and bread, he retired to his room. The lock on the door was sturdy, and he kept the key nearby as he lay on the bed fully dressed, smelling the musty blanket and hearing the noise bubbling up from the common room below.

He couldn't fall asleep, so he stared at the ceiling and watched a moth dance against the panes of glass in the window, seeking to enter the room.

An hour passed, maybe more, and the din from the tavern had not abated when he heard a soft knock at the door.

Ransom's brows beetled as he listened for the sound to come again, and sure enough, the knock was repeated.

He got off the bed and approached the door. With his Fountain magic, he sensed only one person outside. He did not feel any danger.

Ransom unlocked the door, ready to launch into action if the visitor was a foe after all, and saw Cecily standing at the doorway, holding a candle. The Espion gave him a mocking grin. "Is that all the trouble you took to conceal your arrival? Lord Ransom, I'd thought better of you."

"Hello, Cecily," he said, nodding.

"Can I come in? I won't stay long. I have to get back to the palace."

He did not feel threatened by her in any way, so he opened the door wider. There was just the bed and a small table near the windows with a pitcher and bowl on it. Cecily put the candle on the table and sat on the edge of the bed. Ransom leaned back against the door, folding his arms, and watched as she lowered her hood.

"Are my sons in good health?" he asked her.

"Very, considering the amount of climbing they do. They've exhausted everyone set to watch over them, and delight in evading their caretakers and hiding throughout the castle. I did show them some of the Espion tunnels, so they know how to disappear rather efficiently. They think it's all quite a game."

Ransom let out a grateful sigh. "Thank you."

Cecily gave him a serious look. "Why didn't you go directly to the palace? It's early still."

"I came to get information before surrendering."

Her brow wrinkled. "What information?"

He looked her in the eye. "About the Occitanian hostages."

She flinched and looked away. Then she met his gaze again, the joviality drained away. "How could you have learned of it? It is a closely guarded secret."

"Yet still . . . I know. So it's true? They're all dead?"

She bit her lip and nodded.

"Why?" Ransom said in distress. "Why would he do that? He gave up a fortune and will bring curses on himself for this vile deed."

Cecily's eyes fixed on his. "Because he's drunk on his power, Ransom. That's the only way I can explain it. After he won at Auxaunce, he's been a different man. More paranoid if you can believe it. More distrusting. He knew it would be a hugely damaging blow to Estian. You know how long it takes to train a knight. The expense. It will take Occitania years to recover."

"So it was political? It's cold-blooded murder!"

Cecily flinched and looked down. "Yes. It was."

Ransom stared at her. "You participated, didn't you?"

He saw her swallow. "Bodkin made it a test of loyalty," she said. "Within the Espion. Those who balked were imprisoned as Occitanian spies. Some are still in chains." She looked at him. "I'm not proud of what I did, Ransom. We were forbidden to tell anyone. How did you know? Did one of the Espion betray Jon-Landon?"

Ransom let out his breath, struggling to contain his disgust and deep disappointment. He was grateful his boys were alive and well, but their lives were in greater danger than ever before. And so was the whole kingdom with such a king.

"Not the Espion, no. I found out through another source."

"Will you tell me?" she asked.

He studied her for a moment before responding. "Whose side are you on now, Cecily?"

"I've always been on your side," she said, leaning forward. "That hasn't changed. But I have to maneuver a very narrow ledge. When I heard a ship from Glosstyr had arrived at the merchants' docks, I intervened to find you first. Other Espion will be coming for you. If you were intending to slip away, you should do so at once."

"That is not my intention," Ransom said. "I came because the king summoned me."

"He summoned you to arrest you," Cecily said earnestly. "He's going to take Legault from you and Lady Claire. He sent Faulkes there to do the deed. Ransom, you cannot trust Jon-Landon. The king means to destroy you."

Ransom's stomach shriveled. "If I didn't come, he would have every right to."

She shook her head. "He has a grievance against you and Claire. If you enter the palace of Kingfountain, you may never leave it again."

Ransom was sick at heart. "I know."

"Then why did you come?" she asked, perplexed.

"Isn't it enough that my sons are hostages? But even if they were not at his mercy, I have a duty to the Argentine family. If he feels the need to imprison me . . ." He shrugged. "So be it. I will not rebel against him."

"That sounds more like stubbornness than loyalty," Cecily pointed out. Her eyes flashed with disappointment. Had she hoped for something else from him?

"I wish it were only foolish pride and stubbornness," Ransom said, shaking his head. "If that were the case, I might change my mind, but the Fountain bid me safeguard the king's children."

She gave him a quizzical look. "Devon and Léanore?"

Léanore was the king's young daughter, born a year after the heir.

"Yes," he said. "It's as simple as that. I would have come anyway, since the king has my boys, but I've learned that Estian's poisoner, Alix, intends to murder Jon-Landon and his children in revenge for what he did to the hostages."

"They know?" she asked with a gasp. "I thought we'd caught all the Occitanian infiltrators."

"Perhaps you did. They have keen ways of knowing things. I learned of this from Lady Alix herself. She left me a . . . message in Glosstyr. A warning."

"I need to get back to the palace, Ransom. If Jon-Landon doubts me . . . it's much more dangerous now than ever before." She gave him a regretful look. "Benedict would never have ordered anything like this."

Ransom sighed. "No. I can't believe Lady Deborah condoned it."

Cecily shook her head. "She doesn't know. Emiloh might. Since Auxaunce, she's been very ill. It was a hard winter for her."

Ransom stepped forward, away from the door. "What do you mean? Has she been poisoned?"

"I don't think so," she said. "I think her heart is just giving out. She's lost all of her sons, or as good as. Jon-Landon treats her horribly."

He cringed. "Is she still in the Vexin?"

"Yes. He doesn't want her anywhere near the palace. These are dangerous times."

The sound of boots came from beyond the door. The heavy footfalls suggested a group was coming. Ransom felt his instincts tingle with dread. He looked at her.

"It sounds like they sent enough men to tame a beast," she said, shaking her head. "But if I'm seen here, my loyalty will be suspect."

"I'd better distract them, then," Ransom said with the same tingle of excitement he always felt going into battle.

Six more ships arrived at Atha Kleah, each stuffed with mercenaries. Nigh on two thousand soldiers disembarked. They're patrolling the streets and terrorizing the citizenry. One of my nobles, I think it was Brie, was accused of treachery and flogged in the center of town. Faulkes is using fear to tilt the balance of loyalty. I don't know why he hasn't left Atha Kleah and come north to Connaught yet, but I suspect he's biding his time for a reason.

Dearley says we must anticipate an attack by sea and by land. I anticipate sending my daughters to the hunting lodge we have in the woods, but I worry about treachery from the inside. These additional troops show that the king is serious about stripping us of all power.

I've had no word from Ransom since he left Glosstyr. No word about the boys. I fear for them, and yet I must keep my focus on the challenge in front of me, not the one underway across the seas.

Steady, Claire. The people will look to you to see what you do. I don't think I can win this war, but I can make it a costly one.

—Claire de Murrow, Queen of the Fair Isle
(ready to stand alone)

CHAPTER TWELVE

The Sin of Andrew the Ursus

Ransom grabbed his cloak and put it on, hearing the steps coming down the hall. His magic flickered to life, delivering a warning that would have roused him had he been asleep.

"Are you going to fight them all?" Cecily hissed.

"Not if they back down. They've no reason to act against me."

He sensed several men coming to the door. He hadn't locked it since letting Cecily in. Leaning back against the door, he wedged his boot against the edge of a floorboard and pressed his shoulder into the wood.

Cecily rose, looking fearful. She'd feared being caught out of the palace—how much worse would it be if she were caught with him?

"Hide under the bed," he counseled. She promptly obeyed.

A voice grunted, and then several bodies struck the door at once. Ransom held it firm. Another blow came, making the whole frame rattle. The wood cracked, but Ransom did not desist.

"C'mon lads. Hit it harder!" said a muffled voice.

Ransom stepped away from the door to the opposite side of the hinges. When they hit it again, the door flew open with a crash, and three men tumbled inside, landing atop each other. Ransom stepped around them and entered the hall, encountering several more men.

"It's him!" one of the Espion said in surprise.

They didn't state their purpose or explain why they'd come to him before sunrise—rather, four men charged him at once.

Ransom felt the Fountain magic surge inside him, but it was muted, lethargic.

Because his magic was driven by loyalty, and his was being tested. Severely.

He punched the first in the jaw, dropping him. Two of the man's companions shoved him into the wall, but he kneed one in the stomach and threw the second down. The fourth he grabbed by the collar and threw into a neighbor's door. Blood spurted from the man's split nose as he sagged down to his knees.

Flooded with determination, Ransom rushed down the hall as several more Espion charged up the stairs, responding to the noise of violence. Ransom grabbed the railing and kicked the foremost man hard in the chest, knocking him backward into his fellows. Ransom charged down the steps, using his elbows to rush them. As they collapsed in a pile at the foot of the stairs, he vaulted over the railing and landed in the common room amidst startled shouts. Two men stood guard at the door, and both unsheathed long swords.

Ransom drew his bastard sword and marched toward them, anger seething in his chest. Neither of them were knights, and neither wore armor.

The two, seeing his glaring eyes, fled their post while the men in a pile at the bottom of the stairs scrambled over each other in confusion, trying to rise.

"Stop him! Stop him!" came a shout from upstairs.

Ransom shoved his way out of the inn. He saw a knot of horses tied up nearby, each still saddled. The Espions' horses. Ransom grabbed the first, a dusky mare, and swung up onto the saddle without releasing his bastard sword. He severed the rope tying the beast to the bar and turned it toward the sanctuary of Our Lady.

His heart hammered in his chest, part with exhilaration and part with dread. Would he end up in a dungeon now that he'd defied the king's Espion? The men hadn't announced themselves, however, nor had they ordered him in the king's name. He felt a little bit of pride at how easily he'd overpowered them, but he squashed it down as he urged the horse to gallop. Cries came from the inn he'd left, and he heard the men rushing to grab their horses, save the master of the one he'd taken.

The gates to the sanctuary were in the middle point of the bridge, about halfway to the palace. The rush of the falls blotted the sounds of pursuit as he hastened away. When he reached the gates, they were closed, the grounds beyond them darkened.

He swung off the saddle and then sheathed his sword and marched to the gate. The sounds of pursuit came from behind him. He grabbed the bars and wrenched on them, but they'd been locked. The sound of footsteps reached his ears, and the buttery light of a lantern illuminated the sexton as he walked to the gate.

"I see him! He's at the gates of the sanctuary!" shouted a voice. The thunder of hooves grew louder, clashing against the roar of the falls.

The sexton lifted the lantern to shine the light on Ransom's face. "Do you come seeking sanctuary from the king's justice?"

The Espion were nearly to them, and Ransom's heart raced. "I'm the Duke of Glosstyr," he said firmly. "Open the gate."

The sexton's face pinched in surprise, and he lifted the lantern higher. Ransom leaned against the bars, regarding the man without flinching.

The sexton set down the lantern and rushed forward, digging into his pocket for the key. It was then the other horses arrived. Several of the Espion had blood smeared on their faces from the ferocity of his attack.

"Grab him! Take him before he makes it inside!"

The sexton's hands were shaking as he fumbled the key into the lock. The latch released, and he pulled the gate open. Ransom darted inside and helped slam it shut, holding it in place while the nervous sexton locked it again.

One of the Espion reached through the bars and grabbed the front of Ransom's tunic, his face twisted with anger. In retaliation, Ransom grabbed the man's wrist and tugged him forward, bringing him face-first into the bars of the gate. Releasing his grip, he watched the man grimace and rub his mouth.

"You think you're safe in there, Lord Barton?" said one of the Espion in a sneering voice.

"He is protected by the deconeus," said the sexton. "Leave at once. These are hallowed grounds."

The man whose face had been smashed against the bars kept rubbing his mouth. "We'll see about that," he said scornfully.

"If the deconeus orders the bells rung," said the sexton, "we'll see if anyone arrives in time to save you. Do you want to test your faith against the falls? It's a long . . . way . . . down."

The Espion were clearly furious, but the sexton's comment didn't fail to move them. A spark of fear had entered their eyes, and some stepped back from the gate.

"There is nowhere to run, Barton," said the ringleader. "You're in a cage regardless."

It was true. Ransom glared at the man, knowing he could have easily killed all of them. It would have been self-defense, but even so, he knew it would have made him a traitor to the crown for certain.

Should he have surrendered to them without a contest? Perhaps, but it would have made him lesser in his own eyes.

He turned his back on the Espion and walked toward the sanctuary, gazing up at the darkened spires. The fountains on the grounds were silent.

And so were the whispers in his heart.

The accommodations Ransom was given by the deconeus were lush compared to the inn where he'd paid for a room. Because of the hour, the deconeus said they would talk after sunrise and discuss what to do next. He was given food, even though he wasn't hungry, and then he lay awake worrying he'd made things worse for himself.

The bells rang in the morning, awakening him from his fitful sleep. He drank, washed his face, and then went to meet with the deconeus as planned. He was escorted to the man's study, which featured a glass door leading to the rear gardens of the sanctuary. It was lavishly decorated, the floor the same polished marble with offset black and white squares as existed throughout the chapel.

The deconeus, Archibald, was the same man who had been tricked into performing the marriage between Jon-Landon and Léa DeVaux. He was an aging fellow, with thinning white hair and several liver spots on his face, and had served Kingfountain for many years. He sat behind his desk, regarding Ransom with a worried brow, and waved for him to take a seat on the couch, which he did.

"Have you had anything to eat, Lord Ransom?"

"I'm not hungry."

"I imagine not," said Archibald. "Are you ready to discuss the situation? We are not friends, you and I. But you are a man of the world. I'm sure we can speak freely with each other."

"I'd hope so," Ransom said. He felt the urge to pace but remained on the couch.

"I'm expecting the captain of the king's guard to arrive at any moment. The king knows you're here. That puts me in a . . . delicate situation."

"I'm sure it does," Ransom said. "It wasn't my intention to bring trouble to your doorstep, Deconeus."

"Well, trouble has a way of finding us whether we wish it or no. May I speak frankly, Lord Ransom? Is it your intention to claim sanctuary instead of facing the king's justice?"

"No."

Archibald frowned. "Then why did you come?"

"I came because I was going to be falsely arrested last night. It was my plan, all along, to stop by the sanctuary and drop some coins in the fountain. But I'm going to the castle today."

The older man sighed in relief. "That does spare me an unpleasant confrontation with the king. He's become quite unpredictable, of late. I've heard . . . rumors . . . which are quite upsetting. But they were told to me in confidence, so I cannot share them with you."

Ransom leaned forward. "About the hostages?"

The deconeus blinked. "You know?"

"I only heard the tales recently. And I'll speak no more of it. I'm here because the king sent Lord Faulkes to Legault with a writ of summons."

"Yes, I'd heard of that." He grimaced. "I'm sorry, Lord Ransom. You have been so loyal to this family. The king has long resented you, yet he also admires you."

Ransom gave him a quizzical look.

"It's true, Lord Ransom. His petulance outweighs his common sense. By weakening you, he weakens himself. He needs your loyalty more than ever, yet he will stop at nothing to push you away. What he's done to the hostages . . . it's abominable."

"Why did he do it?"

The deconeus looked down for a moment before he met Ransom's gaze. "I don't know. Not for certain. I try not to play politics if I can help it. He has not confided in me, but the deconeus of the palace chapel has noticed a change in the king's moods. He's darker now. More depressed. I think he feels anguish and guilt over what he did. And although he has not confessed to any crimes, he's contributed more to the order than most of our previous kings. He's even talking about establishing a new sanctuary, and you know how much they cost to build. His conscience is panging him."

Ransom imagined so. "Do you think he would violate the right of sanctuary?"

"I hope not. But I cannot be sure."

"Which is why you were relieved to learn that I plan to go willingly."

"My office requires me to accept any pilgrim who seeks protection. But my heart warns me that if you stay, the king will use it as an excuse to do something even worse."

"Wouldn't the people rise up?"

The deconeus held up his hands. "Would they? It's not the people I worry about. It's the punishment."

Ransom looked at him in confusion. "You fear the king's punishment?"

"No. I fear the Fountain's. I've read the annals of history kept by the previous holders of this office. There's a pattern in them, Ransom, a subtle one that began with the reign of King Andrew the Ursus. He began as a benevolent ruler, but he turned into a tyrant and lost everything. His evil actions preceded his fall. But not immediately." He leaned back, steepling his fingers. "The Fountain often delays its punishments. It's written that the hollow crown itself is a foreteller of such doom. In the later years of Andrew's reign, he spoke of the torments and curses the crown had unleashed on him—betrayals, storms, and a dozen different misfortunes. Especially after he executed his first knight, a Fountain-blessed woman who was his chief warrior. He lost everything, and his kingdom was drowned in a flood and remains lost forevermore." His eyes narrowed. "This same pattern has repeated itself again and again—with monarchs who vaulted to the skies only to plummet after being pierced by an arrow of fate. The Elder King's grandfather was one of them. This time, I fear for your life, Lord Ransom."

The deconeus's words weighed heavily on his heart. A pang struck him at the thought of never seeing Claire again. Or his children.

A knock sounded on the door, and the sexton entered. "A delegation from the king has come," he said. "They have an order from the king to release Lord Ransom to their custody."

The deconeus sighed. "That didn't take long."

"I'll go with them," Ransom told Archibald. "Thank you for taking me in."

"I would risk the future to protect you," said the deconeus in a serious tone. "You are a good man."

Ransom shook his head. "The king has summoned me. But it is the Fountain I must obey."

He felt a throb of approval from the Fountain inside his heart. But it was a very small one.

XX

The king's guard had brought a horse for him to ride, and he did so without resistance. People came out from their homes to watch them ride by, and some looked at him worriedly. A few cheers for Glosstyr came, but the scolding looks from the guardsmen silenced them. Sympathy was the expression he saw the most.

He'd come there for the first time as a prisoner, a hostage, and now he was going back as one. They hadn't bound his wrists at least. What were Jon-Landon's intentions? Would he arrest him for attacking the Espion, or some other manufactured offense? His mind mulled it over as he rode up the hill to the palace and dismounted in the courtyard. He entered the palace under escort and strode down the corridors he'd wandered as a boy. They were familiar yet not familiar, the scent of rosemary a surprise.

Part of him had hoped his sons would be allowed to greet him, but there were no sounds of childish glee. No sign of the boys running up to greet him.

When they arrived at the hall, Jon-Landon and the queen were seated on their thrones on the dais. Jon-Landon's goatee had grown since the winter, and he had shadow smudges under his eyes, showing a lack of sleep. It was still morning, and the sun came in through the high windows.

Queen Léa scrutinized Ransom as he entered. She had rings on many of her fingers, and her golden hair was coifed and coiled into an intricate nest. When she caught his eyes, an involuntary smirk came to her lips. Was she enjoying his humiliation? They'd first met when he'd come upon her changing in his room, which Lord Longmont, the former justiciar, had given to her without informing him.

The knights bowed to the king and took up a defensive position alongside Ransom.

The king rubbed his upper lip and said nothing, letting the silence linger.

"Did you have to break open the gates of the sanctuary, Captain?" the king asked, though his eyes were fixed on Ransom.

"No, my lord. He came willingly."

"Oh?" the queen asked with a sardonic smile.

The king kept his eyes on Ransom's face. "Where is the scutage, Lord Ransom? I don't see any chests."

"It's on my ship," Ransom answered. "It's coming."

"Good," said the king. "You attacked members of the Espion last night. What do you have to say for yourself?"

Ransom looked around the room and noticed several of those gathered there had puffy and antagonistic faces. One had a split lip. Another a bruised nose.

"You didn't send enough men, my lord," Ransom answered, and his reply caused a few chuckles among those assembled in the hall.

Jon-Landon flushed with anger. "You are under arrest, Lord Ransom Barton. You are hereby confined to the palace grounds. If you attempt to leave the outer gates by any means, you will be branded a traitor, your lands and titles forfeit, and you'll be hunted as an enemy of the king." The words had come in a rush. Hot emotion flashed in the king's eyes. "Do I make myself clear?"

"What have I done to invoke your displeasure, my lord?" Ransom asked calmly, feeling anger sear his insides. But he didn't let it show on his face or mar his voice. At least Jon-Landon hadn't attempted to strip him of his office. He could have accused him of treason for attacking the Espion—even though it was *they* who had attacked him, without any provocation. He had done his duty by coming to Kingfountain. The only crime he could be accused of was coming a day early.

"Shall I recite all of your ill deeds for you, Ransom? You've thwarted me long enough. And you shall suffer for it. Take away his sword and scabbard. He won't be needing them now."

Ransom's scabbard was irreplaceable. Acquired during his pilgrimage to the Chandleer Oasis, it was a treasure of the Deep Fathoms, one that healed his injuries. He felt the urge to resist, because losing it would be a grievous outcome, but he knew the king would take it as the aggravation he was seeking. Did the king know of the scabbard's magic? Ransom had taken pains to keep it secret.

"As you command, my lord," said the captain. He turned and approached Ransom, reaching for the buckle and strap. Ransom wanted to punch him in the face and defend his own property, but he submitted to the disarming, to the humiliation that Jon-Landon had designed for him.

When the captain took the scabbard in his hands, Ransom felt a hollow sensation open inside his chest, accompanied by a feeling of nakedness and vulnerability.

But he dared not show on his face how much he resented the king for what he'd done.

When the ships were seen coming toward the docks at Connaught, we thought at first they were reinforcements from Glosstyr. But alas, the eejits were sailing from Kingfountain to block our harbor. I've had no news of Ransom since he went to the palace, and now it looks like I'll have none at all. Because of the cliffs, we have the higher ground, and their ships cannot come too near for fear of our catapults. But they shall stop supplies from coming. We are cut off.

Sibyl says the ships are ugly. She told me I should make them go away. Sweet lass, if only I could.

Our scouts continue to watch the road to Atha Kleah. When Dearley returned from his latest journey, he brought news that Lord Faulkes is gathering a force outside the town. It seems many Legaultans have defected to Jon-Landon's side. Perhaps they were enticed by the coins he's paying all those mercenaries. I asked Dearley how many he thinks they have in their camp. He didn't want to tell me, but I demanded an answer. Eight thousand by his reckoning. But the numbers are swelling.

That is a sizable force to bring to a siege. Without reinforcements from Glosstyr, we have about four thousand. We can hold the castle with that many. But eventually we'll run *out of meat, out of grain. Once they surround the hillside, we won't be able to hunt game from the woods.*

Waiting this out doesn't seem to be our best option.

—Claire de Murrow, Queen of the Fair Isle
(all things must come to an end)

CHAPTER THIRTEEN

The Prisoner of Kingfountain

Ransom asked to see his sons, and they were brought to him in the main corridor of the palace, escorted by a slender man with a hooked nose and shaggy eyebrows who couldn't hide the disdain he had for them. The boys greeted their father with a hurried embrace after Ransom dropped to one knee. He was stunned by how much they'd grown since he'd brought them to the palace.

"Are you staying with us now, Father?" Willem asked with excitement.

"Of course he is, don't be an eejit," said Devon, elbowing his brother in the ribs.

Ransom's heart nearly overflowed with relief, and he held his sons tightly, breathing them in. Until now, he hadn't realized how much he'd feared for them. The news about Drew had hit him hard. The boys grinned at him and asked so many questions he couldn't hope to answer them.

"How is Máthair?" Devon asked, using the Gaultic term for mother.

"I miss Lord Toole. Is he well? Did you bring us a treat?"

"Can you come to the training yard with us tomorrow?"

"That's enough," barked the slender man. "Your father is a prisoner of the crown."

The lads stared at the fellow in wide-eyed amazement, then shared a worried look.

"You've seen them, Lord Ransom. That's enough. Now I must take them for their exercise."

Willem rolled his eyes and gave the man a resentful look. "Aldous, we haven't seen our father in months! He can walk us around the grounds."

"Show us the tree you used to climb with Máthair!" Devon enthused. "I think I know the one!"

"No!" Aldous snapped. "If you behave, which I doubt, you'll be allowed to see him later. Come with me, boys."

Ransom rose. He towered over the boys' keeper, but the man didn't look intimidated. His expression was scornful.

"These two are incorrigible," he said. "Always sneaking off and getting into mischief. Come, lads. To the training yard."

Willem and Devon looked at Ransom imploringly, hoping their father would defy the man, but he nodded for them to do the man's bidding. He had little choice. They were not his to command.

Willem sulked a bit, and Devon blasted Aldous with a withering look. They waved to their father before leaving. At least they were healthy. He watched them go, feeling both relief and pain. He wondered if he'd be given permission to write to Claire. If so, he had no doubt the Espion would read every word. He still had the letters she'd written to the boys, but he'd hand those over later.

At least he wasn't being confined to the tower or the dungeon. The king had given him leave to wander the castle and its grounds with absolute freedom. But as he walked around the inner circle of the castle, it felt as if the very walls were pressing on him. He felt the absence of his sword and scabbard keenly, unused to the lack of weight on his hip. It brought back memories of his captivity with DeVaux's men. And the thought of those cold days, starving and alone, drove him to seek out the warmth of the kitchen.

He paused in the threshold, taking in the hanging pots, the bunches of dried herbs, and the delightful aroma of baking bread. The upper windows were bright and cheerful, and flames licked the inside of the ovens. Thick sausages hung from the walls on hooks. He saw the table and benches where he and Claire had sat and talked after the Elder King finally granted him permission to court her. The image in his mind made his chest ache. He worried about what she might be enduring in Connaught. Not knowing was a cruel torture.

"Lord Ransom? Is that you?"

One of the undercooks approached him with a friendly smile.

He nodded to her. "Could I get something to eat?"

"Of course! Come whenever you like. I'll put together a plate for you."

He entered the kitchen, lost in his memories, and sat down at the table, propping his elbows up on it and trying not to let his worries overwhelm him. He didn't know how long he would be a prisoner at the palace. The king could hold him there for as long as it took to attack Legault. Would any of the Legaultans prove faithful? Or would they abandon Claire and leave her to fend for herself?

"Hello, Lord Ransom."

He turned his head and found the prince had just entered with one of his tutors. The boy walked right up to his table, a serious look on his face.

"Hello, lad. Hungry?"

"Master Anthon has been tutoring me in languages. I think better when my stomach isn't empty."

Ransom smiled. "Languages were a struggle to me."

"I've heard you speak Occitanian very well."

"Oh?"

"And that you used to live in Chessy when you were in the tournaments."

The cook brought the prince a scone with a glaze drizzled on the top, her expression fond, and the boy smiled and thanked her.

"After languages, what do you study next?" Ransom asked.

The prince took a small bite from the pastry, his eyes brightening either from the treat or the question. "My favorite subject. Strategy. Perhaps we could talk about it, you and I. I would like that."

"So would I," Ransom said. The ache in his heart had eased just a little. The youngster made him think of earlier days, back when his cares weren't so heavy.

The prince and his tutor left, and Ransom sat alone, deep in thought. He didn't smell the crisped bread and bubbling qinnamon until the undercook slid a plate in front of his nose.

He looked at her in surprise, since the qinnamon spice was a rarity.

She grinned at him. "I remembered, my lord. You and Lady Claire . . . we haven't forgotten you."

The kind action made his throat thick with gratitude. It was a delicacy he and Claire had enjoyed together just after their betrothal— her way of sharing something sweet with him, just as he'd shared the penuche with her.

"Thank you," he said. "I was a child here at the palace."

"I think Siena was the cook back then," said the woman kindly. "She was Gaultic."

Ransom nodded, inhaling the delicious scent of the qinnamon torrere. His mouth watered.

"Those boys of yours are a pleasure," said the undercook. "They sneak in here all the time with the princess."

"Do they now?" Ransom couldn't help but feel a burst of pride in his boys.

"Oh, they drive the Espion to distraction. They're good lads, Lord Ransom. Don't let anyone convince you otherwise. Now eat it before it gets too cold."

Ransom enjoyed the toasted bread with qinnamon, feeling less alone than when he'd entered the kitchen. He had Claire. He had his family. And though they'd been thrust apart for a season, he felt hopeful that they would be reunited.

His wish was granted sooner than he would have thought, for Willem and Devon and a blond-haired little girl came running up from behind him. Their arrival surprised him, for he was sitting facing the entrance to the kitchen.

Willem grinned. "Sorry it took so long to lose him. Aldous is warier than some of the others, but he's still an eejit."

The little girl, whom Ransom assumed was the princess Léanore because of her decadent dress and her resemblance to her mother, looked at him with inquisitive and mischievous eyes.

He turned, seeing no other way into the kitchen. "How did you—?"

"The Espion tunnels," Devon said proudly. "We know them all, I should think. One goes all the way to the king's room! We've spied on him many times."

"Papa doesn't know," Léanore said with a grin. She was quite a bit younger than the boys, smaller, but her amber eyes glowed with liveliness.

"Have you been to the tunnels, Papa?" Willem asked.

"I have," Ransom answered. "But I don't know them as well as you, it seems."

"Cecily taught us," Devon said in a whisper.

Léanore's eyes brightened at the name. "I like her."

They began to regale him with tales of their adventures together, interrupting one another in their haste to share a story or correct a detail from it. Ransom chuckled to himself, pleased with the strength of the connection between the three, which reminded him of his own childhood with Claire and King Gervase's son. Sometimes the boys and the princess were caught and scolded by the Espion. But they escaped censure more often than not and had learned a great deal about the intrigues of the palace through their defiance.

"What of your brother, Prince Devon?" Ransom asked the princess. "Do you leave him out?"

"He's too afraid," Léanore said with scorn. "He doesn't like the dark at all. He came a few times, but he's always with his tutors, and they never want him to have fun."

"He's boring," Willem said with a shrug.

"We offered loads of times," Devon insisted. "But I think he stopped after Léanore fell into the cistern water."

"You pushed me!" Léanore said, shoving his arm.

"You were following too close!"

"No I wasn't!"

Willem started laughing. "She was so wet! The queen was vexed that day."

The princess stomped her foot. "I didn't tell on you, though."

"If you had, we wouldn't have let you come anymore," Devon pointed out.

"The prince was scared half to death. The water wasn't very deep. It was just really cold."

"I should say," said Léanore. She put her little hand on Ransom's arm. "Have you been down into the cistern?"

"I have," Ransom answered. He shuddered at the memory, for seeing the cistern waters in the dark had affected him strangely. It had made him feel as if another existence lay superimposed over his own, the two rippling into each other.

He shook off the thought, returning his attention to the children. The camaraderie between the three of them was endearing, but he couldn't help but see evidence of the queen in her daughter's face.

Jon-Landon had children of his own. How could he have ordered the death of his nephew, who wasn't much older than these children? The thought continued to sicken him.

"Aldous is coming," Devon suddenly said.

Willem stiffened, and the three children scrambled toward the wall. The princess touched one of the stones, and a section of the wall opened up, revealing a dark passage. The three vanished into it, shutting the door behind them just as Aldous stomped into the kitchen, his face flushed.

He stood at the threshold, nostrils flaring, his bushy eyebrows twitching. His gaze ran over the kitchen, but the staff pretended nothing was amiss. Ransom saw one of them struggle not to smile. He remained at his table, gazing nonchalantly at the slender man who had again lost his wards.

Aldous huffed, turned around, and stomped away.

The undercook came back to Ransom with a plate of bread, fruit, and some cheese.

"Still hungry, Lord Ransom?" she asked him with a wink.

✕

Ransom lay on his bed in the dark, hands behind his neck, listening to the creaking timbers. Occasionally he heard a set of boots pass by his door, but they never lingered. It was just the night watch. Even with that knowledge, he couldn't sleep. It didn't matter that he'd been allowed his old room, where he'd spent many nights in the past. It felt like a cage. Still, his first day of bondage had not been as horrible as he'd feared. He'd seen his children, which had been heartening, and all day long he'd met people who were sympathetic to his plight. Lord Kinghorn's son, Dalian, had even asked to meet him in the training yard the next morning. In fact, he felt he had more friends at the palace than the king.

Eventually drowsiness set in, and he fell into a light sleep, which was interrupted when he heard his door handle turn. His eyes shot open, and he reached for the sword that wasn't there, but his Fountain magic assured him that he wasn't in danger. The door opened, and Cecily came inside from the darkened hall and shut the door.

"Are you awake?" she whispered.

"Yes," Ransom said, sitting up. "It's after midnight I should say."

"Later still. The king finally went to bed," Cecily said. "The palace is quieting down. I'm sorry I couldn't come before now, but I was needed to translate for some Brugian guests."

"You could have come in the morning," Ransom said. "Why now?"

"Because I have to attend to them all day tomorrow," she said. "And I thought you'd want to know the news."

Ransom rose from the bed. It was dark, but moonlight streamed in from the window. He motioned to the only chair in the room. "Sit. Tell me."

"I'll wait by the door so I can keep an ear out for the night watch," she said.

He knew the risk she was taking by continuing to help him. And he appreciated it. "Have you news from Legault?"

"Yes, but let me tell you about the Brugians first. Lord Gotz defeated the last bit of resistance and proclaimed himself king. It's taken him this long to consolidate power, but he's now the ruler. The ransom we paid to free Benedict won him the crown after all."

That wasn't a surprise. The duke's ambition had been plain to see when Ransom and Cecily had gone to rescue their king. It seemed a lifetime ago.

"You mentioned you were called on as an interpreter," Ransom said.

"The new Brugian king sent an emissary to Kingfountain to notify us of his coming coronation at the Wartburg. He asked, specifically, that *you* attend the coronation. Gotz wants you to be the emissary of Ceredigion to his new court."

Ransom started with surprise. "Does he know about my fall from grace?"

"It's unclear, Ransom. But he asked for you by name, and it upset him when Jon-Landon said he would send Lord Kiskaddon instead. I was asked to smooth things over with the emissary, but he's furious and offended. Lord Gotz admires power, and he wanted Ceredigion's best knight to stand in for the king. The emissary knows Kiskaddon is out of favor."

"And Lord Faulkes isn't available," Ransom mused. "The Brugians haven't troubled us in years."

"I know. It's been a long time. And now that his contest is won, Gotz is in a position to meddle in other affairs. Like ours. If he finds out that we're sending troops to Legault, he might see an opening, a weakness."

Ransom sighed. "Jon-Landon isn't as shrewd as his father."

"Not by half," agreed Cecily. "Now for the news about Legault."

"Yes?"

"A fleet of ships was sent to blockade Connaught. Faulkes is assembling an army to attack the castle. He controls the lower half of Legault right now and married the heiress . . . Tenthor's niece? Is that right?"

"Yes, that was what we'd heard he intended to do."

"He named himself her guardian and married her within the week."

Disappointment rankled inside Ransom. He'd liked Tenthor, a lot, and would have wished for more for his niece. Dawson would have made a better husband.

"It's the custom in Legault that the wife gets to choose her husband," Ransom said.

Cecily was quiet for a moment. "I can't say this for certain, but I don't think she was given a choice. I've heard one of the Espion bragging that the marriage ceremony was rather . . . short. That she was forced to say yes."

Fury blazed in Ransom's chest. He started pacing, then paused, trying to keep the anger from his voice. "I sent Simon to reinforce Connaught. Do you know if he arrived in time?"

"I don't think they did," she said softly. "The king's fleet was waiting at Blackpool. They would have gotten there first."

Ransom's anguish doubled at the knowledge that Claire was facing immense odds. And she would have to face them alone.

He knew she wouldn't surrender. She would not go back into bondage.

"I must go," Cecily whispered.

Ransom turned. "Thank you," he told her sincerely. "Thank you for everything."

She looked down. "Why don't you fight back? Many would follow your example."

He knew she spoke the truth.

"And that's why I can't," he told her.

In the darkness of the room, he felt his Fountain magic throb. It was just a single pulse, a feeling of agreement. He didn't know why the Fountain had brought him to this prison, but he would not abandon the duty it had set out for him.

Even if his king took everything from him.

⋈

It has been over a fortnight since I last wrote. Simon arrived with reinforcements from Glosstyr. Because of the blockade, they were forced to land on a different part of the island before making their way to Connaught. The additional soldiers were greatly appreciated, and Simon's counsel about the war has been useful.

Our defense comes down to two options. If we remain in the castle, they can pin us here indefinitely while they conquer the rest of the island. I don't care for this approach, although it would enable us to hold out for months. The other option is hiding a large number of our soldiers in the woods. We draw their gaze to the castle itself and then attack them when they least expect it. The danger of this strategy is that our force may not be large enough to defeat theirs, and we risk losing because retreat would be impossible. Our men would be cut off from the castle, and I don't think Faulkes would show mercy. But if we could defeat his army, it would end the conflict and allow us to bide our time for another invasion from Ceredigion while rallying strength from the lords who are still loyal.

Dawson and Simon think that the second plan is worth the risk. Dearley thinks the first has a better chance of long-term success. Faulkes and his army are coming up the road and will be here in three days if not sooner. It is time to decide.

—Claire de Murrow, Queen of the Fair Isle
(fateful choices)

CHAPTER FOURTEEN

Vultures of War

Days turned into weeks, and Ransom found it difficult to keep track of the passing time. He longed for any news from Legault, but what little tidings Cecily supplied were grim. Half of the island kingdom had been conquered, and Faulkes had finally turned his machinations against Connaught itself. More than anything, Ransom wished he were there to face the threat himself. He thought about slipping away from the palace with the boys, but his conscience forbade it. He could not forget Alix's wish to kill the king and his children, to end the game and doom Ceredigion to a watery grave.

Because of the insult to King Gotz, the Brugians began to launch raiding ships against Ceredigion's coast. Perhaps encouraged by their example, the Atabyrions began a series of incursions against North Cumbria. And the Occitanians began building at the ruins of Tatton Grange in order to build a stronghold in Westmarch.

With the threats around him growing, Jon-Landon summoned his council to meet at Kingfountain. Ransom wasn't invited to participate, of course, but he was interested in what was going on. He was walking the inner corridors of the palace, waiting for news from the council, when he heard shouting from inside the great hall. His stomach clenched. The door leading to the great hall was shoved open, and

Lord Kiskaddon stormed out, his face splotched with color. Ransom had never seen the man so angry before.

Kiskaddon marched down the corridor, slowing when he noticed Ransom some distance away. There were servants nearby, exchanging worried looks, but the duke's attention was fixed on Ransom. He approached him, shaking his head in disgust.

"I've never known such a short-sighted man," he fumed.

"I take it the council didn't go so well, Hal."

"He's so fixed on his conquest that he cannot see the damage he's doing. We're being attacked on all fronts by our enemies, but he's still determined to cut off his own right arm! I told him to end this fruitless attack on Legault and restore you to your rightful station. He exploded and began ranting like a madman. You've done nothing to discredit yourself, Ransom. There is no reason for his spite."

"I'm grateful you spoke up for me, but I can see it didn't do any good."

"No, it only made things worse," Kiskaddon said. He looked back at the doors to the great hall and scowled. "He'll probably come after me next."

Ransom sympathized with Lord Kiskaddon, but he suspected he was right. "What have the Brugians been up to? I only hear a little bit now and then."

Kiskaddon shook his head. "We never know when or where they're going to strike because all of our ships are anchored off the coast of Legault. The king seems to think the war he's waging against your lands will soon be over. He won't draw them off until it is. I'm sorry, Ransom." The duke clapped him on the shoulder. "I'd better go while I still can. He's bled us dry paying scutage, and now he expects us to fight anyway, while he keeps the money. Bennett would never have acted this way."

Ransom gave him the knightly salute. The other knight returned it and marched down the corridor.

With nothing else to occupy himself, Ransom continued his walk, and some hours later he was approached by the queen's steward, Master Dyson.

"Ah, there you are. The queen would like to speak to you. Would you come with me, please?"

"Of course," Ransom answered, surprised by the summons. During his confinement, she'd never asked to speak with him privately before. He'd seen more of her daughter than he had of the queen herself.

The steward took him to the solar, where he found Queen Léa sitting on a couch with the prince, whose eyes were puffy from crying. She wore a simple coronet in her braided hair, several rings on her fingers, and a jeweled necklace set with a flashing emerald.

"Thank you, Dyson," she said, then flicked her fingers at the steward to dismiss him.

The prince sniffled, and Léa stroked his back.

Ransom bowed to her. "What do you need, my lady?" he asked.

"I don't need anything, Lord Ransom. I'm a queen. Some news came today. I thought you'd want to know."

His stomach filled with dread. "Yes, my lady?"

"The queen dowager . . . is dead. Her health has been failing of late. Poor Devon didn't know her all that well, but he was really saddened by the news." She rubbed her son's neck. "She was someone special to you, I believe. The one who ransomed you all those years ago."

Grief struck Ransom like a lance to his heart. His first reaction was disbelief, but then a feeling of numbness sapped away his surprise. Had her sickness been natural, or was it contrived? Had Alix poisoned her own mother out of spite and revenge?

"I'm sorry to hear it," Ransom said, keeping his voice steady.

Léa gave him a probing look. "I haven't told my husband yet. How do you think he will take it?"

It shocked him that she'd told him first. How had she learned the news before her husband? Perhaps the message had been delivered to her first deliberately, because the bearer feared how the mercurial king would react.

"They were never that close," Ransom said. "It's difficult to say." The numbness was awful. He wanted to mourn, but he dared not show emotion in front of Jon-Landon's petty queen.

"I wanted your advice," she said. "Whether you believe it or not, you know Jon-Landon better than most people. He still respects you."

"He has an interesting way of showing it," Ransom mused.

She smiled. "He admires strong people. His father was strong, in his eyes. So were his older brothers. And his mother. He was young when his parents' marriage fell apart. Emiloh was shut into the tower, not allowed to see him, and he still feels the lack of having a mother. I think this news will be terrible for him. And because it will be, he won't want to attend her funeral rites. He doesn't like doing things that make him feel uncomfortable."

"It would be dangerous for him to travel to the Vexin right now. Estian would see him coming."

"Yes, indeed," the queen said. "That Wizr board. Maybe it's a trap. I was thinking that we should bring her body to the sanctuary at Fountainvault. That is where the Elder King was sent to the Deep Fathoms. Benedict too. And it's much closer. What do you think, Ransom?"

"I'm surprised you're asking me."

"You shouldn't be. I want you to go with him."

"Me?"

Léa nodded. "If Estian saw your piece and the king's piece moving together, I don't think he'd be as quick to attack. And you'd get to pay your respects as well."

The prince lifted his head and looked into his mother's eyes. "Can I go too, Maman?"

She ran her fingers through his hair. "I don't think so, Dev. It would not be wise for you and your father to leave Kingfountain at the same time."

He pouted. "Would you let Léanore go?"

"No, Dev. This is something for Papa to do alone." She looked up at Ransom next. "Would you go, Ransom? If I asked you to?"

"I would. Thank you for telling me."

"Let me see how Jon-Landon takes the news. That is all." She flicked her fingers at him in dismissal.

Before the week had ended, Ransom found himself on a horse riding toward Westmarch with the king. Being freed from the castle was a relief to Ransom, but he still felt like he was a prisoner. He was allowed to wear a chain hauberk beneath his armor but not to carry a sword, and his scabbard had not been restored to him. It made him feel defenseless, hamstrung, and he wondered why he had even been brought if he wasn't allowed to act the part of defender. Still, he wished to pay respects to Emiloh, and he rode without complaint. They traveled with a group of two hundred men toward Beestone castle, where they'd rest, change mounts, and continue to Fountainvault, on the borders of Westmarch. Arrangements had already been made to bring the queen's corpse from Auxaunce.

It came as no surprise at all that Jon-Landon named his father-in-law, Lord DeVaux, as the Duke of Vexin. The old man had finally gotten what he wanted.

The king said hardly a word to anyone. Judging by his expression, Jon-Landon grieved his mother's death. There was a tightness about his eyes, a permanent scowl on his mouth, and a look of low spirits that plagued his soul. For all the man's faults, Ransom pitied him. The king had never fully reconciled with his mother, and now she was gone.

The scouts had gone ahead to make sure all was in preparation. The Occitanian forces were securing the construction of a new fortress where Tatton Grange had been, and a writ of safe conduct had been granted by Estian for Jon-Landon to see to the funeral rites for his mother. The writ lasted from sunrise to sunset on the day they would arrive.

When they reached the sanctuary, Ransom used his Fountain magic to see if he could sense any threats to the king. He didn't feel anything, although his magic had been diminished of late. Still, he felt some trepidation as he dismounted with the king and followed him into the sanctuary.

Emiloh's body had already been prepared and lay within a canoe draped with lavender-colored linen, propped to waist height atop poles and a funeral bier. Her face was waxy and shrunken, the luster of her hair muted in death. Seeing her like that caused a jolt of pain in his heart. It was her, but it was a husk. As he examined her face, he looked for signs of the incurable poison that had taken the life of her husband and two of her sons. He didn't find any. Although the people who'd prepared her body would no doubt have cleaned any blood that had leaked from her eyes or nose, that particular poison caused a languishing death, and it would have left more signs. He reached into the boat and put his hand atop Emiloh's, which were crossed over her breast. The skin felt rigid and cold.

Jon-Landon, who had already peered into the canoe and moved past it, returned, as if shamed by the respect Ransom was showing his mother. His lips pulled back in a near snarl, but he reached out and touched the edge of the boat with his gloved hand. His breath came in and out quickly as he wrestled with his emotions.

Then, pursing his lips, he breathed out again and retreated a few steps. "There," he sighed out. "Wasn't as bad as I feared."

Ransom looked at the king but said nothing. There was a haunted expression in Jon-Landon's eyes. Now that they'd paid their respects, they assembled a group to carry the canoe to the river. This included Ransom, Lord Jex, who had served as the queen's steward in Auxaunce, as well as other members of her household guard, knights all. They carried their cargo solemnly. Ransom felt his eyes burning, but he didn't let his tears fall. When they reached the edge of the river, the deconeus performed the funeral rites while they stood at attention. When he finished, they lowered the front of the staves so that the canoe slid into the river. Ransom watched as it bobbed downstream. His throat was tight, but he kept a grip on his emotions.

They left after the ceremony to ensure they were clear of Westmarch before sunset. As he rode eastward, Ransom found himself thinking about the past, of all the times he had traveled the realm in service to the various kings. With enemies attacking their shores on multiple fronts, would Jon-Landon's stubbornness continue, or would he finally rely on the man whose loyalty he'd despised?

When they reached Beestone castle again, they were all weary from the journey and grateful for the feast that had been prepared in anticipation of their arrival. Jon-Landon drank heavily during the meal, his mood becoming darker as the night wore on.

Ransom was about to retire for the night when a man hurried into the audience hall and delivered a message to the king. He bent close and whispered in the king's ear. Jon-Landon's eyes widened in surprise. He asked a quick question, listened to the response, and then hurriedly opened the sealed note he'd been given. Ransom watched him read the news, wondering what it was about. Another attack from the Brugians?

The king lowered the page and carefully folded it again. He lifted his gaze and searched the hall until his eyes fixed on Ransom's. The king smirked at the sight of him, gesturing for him to approach.

His stomach twisting in knots, Ransom left his place and approached the head of the king's table.

"Yes, my lord?"

Jon-Landon tapped the note against the edge of the table. "News from Legault," he said.

Another twist in his stomach. "Oh?"

"Looks like our troubles there are over," he said, giving Ransom a vicious smile. "Your wife took a terrible gamble, one that failed. She hid the bulk of her forces in the woods outside the castle and attacked Faulkes's forces. It was a slaughter. Simon is dead. So is Dearley. The castle surrendered two nights ago. I'm glad they did. I would have hated to raze it. What's done is done. I thought you'd want to know."

Ransom stared at the king in disbelief, his emotions churning beneath a veneer of calm. Connaught had fallen so quickly? He'd imagined it would take months to lay siege to it. He'd hoped they'd last long enough for winter to come, forcing Faulkes to withdraw for a season. But Dearley was dead . . . and Simon . . . and this man was *smiling*. His gaze traveled to the sharp knife at the side of the king's plate. For a moment, he considered grabbing it and plunging it into Jon-Landon's neck.

The urge for violence pulsed until he saw red, but he managed to thrust it down, even as it threatened to drive him mad. Jon-Landon wouldn't realize how close he'd come to dying at that moment.

"What?" Jon-Landon scoffed. "You lost. I've defeated you. And you've nothing to say?"

Ransom looked him in the eye, feeling the sear of anger and grief. "My lord, by the Fountain's grace, I have been loyal to you all the while. I came when you summoned me, even though my friends warned me against it. But I didn't want to believe, my lord, this is how you would reward my faithfulness to you and your family."

Jon-Landon lifted his goblet to drink, but it was empty. He thumped it hard on the table and scowled at a nearby servant, who rushed to fill it.

"Then I hope you've learned your lesson," he said to Ransom, not meeting his gaze. "Go. I cannot bear the sight of you." He grimaced with loathing and contempt.

Ransom left the great hall in a daze, anger chafing inside his heart. Disbelief and loss crawling through him. Dearley was dead? Simon too? What of Dawson? Had he remained in the castle to defend Claire? He gazed up at the stars dappling the sky, wanting to let out a roar of anguish.

He only let it out when he was sure there was no one to hear him.

I can scarce trust my hand to write these words. It is over. We have won. The risk was great, which makes the victory all the sweeter. The army of Ceredigion is vanquished, and we have a surfeit of hostages to bargain for peace. I'm in awe at the suddenness of the transformation of our fortunes. Here is our story.

I chose to hide the bulk of our forces in the hunting woods but also another contingent in marshland to the southeast. We cleared all traces of our presence and awaited the enemy's arrival. I had proposed that Dearley defend the castle because I know he isn't as strong at arms as Dawson and also because Elodie is pregnant with their child, but he made an impassioned plea not to be set aside. He swore it was his duty to risk his life for his lord and his lady, that Ransom had suffered grievous wounds on his behalf, and that it was his right, as first knight, to stand in his lord's place. He argued that Dawson, who was the best champion we have, should guard my life with his own and see to the defense of the castle if our plan failed. We discussed it openly, with great candor, and I felt I could no more deny him that right than I could have done to my husband.

Dearley led a rousing speech before they left the castle. He spoke from the heart, sharing the common feeling of loyalty and love that my husband's knights share for him. He said that the Fountain would be with us if they stayed true to their oaths, for they were defending home and hearth from a dishonorable man. Even though we were outnumbered, we would fight with the strength of true lions, not false ones made of thread and worn on badges. I was impressed by Dearley's vigor. He saluted us and led the forces into the woods while Captain Baldwin hastened the younger lads to the marshes. Simon led the reserves, and it was agreed he would choose the best moment to interject them.

Faulkes was blind to our intrigues. His army came like a mighty, lazy bear, so confident in its muscle and claws that it plopped down in the meadow at the foot of Connaught and proceeded to nap. Foragers were sent into the woods to start cutting down trees for firewood. Our archers abducted them in small groups. We watched them build their camp, and we paraded the same men back and forth along the walls of Connaught to make it look as if our entire force were encamped within. We had servants clanging pans and black-smiths denting bits of iron to add to the noise.

At nightfall, Dearley launched his attack from the woods. The bear was roused from its slumber, but it was too disoriented to know where to strike. Nor did he know the land as we do. He attacked and retreated and then attacked again. Baldwin's youths struck from the rear, confusing the bear even more.

By morning, Faulkes found that his mercenaries had abandoned him and half of his Gaultic henchmen had fled in the night. Seeing the disarray, I ordered Dawson to charge down from the castle with the remaining defenders, and he did so, riding Dappled and shouting the battle cry Dex aie! *It felt as if Ransom had returned. The weary soldiers from the marshes and the woods rallied once more and surrounded*

Faulkes's men, who surrendered and begged for quarter. Though they would have given us none had the situation been reversed, we granted it, for we are made of better stuff than they. Faulkes was brought to the castle under guard and unceremoniously chained in the dungeon along with his captains.

Dawson led a counter force of knights to chase after the mercenaries and routed them before they could reach Atha Kleah. Then he marched his prisoners to Atha Kleah and retook the fortress. They were met by a rejoicing mob, as our people had already grown resentful of Faulkes's broken oaths. Simon sustained some injuries in the battle, but he's hale. Dearley, I'm so proud of John Dearley. His victory increased his stature today. He's a new man. I've never seen Elodie more honored.

I'm now in Atha Kleah, ready to mete our rewards and punishments to those who have earned them. I've sent a missive to Jon-Landon to negotiate terms. Now that we're no longer cut off, I've learned the king is facing threats on all sides. He cannot send more knights to subdue us. On the contrary, if he releases Ransom, he can gain the help he desperately needs.

I await his response.

—Claire de Murrow, Queen Once More
Atha Kleah

CHAPTER FIFTEEN

A Key in a Well

Ransom was tormented by the deaths of his friends. When he remembered that Elodie was still with child, the grief nearly broke him. He'd always imagined Dearley would outlast him, that he'd help carry Ransom's funeral boat. It should not be the other way around. Elodie's despair would be limitless. He prayed to the Fountain her child would survive, to keep Dearley's name more than just a memory.

Simon was dead as well. He'd been a trusted friend and confidant since they were both in service to Devon the Younger. What of old Captain Baldwin? Surely he had survived? The old captain was too stubborn to die.

On that hurried ride back to the palace, he managed to keep his composure. He pretended he was made of stone. But inside, he wrestled against a beast that demanded revenge on the last Argentine son. He knew those thoughts would lead to madness, to betrayal, and he fought them, but it seemed as if he battled a mythical beast that only grew stronger the more he lashed at it within his mind.

He worried he would lose his sanity. That he would do something unthinkable.

It didn't help that the knights of the entourage kept giving him pitying looks. At least, that was how he interpreted them. He'd never liked being a spectacle, even back in his tournament days. Each glance made him long to leave more fervently, to go back to Legault so he might comfort the mourning and honor the dead.

The journey finally ended, and they reached the palace. Ransom went looking for his sons to relate the tragic news to them. At least he would be there to comfort them. He searched in the kitchen first, but the boys weren't there. He made a circuit of the castle's interior, stopping servants occasionally, before one finally revealed that she'd seen the boys from a window and thought they were still in the palace gardens. He asked which gardens, was told, and then hurried there, his mood black from the weight of his burdens.

He left the palace and started through the garden, passing the tree that he and Claire had once gotten stuck in. It caused a flash of hurt inside him, but his mind went blank when he heard a cry of pain.

"Let him go!" Willem shouted.

"I'll make him go down into the well to fetch it, I will!" snarled a man's voice, one he immediately recognized as the Espion Aldous. "Maybe you'll drown. You little rake—owww!"

Princess Léanore screamed.

Blood pounded in Ransom's ears as he ran toward the sound. He came around the corner and saw the scene unfold in a flash. The princess was running toward him, her eyes wet with tears. When she saw him, a look of relief dawned on her face. Aldous had Devon by the collar, and they were both by one of the garden wells. It didn't lead to the cistern, for it was lower down the slope from the castle proper. Aldous was pressing his other hand, where there were some flaming-red teeth marks on his skin, to his mouth. Willem's face was contorted in rage, and he was beating his small fists into Aldous's back, but the blows were having no effect on the larger man.

"Lord Ransom!" Léanore gasped. "Help! Help!"

Aldous growled and shoved Willem in the face, knocking him down, and then continued to wrestle Devon to the edge of the well. Aldous's stringy hair a mess, his long nose dripping, he used his greater power to bend the boy toward the mouth of the well.

Ransom sprinted the final steps. Aldous turned on hearing his approach, and then his eyes widened with shock at seeing the boys' father coming at him.

Aldous immediately released Devon and backed away. "Hold there, Lord Ransom, let me expl—"

Ransom caught him by the front of his shirt and continued to push him backward to the nearest tree. Aldous collided with it, his eyes blinking with panic. His huge nostrils flared. Ransom brought his forearm into Aldous's chin, easily overpowering the smaller man, but he sensed danger as the Espion drew a dagger and suddenly pressed the tip against his ribs.

"It's not what you think," Aldous said tightly, his breath coming in quick bursts.

Ransom thought of Drew Argentine's death, and the beast inside his chest snarled to get out. With his free hand, he grabbed Aldous's wrist and squeezed and twisted until pain bulged in the Espion's eyes and he dropped the dagger onto the grass. Willem and Devon came to stand by their father, their eyes full of wrath at their tormentor.

Aldous grimaced. Fear shone in his eyes now that he had been disarmed. "Let me go, Lord Ransom. You don't want this."

He very much wanted to wring the Espion's neck with his bare hands. "They're children," he chided huskily, so angry he was ready to kill.

Aldous didn't seem to care. He didn't look guilty, only fearful for his life. "Release me."

"Or what?"

"There are other Espion nearby. I'll call out to them. Someone might get hurt if Bodkin finds out." His eyes flashed with animosity.

Ransom was tempted to haul Aldous to the edge of the well and pitch him headfirst down the shaft. The fall might kill him.

At that moment he didn't really care. The pressure he'd been feeling had reached a breaking point. What if he'd come too late? What if the man had pitched Devon down the well, as he'd clearly planned? What if he'd been killed?

He didn't know what to do, but his children were both all right. If anything, Aldous had been injured more by the confrontation. Beyond that, he didn't wish to display more violence in front of his boys now that the danger had passed. Taking a deep breath, Ransom released the man's wrist and stepped away from him. Aldous massaged his lower arm and sidled away from the tree, keeping his eyes fixed on Ransom's face, like a fox backing away from a wolf that had recently held it in his jaws.

"They dropped something of mine into the well," Aldous said scathingly. "I'm going to get some people to fetch it out. They may be children, but they're nasty ones."

"Say no more," Ransom declared. "Or I'll break your jaw next."

Aldous flashed a menacing look at the two boys, who met his ill intent with defiance, hands on hips. The Espion left his dagger, and his dignity, and fled the garden swiftly.

Léanore came up sniffling. "I told you we shouldn't have done it," she sobbed. She looked at Ransom guiltily. "It's our fault."

"Hush!" Devon said to her, but it was too late.

Ransom cocked his head to one side. "What did you throw in the well?"

Willem looked chagrined. "A bit of iron from the forge."

Devon threw up his hands. "You're going to tell him everything?"

"We got caught, Dev," said Willem. "Show him."

Léanore sniffled again. "I knew it would end badly. I knew it."

"It was a good plan—it worked," Devon said. "We just didn't count on how angry he'd get." He fished into his pocket and pulled out a key. It had a star emblazoned on the end.

Ransom closed his eyes. Nothing excused Aldous's reaction, but the boys *had* started it. He looked at Devon in disappointment. "That's a key to the Star Chamber." It was the room Lord Longmont had turned into the headquarters of the Espion in the palace. He'd engraved stars on the ceiling to add to its mystique. Only the most trusted Espion were allowed there.

"I know," Willem said sheepishly. "It's the only place in the palace we haven't been in . . . yet."

Léanore spoke up. "We took a used bit of iron scrap to try and make a key, but that didn't work. Then Devon said he could steal Aldous's key and pretend to throw it into the well." She was trembling but seemed relieved to be telling the truth at last.

"So you tossed the scrap into the well instead to make it convincing?" Ransom asked. He was impressed by their resourcefulness but alarmed by the extravagance of their deception.

"It needed to sound like a key as it slid down the stone," Devon said with a guilty look.

"Give it to me," Ransom said, holding out his hand. Devon handed it over, his cheeks flushing with shame.

Ransom pocketed it. "You must take care. The people who run the Espion now are dangerous men," he said. "They're not like Sir Simon." He dropped down to his knee and pulled his children close. They hugged him, and he looked over Devon's shoulder and saw Léanore staring at him as if she, too, wanted a hug.

She was Jon-Landon's daughter, but that wasn't her fault. He gestured with his palm to come closer, and she smiled in relief and hugged him and Devon.

"I have some bad news to share, boys," he said with a sigh.

"What is it, Papa?" Willem asked worriedly.

"I'll tell you later," he said. "What you did today was not honorable. I need to think of a punishment first."

His sons pulled back and looked at each other.

"Very well, Father," Willem said somberly. He looked like he was bracing for the worst.

"I'm glad none of us ended up in the well," Léanore said. "Do I get a punishment too?"

"I'm going to tell the queen," Ransom said. "That is for her to decide."

She bowed her head and looked genuinely regretful.

Devon was still wrestling with his feelings. "I'm sorry, Papa."

"Let me think on it. Go play in the kitchen. I'll come for you later."

The three children nodded, and they walked away together. He looked down at the grass and saw the dagger he'd wrenched from Aldous's hand. Stooping, he picked it up and turned the blade over in his palm. Then, clenching it in his fist, he slammed it into the tree, blade first. He walked to the well and sat down at the edge, grateful he hadn't let his anger overcome him. Although Aldous had overreacted, and violently at that, his children had been in the wrong. Now that he knew the full story, he felt less threatened by what had just happened.

Had he broken Aldous's wrist? It would have been so easy to have done worse. His magic bubbled soothingly inside of him, but he didn't feel worthy of it at that moment. He sensed someone approaching and turned his neck to see Cecily heading toward the well.

When she reached him, she looked over at the tree and saw the dagger plunged into the bark. "Well, at least you didn't pin Aldous there with it. I don't think he's strong enough to have pulled it out."

Ransom felt so weary, he could barely summon a smile. "Are more Espion coming?"

"There's a lost key in the well, or so I've heard," she said.

Ransom reached into his pocket and handed it to her.

Her eyebrows rose in surprise. "A trick? The boys stole it?"

"They threw down a bit of scrap to mimic it. They were trying to get into the Star Chamber."

Her brow furrowed. "I didn't encourage it."

"I almost throttled Aldous. I thought he was trying to drown my boys. I might have killed him."

She sat down next to him at the edge of the well. "No. You wouldn't have."

"I almost did," he said, looking at a nearby shrub. "I've always had this . . . part of me. It's like a beast . . . a ravening monster . . . trying to come out. I think the first time was when James and some of his lackeys tried to humiliate me back when we were training together."

"I haven't heard that story," she said in a kindly way. "What happened?"

"I'd done well in the training yard, performing better than the others. James was the son of a duke, and I was just a lesser nobleman's second son."

"Already a famous one, though," she pointed out.

Ransom held up his hands. "Famous for almost getting hung. They ambushed me. It was four against one. Or five. It was a long time ago. I beat them all. And there was this part of me that delighted in it. I'm good at fighting. It comes naturally."

"So I've seen," she said. "You should be proud of your abilities, Ransom."

"They frighten me, though." He looked at her. "If I ever lost control . . . I'm afraid of what I might do."

They sat there for a moment, uninterrupted, each steeping in their thoughts as a warm breeze rustled the branches.

Finally, Cecily gave him a probing look. "Would you listen to some advice?"

"I'd welcome it."

"You aren't the only one who feels that way, Ransom. There are beasts within us all. I've seen monsters of many shapes and sizes among the Espion. And the knights as well. Yours is an especially powerful one because you are such a good person. You won't defeat it like you would an enemy with a lance or a sword. It's real, a part of you. The only way you can fight it is by walking away. When it rears its head and flashes its fangs, do nothing. Just walk away. It will weaken it. It will starve it. That part of you will not die, fully, until you do." She gave him a sad smile. "Great men have great challenges. Sorry there isn't an easier way."

As she spoke, he felt a feeling of peace settle over him. There was wisdom in her words. He'd always thought of it as a battle to be won, but it was a battle that never ended.

In the past, he'd controlled his monster by devoting himself to a greater cause, to someone more powerful than himself. The difference was that he'd respected the others. He'd trusted them more. And yet, they'd been flawed too, hadn't they? Emiloh had seen it, even if they had not.

"Thank you, Cecily," he told her. "I needed that."

"Well, it's small comfort in comparison to what I have to tell you next."

"What?"

"I heard from some Espion who just returned from Beestone that the king lied to you. He tried one last time to provoke you into rebellion and failed. Claire won the battle. Faulkes has been captured, his army routed and imprisoned. She's written, demanding the release of you and your sons. I don't think the king will send the boys home. He wants more hostages, not less. But I think it's become clear to him that he knows he needs to let you go." She reached out and patted his hand. "Please act surprised when you find out."

He was so startled by her words that he nearly unbalanced and fell into the well.

"What of Dearley? Is he truly dead?"

"No! He was the hero of the day. He led your army to victory in your name. Everything Jon-Landon told you at Beestone was a lie."

He thought of the way he'd looked at the knife by Jon-Landon's plate, tempted to kill the king right then and there. It made him shudder at what he'd nearly done. Although he was disgusted by the king's vicious lie, that dark feeling couldn't gain traction amidst the cascade of gratitude and relief. He hung his head, stunned.

Hearing voices in the distance, Ransom lifted his head.

"I hear the others coming," Cecily said. "Better give them something to find."

With a mischievous grin, she dropped the key into the well.

Stubbornness, thy name is Jon. I had hoped Ransom would be home already, but the haggling over the hostages has taken longer than anticipated. Securing Ransom's freedom was the easy part, but the king has tried a number of tricks to keep my sons behind at Kingfountain. He's tried flattery, saying that his daughter, the princess Léanore, would be heartbroken if they were to both go. He's tried bribery, offering lands to the younger twin, Devon, since he will not inherit Ransom's title of duke. He's tried selfishness, claiming he's fond of the lads himself and suggesting I should want to appease a king in his wretched misery.

Ransom and I have corresponded, and he feels the boys are in no danger, and the king's declarations of affection for them may have some merit. A speck. The boys themselves consider it a grand lark and would like to stay for the time being. The king has also demanded hostages of his other nobles because many have turned on him and stopped defending the borders of the realm. I would like at least one son to return to me, but Ransom feels they are safer together. He says the king will release all the hostages, eventually, in order to appease his nobles.

After what the king did to the Occitanian hostages, we cannot trust his word.

The king's final attempt to sweeten his request to keep my boys was to suggest that I send Sir Dawson to be the boys' chaperone and trainer. I asked Dawson if he would be willing to accept an exile, and he said he would go to the ends of the earth if we commanded it. So he has been sent, along with Faulkes and the ransomed prisoners, to Glosstyr. If the king holds up his end of the bargain, pays for the ransoms we've negotiated, and releases my husband as promised, then this will finally be over . . . for the time being.

Faulkes asked if Orla could be sent to Kingfountain with him. He seems to sincerely want her to be with him, even though he married her against the customs of our people. I asked for her voice in that decision, and she shrank in horror. She will not go with him, not if given a choice.

Legault has proven to be the Fair Isle once more. But it will be made all the fairer if Ransom returns safely.

Still. I shall have no rest until my sons are safe at home too.

—Claire de Murrow, Queen of Legault
Atha Kleah

CHAPTER SIXTEEN

Go in Peace

The negotiations between Jon-Landon and Claire had dragged on for weeks and then months. Finally, an accord was struck, one that would allow Ransom to go home to his wife and daughters without fearing for his boys' safety. Although he had no great trust for Jon-Landon, who had never apologized for the bald-faced lie he'd told Ransom at Beestone castle, he could trust Dawson with his boys.

On the day the agreement was finalized, Ransom was asked to join the king, queen, and their family in the great hall. He had already learned the terms from Cecily, so he wasn't concerned.

When he reached the hall, he found Willem and Devon playing with wooden soldiers on the floor. The princess was on her stomach, her amber eyes glowing with interest as she watched the battle. Her brother, the prince, was also observing the game.

"I blow the horn and summon the reserves!" Devon said eagerly. He grabbed several other miniatures and brought them to the battle.

Léanore squealed with delight and started to laugh. "Will they get there in time?"

"Of course!" Devon insisted. "They all have desert horses. They're the fastest."

"But he can block them still if he moves right," the prince observed.

Ransom quelled a little smile as he approached the dais. The queen gave him a welcoming nod, although the occasion lacked formality, and she sat slouched in her throne. Jon-Landon was watching the game between the children fixedly and didn't seem to notice his arrival until the queen poked his arm.

"Ah, Lord Ransom!" said Jon-Landon, straightening.

The prince was sitting by his father's footstool. The boy looked up at Ransom and smiled and nodded in a friendly manner.

The king rose from his throne and stepped down the dais steps. "The negotiations are complete. I'll be sending you to Glosstyr on the morrow with the agreed-upon treasure. Claire is an able negotiator. She represented you well. Your knight, Sir Dawson, will take your place of honor here at the palace."

From the corner of his eye, Ransom saw his sons knock their fists together in celebration. He would have preferred to bring them both home, but he understood that the king's position was growing more untenable by the day. He'd demanded more hostages to secure loyalty, including James and Maeg's son. Ransom had hoped to see his nephew before leaving, but it wasn't to be.

"Thank you, my lord," Ransom said, bowing.

"There's one more matter to finish, though." The king gestured to one of his servants, who left the room. "Your sword must be returned. Allow my servant to fetch it."

"Left flank! Left flank!" Willem declared, picking up on the prince's earlier suggestion. Although Prince Devon was quiet, he had an authoritative way about him and, it seemed, an eye for strategy. Both qualities lent themselves to leadership.

The servant came rushing in, holding Ransom's scabbard and sword. Ransom recognized both immediately, and as soon as he saw them, he felt the calming feeling of the Fountain ripple through him.

"Ah, here we are!" said Jon-Landon.

The servant approached Ransom. "These are correct, Lord Ransom?"

"Yes," Ransom said, taking the scabbard from him.

"Léa," said the king. "Would you do the honors and gird him?"

"Of course," she said and came to stand by Ransom. He held the sword out to her, and she unbound the strap. Then, coming closer, she wrapped it around his waist before hooking the pin in place. The familiar and dearly missed weight of the blade settled into place. She smoothed the front of Ransom's tunic and stepped back.

"It is done," she said.

The king looked into Ransom's eyes. "Do you still swear fealty to me as your liege lord and king?"

It sounded like a plea for forgiveness.

Ransom dropped to his knee before Jon-Landon. "I do and ever have, my lord." He felt the Fountain churn, felt his stores of magic swell as if waves were crashing within him.

Jon-Landon looked relieved. He took Ransom's hand and raised him up. "You may go home, Lord Ransom. Until I summon you again."

Ransom rose. He went to his sons, who quickly scrambled to their feet to embrace him. He clutched them both, kissing their cheeks.

"Good-bye, Lord Ransom," said the princess, smiling at him.

Ransom tousled his sons' hair and turned and found the prince approaching him.

"F-farewell, Lord Ransom," said Prince Devon. "I hope we shall meet again soon."

A strange feeling passed over Ransom's heart. For a moment, it felt as if he were parting from Emiloh and Devon the Elder, who'd just arrived at Kingfountain with their young children. So much had changed in the intervening years.

"I hope so," Ransom told the boy. He felt a strong swelling of loyalty to the young man. The one the Fountain had chosen to succeed his father. The future king of Ceredigion.

Cecily had been assigned by the king to accompany Ransom to Glosstyr along with an escort of knights and the two wagons full of treasure. It was her job, as Espion envoy, to make sure the hostages were all accounted for and the terms of the agreement upheld.

On the last leg, they traveled overnight due to Ransom's impatience, arriving before dawn. When he saw the lit fortress of Glosstyr, Ransom felt relieved beyond measure. A force rode to meet him, and he recognized Dawson at the front of the cohort of knights.

The two groups met, Ransom gave Dawson the knightly salute, and his knight grinned while returning it. His gaze shifted to Cecily as she approached on her stallion.

"You are Sir Dawson?" she asked.

His mouth gaped when he saw her. Then, collecting himself, he answered, "Yes. I am he."

"Good," Cecily said. "Come inspect the treasure. May I see the hostages?"

"They are at the gate. Shall I escort you?"

Her brow wrinkled in amusement. "I know the way. Your job is to inspect the treasure."

"Yes, pardon me," he said, his cheeks suddenly flaming. Dawson was clearly flustered by her, something Ransom had never witnessed in the usually confident, collected man. Cecily gave Ransom an amused glance before riding off toward the city.

Dawson, who'd turned back in his saddle to watch her go, murmured, "By the Fountain, she is fair! Who is she?"

"She's one of the Espion. Cecily."

"The one who helped you? You never said she was so beautiful."

"Gather your wits, man," Ransom said, amused in spite of himself. "You'll be riding with her back to Kingfountain."

Dawson chuffed. "Then I won't be dreading this exile as much as I thought. Is the treasure in those wagons?"

"Where else? Come on, Dawson. Your duty."

Dawson nodded, glancing back the way he'd come once more before he dismounted and began searching the thick leather chests. He dug through the livres, plunging his dagger into each collection of coins to make sure it was sufficiently deep. He counted one entirely and then expressed his satisfaction to Ransom and returned to his horse.

When Cecily returned, she nodded to Ransom. "All is in order. Faulkes is anxious to depart."

"He can wait," Ransom said. "Let's unload the chests in the city first. Then they may leave."

"Very well," she said.

They brought the wagons the rest of the way, and guards from Glosstyr emerged to carry the chests, so heavy they required two men each, away from the wagons. The wagons would be used to help cart the prisoners back to Kingfountain. Extra horses had been brought for the nobles to ride. Faulkes, who showed no repentance or humility for his role in the attack on Legault, shot impatient looks at Ransom as he waited for the exchange. Ransom ignored him.

At last, the exchange was done, and the prisoners were set free. Cecily gave Ransom a final nod and then brought her horse to Dawson. "Come with me, Sir Dawson. We have much to discuss on the journey back."

"I look forward to it, my lady," he said, giving Ransom a final salute. No doubt he meant it.

By sundown, Ransom was back at Connaught castle.

There were no lingering signs of battle—the castle looked just as it had when he'd left it. They'd come earlier than expected, so no one was waiting for the ship to approach. He climbed the steps of the wharf and then came up the cliff road to the castle as night birds began to call. Torches lit the path as he made his way home, smelling the beautiful sea and greeting the knights and servants he passed, who addressed him with warmth and respect.

"Welcome home, my lord," several of them said to him.

He entered the castle and heard a squeal when Sibyl came rushing into his arms.

"Papa! Papa!"

Then Claire was there, rushing down the steps from the upper rooms. She came into his arms, and he lifted her off her feet, swinging her around. She pressed kisses to his eyes, his cheeks, his nose, then finally found his mouth. Their littlest, Keeva, came toddling up as well.

It felt like his heart would burst with gratitude.

"I wasn't expecting you until the morrow," she said, still suspended off her feet.

"I couldn't wait," he told her, bringing her down at last and squeezing her close. He stroked her hair, which glimmered crimson in the torchlight. They were a spectacle to the entire castle staff, but he didn't care. For that one stolen moment, it was just the two of them again.

"You defeated the King of Ceredigion," he told her after setting her down. He lifted a hand to stroke her chin. "You stopped his invasion of Legault. How does it feel? I am so proud of you."

"I did what you could not," she said. "You had to remain true to him to keep your honor. I had to defend our home. Pray we never need to again."

She leaned up and kissed him again, and the warmth of her mouth unleashed a fierce longing in him and made him shudder in her embrace. She was everything he'd wanted. And she was still his.

"Are you hungry?" she asked him.

"For you," he answered.

She smiled impishly. "You'll have to hold your hunger for a bit longer. We have guests."

He wrinkled his forehead. "Can't that wait? I've missed you, Claire."

Then he saw someone coming down the stairs. His stomach dropped. It was his sister, Maeg, holding the hand of a little child as she carefully came down the steps. James stood at the top of the stairs, his hand gripping the banister. His face was sick with worry.

Maeg had a desperate look in her eyes.

Claire hooked her arm with Ransom's. "What was I to do? Turn them away?"

We have waded through war, we have suffered confinement, and just when it seems that peace is possible, trouble comes finding us once more, threatening to drag us back into the mire. James Wigant and his wife, Ransom's sister, have fled Dundrennan in defiance of the king's orders.

Once more our loyalty is being tested. Ransom loves his sister. But if we shelter these two from the king, then we will all be found guilty of treason. How long must this kingdom endure such internal strife?

Why not call back the Aos Sí to rule once more? Surely not even they could have been this bad.

—Claire de Murrow, Queen of Legault
Connaught Castle

CHAPTER SEVENTEEN

The Woe of Treason

Ransom embraced his sister when she reached the bottom of the stairs, and she clung to him so tightly that he could feel her trembling. He was still getting over the shock of seeing her at Connaught castle when she was supposed to be in North Cumbria. There, she reigned as duchess of the North. But now, in his arms, she was his younger sister once again.

He stroked her hair and looked down at the child, who stared up at him with a frightened gaze. He was a stranger to the boy—an intimidating one—but that did not stifle the affection Ransom had for the lad.

"What do we do? What do we do?" Maeg whispered, her voice thick with tears.

James sauntered down the steps, but it lacked his old confidence. He had a defeated look.

"Hello, Brother-in-Law," James said to Ransom. "Is this a bad time for a visit?"

Claire lowered herself to Sibyl's height and put a hand on her shoulder. "Would you take your cousin Percy to the kitchen? Find out what he likes to eat."

"Yes, Máthair," Sibyl said. She grabbed little Keeva by the hand and then extended her other one to the boy.

Maeg released Ransom from her embrace and nodded to her son to go with his cousins. He looked fearful, but he took Sibyl's hand, and the three children went toward the kitchen. Following them with his gaze, Ransom saw Dearley watching the scene from the doorway.

Ransom felt a flush of pride in his first knight. The two men grinned at each other, and they met in the center of the room in a rough embrace.

"Welcome home, Ransom."

Dearley's success had given him a new—and well-deserved—self-confidence. It felt so good to see him alive and well, especially after the false news from Jon-Landon, yet anxiety squirmed in his stomach. His sister's visit didn't bode well.

"How is Elodie?" Ransom asked in concern, trying to quell his worries for the moment.

"She's ready to burst," Dearley said. "The baby should come any day. She's already abed for the night."

"May the Fountain bless you both," Ransom said.

"Go," Dearley said, nodding to the others. "They've been waiting for your arrival to tell us why they've come."

"You're coming with us," Ransom said.

His old friend shook his head. "This is a family matter."

"You *are* family," he insisted. "Come. To the solar. Everyone."

They all marched up the stairs to gather in the solar. It felt good to see the familiar sights, to reassure himself the castle and his family had suffered no lasting damage in the conflict. Still, he felt the tugging sense that there was more trouble to come.

Once they were all sequestered in the solar, where they could speak without fear of being overheard by servants, Ransom gave Claire a worried look, which she reciprocated. They sat on a couch, while Dearley took a chair to the side of the room. James paced nervously, unable to sit, and Maeg lowered herself onto a divan and buried her face in her hands.

"Does the king know you're here?" Ransom asked, breaking the awkward silence.

James shook his head. "Not yet. We took a ship from Blackpool and came straight here."

"Why?"

James looked at Maeg before shifting his attention back to Ransom. "Do you know what happened to Constance's son at Dundrennan?"

"I know he's dead," Ransom answered bleakly. It was still hard to think on it. He'd promised to be the boy's protector, and he'd failed miserably.

The sun was down, so nothing but darkness could be seen out the window. Although there was a crackling fire in the hearth and a few candles had been lit around the room, it held deep shadows and had a somber look.

James looked disgusted. "Yes. He is. Do you know *how* he died?"

Ransom's stomach soured. "I don't."

"The king made us take an oath not to tell," James said bitterly. "He wanted to conceal his shame. But I'll tell you. I'll confess this Argentine's sin. We're ruined anyway."

Claire reached for Ransom's hand and squeezed it hard. "If you tell us, what good will it do? I think it can only do evil."

"*He* is evil," Maeg said, her voice trembling.

James approached her and put a comforting hand on her shoulder. "I need to tell you because I want you to join us."

Ransom wrinkled his brow. "Join what?"

"An uprising against the king."

A pit opened in Ransom's stomach. "You speak treason."

"I know," James said seriously. "Hal Kiskaddon is leading it."

Claire gasped. "How long has this been going on?"

"Long enough," James said. "It has already started. The lesser lords of the realm are furious with the king for his heavy-handed ways. He's alienated everyone. Kiskaddon is the ringleader. Dalian Kinghorn is our man inside the palace. The royal family will be abducted, and the king charged with violating the sanctuary of the Fountain. He'll be thrown over the falls, and good riddance to him."

Ransom rose from the couch, his nerves tingling with dread. "When?" he demanded.

"Soon, if it has not already happened," James said. "It is only justice, Ransom. We've all watched him humiliate you. He attacked your domain when he invaded Legault, and he did so with treacherous aims. You bore it like a saint when you should have risen up against him!" He shook his head. "I'm no saint."

Claire rose from the couch as well. "By coming here, you've implicated us in your plot."

"That wasn't our intention." James looked down at Maeg. "We had to come. We had to start the revolt now."

"I don't understand," Claire said. "Why now? If you wanted to act before Faulkes was released, you're days too late."

"No one fears Faulkes now after his defeat here." A smug smile had risen on his face, but it fell the next moment. "Our hand was forced."

"How?" Ransom demanded.

Dearley looked greensick at all the talk of treason.

James swiped a hand through his pale blond hair. "After we defeated the Occitanian army and took our prisoners back to Dundrennan, the king came to visit. He asked to see Drew Argentine. Of course I let him. He's the king. He took the boy on a walk to the top of the falls. I went with them, of course, because I was worried. The king had been acting strangely."

"In what way?" Claire demanded.

"Like he had a fever. He had a half-mad look in his eyes and kept muttering under his breath. The three of us climbed to the falls. There's a bridge there, one that straddles the falls. It's a beautiful view." James's voice began to crack. He covered his mouth, his eyes haunted with the memory. "He did go mad. He grabbed Drew by the shoulders and said if the Fountain wanted a boy to be king, then he would survive the fall. He *shoved* Drew off the bridge."

Maeg began weeping, her arms wrapped tightly around herself as she sobbed.

Tears stung Ransom's eyes as he imagined the awful scene. The man who'd held him hostage all those years ago, King Gervase, had been given the opportunity to kill a child to secure his throne. He'd refused and lost the hollow crown in the end. What sort of monster would do such a thing? Jon-Landon had not even been compelled or cornered into doing so—Drew had been his prisoner. The boy had been honorable and kind, much more regal than the man who'd killed him.

"I was so surprised," James said. "I rushed to the edge and watched him vanish in the mist. Some of my men found the . . . body . . . two days later."

"That is terrible," Claire said with revulsion.

"It was an awful scene," James said thickly. "I stared at the king. I . . . I was so upset I nearly shoved *him* off. And every day since I have regretted that I didn't end his miserable life the same day he killed his nephew. Jon-Landon stood there on the bridge, staring at the falls, and he chuckled and said that the Lady of the Fountain wasn't real. That nothing had stopped him. No manifestation had saved the boy's life. He turned to me and made me swear an oath I would tell no one, not even my wife, what had happened. He made me swear it on pain of death."

Maeg put her hand on her husband's, still on her shoulder. "But he did tell me. Later that night, James went on a walk in the woods to hide his face from the king. And the king tried to . . . to seduce me."

Ransom's heart was already blackened by the news, but hearing Maeg's confession made it even darker. He glanced at Claire and saw the cold fury in her eyes.

"I fought him," Maeg said. "Made his lip bleed. He seemed to fancy the taste of blood. I fled and hid in the servants' quarters."

James's eyes were livid. "I didn't know until he'd left for the palace. I've heard since that it has become a habit with him. He preys on other men's wives and daughters. His court is benighted. I think he demanded hostages from all of us because he suspects an uprising. He sent Bodkin, the head of the Espion, to Dundrennan to collect Percy."

Maeg scowled with repressed rage. "I refused," she whispered. "I could not bear him using my only son as a hostage to get me to . . . to submit to him! I *refused*."

"That probably didn't go well," Claire said softly.

James chuffed. "When he demanded why not, she said—probably too hastily—that she'd never trust her son to a murderer who killed his own nephew."

Maeg trembled with grief and rage. "I wouldn't. I couldn't. Not my son."

"Ransom," James said earnestly. "The king has broken faith with all of us. Our borders are under attack by foreign enemies. He's lost the empire his father built. It's just a matter of time before it all crumbles. Join us. With you on our side, it will end before winter. When Kiskaddon takes the palace, your sons will be freed. You have nothing to fear if you defy him."

"Ransom and I need to talk," Claire said firmly. "Give us some time, please. I'm sorry for your misfortunes. Truly. That must have been an awful scene to witness. I'll have nightmares just hearing of it. But we must decide what is best for ourselves."

"Of course," James said, his shoulders drooping. He took Maeg's hand, and they rose to leave.

Maeg looked into Ransom's eyes. "Please, Brother. Please."

He could not give her the reassurances she wanted, however, so he looked down at the floor and waited for them to leave. As Dearley went to leave, Claire motioned for him to stay. He shut the door before turning back to them.

"I'm sick at heart," Dearley said.

"We all are," Claire confirmed as she began pacing the room.

Ransom's stomach was sour. His feelings of animosity for the king had swelled, yet his commitment to protect Jon-Landon's children weighed heavily on him. They'd be present when violence began. So would Ransom's sons. At least they knew the Espion tunnels, and Cecily and Dawson would be there to keep them safe, if that were at all possible.

"They're going to depose the king!" Claire said in wonderment.

"They're going to *try*," Ransom clarified. "The Espion are still loyal to him. And with Faulkes back in play, he has another duke on his side."

"How much does Jon-Landon have in his treasury?" Claire asked. "He could hire a lot of mercenaries."

"He's richer than Benedict or his father from gathering scutage for so many years," Ransom answered. "If they fail to capture him quickly, the whole kingdom will be plunged into civil war."

"It was like this during the reign of Gervase, wasn't it?" Dearley asked.

"We were only children back then," Claire said, looking at Ransom plaintively. "Oh Ransom, what do we do?"

"Before I left Kingfountain," Ransom said, reaching and taking her hand. "I swore fealty to the king. I don't condone what he did. I abhor it." He glanced from Claire to Dearley and then back. "But the Argentine line must continue through Jon-Landon's son. It *must*. The Fountain has made that very clear to me. If we do not protect the boy, we will all pay the price."

Dearley clearly didn't understand all he'd said, but he didn't ask questions. He just nodded, once, and said, "Then we protect the boy."

Claire reached for his hand and squeezed it. "Jon-Landon has done nothing to earn your loyalty, but the boy needs you now more than ever. If you're right, and he's the one who'll eventually bring peace to our kingdom . . . we must save him. Alix could use the upheaval as a chance to destroy all of the Argentine heirs. As little as Jon-Landon deserves our help, we must warn him that his family is in danger."

"I'll send a ship tonight to the palace," Ransom said.

"What about Lord James and your sister?" Dearley asked.

"They must go tomorrow," Claire said. "For their safety as well as ours."

The thought of sending his sister away was a cruel torment to him. If the plot failed, they would be on the run. He hated to think of it, particularly since he knew Jon-Landon lacked any generosity of spirit. He'd looked forward to coming home, to being with his wife and daughters, but it was obvious there would be no rest, no comfort.

"I'll tell them," Claire said, seeing the raw pain in Ransom's eyes.

"No," he said. "I'll do my duty." But duty had never hurt like it did now—it had never felt so very heavy before.

Claire must have known that, or perhaps she simply knew him, because she came to him and held him. He wrapped his arms around her and pressed his lips into her hair.

In his mind, he could see Drew falling off the bridge, hands grasping at nothing. Then he imagined his own sons being tied to boats and sent over the falls at Kingfountain. The thought made him shudder with dread.

As he held Claire tightly, he remembered the king's son, Prince Devon, and the look he'd given Ransom before he left Kingfountain.

"F-farewell, Lord Ransom. I hope we shall meet again soon."

And Ransom realized, once again, that he was all that stood between death and that boy.

I'd wished for Ransom to be home, but now that he is here, I believe it would have been better for all if he'd stayed. The king does not deserve to be saved, but save him we must. Ransom believes Jon-Landon's son is important, and although I still have difficulty accepting that everything I've been raised to believe is a lie, I can do no other than believe in him.

Who will prevail in this contest? There's a saying in Legault—if you plan to injure your neighbor, better not do it by halves. Lord Kiskaddon does not seem to be a man of half measures. But having a plan doesn't mean one will execute it well.

I only pray we will not be forced to take up arms against our friends. Peace is our plan. Let us hope we need not spill blood for it.

—*Claire de Murrow, Queen of Legault*
Connaught Castle

CHAPTER EIGHTEEN

To Murder a King

It was nearing midnight when Ransom went to his room. Claire was still awake, wearing a pale nightdress and shawl, nestled into the window seat, her little book in her lap. She turned her head at the sound of the door. Ransom leaned back against it, listening to the snap of embers in the sinking fire within the hearth.

"I thought you might already be abed," he told her, throwing the lock on the door.

Claire set the book down and rose, her bare feet soundless as she approached and buried her face in his chest. "Why do troubles continue to torment our family?" she whispered, shaking her head.

He held her, stroking her dark hair, admiring the glints of crimson in the dim light.

"I don't know," he answered sadly. "We can never have a moment's peace."

She pulled back, then wrapped her arms around his neck and tugged his face down to kiss him. It was a possessive kiss, one that stirred his blood and made him wish all the world would just leave them alone. He pulled her closer, enjoying the sensation, yet his heart grieved at so much bad news.

Claire stopped and withdrew, clenching her fists. "I want to throw something against the wall and break it."

"A pillow?" he suggested with a wry smile.

She gave Ransom a stern look that quickly softened. "How did James and Maeg take your refusal?"

"With disappointment but not surprise," he answered, running his fingers through his hair.

Claire unfastened his scabbard belt and then propped his weapon against the nightstand. "Sit down. You're exhausted."

He sat on the edge of their bed and started pulling off his boots.

"James asked if Maeg and Percy could stay with us," he said.

"It would still be treason," Claire said. She tossed the first boot down and helped drag off the other. "If we help them in any way. I hope you told them no."

"I did, but I made another suggestion. I thought they might seek shelter in Ploemeur."

Claire tossed the other boot down and gave him a quizzical look. "Do you think Constance would accept them?"

"I don't know for sure, but I believe so. Especially given their connection to Drew. Still, it would be better if Jon-Landon didn't know where they were staying. I don't think Constance would want to take up arms against Ceredigion. But I suspect she'll never forgive us after what happened."

"I feel sorry for her. Truly, such news would have broken my heart. I'm probably not as kind as her. I'd have ripped Jon-Landon's heart out with my own dagger."

Ransom sighed as he leaned back against the pillows, hands behind his head, and stared at the ceiling timbers. Claire snuggled next to him, one hand resting on his chest, the other propping up her head. She gazed down at his face.

"I missed you," he whispered tenderly.

"Tell me about our sons. I'm sure you left out much in your letters. They truly stole an Espion key and threw it down a well?"

Ransom chuckled. "That's true. They're both fearless. And so is the king's daughter. The three of them were always slipping away from their caretakers. But not the king's son. He seemed more . . . timid. But he has a keen mind. I've heard his tutors praise his understanding of law and languages. I've talked strategy with him several times, and he's eager to learn how to prevent a war. In the training yard, he's more uneasy. He doesn't relish violence."

"What do you make of the queen?"

He reached out and stroked the edge of her cheek. "It's difficult to guess her thoughts," he answered. "Does she know her husband is unfaithful to her? Does she turn a blind eye? She enjoys the power of her rank. That much is clear. I don't think she knows everything."

"I'm sorry for her, then," Claire said, stroking his chest. "I would be devastated if you were ever unfaithful to me."

He looked into her eyes. "And I would be the world's biggest eejit." Taking her fingers, he kissed them one by one.

"Are you saying you are *not* an eejit, Ransom?"

"I'm not as clever as you are," he said. "But I'm faithful to you. I always will be."

"I like hearing you say it," she said, then kissed the tip of his nose. "I'm faithful to you, Ransom Barton. This situation with the nobles . . . it's going to turn ugly for everyone. It cannot do otherwise. We might be lucky to stay out of it for a little while, but we'll both be dragged into the fight. I'm not afraid of Jon-Landon. I never was. But even he isn't enough of an eejit not to realize he needs you now more than ever."

Ransom thought the same. He kissed her wrist next. Then he pulled her sleeve up to kiss the inside of her arm.

"You're not too tired?" she asked him, tousling his hair.

"Not if I'd swum all the way from Glosstyr," he said as he leaned over and kissed her neck.

"I'd forgotten how ticklish your beard was," she said with a sigh and lowered herself onto the pillow. "Can we forget our troubles for a little while, Ransom? Can I make you forget them?"

He liked the sound of that. "I love you too much, Claire," he said, kissing her neck again. *"Is breá liom an iomarca duit."*

"Tell me again. And again . . . and again . . ." she whispered, grasping his tunic.

$$\lambda$$

Several days passed in a surprisingly restful manner. Ransom played with his daughters, taking them for rides on Dappled through the meadows and woods beneath the castle hill. He went hunting again with Claire, and they spent a night in the lodge in the woods. She offered to take him to the barrow mounds, but he remembered the way the magic had afflicted him on his last visit and declined.

They waited for news to come from Ceredigion. And when it did not, he wondered if something had interrupted the insurrection. Life had a way of interrupting well-laid plans, something he'd seen often enough in the service of four Argentine kings.

But that stretch of quiet was shattered on the fifth day, when a message came from the king, who had fled Kingfountain and had transferred his court to his fortress at Averanche. The message was delivered by an Espion named Branson Chase, a tall fellow with a bushy black beard and the physique of a knight.

"What does the message say?" Claire demanded. They had brought the Espion messenger up to the solar for privacy, and Ransom had only just finished reading the missive. He handed it to her, and she read it swiftly before lowering the page.

"Kingfountain is lost?"

"Aye, my lady," Branson said. "The king and his family had time to flee with half of the palace guard. The message Lord Ransom sent arrived before the plot could take effect. The king is grateful for your warning."

"Did they flee by horse or ship?" Ransom asked.

"By ship in the dead of night," Branson said. "Some of the knights rode as decoys. They were attacked on the bridge outside the sanctuary of Our Lady. Blood was shed that night, and the knights fought to the last man. No quarter was given or offered. Kiskaddon controls Kingfountain now."

Ransom gave Claire a worried look. "Averanche isn't the most protected castle. He'll be vulnerable there to Alix and Estian."

"The king knows. He's going to ride to Beestone, where much of his treasury is kept. The queen will stay at Averanche with their children. And your sons. They escaped by ship as well."

"And Sir Dawson?" Ransom asked.

"Sir Dawson is protecting them and the queen. He's a good knight. You've trained him well."

"I don't feel Averanche is safe," Claire said, setting down the note. "It's vulnerable by sea."

"The king's fleet is being rallied as well," said Branson. "And Lord Faulkes is securing mercenaries."

"From where? Not Brugia," Ransom said.

"No, my lord. Genevar. That's another reason he went to Averanche. An army from the North is coming down toward Blackpool. Kiskaddon attacks from the east. It won't be long before the Black King of Occitania meddles as well."

"You should sail for Glosstyr," Claire told Ransom. "You still have a garrison there. You could form a wall and stop that Northern army from coming down."

Ransom didn't want to fight James, but he felt that the sooner he confronted him, the more bloodshed could be avoided. He gave the Espion a weighing look. "Would the king accept my help?"

The man grinned at him through his beard. "He'd be most grateful, my lord. I was sent to give you the information and see if you were willing to help. After all the king has done to you, he wasn't certain."

"If we continue to fight amongst ourselves," Ransom answered, "we make our kingdom even more vulnerable to our enemies. I don't want to fight a war. I want to try and stop one."

Branson looked skeptical. "Kiskaddon won't relent. He's risked his fate on defeating the king."

"And I'll risk mine on helping him keep his crown," Ransom answered. "I'll go to Glosstyr straightaway. Have the king send word on where he'd like to meet me."

Chase breathed a sigh of relief. "My lord, he'll be most pleased to hear this news."

"Then hurry and tell him," Ransom said. The Espion nodded and left the solar to return to his ship.

Claire picked up the letter and crushed it in her fist. "I hope he realizes he doesn't deserve your loyalty."

Ransom approached her, taking her shoulders in his hands. He kissed the top of her head. "I don't want to fight other knights of Ceredigion. Each man we lose weakens us all the more."

She looked up at his face. "You may not have a choice. You're facing two duchies with only one. Not to mention all the other lords who have defected, according to the king's letter. He has Faulkes, you, and mercenaries if they can arrive in time. They will be using their full strength. Be careful."

"I'm going to try and argue for clemency," Ransom said. "If it comes to a pitched battle, we could lose."

"You? Lose?" Claire asked with a mischievous smile. "Not my husband."

"If there is a battle, we lose no matter who wins," Ransom said. "Every person we lose is a kinsman."

"Maybe you could offer to go to King Gotz and sue for peace," she suggested. "Jon-Landon refused to send you before out of pettiness. You can make an alliance or at least prevent Gotz from joining Estian."

"It's a good suggestion, but until we find a way to stop fighting amongst ourselves, an alliance won't last. I need to persuade Hal to back down."

Claire pursed her lips. "How do you plan on achieving that? He was loyal to Benedict, and he's plotted to murder Jon-Landon."

"His back was to the wall," Ransom said. "I'm going to ask Jon-Landon to pardon him and James."

Claire studied him with a look of disbelief. "Be serious, Ransom."

"I am. And I'm going to try and get Lady Deborah on my side. If we cannot make the king see reason, then none of this matters. If he's determined to fight to the end, well . . . the end will come much sooner than he thinks, and he'll lose the crown. If that happens, he'll deserve it."

Claire looked at him seriously. "Then who would be king? The boy?"

Ransom met her gaze. "Yes." The Fountain had told him as much, although it had not given him enough information to know when Devon was to become king.

"A child king," Claire said thoughtfully. "What if Kiskaddon balks? What if he won't swear fealty? He could try to claim the throne himself."

Ransom shrugged. "I don't want to fight him. But I will if I must."

She threw down the paper and took his hand, leaning her forehead against his chest. "This feels worse than what we went through with the Elder King. Or even with Benedict when he was away at war. I don't trust Jon-Landon, and neither should you. Promise me you won't be foolish."

He squeezed her hands. "I will do my best. And I'll try to bring our sons home with me."

She looked up into his eyes. "Come back to me, Ransom. I couldn't bear it if I lost you."

Her words sent a ripple of apprehension through him. He lifted her hands and kissed her knuckles. "I will come back."

"You'd better," she said with tears glistening in her eyes. "There's a legend that the Aos Sí had the power to raise the dead for one night a year." Her tearful smile told him that she didn't truly believe in it. That maybe she truly was beginning to believe in what he had seen and heard. In what he knew in his heart to be true. "Don't make me use heathen magic on you, Ransom Barton. Come back to me!"

"I promise," he whispered huskily, trying not to focus on the sliver of doubt in his heart.

The morning was clear the day Ransom left for Glosstyr. And then, around midday, a wind rose from the sea that felled trees in the meadow and damaged the turret roofs at the castle. The ships at harbor were battered against the docks, and many took heavy damage. It came from nowhere. It is still summer, so the storm was unusual. An omen that makes my heart shiver with dread.

Ransom was at sea when that storm struck. The felled trees are being axed into wood to help prepare for the coming winter. And I must wait to learn if my husband arrived safely. Why does my heart murmur so? Why does it whisper that he may not be coming home?

—Claire de Murrow
Fair Isle
(in weather foul)

CHAPTER NINETEEN

The Drowning of Leoneyis

The cog lurched down another swell, and Ransom gripped the edge of the table, catching his goblet before it slid off the top. His stomach clenched and heaved with the heavy pitching. It was an unseasonable storm, one that shoved and tossed the cog mercilessly. Unable to bear sitting, he rose to his feet and stumbled to the door, his footing like that of a drunkard.

He opened the door to his stateroom and gripped the handrails as he shuffled down the corridor. It took some effort to mount the stairs, and when he reached the deck, he was surprised to see the sail had been lowered. The wind and waves pounded the cog, and the crew wrestled with ropes to try to bind down the cargo. Some of the barrels had already been smashed, and the stink of pickled herrings rushed to his nose.

The main mast creaked and groaned, and sailors shouted at one another. Ransom stumbled forward, trying to reach the helmsman deck where the captain gripped the tiller with both hands and leaned against it with all his weight. Wind buffeted Ransom like an invisible giant. His hair whipped about, and his tunic rippled against the current as he struggled his way to the ladder and climbed it to join the captain.

"Did you throw a coin in the well before leaving, Lord Ransom? For safe passage?" the captain shouted against the wind. "Methinks not!"

Ransom hadn't, but it was never too late to petition the Fountain for safety. He clutched the railing and watched the sea collide with the hull, sending a huge spray up onto the side deck.

"Feels like a winter storm!" Ransom shouted back.

"Aye, except the air is too warm for it! The Deep Fathoms must be angry. I see no other cause for it."

Ransom looked into the distance, eastbound, and saw cliffs and shore. "Where are we? How far off Glosstyr?"

"These devilish winds are blowing from Glosstyr, I think!" said the captain. "Had to lower the sails, or they would have torn apart. We're not making any progress at all."

"How far, though?"

The captain shrugged. "At this rate, my lord, we'll *never* get there." He pointed to the south. "That way be Averanche. We've a better bet of getting there, but if this storm keeps up, we might shipwreck before we reach shore."

Ransom frowned and shielded his eyes. The day was waning quickly. The thought of fighting the storm all night filled him with dread. "What other options do we have?"

The tiller yanked out of the captain's hands, and it took the strength of both men to get it under control again. The captain's eyes blazed with fear.

"The cliffs yonder are dangerous, but there's a sanctuary over there. St. Penryn. Have ye been there?"

Ransom nodded slowly. It was a visit to St. Penryn that had sent him on his quest to the oasis. "Aye. Years ago."

"They have a cove that might shield us from the worst of these winds. We could drop anchor in there, and you could take a horse to Glosstyr from the sanctuary. Seems less reckless than trying to sail against the wind."

"I agree," Ransom said. "Take us there."

"I'll try to coax her there, my lord, but the cog is going where she wants to go."

"Good man," Ransom said, clapping the captain on the shoulder. He decided against trying to walk back down to the lower deck after watching a sailor slip, slide to the edge of the ship, and catch himself before he tumbled over the deck. Much better to stay put, with a firm grip on the railing. The captain steered to the new course, and the waves began to hit them from behind.

Spray smacked Ransom in the face. His tunic was drenched already.

They fought the storm every bit of the way, but at dusk they finally reached the cove with the sanctuary of Our Lady at St. Penryn. Fires were burning from the upper cliffs as well as the lower ones, a welcoming beacon to the weary seamen.

"It was good of the deconeus to leave the lower lights burning!" shouted the captain. "We can see the cliffs much better!"

As soon as they entered the cove, the wind calmed considerably, and the fear inside Ransom's chest began to ebb. The crew used oars to row with the current. Ransom looked up at the shining spires of the sanctuary and felt moved to offer a silent prayer of gratitude for having made it to safety. Two other ships were in the cove, both larger vessels with the markings of Genevar. It seemed they'd had the same idea.

After sunset, they reached the dock in calm waters and moored the cog in one of the berths. A sailor fixed the plank for Ransom and his knights to cross, and when they did, Ransom's stomach finally settled from the seasickness that had plagued him. The Genevese ships had crews aboard, and he recognized the sound of their language as he heard them talking amongst themselves. He walked down the dock and led the way up the path to the sanctuary. He was met partway up by an acolyte bearing a covered lantern.

"Greetings, travelers!" said the acolyte. "Where do you knights hail from?"

"We were blown off course from Legault on the way to Glosstyr," Ransom said. "Would you tell the deconeus that the Duke of Glosstyr is here?"

"You're Lord Ransom?" asked the acolyte with interest.

"Yes. It's been a long and wearying day."

"Come with me. I'll be your light and will tell the sexton to prepare rooms for you all."

"Thank you."

They trudged up the steps until they reached the upper cliffs, from which the massive torches illuminated the evening sky. A quiet hush fell over his heart upon seeing the familiar walls of St. Penryn. The last time he'd come here, it had been with a broken heart. He'd just been dismissed by Devon the Younger, and the deconeus had sent him on a journey that had ultimately brought him here, to this day. He dropped his hand to his sword pommel, feeling the comforting bulk of the scabbard he'd been given on that pilgrimage.

When they entered the sanctuary, there were plenty of guests already in attendance. The acolyte announced them to the sexton, who quickly summoned the deconeus. The man emerged promptly and offered a warm greeting. It was, Ransom realized, the same man who had advised him all those years ago.

"It's good to be back," Ransom said, bowing to the elderly man.

"Have you been here before, Duke Ransom?" asked the deconeus.

"Long ago," he answered. "Thank you for giving us shelter."

"Benevolence is one of the aspects of the Lady," said the deconeus. "A Genevese merchant ship was blown off course . . . this is the captain, Weyrich. And we've other visitors too. A ship of mercenaries, bound for the king, was also unable to reach their port. Are you going to the king as well, my lord?"

"I was going to Glosstyr," Ransom said. "I left Legault this morning."

"Perhaps it is the Fountain's will that you were waylaid by the storm. Come have some supper. You and your knights must be hungry."

The acolytes set up an extra trestle table and chairs for Ransom and his knights. After a short wait, plates of venison and vegetables were brought out. The meat was sparse, so midway through the meal some peppered fish was brought out to accompany it. Ransom enjoyed every bite of the meal, and the wine served with it had a mellow, pleasant flavor.

The captain of the merchant ship raised a cup to toast the deconeus's hospitality. "A cheer for our gracious host!" said Captain Weyrich. "Hup, hup!"

They all joined in the recognition, and Ransom leaned back in his chair. He'd thought about riding on to Glosstyr that night, but he was exhausted from the journey, and his knights looked as if they were content to stay at the sanctuary for the rest of the night.

"A blessing on your various journeys," said the deconeus after things had quieted.

The captain knocked on the table. "Is this not the oldest sanctuary built in devotion to Our Lady of the Fountain?"

"It is, Captain Weyrich," replied the elder man. "It is the last and the first."

The captain's brow wrinkled. "How can it be last and first? Explain this riddle."

The deconeus was at the other table, but he was close enough that Ransom and the others could easily hear him.

"It was the only sanctuary to survive the flooding of the ancient kingdom of Leoneyis," he said. "Because it was built on higher ground. All who fled here were spared."

"The drowned kingdom is only a myth, Deconeus," the captain argued.

The deconeus gave him a pointed look. "Is it? Our fishermen continue to pull artifacts from the sea. Helmets with barnacles. Swords cankered in rust, brittle except for the hilts. If you would see evidence, Captain Weyrich, I can show you."

The captain shook his head. "Of course one would find such things. Many wars have been fought in this land and along its shores. It proves nothing. But if you wish to believe a kingdom was once swallowed by the sea, I will not mock you for it. Even in Genevar we have heard the tales of King Andrew." He raised his cup again in salute and took a sip from it.

If the deconeus was bothered by the comment, he didn't show it. "And do the stories you've heard in Genevar speak of the prophecy of the Dreadful Deadman?"

"Are not all dead men dreadful?" quipped the captain.

Ransom leaned forward in his chair. He'd felt a throb in his heart at the deconeus's words.

"Alas, many are," said the deconeus. "So you have not heard the prophecy?"

"Enlighten us," said the captain with an indulgent smile.

"King Andrew was mortally wounded during a battle with his bastard son. He had dismissed his first knight, who was falsely accused of seducing the queen, so he had no champion to fight his battle for him."

A shiver went through Ransom's heart. He wasn't hungry anymore.

"A king without a champion. A sorry thing indeed," said the captain.

"Alas, that is not the worst of it. The king had many artifacts of power that should have preserved his life. He had the hollow crown, which could control the weather. He had the sword Firebos, which was sharp and strong and could summon a holy fire. But his greatest treasure was a scabbard. It had the marking of his kingdom on it." The deconeus turned at that moment and gazed at Ransom. He did not look at Ransom's scabbard, only his eyes, but the gaze was full of meaning. "With that scabbard, he could not be slain in battle."

"I see," said the captain with uncertainty. "Yet he was wounded. He was killed."

"The scabbard was stolen before the battle," said the deconeus, turning back to the captain. "A decoy was put in its place. One that lacked the power to save the king. But even then, he did not die of his injury. He was put on a boat and sent over a waterfall in Leoneyis. Three days later, the flood came and submerged the once powerful kingdom. King Andrew survived, and an artifact of great power, the Gradalis, sent him to another world to heal and recover."

"Another world?" scoffed the captain. "You mean the Deep Fathoms?"

"No," said the deconeus. "Another world, like ours. A world where they carve faces into stones."

Ransom swallowed, remembering the barrow mounds in Legault. There'd been faces there, full of a power that had felt threatening before he entered the space. Constance had told him they were also carved in caves on the shores of Ploemeur. He felt an itching curiosity about what the deconeus had told him earlier. It was no accident that he was there that night.

"And the prophecy?"

"The Dreadful Deadman will be Andrew reborn, from the same line of kings. Like his forebear, he will unify his land with the help of his champion."

The captain shrugged. "I've heard many stories during my travels, Deconeus, and the one unifying factor is that everyone believes their own stories to be true. The Brythonicans like to say their jeweled glass is priceless because it comes from the ruins of Leoneyis. I say the legend makes them rich at the expense of the gullible."

The deconeus sniffed and held up his hands. "Many do not believe in the prophecy of the Dreadful Deadman. Some lack eyes to see what is still far off. So be it. You are not the first. But I've given you the answer to the riddle. This sanctuary was the last standing after the terrible flood. And it was the first after it."

"Thank you for the explanation," said the captain. "And for your generous hospitality." Despite their differences, he appeared to mean it.

"You may thank the Lady for that," said the deconeus, bowing his head.

"I shall put a coin in one of her fountains," said Weyrich. "A tribute for fairer skies tomorrow."

The sexton approached Ransom's table. "I can take you to your room when you are ready."

He glanced at the deconeus, who'd already risen from his chair. He felt a powerful compulsion to speak to the man. "Take my knights. I'll join them later."

"As you wish," said the sexton.

Ransom caught up with the deconeus as he reached the pillars at the far side of the guest hall. The older man paused and turned, hearing the sound of Ransom's boots.

"Yes, Lord Ransom?" he asked, his eyes sharp and clear.

"I believe what you said."

The deconeus nodded. "Some will always reject the warnings of the Fountain. You, on the other hand, do not. I recall your visit, you know. Sometimes my memory just needs a little jab." He glanced at Ransom's scabbard. "Did you find what you were looking for?"

"I did," Ransom confirmed.

The deconeus nodded. "And you've kept it secret, I see. Good. I feel impressed to say one thing more to you. One part of the legend, which I rarely share." He reached out and put his hand on Ransom's shoulder. "The prophecy of the Dreadful Deadman will be fulfilled here, in this very sanctuary. On a night during a great storm, the child will be born *here*." His expression was one of fierce determination. "Your scabbard will also be here at that time. You are part of something greater than yourself, Lord Ransom. Many are called by the Fountain. But few choose to heed the call because the road is never easy."

Ransom swallowed, feeling his knees tremble at the deconeus's strange words. "I will do what I can."

"There was a man, years ago, who drowned in the cove," said the elderly man. "He and his son were looking for clams and had wandered too far along the cliffs before the tide came in. It came swiftly. They tried to swim, but the waves kept smashing them against the cliffs. They were both going to drown. But the father hoisted the lad up onto his shoulders and pressed himself against the cliffs. His son grabbed the higher rocks and hung there until the water covered his father's head. The father drowned. The boy lived."

Ransom's heart clenched with dread. "That is a terrible story."

"I was the boy," said the deconeus. "And I have given my life to serve the Fountain since that day." He patted Ransom on the cheek and walked away.

I was relieved when the cog came back to Connaught with a message from the captain and a note from Ransom. The storm prevented them from reaching Glosstyr, but they found shelter at St. Penryn along with some Genevese ships. The king is at Averanche, and Ransom should be there by now.

I've heard that Estian sent the Duke of Garrone to attack Southport by sea. No one has stood up to counter the invasion because the duke, Lord Faulkes, left Southport with his mercenaries and is waging war against North Cumbria at present. Surely Estian is using the Wizr board to see where we are most vulnerable. Lord Kiskaddon still holds the palace and East Stowe and has done nothing to stop the incursion. Perhaps he even welcomes it.

I hope Ransom can convince the king to treat with his nobles. If not, the kingdom of Ceredigion may be no more.

—Claire de Murrow
Connaught
(calmer seas)

CHAPTER TWENTY

The King's Favor

This was the second time Ransom had gone to Averanche in search of Jon-Landon. The first time, the then prince had been hiding while attempting to mount an insurrection against his brother. Now he was a king seeking shelter from an insurrection against him.

Ransom saw the castle from afar, and it brought back other memories. This was where he and James had trained as knights under Lord Kinghorn. How strange that the man who'd been his enemy had become his kinsman, only for this fissure to come between them.

The deconeus of St. Penryn had dispatched a messenger to the king to inform him of Ransom's arrival and ask if he wished to meet with him. The return reply came from one of Jon-Landon's personal bodyguards, who told Ransom emphatically that he was most welcome, and the king would be gratified if he'd travel the short distance to Averanche to meet him in person. So Ransom had brought his entourage of knights back to Averanche with the king's bodyguard.

His magic pulsed within him, slow and steady, as he closed the distance to the castle, his loyalty to the king the source of its strength.

When they arrived at the main gate, it was opened to greet them. The knights standing guard at the bulwark shouted down at them as they approached.

"It's Lord Ransom! He's here!"

"A cheer for Glosstyr! *Dex aie!*"

The knights above them flashed the knightly salute, which Ransom returned, feeling a flush come to his cheeks at the unexpected welcome. They rode beneath the portcullis, through the open gate, and into the courtyard. Eight sturdy, fortified wagons waited there. Each had huge wheels, rimmed with iron, and teams of horses were tethered within the courtyard.

"What's this?" Ransom asked the bodyguard who had accompanied him.

The knight smiled. "It's two hundred thousand livres, more or less. The royal treasury, all in one place. The king feared the castellan of Beestone might revolt, so he had the coins that were stored there sent over, in addition to the treasure he brought from the palace. If Estian knew it was here, we'd be in trouble. The greedy savage!"

Ransom was agog at the number of wagons, each with its own guard. Big, sturdy locks were fixed to the rear doors, intended to deflect an axe blade. Ransom and his knights dismounted, and they passed through the ranks of mercenaries already assembled in the courtyard. He saw encouraging nods and smiles from several of them and wondered how many had previously served under his command.

They were greeted at the inner doors by Lady Deborah of Thorngate castle. The diminutive woman's hair was now more gray than nut brown, and her smile was welcoming and relieved.

"Lady Deborah," he said, bowing to her. He turned to his knights. "Get some food and rest. Tend to the horses."

His command was obeyed, and he stayed outside with Lady Deborah while the bodyguard who'd accompanied him entered the castle. "I'll tell the king you're here, Lord Ransom," he called over his shoulder.

"You're a long way from Thorngate," Ransom said to Lady Deborah, smiling.

She shook her head. "With all the chaos happening in the North, I thought I would be of most use if I came here and tried to reason with the king. You couldn't have come at a better time, Ransom."

"What's going on?" Ransom asked.

"I'll let the king tell you his troubles. Do you have a plan? I've never seen the realm in such a precarious position. If we don't act together, Ceredigion will fall to its enemies. I'm certain of it. Our nation will be no more."

"I agree," Ransom said. "Shall we go inside?"

"Yes. So many are staring at us. Come."

They entered the castle and started walking down the main corridor. Servants bustled about, carrying chests in both directions. Baggage had been arranged in haphazard stacks, and they were attempting to organize the chaos.

"What are your intentions?" she asked him as they moved along.

"We cannot afford to squabble amongst ourselves when the kingdom is so vulnerable," he replied. "I was going to offer to go to Lord Kiskaddon and negotiate a truce."

"Impossible. He'd never relent."

"He might if he feels there is reason to hope there will be no reprisals against him and that things will be different going forward. The king's behavior has ruined trust among the nobles."

"Such things are not repaired so easily. How can you mend trust once it's broken?"

"Maybe it is beyond the point of repair, but if we do nothing, we die by suicide. You think Kiskaddon believes he'll get better terms from Estian?"

"I'm convinced of it. Though you know, as I do, that Estian will promise silver and deliver dross." She shrugged. "But at least he hasn't betrayed his own nobles."

"Then help me persuade the king that it serves his own interests to be forgiving. That he caused this contention, and he will lose everything, including his life, if he persists in alienating those who serve him."

"He will bristle if you put it like that."

"I'm a plain-speaking man and always have been. If he cannot stomach the truth, then he'll continue to sicken on his own pride. Can I count on you to help me talk sense into him?"

"Of course, Ransom. That's why I'm here as well. I think . . . it's possible even the queen will support you. She's young, but she's not as naive as she seems. She asked me, privately, if I knew that Jon-Landon had ordered the deaths of all of the hostages. I still don't know who told her. I've tried to enlist her help, but she is too worried about hurting Jon-Landon's feelings. Your arrival could alter things. No. It *will* alter them."

"Thank you," he said. "I'll do my best."

They reached the great hall, where Ransom found the king pacing nervously, his hands clasped behind his back. He wore a short sword and a dagger, and Ransom saw the glint of a hauberk beneath his elegant tunic and a chain hood pulled down around his neck. When he saw Ransom, he swallowed and offered a strained smile, the look of a man besieged on all sides and struggling to hope.

Ransom approached Jon-Landon and dropped to one knee before him. "My lord, thank you for granting me an audience."

"Rise, Ransom—rise!" He took Ransom's hands and squeezed them. "It is good to see you again!"

The show of affection, which seemed genuine, shocked him.

"Come to the solar. Léa is there. Your sons are here with Sir Dawson—a very capable knight. I asked if he'd be captain of my guard, and he refused me outright, saying his loyalty was to you. Should I be jealous?" he added with a chuckle, but he wasn't being vicious.

"I should like to see my sons, but let's talk first. In the solar if you prefer."

"I do. Come." He put his hand on Ransom's shoulder as they walked. "You as well, Deborah. You know I value your counsel." He lowered his voice a little. "I'm sorry about the storm that caught you at sea, but it hastened our meeting. I'm grateful for that. I've always known I could count on you. You said as much, before I sent you back to Legault. How is Claire?"

"Worried, no doubt," Ransom answered. The transformation in Jon-Landon's mood was startling. But his easy manner and grace, compared to the way he'd always received Ransom in the past, were grating. He could practically hear Claire telling him that Jon-Landon was only acting pleasant because he needed Ransom. "Things are calmer now in Legault."

"She's a canny woman. I've always admired her. You chose well. No, actually, I believe she chose *you*. Clever lass. I don't think she and I would have mixed very well. I'm quite happy with Léa. Do you remember when you found us, walking hand in hand, along these very shores?"

"I do, my lord."

After leaving the great hall and climbing the stairs, they reached the solar. The space was familiar, yet it had changed quite a bit from when Lord Kinghorn had lived there. There were more decorations, fewer books. The window was open, letting in the sound of the surf crashing outside. The queen was playing a game of Wizr with her son, who smiled at the sight of Ransom. His little hand lifted in a wave. The princess wasn't there. A tall, gaunt man with long hair and bloodshot eyes stood in the corner. Ransom recognized him as the head of the Espion. Bodkin had the look of a murderer.

The queen rose from her chair and inclined her head to Ransom. She wore her jewelry—a decorative crown, necklace, and rings on most of her fingers. She looked too young to have had two children already. For a long moment, she just stared at him without speaking, giving him a curious look, as if she were weighing him in her mind.

"You did come," she finally said.

Lady Deborah shut the door behind her and went to the brazier to warm her hands.

Jon-Landon kissed his wife on her forehead, actually on the band of the crown, and turned, grinning with eagerness. "I must say, Ransom, you've come at a desperate hour."

"So it seems," he replied. "What is the state of things?"

The king turned to the Espion. "Bodkin—you tell him."

The Espion leader straightened, his narrow shoulders drooping. "At your command, my liege." His voice had a nasal inflection and was slightly high pitched. "Where to start? Southport has been taken. Some of the people fled, some stayed and begged for their lives. I wonder how long the Duke of Garrone will suffer them to live? That gives him a stronghold within striking distance of Kingfountain. Which . . . as you probably already know . . . is being held by the *blackguard* Lord Kiskaddon." His eyes narrowed, and his lips twisted into a sneer as he said the name. "Atabyrion is attacking North Cumbria from the east and Lord Faulkes from the south. Wigant is caught between them. Won't end well for your brother-in-law."

"Bodkin, hurry up," Jon-Landon said.

"East Stowe has been harassed by Brugian ships, but Kiskaddon hasn't suffered them to take it. There's not much he can do, with the riots happening in Kingfountain. The people resent Kiskaddon's treason. He dares not cross the bridge for fear of being thrown off the falls. I would that he drowned. But it would make the city vulnerable if the Occitanians were to press north. I advised His Majesty to send one of the Espion, I think you know her, back to Kingfountain to end Kiskaddon's treachery discreetly. He might choke on a pie, you know. That would end the worst of our problems." He flashed Ransom a ruthless smile.

"I was intending to send her to Pisan," Jon-Landon said. "They won't reveal any of their secrets unless we train someone. You know of whom we speak, Ransom. The girl Cecily. I was on the verge of sending her, then I learned that Kiskaddon intended to murder me." His face twisted with resentment. Ransom regarded the Espion master coldly, thinking about the many, many deaths this man had orchestrated. So many hostages killed without honor, without mercy. He caught a glimpse of the queen and realized her eyes were large with worry and fear, her nostrils flared. She clearly didn't like Bodkin very much either.

Ransom sighed. "My lord, the situation is bleak indeed."

"I know," the king said with desperation. "I had everything in my hands, and now it's all slipping through my fingers like sand." He clenched his hand into a fist and shook it. "The harder I clutch, the faster it spills."

"Power is like sand, my lord," Ransom said. He held his own hand out in a cupping shape. "If you hold it like this, then less of it spills."

Bodkin snorted, and Ransom repressed the urge to punch him on the jaw. Ignoring the Espion, Ransom regarded the king. "My lord, your advisors have misled you. Authority doesn't come from the hollow crown. Nor does it come from forcing others to do your will. I've watched your family struggle with power for years. Power must be coaxed. Respect must be earned. I don't think it is too late."

"And what do you know about power?" Bodkin said with derision.

The king's eyes were fixed on Ransom, like a starving man offered a feast.

"Make peace with your nobles," Ransom said. "If we stand together, we *will* prevail. Send me to Kingfountain. I will speak to Kiskaddon on your behalf. Let me see if I can persuade him to reconsider his actions. Your father once sent me to Auxaunce to make peace with Bennett. I didn't succeed then, but I'm more experienced now. I think I could persuade him."

"How?" the queen asked, her voice tremulous. "What he's done is worthy of execution. He knows it. They all do."

He turned his gaze on the queen. "What happened to your father after he attempted to kidnap Queen Emiloh? Was he put to death?"

Léa's mouth turned down. "No."

"We were both there, my lady," Ransom reminded her. "The king, as angry as he was at your father's actions, forgave him. One of the Elder King's most loyal men, Lord Rakestraw, was killed in that conflict. I watched him and his knights get slaughtered. But the Elder King still forgave the insult because his goal was to make his kingdom more stable, not less. If he had persecuted Lord DeVaux, he would have made himself vulnerable to attack from others. Which is exactly what's happening now."

Jon-Landon nodded with interest, the story working a spell on his mind. "So I must pardon Kiskaddon?"

"And Lord James. All of them. Give them a reason to hope, my lord."

"Your Majesty," Bodkin interrupted, "if you pardon them now, you will lose face. No one will respect your authority after this. You'll be seen as a puppet king, weak and ineffectual."

"It is not weakness; it is wisdom," Lady Deborah said, coming forward. "You were too harsh with Lord Ransom. You flexed your royal power, and you frightened the lords. Your father didn't persecute his nobles. He rewarded them."

"Yet still he lost," said Bodkin.

"He lost because he wouldn't share enough of the power he hoarded," Ransom said to the Espion. "He didn't trust it in anyone else's hands." He looked back at the king. "Not even his own sons. My lord, think of the consequences should you do the same."

"I've tried, Ransom. Truly, I have," said the king. "I don't think Kiskaddon would forgive me. And James . . . what he . . ." He paused, wrestling with his emotions. "I cannot undo what's been done. We cannot go back and change the past."

"Nor should you," said Bodkin angrily.

"You're wrong," Ransom said. "Regret encourages us to try and do better. I've made my own blunders. Just like the king has stumbled, in heeding your advice. My lord, if you trust this man, your kingdom will end. It will perish like ancient Leoneyis."

Bodkin snorted. "You actually believe that myth, Lord Ransom? A child's tale."

"No, it's the truth," Ransom said. "I was just at the sanctuary of Our Lady at St. Penryn. The deconeus knows the tale. It is a warning to all of us." He looked at the king imploringly. "You've seen the Wizr board yourself. We stand at the brink of losing the game, my lord. Step back from it. If we lose, we lose everything."

Jon-Landon glanced at his wife, who nodded to him.

"Lady Deborah, do you believe Lord Ransom?" he asked.

"I do, my lord. I cannot save your kingdom. But he can. He is the only one they would trust."

Bodkin clenched his fist. "This is—"

"Enough!" Jon-Landon snapped. He gave Bodkin a withering look. "I'm here because of you. Everything that has gone wrong is because I listened to you. I will listen to Lord Ransom now." He turned to Ransom with a determined expression. "Go to Kingfountain. If you can persuade Kiskaddon, do what you must. I will pardon him. I swear it on the soul of my father."

The queen gripped Jon-Landon's arm. "What if he . . . what if he demands a hostage?"

The king's countenance fell.

"I won't allow it," Ransom said. "I'll find another way."

The king sighed in relief. "Go, Ransom. You are my only friend. You have my authority and my commission. Save us!"

$\bigvee$

Fate is now on our side. Ransom has spoken to the king, and he will journey next to Kingfountain to try to talk Lord Kiskaddon around. I know this from a note, written by Ransom and delivered by the king's own courier. I don't know how Ransom will be able to set this to rights, but he will try. Having so many enemies now, Jon-Landon must be grateful to have one ally, even if it's the man he persecuted most.

I'm nervous about what will happen. I have to go to Atha Kleah to hear petitions for justice. One complicated case is that of Lord Faulkes's wife, Lady Orla, the heiress of Lord Tenthor's estate. Some nobles, who want a chance to win her inheritance, are arguing to invalidate the marriage since it happened under duress. Faulkes isn't here to defend his cause, but he sent his first knight to argue on his behalf. Turns out he actually loves the lass, poor sot.

The decision could impact the tenuous peace with Jon-Landon, for Faulkes is a favorite. Or has that changed? It matters not. I will listen to Lady Orla, and if she feels her rights to choose were denied, I will dissolve the marriage. Justice is not justice if it is only convenient.

—Claire de Murrow
Connaught
(preparing to journey to Atha Kleah)

CHAPTER TWENTY-ONE

Castles of Sand

After leaving the king and queen's presence, Ransom instructed his knights to prepare for departure to Kingfountain, then made his way to the familiar stone steps he'd once climbed with James. The king had told him the boys were playing on the beach, and he wished to see them before he went on his way.

The day was bright and full of sunlight, although errant clouds bloomed in the sky to the east. As Ransom walked down the steps, he saw his boys parrying and lunging with sticks instead of swords. Dawson was with them, showing the boys some techniques on how to hold the sticks, how to defend. Although Ransom couldn't hear his voice, he recognized the effort he was taking and appreciated it. He spied Cecily sitting in the firm, wet sand with Princess Léanore, using sticks to carve little trenches. Léanore's hands were sculpting the wet sand into mounds as if she were building a castle, and she had placed an assortment of shells and even a colorful starfish gathered around them. They were near enough the boys to witness the dueling.

Ransom's heart thrummed with gratitude that the boys seemed hale and appeared to be having a good time. He trudged forward into the sand, feeling a weariness in his shoulders from the quick journey from St. Penryn. It would be another two days' ride to the palace. So much of his life had been spent racing from one end of the kingdom to the other.

As he neared the noise of the clashing sticks, Willem saw him first. He threw down his stick and yelled in surprise and started to race toward him. Devon whirled around, recognized Ransom, and came charging after them, fake sword still in hand. Ransom dropped to a knee, feeling a little stab of discomfort as he did so, and waited for his sons to reach him.

"Did you see us fighting? Sir Dawson has been teaching us!" Willem said eagerly.

"Father!" Devon cried, coming up right behind his brother. They embraced him, and he hugged them tightly, smelling the scent of the sea in their hair. His emotions were so powerful at that moment, he couldn't speak. He gripped them both, one in each arm.

Dawson approached with a smile. "Welcome to Averanche, my lord."

Ransom tousled Devon's hair. "Have you been giving Dawson a difficult time?"

"No! He's not some badger-brained Espion," said Willem proudly. "He's a knight of Glosstyr!"

Dawson chuckled. "Truth is, Lord Ransom, I work them so hard during the day that they're both exhausted by nightfall. The cooks complain about how much they eat. They're growing like beanstalks."

Ransom had noticed they both looked thicker. Devon tugged on Ransom's tunic. "How is Sib? And Máthair?"

"They miss you," Ransom said. "Sibyl wanted to come with me."

"I love the beach here," Willem said, kicking up some sand. "Averanche is fun. We've gone to the village with Sir Dawson. Can I have some livres, Father? I don't want to keep borrowing them."

"Me too!" said Devon. "I want some livres."

Ransom nodded, and both boys giggled with excitement as he opened the money pouch on his belt and pulled out five livres for each. Once they'd seized the coins, they took off running.

Rising, Ransom looked at Dawson. "They're so young."

"They're good lads, both of them. And they'll make fine knights someday. I don't think you could persuade either of them not to pursue it."

"I wouldn't dream of it," Ransom said, watching the boys tear after each other. Léanore shouted at them to stop running and kicking up sand.

"Have you and Claire thought about where to send them to train? I don't think they should be together. They need some space to become their own people."

Ransom shrugged. "It's too soon to decide. They're still boys."

"Willem is your heir," Dawson said, "but I'd be honored to train Devon when the time comes. I've grown fond of both of the lads, but particularly Devon. I imagine him as you as a child. Well, I thought I'd mention it."

Ransom held Dawson's gaze, pleased by the request. "I'll talk to Claire about it."

Dawson smiled and then sighed, looking over his shoulder at the princess and Cecily. "The princess gets along so well with the boys. She'll be devastated when they go back home. Sometimes the boys fight over who is going to marry her."

Ransom gave him a startled look.

"Boys will fight over anything. But the rivalry is fierce. They like to perform for her, to win her praise. They're children, I know, and she's the king's daughter. But I thought it worth mentioning."

"Thank you," Ransom said. He saw Devon tackle Willem, and soon they were both wrestling in the sand. The sight made him laugh.

Dawson scratched his neck. "I'm grateful you assigned me to come here, my lord. It's different than any other duty you've given me. I've gotten to know Cecily fairly well. She . . . she astounds me. She knows so many languages—she's been teaching me Brugian! And the court gossip she shares keeps me informed of what's going on in the realm. I know she's a little older than me, a few years only, but I think . . . I hope . . . that she sees potential in me. I'm rambling."

Ransom saw that Dawson's gaze hadn't left Cecily. It warmed his heart.

"You care for her?" Ransom asked, unsurprised.

"That word doesn't do my feelings justice. I'm *bewitched* by her. I tell you truly, Lord Ransom, I've never been jealous of John Dearley and Elodie. Until now. Cecily is no duchess. But she is one to me. I'd give the world if she would have me."

Ransom clapped Dawson on the back. "That happened fast."

"I know. It scares me out of my wits. I'm a soldier, not a poet. I can't woo her with words. I don't even know how she feels about me."

"I can't help you there, lad," Ransom said with a smile. "You'll have to tell her how you feel, I suppose."

Dawson looked greensick. "I'd rather fight unarmed against six knights."

Ransom gave him a friendly shove. "Courage, lad. Tell her your heart." He looked over at Cecily and Léanore. "I should talk to her before I go."

"I'll stop your sons from killing each other," the knight replied, glancing at Cecily with a thoughtful expression. "Think they need to race along the shore for a bit."

Ransom nodded, and they parted, Dawson going off to break up the wrestling match and Ransom approaching the pair building sandcastles.

Cecily peered up at him, her dress slightly damp from the wet sand. Her shoes were off, and her bare feet looked gritty.

Léanore was kneeling and had sand in her hair and on her cheek. She glanced up at Ransom. "I'm building a castle," she said matter-of-factly.

"Do you think it will survive when the tide comes in?" Ransom asked her.

"Cecily is digging a moat to protect it. I want to play here again tomorrow."

"I've tried to tell her that the sea is powerful," the Espion girl said. "She doesn't believe me."

"Make it deeper!" the little girl ordered.

Cecily gave the princess a bemused smile and kept scratching at the sand with her stick. The trench she'd dug surrounded half of it so far.

"How long does the king intend to stay in Averanche?" he asked her.

"It depends on how long it takes Faulkes to defeat Lord James," she answered. "Bodkin said that Dundrennan would be a stronger defense if the rebellion lasts a long time. But your presence here tells me that it may not last as long as Bodkin hopes."

"Hopes?" Ransom pressed.

She gave him a knowing smile. "He wants Wigant to fall. And Kiskaddon. And you if I'm being honest."

"Bodkin is a seagull turd," Léanore said, patting more sand to add to the tower's height.

Her simple comment made Ransom and Cecily laugh.

"I'm going to Kingfountain," Ransom said after the amusement had faded.

"If anyone can convince Kiskaddon to end this mad conflict, it is you. But it won't be easy. Trust has been broken. A mirror can't be fixed. It must be remade."

"That takes time," Ransom admitted. "The king is vulnerable here," he said. "I'd rather he stay in Glosstyr. I suggested it to him when we met, but he hasn't come to a decision."

"It's a stronger fortress, for certain," she agreed. "But there are memories here between Jon-Landon and the queen. And new memories being forged," she added, giving the princess a meaningful look.

"Mama wants to go to Auxaunce," said the princess. "But it would be too dangerous. I think we could lose the Vexin."

"Why do you say that?" Cecily asked her, continuing to dig the trench.

"Because my grandfather the duke is an eejit," said the princess. Ransom tried not to smirk and failed. His sons' choice of words had clearly influenced the girl's language. "If Papa dies, Grandfather will swear loyalty to the Occitanians, I think."

It was a cynical statement for such a young girl. However, Ransom didn't think she was off the mark.

"Can we speak privately?" Ransom asked Cecily.

"Hurry back and keep digging," Léanore said firmly and with a tone of disapproval.

"As you wish, my lady," Cecily said. She brushed off her hands, and Ransom reached down to help her rise. They walked closer to the surf, which was creeping up again. The foamy bubbles on the shore popped, and little brown crabs scurried up after the water receded.

"Bodkin is falling out of favor, I think," Ransom told her.

"He's the king's darkest self," Cecily said, her voice dropping lower. "He's the one who advised him to murder the hostages. I wish the king would exile him, but I don't think he dares. He knows too many secrets. Secrets Jon-Landon wouldn't want shared."

"How about a dungeon, then?" Ransom suggested wryly.

She smiled at him. "I'd support it." Then her smile faded. "If you don't conjure a miracle, Ransom, Jon-Landon's reign will end. No one will support Prince Devon as the new king. And if that happens, the flood comes, correct?"

"*I* will support him," Ransom said firmly.

She gave him a sad smile. "No one but you." She folded her arms and gazed out at the sea. "I think there's a chance the Argentine dynasty will fail. We must all be prepared to flee if it does. There was hope when Benedict was king, but the Occitanians poisoned him, and I fear the same will happen to Jon-Landon. We can't hope to protect him here as we would at the palace." She sighed. "The king wants to send me to Pisan." She glanced at him. "I'm afraid it will all be over before I could return."

"Do you want to go?" he asked.

"Yes, actually," she said. "I think I would be good at it. But I am afraid. If I went there, I would be a target of Lady Alix. That would frighten anyone."

"Anyone with sense," Ransom said. "If the king stays anywhere for too long, it gives her an opportunity to strike. The fountains here at Averanche are being guarded? The poisoner promised to come after his children too."

"Of course," she said. "The king is paranoid about being poisoned. He should be. We have guards night and day."

"Good, because I'm not entirely sure her ability to travel is linked to the fountains. Claire once saw her disappear on land."

Cecily's eyes widened. "Lady, let us hope not. If Alix could do that, though, I suspect none of us would still be alive."

He expected she was right. It was the only thing that offered him any comfort.

"You know, the king has tried to win over Sir Dawson. Offered to make him captain of his guard. Did he tell you?"

"The king himself told me," Ransom said. "Dawson refused."

"I respect him more for it." She inclined her head toward Ransom, studying him. "When the two of you were talking over there, were you talking about me?"

Ransom smiled and shrugged. "What gave you that idea?"

Cecily arched her brows as if Ransom were being foolish. "He's a good man, Ransom. You've done well by him. But I have ambitions of my own. I wouldn't be content sitting in a castle and working on embroidery while he was off having adventures."

Ransom shrugged. "I don't imagine you would be."

She sighed. "So you're not going to tell me?"

"I would never betray his trust," Ransom said. "Ask him yourself."

"Maybe I will. I like to see him flustered."

"Cecily!" complained the princess. "The water is almost at the edge! Hurry!"

Ransom gave her a sidelong look. "You're digging a trench that you know will get washed out within the hour?"

She arched her eyebrows again. "She didn't believe me. What better way to teach her than to let her watch it happen herself?"

He gave her an approving nod. "Very wise."

A grin, a genuine one, lifted her lips. "Thank you, my lord. Good luck on your mission to Kingfountain. You will need it."

He turned his gaze to his sons, who were racing back from the run Dawson had assigned them. By the footprints, he saw they'd run to a boulder speckled with guano and then back. They were racing hard, and Devon was slightly ahead. Willem's face was contorted with the grimace of one who might lose. It spurred him on harder.

"Run, Willem! Run!" Léanore shrieked.

And that incentive was all Willem needed to put in a final burst of speed and reach Dawson first. Both boys dropped to their knees, gasping for breath.

How would their lives play out, Ransom wondered. Whom would they marry, and what sort of men would they become?

A shadow passed over his heart. He had the dark suspicion that he wouldn't live to see it.

XX

When I returned to Atha Kleah, I was surprised to find Lord Toole had come. We hadn't spoken since he abandoned us in our hour of need. He sought forgiveness, not his former position. He said he was wrong for losing confidence in our rule.

There has been a rift between us, but I thought of what Ransom would do. What he's done. Some rulers would have left the aging man on his knees and humiliated him in front of the onlookers. But I went to him and raised him up. I told him all was forgiven and asked him to take a seat, once more, in my council. The look on his face, I will never forget it. Nor will I forget how it felt to be merciful.

Lady Orla addressed the council. She is with child, which we didn't know, for she has concealed that fact from everyone including her husband. That complicates the situation. I asked her if she was forced into marriage. She said that she was. It is against Gaultic law, and so, accordingly, the marriage can be made void. It is a difficult situation, as I feared it would be. The right is on her side. But if I champion her right to void the marriage, it could destroy the peace.

I told her to give it thought for three days. I will support whatever she chooses. She had no choice going in. But by the Aos Sí, she'll have it going out.

—*Claire de Murrow*
Atha Kleah
(justice)

CHAPTER
TWENTY-TWO

A Game of Wizr

As Ransom and his knights made the fateful journey to Kingfountain, he gazed at the well-worn road and thought about facing Lord Kiskaddon. What would he say? How would he convince him to stand down?

The rebellion might not have started out as planned, with the king's capture, but the results could not be denied. The problem was that there was no heir in Kiskaddon's pocket, no alternate king who possessed Argentine blood. And if the Argentine line failed, the Wizr game would end. The price they would have to pay, Ransom feared, would be in blood.

It was still late summer, but there was no heat to scorch them. The breeze on Ransom's face felt mild, a warning of an early autumn perhaps? After their journey, they reached the edge of the city and found the gates barred. There had been a few wagons heading that way, but they'd not been allowed in either, and merchants were lingering outside. Many of them regarded Ransom and his men with angry stares as they passed.

Once at the gates, Ransom looked up at the guards.

"Is that you, Lord Ransom?" asked one of the knights. "We had reports that a band of knights was on the way. The order was to close the gates."

"It is I. Who is your captain?" Ransom shouted back.

"We have no captain. We're paid by the mayor and the city aldermen to defend the town. What is your purpose?"

"I'm going to the palace."

"Are you joining the rebels, my lord?" asked the knight warily.

"No, I come in the king's name. I just left him and travel with his authority."

Another man, not in armor, approached the knight and said something to him.

"May one of the aldermen speak to you, Lord Ransom? At the gate?"

"Yes," Ransom answered.

"Have the merchants draw back a pace. I know they're eager to come in, but they'll have to wait until we sort this out."

Ransom saluted the knight and motioned for his entourage to come forward. His knights urged the merchants at the gate to stand aside, and they obeyed, although some did so sullenly.

The hinges of the gate groaned as the doors were pulled open from within, but they were only parted a few feet. Several knights stood in the gap, watching Ransom's knights with concern. The man who had appeared above came down, puffing for air. He was surprisingly young to be one of the city elders.

"Lord Ransom, my name is Nathan Ashcraft," he said, huffing and wheezing. "I recognize you. Are you aware of the situation here?"

"Tell me what I should know," Ransom said, looking down at the man from his saddle. He reached out with his Fountain magic but didn't feel any risk.

"Lord Kiskaddon has taken over the palace. The people are angry at him and demand he be captured and thrown into the river. There have been riots, my lord. We are not enough to keep the peace. Some thieves are taking advantage of the unrest and robbing merchants who come through the city."

Ransom looked at the alderman with concern. "Thank you. Who controls the bridge?"

"The deconeus," came the answer. "Neither side is allowed to cross to the other without permission. Duke Kiskaddon has the king's docks and uses them for supplies. He's threatened to take the bridge and subdue the town to restore order, but so far he hasn't acted."

"Then I will go to the sanctuary of Our Lady and advise with the deconeus," Ransom said. "Let me through."

"Very well. I just wanted to warn you that a mob may form. If we let you in, we must also allow entry to the merchants. They would feel safer if you went in first. We need the food they bring."

"Agreed," Ransom said. He signaled to his knights to gather near him. As the guards turned their attention to opening the gates, he addressed the others in a low voice. "Don't draw your swords. There may be trouble, but let me see if I can calm it. We're going to the sanctuary."

He saw nods of agreement. By then, the gates had been opened, and the merchants were hurrying to prepare their wagons. Ransom waited until most of them looked prepared for the journey, then nudged his mount to continue into the city. The sound of the falls thundered in his ears as he rode through the gates. Despite all the trouble he'd lived through, Kingfountain itself had never felt this dangerous. The streets were mostly empty, but he saw people watching from their windows as they rode by. Several buildings were damaged, burnt by fire, and debris littered the street. With a watchful eye, he led his men down the main street toward the bridge leading to the sanctuary.

The mob found them before they got there.

It was a rabble of men, armed with clubs and some with sharper weapons. There were about a hundred, if Ransom had to guess, all ill-trained and violent, their faces bruised and dirty. His magic reached out and sensed their hostility, the danger of the situation. They blocked the street in a mass. Ransom had thirty knights with him. A mob, even one of that size, would not last against trained men. But Ransom didn't want to hurt them.

He continued to approach and then gently tugged the horse's reins to stop him.

"Who are ye?" asked one of the rabble, a man with silver in his beard and a suspicious look.

"Ransom Barton," he answered. "I come in the king's name."

"You?" said the man doubtfully. "Why hasn't the king returned with an army?" He looked pointedly at the knights following Ransom. "That's not enough to take on Kiskaddon; may the Fountain curse him!"

"I didn't come to fight him," Ransom said. "Or you. Our enemies prowl like wolves outside Ceredigion. We must band together to protect against them. Stand aside, and let us pass."

"What if he's tricking us?" another man asked the one who seemed to be the leader.

"No, he's Lord Ransom," said the bearded man. "I know his face. He'd not lie to us."

"All nobles lie," spat another man.

"Not this one," insisted the leader.

"Disband," Ransom ordered. "In the king's name. Go back to your homes."

Ransom felt a thrum of Fountain magic come to him, unbidden. Power surged in his chest, and his words, his warning, rustled through the crowd. The people began looking at one another in confusion.

"Go back to your homes," he entreated.

As if a spell had been cast, the mob broke apart. Within a few moments, the street was clear, and he could see the gatehouse of the bridge ahead.

He looked back at his knights, smiling encouragingly. Sir Casey, one of the newest members of his mesnie, had a look of awe.

When they reached the bridge, the thunder of the falls grew even louder. The bridge was normally swollen with merchants and business, but it was completely empty. They stopped at the closed gate, and the acolyte who stood behind it peered at them.

"Who are you?" he asked.

"Lord Ransom of Glosstyr," he said. "I've come to speak to the deconeus."

"The deconeus has forbidden violence on the bridge," said the acolyte. "On pain of excommunication. Will you abide his edict, Lord Ransom?"

"His authority does not reach past the sanctuary grounds," Ransom reminded him. "But we declare our peaceful intentions. The king sent me to represent him."

"I need to seek permission," said the acolyte.

"Hurry, then," Ransom said, waving him on.

As they waited, Ransom listened to the roar of the falls and felt his Fountain magic swelling in his chest, filling him with strength and purpose. Assuring him he had done right to come here. Even his ears started tingling with it. After a short while, the acolyte returned and opened the gate.

"The deconeus will meet you in the sanctuary. You may proceed."

Ransom nodded to the young man, who shut and locked the gate after they passed through it. He could feel the tremor caused by the river rumbling beneath the bridge stones.

This is the river that King Gervase was sent into. It is where your body will join his.

He heard the whisper from the Fountain and felt his heart clench with dread. It was an awful burden of knowledge. Although there'd been no whispers of *when* it would happen, he had the presentiment he would not die an old man. The possibility of failure, of death, had been pressing in on him of late, and this confirmed it.

Thoughts of Claire and his children rushed through his mind, nearly bringing tears. He struggled against the surge of emotion, determined to do his duty whatever the cost. But the soreness in his heart was real.

I submit, Ransom answered in his mind.

When they reached the gates to the sanctuary, he gazed up at the spires and felt a swell of pride. The gate was already open, and the sexton greeted him warmly.

"Welcome back to Kingfountain, Lord Ransom. Your visit is unexpected and greatly appreciated. Come with me. Are your men hungry from travel? The day is getting late."

"Yes, we're all hungry," Ransom said.

"We will provide for them. Enter the protection of Our Lady of the Fountain."

Some of the knights stayed behind to tend to the horses, but Ransom dismounted and followed the sexton up the steps into the grand building. The alternating white and black marble floor tiles were scrubbed and polished. The statues depicting the Lady were immaculately clean, as were the majestic fountains filled with coins. There were no visitors now except for Ransom and his knights.

He was escorted to the deconeus's personal study, where the old man waited.

"Lord Ransom," said the deconeus with a chuckle of surprise. "This is unexpected."

"I've come from the king," he replied. "I'd like you to send a messenger to the castle to inform Lord Kiskaddon I'm here and wish to speak to him. Would you broker the conversation, Deconeus?"

The deconeus leaned back in his chair, pressing his hands together. "I don't know if he will come. He's afraid of excommunication. And rightfully so." A look of anger flashed in the deconeus's eyes. "He began this without having a legitimate heir on his side who could claim the hollow crown. I fear he will try to take it for himself. Doing so would unleash the Fountain's wrath."

Ransom leaned forward and put his hand on the desk separating them. "I've come to end this conflict."

"How?" asked the deconeus skeptically. "Power is on Kiskaddon's side, and he knows it. The king . . . skulks in Averanche. He has money but no loyalty. The nobles have all fled him."

"He has *me*," Ransom reminded him.

"True. And having the Duke of Glosstyr on his side is more than he deserves. I commend you for your loyalty, my lord, but Kiskaddon will not risk losing everything. He's made his choice. And whatever his intentions were, we all suffer for it."

"Help me put a stop to this," Ransom said.

"I'll send for him. But don't be surprised if he refuses. Or if he demands you come to the palace. How many knights did you bring with you?"

"Thirty."

"Not enough," chided the deconeus. "You won't take back the palace with so few."

"I don't intend to lay siege to the castle," Ransom said. "Well . . . not yet."

The deconeus tilted his head. "I've heard rumors that some implore *him* to seize the hollow crown. Others say he should invite Estian to be our king."

"It cannot be allowed to come to that," Ransom said, shaking his head. "There is much more at stake in this. Are you familiar with the legends of the fall of Leoneyis?"

The deconeus was a more worldly man, and he looked unconcerned. "What of them?"

"Summon Lord Kiskaddon, and I'll tell you both together."

"I will try, my lord. But don't cling to hope too tightly. There is little to hope for these days."

Kiskaddon didn't come that night. Nor did he come by the next. It took three days of waiting at the sanctuary before the reply came. The duke would treat with Ransom, on the condition he was granted safe conduct and allowed to bring an escort of forty knights. It was slightly more than what Ransom had brought, but he agreed to the terms anyway. He knew Kiskaddon feared he was walking into a trap.

The waiting had taken a toll. Ransom had spent hours walking the grounds, chafing with nervousness about the upcoming meeting and the premonition he'd been given upon arriving at Kingfountain. He'd written to Claire and the king, of course, to tell them of his arrival, so he knew both were waiting anxiously to learn the result of his first discussion with Kiskaddon.

At last the time arrived, and word came that a band of knights was approaching from the palace. Ransom hoped that there would be no trickery, but he thought that perhaps Kiskaddon was the more worried of the two of them. He waited at the sanctuary gates with the sexton and a few of his men. The other knights had gathered and stood a distance away, having been given the explicit order not to cause trouble.

The noise of the approaching horsemen caught Ransom's attention, and he stopped pacing and stared at the gate. He noticed Lord Kiskaddon at once. He rode atop his charger, wearing a tunic over his hauberk and bearing a sword as any knight would. Ransom nodded to him and then noticed the knight serving at Kiskaddon's side. It was Guivret. The shock of recognition stunned him. He'd thought all the hostages had been killed. How was he alive?

Guivret's eyes met Ransom's and then lowered, his face inscrutable. Then he dismounted, as Kiskaddon had done, and the two approached the open gate. The other knights followed suit. Judging by Kiskaddon's complexion, Ransom could tell that he was uneasy. He looked like a guilty man tormented by his sins.

"Thank you for coming, Hal," Ransom said, giving him the salute of a fellow knight.

Kiskaddon returned it reflexively, then lowered his hand to his sword hilt. "Are you here to arrest me, Ransom? Charge me with my crimes?"

He shook his head. "No. We're going to talk, just as I promised."

The other man sighed. "I wasn't sure whether or not to believe you. Have you had any word from the North?"

"None," Ransom answered honestly.

"I haven't heard back from James after I told him you'd come. But the road might be impassable by now. You'll need to treat with both of us, and from what I understand, you spurned his offer to join us."

"I did," Ransom agreed. "Shall we go inside the sanctuary? Do you trust your knights to keep the peace?"

Kiskaddon turned to Guivret. "Keep the men apart," he ordered.

"Aye, my lord," said Guivret, and his familiar voice reminded Ransom of the past. The rift between them was painful. The last time Ransom had seen Guivret, he'd been a prisoner at Beestone castle. Dawson had attempted to speak with him that afternoon, but Guivret had stared at the ground in defiance and refused to speak. They'd been sent away so quickly that Ransom hadn't had a chance to seek him out. Somehow he'd found his way into Kiskaddon's service. Did the duke's sudden reluctance to meet with him have anything to do with Guivret?

"Shall we?" Ransom said, gesturing to the sanctuary.

The dukes walked side by side as equals and mounted the steps.

"I don't like being this close to the falls," Kiskaddon said with strained nerves. "I know the consequence of treason is to go down them . . . alive."

"I didn't come here to do that," Ransom said.

"But if the king ordered it . . . you would." Kiskaddon gave him an accusing look. "If he whistles, you'd come like a wolfhound."

"No," Ransom said, shaking his head. "I chose a different path than you did when things turned against me. But I see the guilt in your eyes. You're haunted by it."

Kiskaddon glowered. "Don't mock me, Ransom."

"I'm not. If the river surged and destroyed the bridge that connects the palace to the city, it would need to be rebuilt. It would take time and care. But it could be done if there was a will to do it. I came to build. I didn't come to destroy."

"If you think that I will ever trust Jon-Landon again, you are sorely mistaken. He's unworthy of my respect or your loyalty."

"That may be," Ransom said, clapping him on the shoulder. "But what is at stake is more dire than the worthiness of Jon-Landon Argentine to be our king."

Kiskaddon wrinkled his brow. "What do you mean? It is *all* about that."

They reached the deconeus's private chamber. There were two chairs arranged, face-to-face, in front of a table with a Wizr set on it. Ransom had asked the deconeus to provide it. The board was not set up for the beginning of a game.

It was set up for the ending of one.

Lady Orla asked to speak with me privately. She is terrified of her husband and wishes to be freed from the marriage. She also sees the conflict my decision may bring to Legault. Now that I know her true feelings, I've told her that I will do her justice and dissolve the marriage. The child will be hers regardless, to give away for another to raise or for her to raise herself. Orla said that she doesn't blame the babe, that she will care for it.

I've sent Ransom a letter to inform him of the situation. I don't want him to be taken unawares. Who knows what that brainless badger of a king will do because of this.

Also, I thought he'd want to hear the good news. Elodie gave birth to a daughter. It was a difficult delivery, and I especially worried since Ransom was not there to use the scabbard, but their deepest wish has been given.

—Claire de Murrow
Atha Kleah
(a lady's freedom granted)

CHAPTER
TWENTY-THREE
The Power of the Falls

Duke Kiskaddon leaned back in the wooden chair, rubbing his upper lip and gazing quizzically at the Wizr board. Ransom seated himself across and examined the board himself. The deconeus stood to one side of the room, watching them, his expression grave.

"The board isn't set up properly," Kiskaddon observed. "I think that's deliberate. What are you playing at, Ransom?"

The piece representing the king was at the edge of the board with just one smaller pawn next to it. The other king was surrounded by two castle pieces and the Wizr piece.

"Bennett had a Wizr board," Ransom said seriously, looking across the table at Kiskaddon. "A special one. Did he ever tell you of it?"

"He wasn't fond of such games." He shrugged without concern. "He didn't have the patience to master them. But I do recall . . . he did mention he had a set that had been stolen from King Estian. That's all I know."

"I'm the one who took it from Estian," Ransom said, folding his arms. "Although it was made of stone, it was imbued with the power of the Fountain."

Kiskaddon snorted. "To what purpose?"

"It's a relic from the days of King Andrew and Queen Genevieve. The pieces can move themselves. They represent the different factions within a kingdom—*two* kingdoms. The game being played was a game of conquest between Ceredigion and Occitania. One that impacted the real world."

"You seem serious, but I find the story absurd."

"Hear him out, lord duke," said the deconeus gravely.

Kiskaddon waved a dismissive hand at the board. "Go on, then."

Studying him, Ransom said, "It is played between two rulers, each seeking to dominate the other. I believe Estian's forefathers inherited the game after the drowning of Leoneyis."

"You believe that really happened?"

Ransom ignored his doubtful tone. "The Vertus family wishes to create their own dynasty, one to rival the glory of King Andrew's domain. There's a reason why so many of those legends were written down in the old tongue. Passed on and dimmed with time. They wanted us to forget. But we mustn't. The board is real, and so are other artifacts from that time."

"I fail to see your point."

"Then let me make it. This piece represents Jon-Landon. If he dies, then his son is the last Argentine heir. If his children are killed, the game ends."

"Every game must end eventually," Kiskaddon said with a snide smile. Ransom could see he had little love for the king or his offspring, not that he was surprised. Jon-Landon had done nothing to earn goodwill.

"That's the problem. When this game ends, Ceredigion is destroyed."

Kiskaddon's brow wrinkled. "It's only a game. Threat and mate. It ends."

Ransom shook his head. "In Wizr, we always stop before the king is taken. That is the rule. The game ends when you say 'threat and mate.' But that's not how that board works. When the king piece is taken, if there are no heirs left, the kingdom is destroyed by flood."

Kiskaddon glanced at the deconeus and then back again, as if he thought they were jesting. When he saw they were quite serious, he asked, "Why didn't that happen when Gervase died? Or his son?"

Ransom opened his palms. "Because Devon Argentine was the true heir. His mother was named heir, but Gervase claimed the hollow crown before it could be given to her. That started the civil war. The board is real. I've seen the pieces move on their own accord. And I've seen the Argentine heirs move them. It was a closely guarded secret."

"Can you prove it? Where is the board now if this isn't it?"

"When Bennett was murdered, it was stolen back by Estian and his poisoner, Lady Alix. They are intent on ending the rivalry between us. Permanently."

Kiskaddon scratched his eyebrow. "You came all the way from Averanche with this childish tale, hoping it would convince me that I need to *trust* a man who has no more honor than a pile of horse dung?"

"If the game ends, the people will die. You as well."

"Why didn't I know about this? Why were you the trusted one?"

"Because I'm Fountain-blessed," Ransom said simply. Although he'd anticipated Kiskaddon's response, he was frustrated by it.

"Another legend," Kiskaddon said with a wry smile. "May I be completely honest with you, Ransom?"

"I encourage it," Ransom said.

"I've often wondered why you cowed to Jon-Landon. Why you, a man so principled and honorable, would suffer himself to be kicked like a dog by a ruthless master."

Ransom bristled at the comparison, but he kept silent and listened carefully.

"I believe Jon-Landon knows of some crime or indiscretion he is holding over you. Some knowledge gained from the Espion that, if revealed, would tarnish your reputation. So you surrendered to that cruel tyrant to avoid the truth being known. If not for your clever wife, you'd still be the king's hostage. That is what I think."

Ransom's mouth was dry with anger, but he kept his voice controlled. "And what do you believe the king has been holding over me?"

"I'd rather not say in front of a deconeus." Kiskaddon's smile was smug, and Ransom squeezed his hands into fists to subdue his growing anger.

"I think I'm familiar with the sordid rumors," Ransom said. "There have been plenty."

"There have," agreed Kiskaddon. "First, there was the Younger King's wife. Then, after your marriage to Lady Claire, you ran off to visit Goff's widow, Lady Constance. I even heard from Bennett's chancellor that you seduced the masked emissary of the East Kingdoms and persuaded her to quit Brugia and stop bidding on the king's ransom." He reached out and tapped his forefinger on the Wizr board. "That's why you're here, doing the king's bidding once more. He has you in his fist, and he's squeezing you hard. Isn't it also said in the legends that King Andrew's first knight seduced his queen?"

The anger in Ransom's heart nearly spilled out. He wanted to strike the Wizr board to the ground, to let the whole kingdom drown in infamy. It burned like a brand to hear that the rumors persisted still. The cruel and false tales about him had proliferated like weeds and hid in the stalks of truth. But he kept his emotions in check, refusing to let Kiskaddon goad him.

"Guivret knows about the Wizr board," Ransom said. "He was with me when I took it."

Kiskaddon chuffed and gesticulated. "He's the one who told me of your affair with the Duchess of Brythonica! You can hardly count him as a witness of your honor!"

Ransom looked at the deconeus, whose eyes were wide with aston-ishment. He looked discomfited by the sordid tales.

"I have always loved Claire de Murrow," Ransom said. "I've never betrayed her, and the accusations you throw at me are false. Estian's sister was the one who tried to dishonor me, and I rejected her both then and in Brugia. *She* was the masked lady, and it was her conniving with her brother that led to our war with the East Kingdoms. I unmasked her, and she fled. As for the Duchess of Brythonica, I never laid a finger on her. She is the most honorable person I know, and the accusation of your knight must be roundly denounced."

Ransom's forceful speech had shocked Kiskaddon into silence.

"I see you are in earnest," he said after a long pause, his eyes serious.

"There is only one thing a knight can do when such accusations have been leveled against him. I must defend my honor and my reputation. I challenge Sir Guivret to single combat. A trial of the sword. May the Fountain judge between us."

Kiskaddon nodded. "That is just, although your reputation as a warrior would make any man balk. I will relay your challenge to Guivret. If he continues to denounce you, then you will both fight, without armor."

"There will be no blood shed on these grounds," the deconeus said firmly.

"We will hold the challenge on the bridge, before the gates of the sanctuary," Kiskaddon offered. "Do you agree, my lord duke?"

"I do," Ransom said, rising from his chair. He gave Kiskaddon a knightly salute.

It was returned.

The duel was arranged for later that afternoon. It was not a fight to the death, but a fight to submission. It would end with one man lying on his back, a blade to his throat, and declaring guilt. The knights who had come with Ransom lined the street on one side. The knights who had come with Kiskaddon lined the other. Ransom and Guivret faced off in the space in between. The roar of the falls blocked out all other noises.

Ransom stood alone, hand on his pommel, but he felt the support of his knights behind him. Guivret was speaking to Kiskaddon, but he left his mesnie and approached Ransom on the street.

Ransom wore a thin undertunic, open at the front. He was older than Guivret, more experienced, and he felt the confidence of his Fountain magic thrumming through him. The knowledge that he was in the right. Reaching out with his magic, he gauged Guivret's abilities and found him to be highly skilled. The lad had always worked hard on his drills, and he was fearless by nature. But Ransom sensed a shadow in the young man's soul, a taint undoubtedly caused by Alix's strange gift of persuasion.

Ransom sighed. "I am innocent," he said to the young knight.

"I know in my heart that you are a liar," Guivret said with emotion. He looked conflicted, though, ravaged by distrust and the time he'd spent as the Occitanians' prisoner.

Ransom felt a twinge of guilt. Had he managed to rescue Guivret, he could have saved him the pain of being a prisoner, of having his mind twisted against his friends. But Alix had never intended to let that happen. This was just another piece of unfairness in a world that sometimes felt harsh and uncaring.

"May the Fountain judge between us."

"It will," insisted Guivret. "You've always been better than me, Lord Ransom. But I believe in the Fountain. I believe it will deliver you into my hands."

Ransom nodded and drew his bastard sword. He had the Raven scabbard and didn't fear injury, but he didn't want to hurt Guivret, and the young knight seemed ready to throw himself fully into the fight.

The deconeus and the sexton and their many acolytes had gathered at the gate to watch.

Guivret drew his weapon, also a bastard sword. His chest heaved as they faced off.

"I'm ready, lad," Ransom said.

With a cry that sounded like an animal's guttural roar, Guivret rushed him, swinging his sword in a blizzard of swirls. Ransom sensed what he would do, however, and he easily backstepped and deflected, the noise of their clashing blades ringing out on the street. They switched sides, circling each other. The whistle of the blade came for Ransom's neck, but he raised his own weapon and parried. Guivret's mouth contorted with anger and another emotion—guilt?—and he charged on, coming at Ransom with the energy and fury of youth.

Ransom felt calm and peaceful.

Before long, the younger man's attack began to slacken, his energy spent.

It was then Ransom commenced his assault. In three swings, he sent Guivret's sword skittering across the cobblestones until it rested far out of reach. Guivret's eyes shot wide with terror and surprise. He dropped to his knees before Ransom and lifted his head, exposing his throat.

"Kill me, Lord Ransom, I beg you!" he groaned.

"I'll not kill you, lad," Ransom said.

"Please!" Guivret opened his arms, offering his life. "I cannot . . . bear . . . to live. Not when the boy . . . is dead. My heart cannot endure it. Kill me."

Ransom lowered his sword. "Do you revoke your accusation? I did not dishonor anyone."

Guivret's shoulders slumped. Tears began to mix with the sweat on his cheeks. "I bear witness, before you all, that Lord Ransom is innocent!" he shouted. He began to sob.

A feeling of peace swelled in Ransom's chest. He felt nothing but forgiveness and empathy for the young man. Reaching out, he laid a hand on Guivret's shoulder.

"It's not your fault," he said. "Alix is blessed as well. Her words are magic. Even I have fallen under her spell and believed things that were not true. I forgive you, lad."

Guivret looked up at him, the confusion and guilt fading from his eyes. He took Ransom's hand and kissed it.

A surge of Fountain magic manifested, stunning Ransom in its intensity. And suddenly the river overwhelmed the grounds of the sanctuary. Everyone turned in surprise as a wall of water tumbled through the gardens, surged past the sanctuary, and then came spilling through the gates, drenching the hem of the deconeus's robes. The river cut through their group, about as high as their knees, before surging against the buildings on the other side of the bridge and spilling down the alleys in between them until it dumped off the bridge.

In all his years, Ransom had never heard of the river overtaking the sanctuary. The surge ended, and everyone stood staring at the wet cobblestones, stunned by the dramatic display of the river's power. Guivret stared down at the water, then pressed his palms against the stones and bowed before Ransom.

"You *are* Fountain-blessed," he said hoarsely.

Ransom turned and saw that his knights had dropped to a knee before him. Whirling around, he saw Kiskaddon and his men had done the same.

The miracle of the surging river had been witnessed by everyone. It had washed away any last doubts or defiance.

The gate leading to the sanctuary creaked as it opened, and the deconeus and sexton came out onto the river-soaked street. The deconeus had a feverish look in his eyes as he approached Ransom and came to a stop in front of him. "We've all witnessed it. The Lady of the Fountain has proven Lord Ransom's innocence."

Duke Kiskaddon rose and approached Ransom with a look of respect and chagrin. When he reached them, Guivret had come to his feet, his pants and boots soaked by the water.

"Everything you've said is true?" Kiskaddon asked.

"It is," Ransom answered. "I've come in the king's name. You will be pardoned if you submit to him again. I promise you."

Kiskaddon sighed. "I trust you, Lord Ransom. It is the king I do not trust."

"May I propose a solution to this conundrum?" said the deconeus.

"Please," Ransom answered.

The deconeus squared his shoulders and assumed a dignified authority. "I propose a charter, to be signed by the king and his nobles across the land. It would diminish the king's authority to punish the lords of the realm. Any noble accused of treason will stand trial by their peers and not the king himself. Only if the peerage finds guilt can the king execute the penalty for treason. It will prevent the king and his heirs from being arbitrary. If the king does not uphold the charter, then all nobles will be released from their vow of allegiance to him and suffer no forfeit of land or life."

Kiskaddon studied the deconeus before speaking. "I would sign such a charter. I would rather let my fate be judged by my peers than a capricious king. But will Jon-Landon willingly give up some of his power?"

Ransom thought carefully. "If it unifies his realm and ends the war, I think he might."

"Will he not forsake his word later?"

"If he does, then it will no longer be treason to rebel against him. I think it is fair. What will we call these courts? These trials by the peerage?"

The deconeus said, "The Assizes. The Elder King used a similar arrangement to settle land disputes without his direct involvement. Only we'll be using them to resolve issues involving life and property."

"The Assizes," Kiskaddon said. "May we have your help, Deconeus, in crafting this charter so that Ransom might return to Averanche with it?"

"Indeed you may," said the deconeus proudly.

The noise of clopping hooves came from the direction of the palace, and Ransom and Kiskaddon both turned in concern.

The far gate had been left open, and a knight came charging up with a worried expression.

"My lords," he said breathlessly. "The docks are under attack! The Occitanians have come!"

I've not heard back from Ransom, but I imagine it will take days yet. Instead, I received a message I was not expecting, from the Duchess of Brythonica. She has never written to me before, but she said the fate of Ceredigion is hanging by threads. King Estian will attack on multiple fronts to destroy Jon-Landon and all the Argentine heirs. With the kingdom in chaos, it cannot survive unless we band together and remember to trust one another.

She knows, somehow, that the Occitanian fleet will attack Kingfountain, and Estian and his knights will strike at Averanche. I am in a position to defend the palace if I send enough ships to the rescue. But that would mean leaving Legault vulnerable.

I must make this choice without Ransom here. I've always had a strange feeling about the duchess. Is she seeking to make Legault defenseless to her own duchy, or is she trying to assist us however she can?

Ransom trusted her. Now I must decide if I can.

—*Claire de Murrow*
Atha Kleah
(fateful news from Brythonica)

CHAPTER
TWENTY-FOUR

Coming of the Times

Fire from the burning docks could still be seen at midnight. Ransom was weary from the fighting of the day, which had claimed the lives of many, including some of the knights whom he'd brought with him. The Occitanian surprise attack on Kingfountain would not soon be forgotten. But it had been repelled.

Ransom and Kiskaddon were in the great hall of the palace, a map of the realm spread out on a trestle table in front of them. On it stood figurines representing the different forces at work. Faulkes was fighting James in North Cumbria. Kiskaddon's troops were split between Kingfountain and East Stowe, but with the Occitanian ships still in the harbor, they could not send word to the port city by sea. A piece representing Jon-Landon was at Averanche. The other nobles were positioned in various places. There was no strategy to it, only chaos.

They both pored over the map, and Ransom felt a pinch of unease at the sight of Jon-Landon alone. Averanche was close to the border of Westmarch, which was currently still Occitanian territory. If only they had the Wizr board to advise them of Estian's plans.

"I'm exhausted," Kiskaddon admitted after slurping down some wine. His eyes were bleary. They both still wore their armor from the combat earlier in the day. Guivret stood with them, as well as some of Ransom's knights. The chairs where the king and queen usually sat had been removed from the room. It felt strange being in the palace, knowing the precariousness of the situation.

Ransom pointed to a spot on the map—the city of Kingfountain. "Is this the only place where Estian has attacked?"

"I have no way of knowing," Kiskaddon said. "With the mobs in the streets on the other side of the river, we can't send messengers by foot. All of our information has come from ships."

Ransom tapped the spot. "Estian has spies in the city, no doubt. I don't think Kingfountain is his only target. The king—he's going to go after the king."

Kiskaddon tilted his head and looked at the map quizzically. "I think you're right. He attacked us here to keep our focus off his real assault. Averanche is too vulnerable. Where do you think the king should go? Glosstyr?"

"It's near enough," Ransom said. "If we follow the coast, that's the quickest way."

"What about by ship?"

Ransom shook his head. "I think it would be safer to stay on land. A freak storm struck us during my crossing from Legault. The season is turning early this year, I fear."

The duke looked at the map and nodded in agreement. "What about the fortress at Beestone?"

Ransom looked at the map again. "With all those wagons full of treasure, it would be slow going. And Estian would be able to predict the destination, so he could send his army to cut off the way. We don't have much time to react."

"Do you think, Ransom, that he will accept the terms of the charter?" There was a hint of doubt in Kiskaddon's tone.

"I do. He has little choice."

Kiskaddon looked wary still. "No king willingly relinquishes power. Not the Elder King. Not even Bennett. If Jon-Landon doesn't sign the charter, we're all doomed. That is, if you're right about what happens when the Wizr game ends. After what I saw on the bridge today, I have to believe what you said is true."

Guivret approached the table and stood between them. "It is true," he said. Something within him had altered, as if the last of Alix's influence had slithered away. He seemed like his old self again. "I've no doubt on that score, my lord."

Kiskaddon looked at Guivret thoughtfully. "You both have more confidence in the king than I do. But I agree, what else can he do? The charter will change the affairs of the kingdom permanently. If Jon-Landon accepts it, then I'll unite with him. I need your promise, though, Ransom, that he will not condemn us for treason."

"You have it," Ransom answered. "If he signs the treaty, I'll hold him to it. He sent me here to work out a truce. What we propose is fair."

"Fair, but he'll be tempted to tear up the charter after we've stabilized the realm."

"It's more than words on a page," Ransom said. "If he agrees, it will bind not only him but all future kings of Ceredigion. It feels right, doesn't it?"

Kiskaddon sighed. "It does. I'd like to send one of my knights with you, though. To see firsthand how he reacts to the terms. Would you be opposed to me smuggling someone in with your group?"

"Let me go, my lord," Guivret asked.

Kiskaddon smirked. "You were the one I was thinking of, lad. What do you say, Ransom?"

"I agree." He gave Guivret a smile. "The deconeus said he'd have the charter ready by dawn. I'll take my knights to Beestone and gather some of the garrison there to defend the king."

"How many are left?" Kiskaddon asked.

"Five hundred, I think," Ransom said. "Many were sent north with Faulkes. If the king signs the treaty, I'll have him call Faulkes back. You can tell James about the charter. I don't care how you accomplish it."

"Well enough. Dawn will be here soon, and we both need some rest to prepare for what's ahead. My knights are guarding the docks that haven't burned. I'll see you in the morning before you leave."

They gave each other a knightly salute, and Ransom left the audience hall and found his way to his bedchamber, which had been cleared for his arrival. He lay down in his clothes, his mind weary, and fell asleep in moments.

The next morning, a messenger from the sanctuary arrived with the news that the charter was finished and ready for inspection. Ransom and Kiskaddon ate together and then rode down to the bridge with the rest of Ransom's knights and Guivret. The deconeus met them at the gate and, with a solemn look, lifted the long round leather case he held.

"This is the charter, my lord. I've never written such a document before. It requires the king's seal to be valid, which he keeps with him. After he has approved it, it will become the law of the land."

The deconeus undid the cap and took out the charter, which had been written on parchment instead of paper. That would help it last longer. As he unrolled the document, Ransom felt a throb of approval from the Fountain. Standing side by side with Kiskaddon, they read the small, elegant script. It was in the old speech, which Ransom had learned years ago in his training. As he read the document, he marveled at the significance of what they were doing. The king, if he stamped it with his seal, would no longer be above the law—he would be subject to the laws of the realm. The deconeus had written the terms of the Assizes too, including how justice would be meted out.

After Ransom finished reading, he looked over at Kiskaddon, who was still poring over the words. When he finished, he let out a sigh.

"If he agrees to this," Kiskaddon said, "everything will change."

The deconeus smiled. "I did feel the influence of the Fountain on my pen," he said. "The charter wrote itself into existence." He rolled up the parchment and inserted it back into the leather case, which he handed to Ransom. "My lord, I entrust this to your hands. It is your duty now to persuade the king to validate it."

Ransom took it and slung it around his back with the strap. "I will do my best. I assume this is not the only copy?"

The deconeus smiled. "No, I had it transcribed."

"Then summon the aldermen of the city to the sanctuary and show it to them. If the king adds his seal, we can end this conflict at once. No more threats to throw Lord Kiskaddon into the river."

"I would greatly appreciate that," said the duke with a chuckle.

"I'll send word as soon as I can. Guivret will come in person."

"Good. May better days be ahead. Go with the Fountain, Ransom."

They parted ways, and Ransom and his knights rode through the gate, admitted by the acolyte standing guard. It was early still, and people remained indoors. The view of the Occitanian fleet down in the harbor below was a menacing sight, and the steady noise of the falls offered little comfort. Once they reached the gates of the city, they left Kingfountain behind and rode hard toward Beestone. Two knights rode ahead to alert the castellan of Beestone that they were coming.

Although the wind blew from the north with an unusual chill, and storm clouds hovered over the western skies, they kept a quick pace. Still, Guivret rode at Ransom's side, and they were able to speak in spurts. They discussed Guivret's time in captivity, and Ransom informed him that it was Lady Alix who had murdered Keeva. That knowledge darkened Guivret's countenance. He hadn't known. Lady Alix had told him she was dead but inferred that Ransom and Claire were responsible. Her Fountain magic had convinced him of the lie, just like it had convinced him that Ransom was guilty of adultery and unworthy of the title of knight.

Prior to the battle at Auxaunce, Guivret and a few other knights had been sent to protect Drew Argentine, to prevent him from being freed by the duchess or Ransom. The boy had been homesick for his mother and his duchy, but he'd managed to overcome it and find ways to be helpful and happy. But after the Occitanian prisoners were brought to Beestone, Guivret was sent away from the prince and given to Kiskaddon's custody.

"How did you survive when all the other hostages were killed?" Ransom asked.

A look of grief flashed on Guivret's face. "I was part of the duke's household by that time," he explained. "Not a prisoner. On the day the Espion came to murder me, the duke felt something was amiss. One of the castle servants had died that day of a bleeding ulcer. His corpse had been laid out in a canoe. The Espion didn't know what I looked like, so when Kiskaddon told them I'd died that day, they were shown the dead body of another man. The Espion fell for the trick, and I've been in disguise ever since."

"Thank the Lady," Ransom said in astonishment.

"Aye. If that chap hadn't died, I would not be with you right now. When the duke told me of Drew's death, I felt such a rage. I was willing to murder the king myself out of revenge."

"Do you like serving Lord Kiskaddon?" Ransom asked.

"I had happiness in my service to you and Lady Claire," he said. "But I've sworn fealty to Lord Kiskaddon. I cannot break it. Only he can."

It took twice as long to reach Beestone with the extra patrols needed, and they arrived weary from the journey and anxious for a good meal and a place to sleep. The castellan, Sir Iain, was an aging man. He had served the Elder King and his wife for many years as chamberlain and was given the post of castellan after her death, and although he was no longer capable of riding into battle, he was a keen strategist and had been charged with defending the castle.

"Well met, Lord Ransom," he said. "The stateroom is ready for you, but I presume you'd like some roast pheasant first?"

Ransom's stomach growled audibly, and the aging knight laughed.

"What is that strapped to your back, if I may ask?"

"A portent of better days to come," Ransom answered. "It's a peace charter. I'm bringing it to the king."

"Wouldn't that be a relief!" he said, tugging his white beard.

"How many in the garrison, Sir Iain?"

"We have four hundred. Enough to defend the castle if trouble comes. They're still building up Tatton Grange. I wish we had enough men to halt their progress."

So did Ransom, but attacking Occitania wasn't possible at the moment. "Let's have some of that pheasant you mentioned." He clapped the knight on the shoulder and went inside with him while the knights took care of the horses.

The feast was plenteous, and the knights were all grateful for the food and drink and a chance to rest. Most of them would bed down in the great hall for the night.

Ransom spoke candidly to Sir Iain after they finished eating in the solar. "I need to take some of the garrison with me to Averanche."

Sir Iain frowned. "We have hardly enough to defend the castle, my lord. Why not bring your own men down from Glosstyr?"

"I'm planning to escort the king *to* Glosstyr," he said. "I have a feeling that Estian will attack Averanche. I only brought thirty men with me, and I lost several at Kingfountain when the Occitanian fleet attacked."

They'd discussed the attack over dinner, so the castellan merely nodded. "Is Averanche secure?"

"For now," Ransom said. "If we encounter any of Estian's army before we get there, I'll need to fight my way through. Can I have two hundred?"

Sir Iain blanched. "My lord . . . that takes away half of my defenders."

"You could defend this castle with fifty men, Sir Iain. We both know that. After we've reached Averanche safely and brought the king to Glosstyr, I'll send them back with reinforcements."

Sir Iain quickly agreed, then summoned his steward and told him to prepare two hundred men to travel on the morrow.

All was going to plan. Ransom should have felt relieved, but an uneasy feeling stole over him as he sat and drank from his goblet. He looked around the room, trying to determine the source, but the hall was full of his knights. Maybe it was simply worry for the safety of the Argentines. The king and his two children were at the same place. He trusted Cecily and Dawson would act for their protection, but he wished he were back there already. No doubt Estian was looking at the Wizr board and knew they were at Beestone.

Before retiring, Ransom ordered the captain of his knights to have a watch that night and alert him if there was any trouble. He knew Alix could enter the castle through the fountains, but that warning had already been given, and guards had been posted to prevent her from entering that way.

He brought a candle to his room and bolted the door. Taking off his sword belt, he set his scabbard next to his bed. He was about to take off his hauberk too, but felt that same wariness as before and didn't remove it. That feeling compelled him to examine the room more closely, but he saw nothing out of sorts. Still, he could not help but wonder if the hidden passages in this castle were as widespread as they were in Kingfountain. He tried to reach out with his Fountain magic, but there was nothing. The window was high up on the wall, too small for a person to get inside.

Gripping the leather tube in his hand, he sat down at the edge of the bed and blew the candle out. The smell of its smoke stung his nose. He lay down, weary, and rested the tube against his hip, his hand covering it protectively. His muscles ached, and he felt his body succumb to its need for sleep. It was a new moon that night, so the darkness was complete.

How much time passed, he didn't know. But he awoke to a surge of Fountain magic, warning him of danger. His eyes popped open, and he sat up. He reached for the tube with one hand and his sword with the other.

Suddenly a shielded lantern burst, blinding his eyes and making him involuntarily look away. Fear bloomed in his heart. As he reached for the hilt of his sword to draw it, he heard a voice coming from behind the light.

"If Lord Ransom draws that blade," said Bodkin, the head of the Espion, in a voice dripping with amusement, "shoot him."

I awoke in the middle of the night with a spasm of fear. This has happened before, but this time the sensation was so strong, so fierce, that I could hardly breathe. I felt Ransom was in danger, yet I could do nothing—nothing!—to aid him. I sat up in the dark, the new moon making everything invisible. I gasped and I pleaded with the Aos Sí to protect him. He has the Raven scabbard, so why am I this afraid?

I lit a candle and decided to write to calm my emotions. I've sent ships in response to Constance's warning. Now I pray they return before Legault is imperiled. We wait for news. We worry for it.

—Claire de Murrow
Atha Kleah
(in the darkness)

CHAPTER
TWENTY-FIVE

The Rising

Ransom's eyes gradually adjusted to the glare of the lantern. He'd involuntarily raised his hand to protect his eyes. He couldn't see how many there were, so he reached out with his Fountain magic. Six men had come, including Bodkin, and one held a crossbow aimed at Ransom's chest. At that short distance, it would skewer him even with his armor. His sword was just out of reach.

The magic revealed that these were highly trained men, including Bodkin himself. Ransom felt confident he could defeat them, but not with that crossbow aimed at him. If the man was startled, he might release the bolt and put a quick—and permanent—end to things.

"What shall we discuss, Lord Ransom?" said Bodkin in his infuriating confidence. "How about . . . that leather tube. I'd be grateful if you'd hand it to me. It looks rather important."

"It is," Ransom said, his voice throbbing with anger. His instincts screamed at him to lunge for his weapon, but he didn't dare. "It is a truce, awaiting the king's seal."

"Let me see it," Bodkin said flatly, holding out his hand.

Ransom lowered his hand, shrinking slightly from the stab of light, and closed his other around the leather case. It was then he noticed the hole in the floor at the corner of the room. They'd come in through a trapdoor.

"Don't try anything foolish," Bodkin warned. "You may have bested my men before, but I've taken care this time. We wouldn't want any *accidents* now, would we?"

Ransom took it as the threat it was. He extended his hand and offered the tube to the Espion chief. From the glint of light on metal, Ransom saw Bodkin had a dagger tucked in his other hand.

"Thank you for being reasonable. What have you brought?" He slid his dagger into his belt and twisted the cap off the case. As he shook out the rolled parchment, Ransom glanced at the other Espion. All of them were armed. He listened keenly for the sound of anyone outside, the night watch. What would Bodkin do if he cried out?

Bodkin motioned for the man holding the lantern to bring the light closer to the unfurled parchment. His dark brows beetled closer as he began to read the deconeus's words. The furrows deepened, and his lips pursed with disgust.

"This won't do," Bodkin said. "This won't do at all."

"There is another copy at the sanctuary," Ransom said. "But it means nothing if the king doesn't stamp it with his seal. I'm bringing him options as he commanded me."

"You're a sliver under his skin," Bodkin said with a sneer. "This is an abomination."

"It is the only way the kingdom can survive," Ransom said.

"I don't think so. The king has two hundred thousand livres. I advised him to flee to Gotz in Brugia. He can live comfortably enough in Callait. Let the dukes squabble and bleed each other for a season. He was listening to me. Until *you* returned."

"You are suggesting he flee the realm during this crisis?"

"Why not? As long as he wears the hollow crown, it doesn't matter where he rules from."

"And you presume he'd be safer in Callait?"

"Of course. We need time to get our own poisoner. I think he would be very safe. I'm sorry, Lord Ransom, but this won't do." He rolled up the parchment again, shaking his head.

The sound of boots came down the hall. One of the Espion hissed in warning. The man with the crossbow looked nervously at Bodkin, but his weapon was still aimed at Ransom's chest.

Bodkin pursed his lips and put a finger to them, a signal they all understood.

Ransom gripped a fist around the blankets, feeling sweat trickle down his back. He glanced at his sword again. The only thing that stayed his hand was the memory of the Fountain's whisper—*This is the river that King Gervase was sent into. It is where your body will join his.*

The guard's bootfalls passed by the door and continued down the hall.

"You were wise not to shout," Bodkin said, giving Ransom an approving look. "I'd rather not kill you, but I'm willing to. In fact, your death would make my plan the better option."

"What is your intention, then?" Ransom said.

Bodkin withdrew a little vial. Ransom's stomach shriveled when he saw it. "You are going to get very sick. Delirious even. I'll return and tell the king you've been poisoned. By the time you revive, we'll be on our way to Brugia."

The time to act was upon him. Would his reflexes be quick enough?

"Hold him down," Bodkin ordered curtly.

Three of the Espion lunged at him. As soon as they blocked the sight of the crossbow, he fought back. He swung his legs over the edge of the bed, grabbed the first man by the collar and threw him into the wall. The other two collided with him, both of them very strong and very heavy. He reached for his scabbard as it toppled to the floor, but missed, and suddenly the weight of more men slammed into him.

Ransom used his forehead to smash the nose of one of his assailants and heard a bark of pain. He tried to punch, but one of the Espion managed to capture his arm with both hands, and soon he was pinned on the bed. Anger raged inside him.

"Quickly, quickly," Bodkin said, coming closer with the vial. "Force his mouth open."

Ransom clenched his teeth shut and strained against the weight of his attackers. Fingers prodded his mouth and squeezed his cheeks to part his lips. He kept his jaw closed and continued to struggle.

Bodkin loomed over him, his eyes livid with eagerness. Suddenly he knew. This was the man who'd persuaded the king to murder the Occitanian hostages, to remove all obstacles to his succession plans. There was no sympathy in him, only concern for his own greedy ends. If Ransom could have bitten him, he would have. Bodkin unstoppered the vial and began to reach through the mess of limbs to bring it to Ransom's mouth.

A heavy weight struck the door, startling everyone. The lock held. The Espion master glared, but he persisted in pushing the vial to Ransom's lips. A sickly-sweet-smelling ichor began to dribble out.

The crossbow twanged.

Bodkin roared in pain. The vial fell from his fingers as he arched his back. The men who were restraining Ransom looked bewildered. The man with the crossbow lowered it and rushed to the door to unbolt it. When it opened, Guivret charged in with a sword in hand, along with three other knights.

Bodkin continued to writhe and howl. One of the Espion tried to rush for the trapdoor, but one of the knights stopped him at sword point.

"Unhand him now!" shouted Guivret.

The other Espion backed away, but the one holding the crossbow was standing next to Guivret, a satisfied smirk on his mouth. When Ransom turned his head, he finally registered that Bodkin was the one who'd been shot.

In the arse.

The Espion chief trembled in pain, groaning loudly as he gasped air in and out. Sweat streaked down his brow, and his eyes glittered with fear.

Ransom came off his bed and grabbed his fallen sword, then strapped the scabbard around his waist.

"Your timing . . ." he said to Guivret, shaking his head.

"What shall we do with these blackguards?" Guivret aimed the point of his sword at Bodkin's back.

"Take them to the dungeon, under guard. And get a barber to remove his new tail."

The Espion were ushered from the room, Bodkin moaning as two of his men helped him move. There was blood on the floor, but not a copious amount. The vial lay there as well, its contents leaking out. Ransom took it and stared at it a moment.

The Espion who had held the crossbow on him was still there, looking rather pleased with himself.

"Thank you," Ransom told the man.

"Thank Cecily as well," he said. "When Bodkin was in a hurry to leave Averanche, she suspected treachery. I warned some of your knights about the plan."

Guivret nodded to him. "For that, we are grateful." He turned back to Ransom. "What are you going to do with Bodkin? You could execute him, you know."

"I'm going to bring him back to Averanche to face the king's justice," Ransom said. "It won't be a comfortable ride, but he'll manage the pain somehow."

"Oh, it'll hurt," Guivret promised. "A great deal."

Ransom examined the vial again. "Where did he get this, I wonder?"

The Espion who had saved him shrugged. "I don't know, but he's been in contact with Pisan to make arrangements for Cecily to go there. Twenty thousand livres. A hefty sum."

Perhaps they'd given the concoction to him as a boon, a message of goodwill. Or had he gotten it from Alix?

He sighed. "I don't think I'm going to be able to sleep the rest of the night."

"Come to the great hall," Guivret said. "Rest among those who are loyal to you."

Ransom agreed and rolled up the parchment and put it back in the tube. He went back to the great hall with the others, relieved that he'd managed not to be poisoned . . . or worse. There was still a fire in the hearth, and he took a chair by it with Guivret and his new Espion friend.

"What's your name?" Ransom asked.

"Hans Dragan," said the fellow.

Something about that name sounded familiar. He felt a strange connection to the man without quite understanding why. Then again, he'd become accustomed to such things. He'd felt this way before, especially in the palace cistern, where he'd seen a flash of a boy and a girl. It had felt like he was being given a glimpse of another life. Another possibility. But the meaning of it eluded him.

They sat by the fire, talking in low voices so as not to disturb the sleep of the knights, but a howl of pain pierced the quiet. Guivret raised his eyebrows. "The barber must have pulled out that quarrel just now."

"It was barbed," said Hans.

Some of the sleeping knights lifted their heads from their pallets, looking around the great hall in confusion, and Ransom found himself chuckling.

$$\text{\Large \reflectbox{M}\kern-0.3em M}$$

They reached Averanche after two more days, a slower journey than normal because of the prisoners. Bodkin and the Espion who had attacked him traveled in irons, surrounded by knights at all times. By the time they arrived, Bodkin was weak from pain and blood loss and looked feverish. They left the lesser Espion in the courtyard under guards, while Ransom, Guivret, and Hans Dragan took Bodkin to see the king. There was no attempt to bribe or threaten them. The Espion master was completely miserable, his eyes haunted by what he knew must be coming.

They were told the king and queen were waiting for them in the solar, and so they made their way up the stairs. Bodkin whimpered as he went. Ransom saw the queen and the prince first, standing close to each other. The king was pacing nervously. When he saw Bodkin in chains, his brow furrowed with worry.

"What's the meaning of this?" he demanded of Ransom.

"He attempted to stop you from achieving peace with your dukes," Ransom said, unslinging the leather tube and extending it to the king. "I arrived at Beestone two days ago, and he ambushed me in the middle of the night and tried to poison me. He'd been skulking beneath the castle."

Jon-Landon's eyes shot wide, and he regarded Bodkin with a look of betrayal.

"As I understand the situation," Ransom continued, "he had tried persuading you to leave the kingdom. To seek refuge in Callait with your treasure."

The king scowled. "That plan was supposed to be secret. He tried to poison you?"

Ransom removed the vial from his pocket and showed it to the king. The queen studied it too, then glowered at Bodkin.

"He planned to destroy the charter, my lord," Ransom said. "The one that will ensure peace with your dukes."

"But at what cost?" the king asked.

"Open it," said his wife eagerly.

He twisted open the cap and took the rolled parchment over to the table. After spreading it out, he and his queen pored over the tiny writing. Ransom looked at Bodkin and saw defeat on his face. He hadn't even tried to speak in his own defense.

The prince, Devon, came to the table and joined his parents. "What does it say, Maman?"

She told him to wait for her to finish. Ransom watched Jon-Landon's expression as he came to the end of the document. It held a mixture of disappointment and relief. He shook his head in wonderment.

"This charter . . ." he said with a pause. "It *binds* me."

Ransom said nothing, but he gave the king a hard look.

"This would apply to all the nobles of the realm?" Queen Léa said. She didn't look entirely pleased by the prospect. "Even those who did not rebel. My father?"

"Yes, including him," Ransom said.

"My father would never have agreed to something like this," Jon-Landon said with bitterness.

"You're right. And he lost the hollow crown and died."

Léa took Jon-Landon's hand and squeezed it. "You have no choice."

That was an encouraging sign. Ransom dared to hope.

Jon-Landon rubbed his eyebrow, which had started twitching. "This decision affects not only me. It will bind our son. It will bind future kings."

"It will," Ransom said.

"But at least you will still be king," Léa said coaxingly. "I don't like Lord Kiskaddon either. It will be insufferable to bear his gloating, but we risk losing everything if we refuse."

"He's not gloating," Ransom said to pacify her. "The Occitanians have attacked Kingfountain by sea. I believe they will strike you here, my lord. You must decide and then live with the consequences. Just as your brothers have. Just as your father did."

"Kingfountain is under attack?" Jon-Landon asked worriedly.

That he didn't know meant he'd lost control of his own Espion.

"Yes, but Duke Kiskaddon is defending it. There are armed mobs in the city, rioting in your name. If you end this, we can defend the city together. I've brought two hundred knights with me from Beestone to bring you safely away."

"I am safe enough here," Jon-Landon said.

Ransom shook his head. "No, I don't think so. If Estian is coming with his whole army, we do not have enough men to defend Averanche by land and sea. I advise to flee north, to Glosstyr."

Léa gazed at her husband imploringly. "Please. Heed him. He has done what you asked. The people will rally if they know Lord Ransom stands by you."

The king scowled, but the desperate situation was compelling him to act wisely. "I will go to Glosstyr. I'm loath to give up another castle to the Occitanians." He took Léa's hand in his own and squeezed it, and for a moment Ransom believed he still cared for her, despite his bad faith. "Especially this one. There are memories here that I don't want Estian to steal."

Léa smiled at him and kissed his mouth. "He cannot steal those, my love."

"We should go, then, without delay." The king glared at Bodkin. "Thank you for bringing reinforcements. I've heard nothing in days about the state of Occitania's armies. Now I know why."

The Espion master's shoulders slumped.

"Put him in the river," Jon-Landon said angrily, motioning for Bodkin to be taken away. "Let the sea claim his bones."

Guivret and Hans Dragan hastened to follow his command and dragged the man from the room.

"What of the charter?" Ransom pressed.

Jon-Landon turned and went back to the table and looked over the charter again. He glanced down at his son, who'd come to stand by his side.

"What do you say, young prince? This charter will affect us both. Should I stamp it with my seal?"

"Will it end the war with our lords?" the prince asked.

"Aye, lad, it will. And Lord Ransom advises it."

"If Lord Ransom advises it," said the boy with great solemnity, "then I think you should, Father."

Ransom felt the tingling sensation of the Fountain go up his spine as he looked from father to son. Jon-Landon nodded in agreement. From a pouch at his waist, he withdrew the king's seal. It was the same one the Elder King and Benedict had used. He stared at it a moment, lost in thought. Then the queen brought him an ink sponge, and he pressed the seal into the ink. Ransom felt the tingling turn into a rush of power. The Fountain approved of this moment. He felt giddy inside as he watched the king press the seal to the parchment.

"It is done," he said. "It cannot be undone."

The boy took his father's hand in a trusting way. "It is done. It cannot be undone."

The queen smiled at both of them. "I wish your sister could have been here to see this," she said. "It affects her as well."

A muffled noise came from the curtain, and Princess Léanore huffed and came out, exposing her companion. It was Willem.

"I was here, I was here!" she said with glee and a mischievous smile.

The king and queen looked surprised. Ransom was about to go to the curtain, but Willem came out of his own volition. "Devon's here too," he said.

Another curtain rustled, and the other lad emerged. "You didn't have to tell, Will!"

Ransom laughed despite himself, amused by their daring.

"Sorry, Father," Willem said.

"I'm not sorry," Devon said. "Can we watch Bodkin go into the river? Please?"

Jon-Landon smirked at the boys and then raised his eyebrows at Ransom. "I have another suggestion. Rather than watch an execution, perhaps they might enjoy traveling to Glosstyr with Sir Dawson. And then . . . back to Legault. I think Lady Claire misses them."

"I want to go to Legault too!" implored the princess.

The boys exchanged eager looks and rushed to Ransom for an embrace. His heart felt swollen in his chest. He looked at the king in gratitude.

"You've proven your loyalty beyond question," the king said. "Take your sons. Send them home."

I returned to Connaught after all the petitions were judged. And to my utter surprise, I found Sir Dawson had just arrived with Willem and Devon. You can imagine my astonishment. I hugged those big boys tightly, amazed at how much they'd grown, and smothered them with kisses that they patiently endured. Sir Dawson related the news as quickly as he could but then gave me a letter Ransom had written the day before. I cannot express my relief and joy at the possibility that peace might come at last.

Ransom has brokered an agreement between the lords of the realm, Kiskaddon included. They call it the Charter of the Noble Assizes, and the king has added his seal to it. It means that Legault cannot be stripped away from me without a trial of our peers called the Assizes. And that Ransom's duchy is protected and can be handed down to our heirs in perpetuity. He told me of a miracle that happened at the sanctuary of Our Lady. The river swelled over its banks after his duel with Guivret—who is alive!—to signal to Kiskaddon that Ransom had spoken the truth. I don't think my heart can take in so much good news at once.

The king's family and his treasures are being moved to Glosstyr. Riders have been sent north to stop the fighting between Faulkes and James. I've not heard what has happened to the ships I sent to Kingfountain. But this may truly be the end of dark times. I rejoice. I wish Ransom could have come in person, but he's protecting Jon-Landon and guarding them on their journey. Sir Dawson has asked leave to return to Glosstyr to meet them there. I think he also wants to go back because there is a certain member of the Espion he fancies. I'd like to meet this Cecily and thank her for saving Ransom from abduction. I don't pity Bodkin. His death was deserved.

—Claire de Murrow
Connaught Castle
(rays of hope)

CHAPTER
TWENTY-SIX

A Will Stronger than Iron

The wind howled from the north, and the gusty bursts made Ransom's cloak flap behind him. He missed Dappled, but he rode a sturdy destrier and carried a lance, guarding the wagons with his knights as they lumbered north to Glosstyr. At the slow pace of the heavy wagons, it would take three days to reach the fortress.

Guivret had returned to Kingfountain to tell Duke Kiskaddon that the charter had been signed, that he had seen the king's seal with his own eyes. Ransom would have preferred for the knight to stay—he trusted him implicitly now that he'd been lifted from Alix's spell—but it was imperative the message be sent by someone reliable. And Ransom could not delay getting Jon-Landon to safety. A warning rippled through his mind. His magic had been stronger than usual lately, rendered so by his acts of loyalty to the Argentines. To the Fountain itself, brought on by his Fountain magic, which had filled him to the brim to reward him for his loyalty to the crown.

"Sir Galt," Ransom said to one of his knights nearby.

"Aye, my lord?"

"Take ten others and go back to Averanche. Scout our retreat and all roads leading there. I don't want to be taken unawares."

"The last scouts saw nothing," Galt said with confusion. "No sign of the enemy at all."

"Do it again," Ransom ordered. "I have an ill feeling in my bones."

"As you command, my lord." The knight gave him a salute and rode off to gather his fellows and depart from the host.

They expected to arrive at St. Penryn by nightfall, and Ransom had sent a knight ahead to warn the deconeus they were coming. There was still no word from North Cumbria or Kingfountain, which would have been nearly impossible to get back so soon. He hoped news of the charter had arrived in time to prevent more bloodshed.

As the sun waned in the sky and the blustering wind began to spatter occasional blasts of rain, half the knights he'd sent south returned, riding at breakneck speed to catch up with the rear guard.

Ransom turned his destrier and went to meet them.

Sir Galt's face was pale with fear, which made Ransom's stomach tighten and twist like ropes.

"Well?" Ransom asked.

Sir Galt wiped the sweat from his face. "You were right, my lord. There is trouble. The Occitanians have invaded. An army is coming behind us."

Ransom stared at him in dismay. "Where is it?"

"Part has stopped to lay siege to Averanche."

The coil in Ransom's stomach tightened. "Part, you say?"

"The rest are coming after us," Galt said with worry. "I lost three men trying to escape. A fourth never came back from his road, so I assume he's been captured. They've chased us all the way back here."

"How many chased you?"

"Fifty. They broke off when we came within sight of you. They'll rejoin the others."

"How many knights?"

"Eight hundred, maybe? More? They also have foot soldiers and siege engines and wagons. I've never seen a host so large. Several thousand at least."

This was the news he'd been dreading. The attack on Kingfountain had been a feint—Estian had been preparing for this effort all along. His pieces on the Wizr board were circling around Jon-Landon and his children, preparing to knock them down once and for all. This was the end of the game—the final threat and mate.

He looked at the other knights who had ridden with Galt. To a man, they appeared fearful and chastened.

With over eight hundred knights bearing down on them, they wouldn't be able to reach Glosstyr in time without abandoning the king's treasure, which would then fall into Estian's hands.

"Thank you for your service," Ransom said to Galt and the others. "Stand ready to defend the king's family."

"Aye, my lord," said Galt with conviction.

Ransom turned and struck his destrier's flanks hard to encourage a gallop. He passed the creaking wagons and the unwitting drovers. Then he hurried past the queen's wagon, catching up to the king and his son, who rode before it.

When he reached them, Jon-Landon nodded a greeting to him. "How far to St. Penryn? Will we be there after nightfall?"

"We can't stop at St. Penryn," he blurted.

The king's look darkened. "What is it?"

"I sent knights earlier today to go back down the road toward Averanche. The Black King is coming."

"How many?"

"Thousands."

Jon-Landon's eyes widened with shock. "By the Lady! So many?"

"My lord, we must abandon the wagons. Their advance scouts are already on our heels."

"I will not!" Jon-Landon said sharply. "I've gathered it and preserved it and—"

"It will do you no good if they catch us!" Ransom interrupted. "My lord, the peril is real. If we left yesterday, we'd be halfway to Glosstyr already."

"You condemn me? This is my fault?"

"No, my lord. I'm saying eight hundred or more knights are bearing down on us. We're outnumbered, and our baggage makes us slow. The storm that's coming will turn the road into a mire."

Jon-Landon's scowl was fierce. "No! I did not come this far to lose everything I've saved to Estian. I'll not lose an even greater ransom than what he took from Bennett."

Ransom stared into his eyes, trying to get through to him. "Maybe it's not the treasure he wants. It's your life."

The king glowered. "You must buy us time. Take my knights and add them to yours. Hold the road. Give us time to escape."

Ransom's feeling of danger, of unease, seemed to double. "My lord, we might hold them off for a time, but I can't stop the full host."

"But most of them will be on foot," Jon-Landon countered. "We must try, Ransom. I command it."

Ransom lowered his head in anger. The coins meant nothing to him. But he knew what it felt like to lose everything. He recognized the king's look of desperation, his fear of failure, and he saw the same emotions in the prince's eyes. The boy was listening keenly to their conversation, glancing back and forth between them as they spoke. Then Ransom's gaze caught something behind the prince—massive thunderheads coming from the north. He didn't recall seeing them earlier.

"As you command, my lord, but at least send the women ahead on horseback. Get them to safety."

"Where? St. Penryn?"

Ransom shook his head. "I don't trust Estian to honor the right of sanctuary."

"He won't," Jon-Landon agreed. "Glosstyr is still too far away."

"And that's where they are expecting us to go. They might send outriders to stop our flight."

"You're right. Wait—Lady Deborah's castle is even closer! Thorngate. It's to the east. That may work, but they don't have a strong garrison. We'd need to send some knights ahead to bolster it."

"Of course," Ransom agreed. "Come, let's tell the queen what's happening."

They circled back and approached the wagon, the prince coming with them.

"What's happening?" the queen demanded.

Rain began to plunk on the roof of the wagon, and the wind howled in accompaniment.

"Estian is behind us," Jon-Landon said. "With an army bearing down on us."

The queen's eyes blazed with concern. "And we're too far from Glosstyr."

"Thorngate castle is nearby," Lady Deborah suggested immediately.

Ransom smiled at her. "We were thinking the same."

"Yes," Jon-Landon said. "We'll send you with some knights, on horseback, to Thorngate. Lord Ransom will stall their advance while I accompany the remaining wagons to Glosstyr."

"No, Jonny!" the queen said worriedly, her pet name for him slipping out. Ransom had never heard her use it before. "Come to Thorngate too!"

He shook his head adamantly. "I'll not forsake the treasure. I'm bringing it to Glosstyr. I just need you all to be safe."

"But Papa, it's raining!" said his daughter, perplexed. "Are we to ride in the rain?"

Cecily put a hand on the princess's leg. "It'll be an adventure. Think what you can tell Willem and Devon."

The princess smiled, but it didn't quite reach her eyes.

The queen made a grab for Jon-Landon. "Please! Don't leave us!"

"Where will I go?" asked the prince.

"You'll stay with me," said the king. "As before. If we must, we'll ride on to Glosstyr together, just us."

The prince nodded bravely, though he looked sick with fear.

A memory burst into Ransom's mind. The Elder King and Jon-Landon had escaped the burning ruins of Dunmanis with just a handful of knights after the fortress fell. It did not seem to bode well that it was still in Occitania's possession.

Lady Deborah looked at the king. "It would be more prudent if you came with us. A castle is a better defense than a road."

He shook his head stubbornly. His will was like iron at times. "He has siege engines and wagons. We'll need all of our strength to repel him. If I can get Faulkes and Wigant down here with their men, then we may be able to even the odds. No, I'll not be bottled up in a siege. I'll come to your rescue. I promise."

Lady Deborah seemed to have misgivings, but she did not speak them. "We'd best get horses ready, then. I'm a fair rider, but not in the dark."

The king gave Ransom an encouraging look. "Get your knights ready to defend the road. I'll send some of my guard to take the women to Thorngate. Send word as soon as you can."

"I'll also send a man ahead to Glosstyr to warn them of the situation. They can bring fresh horses to relieve our beasts. We must rest them, my lord. They've been going all day. If we don't rest them, we'll cripple them."

"I know, Ransom. I'm not a fool."

Ransom gave him a tight nod, attempting to ignore his tone. "I'll do as you say."

A streak of lightning flashed through the sky, and the rain began to pour down in earnest. Thunder boomed overhead. By the next day, the roads would be a muddy mess. Saving the wagons was a fool's errand, and the king was an eejit for persisting in his plan.

Ransom gave Cecily a warning look. The queen and princess needed protection, and not just from the Occitanian army. Cecily was the closest thing they had to a poisoner, and she would need to accompany them to Thorngate. Jon-Landon ordered the wagon to halt, and Ransom turned back and went to his men. The dusk was soon overpowered by the rain and the storm. He sighed with weariness, knowing it would be a long night.

When he reached his mesnie, he reined in. "Did you tell them?" he asked Sir Galt.

"Yes, my lord. What does the king command?"

"He's asked us to defend their escape. We are going to ambush the Occitanians on the road. It's not a fight we can win, but we'll hold them back and provide the royal family a chance to escape. Right now, we must rest our horses and prepare to fight. I don't think they're going to stop, so we can expect them to arrive at the darkest hour of night. We'll use the darkness to our advantage."

The rain sluiced through his hair. He felt it dripping from his beard. The knights were giving him fierce looks, although he saw courage in their eyes, not dread. They had confidence in him and his ability to do the impossible.

"We stand as men of Glosstyr," he said with conviction. "We stand to defend the Argentine family and our own. This is *our* land, not theirs. We do not know weariness; we do not know pain. We do not falter; we do not give ground. We make the Black King fight for every furlong. We are the men of Glosstyr." He raised his fist to the sky. *"Dex aie!"*

"Dex aie!" they shouted as another streak of lightning sizzled in the sky overhead.

I sent Dawson to Glosstyr and finally heard back from Ransom. The Occitanians have invaded and laid siege to Averanche. It is certain to fall, which is another loss in Westmarch that we can ill afford. Jon-Landon is taking his treasure to Glosstyr, where he will convene another council with the estranged lords of the realm.

If he makes it.

An army is coming, and it will converge against Glosstyr. Ransom has asked for ships, which still have not returned from Kingfountain. I need to send men to help, but I don't have enough of them available to bring more than a token force, which will be led by Dearley, who felt duty-bound to hurry to Ransom's aid. The boys want to go to Glosstyr as well. They want to join in the fight, even though they are so young. They both have their father's courage.

—Claire de Murrow
Connaught Castle
(the Wizr pieces are moving)

CHAPTER
TWENTY-SEVEN

The Reach of the Sea

Ransom divided his knights into three companies, but he didn't arrange them in a standard battle formation with a vanguard and right and left flank. Each company was its own vanguard and would attack independently of the others. The goal was for one company to strike fast and hard, then withdraw before the enemy's reinforcements could arrive. The next would attack Estian's army from another side, seeking to draw the bulk of the enemy soldiers that way. While they were reeling from that attack, the third would slam into the front of the group, hitting the divided force like a wedge in a stump, seeking to crack Estian's army in half.

It was a desperate gambit. And it worked.

By dawn, with rain pummeling them all and turning the road to mud, they'd fought four skirmishes with the Occitanian force. They had overturned supply wagons and frightened the foot soldiers with raids punctuated by streaks of lightning. Ransom was exhausted from the constant hit-and-retreat maneuver, but they'd succeeded in stalling the Occitanian advance and providing more time for Jon-Landon's wagons to flee. With dawn a gray smear in the eastern sky, Ransom gave the order for a final retreat and led his knights in a flight toward the wagons.

The Raven scabbard was glowing, but he felt no pain, only weariness. His lances had all broken, and there were none to be found on the road.

"My lord," said Galt, "we had them chasing shadows all night long. It felt good to see them so confused."

Ransom smiled. "Aye, it did. How many do you reckon we have lost?"

Galt scratched his beard. "A score or two? I saw some pikemen take down Sir Connor's horse. It was a bloody mess. He's captured or slain; I don't know which. Sir Barnaby was skewered on an Occitanian lance. But he hurt them in return. I'll warrant they suffered more losses than we did."

"They can afford to," Ransom said with weariness. The onslaught had been relentless, despite their early successes, and in the end, there'd been no choice but to withdraw.

As they rode their exhausted horses up the road, they spied a deserted treasure wagon in the rain-soaked haze.

"Go investigate," Ransom said to Sir Galt, and the knight complied. The axle had broken. The back of the wagon was open, and the treasure had been removed. The team of horses, save one, had been loosed. The other lay dead, slathered in mud and froth. The ruts from the wagon wheels were clearly visible in the fresh-churned mud.

Ransom whistled for his men to ride on, and they caught up to the wagons shortly afterward. The king was soaked, his armor spattered in mud. His dripping hair was plastered to his forehead beneath the chain hood he wore for protection. His eyes were feverish with worry as he approached them on his weary destrier.

"Ransom!" he said with a hopeful smile. "What news?"

A pit of disappointment had hollowed out Ransom's stomach. They'd caught up to the king much too soon. The progress during the night had undoubtedly been stalled after the failure of one of the wagons.

"I'd hoped you'd be farther along, my lord," Ransom said.

"We had a problem with one of the wagons."

"I saw it abandoned."

"Yes, well, I couldn't just leave it like a plum for Estian, could I?"

Ransom shook his head. The prince swayed wearily in his saddle as he rode his horse up next to his father. His cheeks were chalk white.

"You think me foolish?" growled the king.

"We're still too far from Glosstyr, my lord. We blunted the advance, but we couldn't stop it. My men are weary from fighting all night."

"They did their duty," said the king.

It was true, but Ransom didn't want to comment on that. "We need to rest. But their knights might catch us before nightfall, and then we lose the advantage of darkness. Any word from the North?"

"None," said the king, his shoulders slumping. "I've not heard back from any of the knights I sent. I can't afford to send more, we're vulnerable enough as it is."

That was true. Ransom wished the storm would pass, but the sky was overcast, and the day ahead of them promised to be every bit as miserable as the one behind them.

Jon-Landon wiped his mouth on his sleeve and smeared some mud into his goatee and lips. He grimaced. "Pfah! Disgusting. What else can we do?"

Ransom wanted again to suggest abandoning the wagons, but he knew the king wouldn't consider it. It would be impossible to stay ahead of Estian's knights, but man for man, Ransom thought his own force to be superior and more motivated. It was the foot soldiers that were the real threat. They could march faster than the wagons could move, and once they caught up, it would be over. There would be no choice but to flee and abandon the treasure.

"Keep the wagons going. Have men help push. I'll leave one of my companies with you to protect you in case they flank us. We'll rest here and lie in wait for their knights."

The king nodded with eagerness. "Good! How far are we from Glosstyr?"

Ransom sighed. "The road bends about a league ahead. You can see the ocean from there. After that, it's one more league to Glosstyr. We're close, my lord." Not wanting to give the king false assurances, he added, "But they are even closer behind us."

"Hold them back," the king said angrily.

"I will do the best I can," Ransom promised.

The king gave him a salute, turned his destrier, and rode back to his wagons. The prince waved at Ransom before turning his horse and following his father. Ransom watched the boy, the final hope of the Argentines, and ordered one of his companies to follow the king and the prince. Their horses wouldn't be able to rest, but at least the pace was slower. That group looked at him with misery, but they obeyed his command.

One company would rest while the other stood guard. They ate some meager rations and huddled beneath trees on each side of the road. Ransom's company were the guardians. He would be the final knight to go to sleep.

The reprieve didn't last long.

Ransom stabbed with his bastard sword and found the chink in his foe's armor. The man let out a groan of pain and then slid off his saddle to land in the muck with a heavy splash. His men had formed a wall to block the road, and they'd held off three attacks from the knights of Occitania. In each attack they'd been outnumbered, but the enemy had not broken through, not with Ransom himself holding the wall.

His other company was preparing a flanking maneuver, getting ready to strike from the trees.

And then the foot soldiers arrived, marching through the mud with diligent purpose, a wall of pikes coming directly at them.

"Curse them!" muttered one of his knights.

The noise of their boots in the mud was an eerie sound, one with a frightening reach. Their tunics were all stained, but their faces were determined and hateful. On they came.

"Fall back," Ransom said to his knights. Staying would only increase the number of dead.

The Occitanian knights were regrouping to give chase. Ransom hoped his other company, the one that had planned on flanking the enemy force, would forbear attacking. He could sense with his dwindling Fountain magic the insurmountable host coming at them. Although he could not see the sun, he knew it was roughly midday. The pit in his stomach yawned. The front ranks of these men would reach Jon-Landon's wagons by nightfall.

As he led his knights into a retreat, a battle cry sounded from behind. The Occitanian knights had rallied again, and they obviously intended to slow their escape until the foot soldiers reached them. He shouted to increase the pace, to win some distance. But it wasn't enough. They were overtaken by a group of knights that appeared from the woods on their right. They'd been outflanked.

"*Dex aie!*" Ransom shouted in warning, brandishing his bastard sword.

The two groups clashed on the muck-strewn road, puddles oozing gray water from the wagon tracks. Ransom heard some of his men fall. He gritted his teeth, slashing against the foes seeking to stall them. His own destrier was sluggish to respond. Although a good beast, it was no Dappled, and the stress of the constant fighting and the difficult terrain had weakened it terribly.

He looked back, seeing the foot soldiers coming toward them. There was a hunger in the soldiers' eyes. A desire to kill the knights who had plagued them.

"Dex aie!" came a shout from the other side of the road, deeper in.

The hidden company of Ransom's men had seen their distress and come to the rescue, mounting an attack on the foot soldiers. Pikes wavered, soldiers turned in confusion. The knights on horseback had a decided advantage in everything but numbers. As he watched his men stanch the foot soldiers' forward progress, a spark of triumph lit within Ransom's breast. He redoubled his attack on the knights, and soon they fled back into the woods to rejoin the advancing army.

It was a reprieve, albeit a brief one. Ransom ordered his men to withdraw again, and the company fighting the foot soldiers turned as well. But many of his knights had been yanked from their horses. It was a brutal conflict. Two sides determined to vanquish. Neither side willing to yield.

They escaped with no one giving chase. Ransom's mind was a fog of weariness. He knew his men were at the breaking point. He could see it in their fearful and determined looks. But their eyes found him, a source of strength, and he rode on without flinching, without flagging. His example lent them strength.

He gave them the courage to keep going despite their weariness.

It was all they had left.

The drizzle persisted all day, and it seemed another storm was on the way. Although the sun had not made an appearance all day, he sensed it was waning, and they'd reached the bend in the road that would bring them within a league of Glosstyr.

Where he expected to find the king's wagons.

Messenger knights had come with the warning that the wagons were all stuck in the mire by the sea. Horses had perished with exhaustion, unable to budge the massive wagons any farther. The conclusion seemed obvious to Ransom—the treasure would need to be abandoned. They couldn't hope to protect it any longer. He told the messenger to return and bring the king to Glosstyr posthaste.

And the knight had returned, miserably, to say the king refused to leave and that he'd drawn his sword when they tried to compel him.

Thick looming clouds continued to blot out the sun. As the trees became sparser, enough so he could see the distant cliffs of his duchy, he heard the sound of the surf and the screech of gulls. He sensed the presence of someone Fountain-blessed ahead. His heart immediately shuddered with fear, but he did the only thing he could. He pressed onward with his men.

He saw the beach finally, the white caps of the surf. But there were no signs of the wagons, horses, or . . .

Where was the king?

Ransom spurred his horse faster in the direction he felt the presence. Sand had come to settle on the road, which was covered with mounds. There were no hoofprints, no tracks at all. The mounds, he realized, were dead men. There were maybe twelve in all. He saw a sword, half-covered in grit. A gray hand was reaching out from beneath a blanket of wet sand.

The horses' hooves, which had been sucking in the mud, now gave wet hisses as the ground changed to sand. There was no sign of the treasure, no spilled caskets or chests. He searched frantically for the king, for the prince.

"What happened here?" asked Sir Galt in confusion.

Ransom sensed the presence coming from the direction of the water. There was a man slumped by the sea, kneeling in the sand, getting doused by the waves as they glided up the shore. But that was not the source of the feeling, which was coming from farther away, where the cliffs of the cove were murky in the dimming light.

Urging his horse to gain speed, he approached the man kneeling at the water's edge and recognized him to be Jon-Landon. There was a sword next to him, but the sea was burying it rapidly with each wave.

Many of Ransom's men were resting, slumped forward in their saddles from the arduous ride and relentless fighting. Others were going through the sand-strewn wreckage.

The presence he'd felt was still farther ahead. Ransom peered into the gloom, trying to see, and caught the sight of a woman walking away from them with a little boy. His stomach lurched with dread.

Jon-Landon lifted his head and gazed at Ransom in confusion. He looked delirious.

"Attend to the king," Ransom shouted to Galt.

Ransom left them and rode after the woman and the boy in desperation.

Dearley left with a storm on the horizon. Now, from a distance, it seems as if all of Ceredigion is smothered beneath the ill weather. Is this the end of the Wizr game after all? My heart yearns for Ransom. Whatever is happening, he is thrust into the middle of it. I fear I will not see him again, and that thought makes my waking hours torture.

—Claire de Murrow
Connaught Castle
The end of the game

CHAPTER
TWENTY-EIGHT

The Ondine

Ransom's heart pounded with fear as he rode along the glistening shore toward the retreating figures of the woman and the boy. He gripped the hilt of his bastard sword but did not draw it.

They were walking just at the edge of the water, and as he drew nearer them, he noticed the sea never touched them, even though they were walking within its reach. The lapping waters always reoriented themselves to leave a gap for them to continue their journey. The foamy tide reached his own horse and the rest of the beach behind him.

After he closed the distance between them, the woman finally turned to look at him.

It was not Alix.

He was stunned by her otherworldly beauty, the serious eyes, the somber mouth. She was barefoot, and he saw the glimmer of jewelry around her ankle. Devon, who had been walking alongside her, carried a satchel around his shoulders and supported it with both hands. He, too, turned. His eyes had a glazed look, as if he were sleepwalking.

"Who are you?" Ransom asked, his voice suddenly husky with fear. She was powerful with Fountain magic. He sensed it thrumming inside her, while his had been diminished from the efforts of the escape.

"The game is nearly over," she said, her voice rich and melodious but full of significance. "If it is allowed to end now, with the Argentine line failing, the kingdom of Ceredigion will drown in a flood. Not from the sea, as before. It will perish in a storm that will last a hundred years."

His throat caught at her pronouncement. "You speak prophecy."

"I have the mantic gifts," she answered.

He swallowed. "The end you see . . . I have tried to prevent it. I have done all that the Fountain has asked of me."

"It is not enough. Would you give even more?" she asked him, tilting her head. Hair the color of copper rustled with the wind. Again the water from the crashing surf slid up the beach to reach him, but it stopped just short of the pair before him.

The painful throbbing of his heart made him tremble. "What must I do?"

She looked at him without sympathy or judgment. "You can escape the fate of Ceredigion two ways. You can return to the Fair Isle. Take as many as will come. You will save your family and any who come willingly. But Ceredigion will fall. Or you can once again face the Black King's army in battle. If you choose that end, you will die. Your children will be left without a father. Your wife without a husband. But Ceredigion will be saved. The fate of the kingdom and the game will be determined by the move you make on the board. It is your choice, Sir Knight. It always has been."

Her pronouncement smote him between the ribs. He'd sent his sons back to Legault already, and he believed Claire was still there. Whatever came next, his family was safe. That was for the best, but he missed them terribly. The thought of never seeing them again filled him with the deepest anguish he'd ever experienced.

He could hear the distant sound of his men on the beach behind him. Voices were crying his name, but he could not break his eyes from the gaze of the otherworldly woman. Everything within him was fixed on that moment, on her fateful demand.

"Are you the Lady of the Fountain?" he whispered. The power and majesty of her person overwhelmed him, as if she were made of lightning and storm. He trembled with emotion.

"No, Sir Knight. I am an Ondine. A water sprite of the Deep Fathoms."

"Do you serve the Lady?"

A smile flickered on her beautiful mouth. "The Lady you speak of is not what you think. Your people have conjured some strange beliefs about our world."

He stared at her in confusion. "Are you one of the Aos Sí, then?"

"Again, no. That is another conjuring. A fable told and believed and twisted." Her brow softened. "I serve the Essaios—that is their true name. The Unwearying Ones. There was a time when the truth was taught plainly, but even then there were those who would not believe it."

He was confused, but her words were confirmed by the gentle assurances of the Fountain magic inside him. He nodded in acceptance.

"So the Aos Sí are a legend too," he said.

"Yes. A legend from another time. No one was banished beneath the waves. The first man and first woman came to these shores as exiles, half-drowned and hungry. All of this you will learn when your time is finished. After your choice is made." She gave him a meaningful look.

He heard more shouts behind him, along with the crashing of water as the tide came in faster. Still, he could not look away from her.

"If I choose to stay," he asked, "then Devon will live? And his sister?"

"Yes, Sir Knight. And many more."

The awful burden settled on him. He shifted his gaze to Devon—taking in his vacant look, his small hands gripping the leather strap of the satchel. His vision blurred, and he saw another little boy with a spot of white in his hair, clinging to a satchel. Then the image cleared, and it was Devon again.

"I will," Ransom told her. "On my honor as a knight. I will."

Her neutral expression melted into a tender smile. "Until we meet again, Sir Knight. In the Deep Fathoms."

Suddenly a surging wave crashed into his horse. Some of the spray stung Ransom's eyes and drenched both him and the beast. He lifted a hand to wipe his eyes, and when he lowered it, she was gone. Devon had been knocked over by the surf and was sputtering on his hands and knees.

"Lad, come to me!" Ransom called. They were near the cliffs, but there was still a stretch of beach ahead of them.

Devon lifted his head. "S-sir Ransom?" he called in relief.

Another wave was building, this one larger.

"Hurry, lad!"

The prince picked himself up from the gritty sand and came to Ransom, who reached down and pulled him up into the saddle as the next wave struck them. His horse nickered worriedly and adjusted to the force of the wave, which had struck it broadside. As Devon settled on the horse behind him, his little arms wrapped around Ransom's waist.

"I was so scared," the boy said. "Papa told me to take the crown and hide by the rocks. He said she would kill me."

"Who?" Ransom demanded, turning. His knights were waving at him and shouting, but he couldn't hear their words over the wind and the waves.

"The poisoner came," Devon said. "She stabbed Papa. I saw it. Then I ran."

Another awful blow.

Ransom rode away from the pummeling waves, back up to his knights. The king was sitting on the saddle of a horse now, doubled over in pain. Relief filled his eyes when Devon poked his head out from behind Ransom.

Sir Galt approached them first, his face showing alarm. "My lord, that was a water sprite! She was luring you into the waves!"

Another knight spoke up. "We cried for you to come back. Did you hear the music?"

"What music?" Ransom asked.

"It was the strangest music," Galt said in wonder. "Yet you broke her spell."

Ransom wrinkled his nose in confusion because their words didn't make sense to him. The Ondine had saved the boy by taking him away from Alix. She'd warned Ransom of what was to come. However, he thought of the superstitions of his people. Of course they had believed his life was in danger—after being raised on legends of creatures of the Deep Fathoms who could lure men to their deaths with their song.

He looked at the king, but his Fountain magic affirmed Devon's words were true. He could sense the wound. "You're injured," he said.

"Aye," said Jon-Landon. "And the poison is already working. This . . . this is how my brothers died." He grimaced with pain.

"What happened?" Ransom asked in despair.

The king's nostrils flared. "The wagons got bogged down. They were right here," he said, extending his hand and waving it around the beach. "I ordered the knights to dig them out, but they wouldn't obey me. All was lost. I should . . . I should have gone with them to Glosstyr."

He turned his head and gazed at the empty beach. "Gone. It's all gone now. I've lost." He groaned in pain. "Each . . . breath . . . burns."

"When did Alix come?" Ransom asked.

The king looked at him in misery. "Not long ago, riding with a band of knights. They killed my guards. I put the crown in a satchel and gave it to Devon. I see he still holds it. I told him to flee to the rocks, to hide until you came." He grunted again, and Ransom saw a bit of bloody spittle come from his mouth. Alix had plunged the knife in deeply. He'd been dealt a mortal wound, which was perhaps a blessing. The poison would give him a worse death.

"They were about to ransack the wagons," Jon-Landon said with a wheeze. "Then . . . then a wave came, a monstrous wave. I've never seen one so huge. Alix fled with her knights, and the water smote me. I was drowning, Ransom. I choked on it, believing it would carry me down under to the Deep Fathoms." Naked fear blazed on his face. He didn't meet Ransom's eyes, just stared vacantly as if reexperiencing a nightmare.

"The wave buried everything in sand. When it retreated, I was still alive. That's where you found me. The wagons were gone. Everything was gone. I thought my son was dead." He looked up at Ransom. "I'm dying. I don't think I can make it to the castle."

"You will," Ransom said with determination. His heart was sick with grief. He'd watched the man's two brothers and their father die from the same poison. Alix claimed to have a cure, but he'd never seen evidence of it. Nor would she give it to him for any price he was willing to pay.

Ransom looked to the knights who had gathered around them. "We hasten for Glosstyr. Sir Galt, ride ahead and tell them to bring a barber to attend to the king."

"I will, my lord," Galt said. He kicked his horse and started up the slope of sand.

But Ransom no longer held hope that Jon-Landon would survive the night.

As they rode with determination, the rain began to fall again in earnest, coming in heavy, drenching sheets. Night had fallen, and they were all hungry and miserable, but Ransom could see the lights of Glosstyr in the distance. He'd sent a company back to waylay the Occitanians, and the men had returned with word that Estian's army had turned inland and were heading to Thorngate castle, where the queen and princess had taken shelter with Lady Deborah and Cecily. They were no longer giving chase to the king.

Perhaps Jon-Landon's piece had already been removed from the Wizr board . . . or Alix had simply reported her deed. Had Devon's piece disappeared from the board too when he was with the Ondine? That would explain the shift in strategy, for Estian would believe—at least for a while—that Princess Léanore was the last Argentine. And since Jon-Landon had murdered all the Occitanian hostages, Ransom thought it realistic that Estian would not spare anyone either. Even women and children. He'd once threatened to execute everyone in Josselin castle in front of Ransom's very eyes.

The king was so weak that they had him mount behind one of the other knights and ride double. He groaned with agony, suffering from the dagger wound as well as the poison ravaging his system. Ransom thought about his promise to the Ondine—to the Fountain—to sacrifice his life so that the boy could survive. He believed the prince would be a better king than his father, if given a chance, but he hadn't done it just for him. He'd chosen to save the people of the kingdom.

When they were still about a league away from Glosstyr, they encountered riders coming from the castle, led by Sir Dawson. They'd brought fresh mounts as well as some bread and wine.

"I'm so grateful we found you!" Dawson said. "Where is the king?"

Ransom nodded to the horse next to him. Jon-Landon's cloak had concealed his identity. In the torchlight, the king's face had a sickly pallor.

One look at the king, and Dawson blanched. His eyes met Ransom's, and they shared an unspoken understanding. The king was nearly dead.

"Is there a barber waiting?"

"I thought there might be wounded men, so I brought him with us," Dawson said. "Come forward!"

While the knights took a brief rest and ate amidst the rainstorm, the soaked barber followed Ransom and Dawson as they brought the king beneath a tree. The light was brought up, revealing the crimson stain spilling from his lower ribs. The dagger had pierced his hauberk. Devon crouched by his father's side, holding his hand and speaking comforting words to him.

Dawson shook his head. "He's almost gone," he muttered to Ransom.

"The blade was poisoned too. She took no chances."

Dawson swore under his breath. "How far back is Estian's army?"

"They broke off the chase," Ransom answered. "They're going to Thorngate now."

"Why?" Dawson demanded.

"That's where the princess is. I don't think they realize the prince escaped. He was guarded by a water sprite at the cove back yonder. All the treasure is gone. It's been dragged out to sea."

"He should have left it," Dawson said with a snarl.

"I can't argue. Tell me—how is Claire? How are my chil-dren?" His voice caught as he spoke. The pang of losing them struck him hard. He felt tears sting his eyes, but the raindrops dripping down his face masked them.

"The boys wanted to come with me!" Dawson said with a grin. "Claire is hale. It was good seeing her again. She sent ships to drive the Occitanians away from Kingfountain. We're still waiting for word on what happened. Your daughters are also well. It was good to see the boys with Sibyl again. But they miss the princess. Willem keeps talking about when they'll see her again and what mischief they'll do!"

Ransom chuckled at that, and then the pain hit his chest so hard he choked and began to weep.

Dawson looked at him in concern. But he didn't ask what was wrong. "There's more news, Ransom. None of it good."

He nodded for Dawson to speak, unable to get any words out.

Dawson sighed and shook his head. "News from the North."

Ransom's stomach clenched. He wondered if he'd fall to the ground. "What?" he croaked.

Dawson's lips were pressed into a tight line. Then he spoke. "Wigant and Faulkes had a battle before news of the charter arrived. They fought for two days, neither side relenting. By the time your messenger arrived, only a few companies had survived the carnage. Both men survived, but their armies were destroyed."

Hearing the words, he felt a surge of darkness within him. He'd been counting on Faulkes's and James's knights to help drive Estian out of Ceredigion. The truth bludgeoned him.

He would be facing Estian alone.

A ship from Genevar sought safe harbor today. It had fled Blackpool two days ago and was nearly torn apart by the storm. It will limp down to Atha Kleah for repairs. The waters around the Fair Isle are much calmer. But the news the captain brought made my heart chill. He said Faulkes and James nearly destroyed each other in their fight before the charter was revealed. They lost, between them, about one hundred and sixty knights and hundreds of foot soldiers. The Genevese ship was sent to bring mercenaries to join the fight, but they've judged the odds to be stacked against them, and they want nothing of it now.

Occitania has invaded Ceredigion. And Ransom is facing the onslaught by himself. I have no ships to send. What I had, I already did, and I've still not heard from the fleet I sent earlier. I fear they might not return. Ransom, if I could walk on the waters between these lands, I would, to come to you.

I'm sick at heart. Please, beloved. I love you too much for you to die.

—Claire de Murrow
Connaught Castle
(on the fate of a Genevese ship)

CHAPTER
TWENTY-NINE

A Final Breath, Then Dawn

Ransom startled awake and realized he'd fallen asleep in a chair at the table. His eyes felt puffy, and he could feel the grit of the sand still chafing his skin beneath his clothes. The only light came from the hearth, which crackled with some fresh logs.

"You're awake," Dearley said with a smile in his voice.

Ransom blinked at the sight of his friend sitting in a stuffed chair by the door leading from the solar. They'd finally made it to the fortress of Glosstyr, soaked to the bone, but Ransom hadn't expected Dearley. At least not yet.

"When did you get here?" Ransom asked, stretching and hearing little pops in his back.

Dearley shrugged. "By midnight. The waves were too fierce to bring the ship closer, so we came on smaller boats from the harbor. I've got a hundred men with me."

That wouldn't be nearly enough to overcome the force Estian had brought.

"Is the king still alive?" Ransom asked.

"He's struggling to breathe, but yes. When I saw him, he looked like a corpse."

"I should go to him," Ransom said, pushing himself to stand.

"James is here," Dearley said. "Dawson came to tell you, but I thought you needed some sleep, even if it was on a tabletop. Simon arranged a bed for the duke."

"Thank you." He gave Dearley a probing look, and his heart suddenly seized with pain. "How is Claire?" He barely managed to get the words out.

"Worried about you. So am I. If I understand the situation, it's pretty hopeless. Jon-Landon is about to go to the Deep Fathoms. Two duchies nearly choked each other to death. And Estian has laid siege to Thorngate, where the queen and her daughter have sought shelter. It won't hold for long. There's also news of some charter the king signed. But what good is it now?"

Ransom rubbed his eyes. The memory of the Ondine's words pulsed within his mind. It was painful realizing he was going to die. He wanted to tell Dearley, but he felt a throb of warning not to. It was his burden to carry.

"Are you all right?" Dearley asked softly.

"I don't think I've been in a more terrible situation," Ransom said. It was a struggle, but he composed himself. "We have to go defend Thorngate. But first, let me congratulate you on your daughter's birth. I'm happy for you and your dear wife."

Dearley rose, and the two men embraced. Even though the situation felt hopeless, there were still blessings worthy of rejoicing.

They talked for a few more moments before Ransom excused himself. "I should see how the king fares," he said, clapping Dearley on the back before he turned to leave the room. As he made his way to and up the stairs, he double-checked to ensure the guards were in their places. They'd been posted at regular intervals.

When he arrived at the king's sickchamber, he recoiled from the stench of death. He'd witnessed this kind of languishing death before with Jon-Landon's family. How grateful he was that Duchess Emiloh had not lived to witness her final son's murder.

There were two knights standing guard at the door, and they nodded to Ransom as he passed. The barber sat at the king's side with a goblet of wine in his hand. The poison had progressed quickly, and Jon-Landon's eyes were bleeding. Ransom clamped his mouth shut, noticing Devon curled up in a chair, fast asleep, breathing softly. What a horrible scene for the lad.

"Lord Ransom is here," said the barber.

"Is he? Truly?" The king suppressed a cough.

"I am," Ransom answered. The barber rose from the bedside and shook his head, indicating there was no hope left.

"I feared . . . you'd forsaken me," Jon-Landon said. "But I knew . . . I knew you wouldn't."

"I fell asleep in the solar," Ransom said. "I'm sorry. I would have come sooner."

"I know. I'm not scolding you. You were there . . . *unngh* . . . when the first Argentines died. Fitting . . . *fitting* that you'd still be here when it's my turn."

Ransom gestured for the cup, and the barber gave it to him. Sitting by the edge of the bed, he brought his palm behind the king's neck and lifted him slightly. "Drink this."

The king took a very little sip and grimaced. Each breath seemed to pain him. "Thank you. Send the barber away."

Ransom set the goblet down on the small table near the bed. He glanced at the barber, but he'd already risen to leave, likely grateful to have been relieved of his post.

"Is my son . . . still here?"

"He's asleep on the chair."

"I told him to go to bed, but he wouldn't leave my side. I'm . . . glad he's asleep. I didn't want him to watch . . . me die."

Ransom put his hand atop the king's and gently squeezed.

"I can't see. My eyes are . . . too sticky. But you're here. You will . . . you will see that my son is made king?"

"I will," Ransom answered.

The king exhaled a ragged breath. "I don't know which pain is from the dagger and which is from the poison. Is she really my . . . my half sister?"

Ransom's heart squeezed again with pain. "She is. What happened to your mother was terrible. But it was not her fault."

"I . . . I wish I had known Mother better. Like you did. You served her for so long. I . . . was too resentful. My father poisoned me against her."

"I know," Ransom said sadly. "He shouldn't have."

"He was a proud man. You knew that." His breath was coming in shorter and shorter gasps. His lips were turning blue.

"He was indeed," Ransom said with a chuckle.

"He just . . . he wanted her to be proud of him. My mother. He wanted her . . . *unnghh*, respect." The king weakly reached with his other hand and put it on Ransom's. "Please . . . I don't want . . . to die."

Ransom could have used the scabbard to heal the dagger wound, just as he had used it to stanch Elodie's bleeding during childbirth. But it did not work against poison, and it was the poison that would have prolonged the king's death, making it even more painful.

"We all must go to the Deep Fathoms in our time," Ransom said.

"I'm afraid," Jon-Landon said with desperation.

"What of?"

"I didn't believe . . . I didn't want to believe. But I saw the flood come. I saw the wave that struck us. It's real. The Fountain. The Lady. It's real. And what will happen to me? Ransom? What if I'm cursed?" The panic in his voice was awful to hear.

Ransom waited, thinking, watching the gasping breaths come. It wouldn't be long now.

"I don't know what happens there," Ransom said. "But I know that things do not end. When I served your father, one night in the palace I heard a voice calling my name. A quiet voice in the still of the night. I went to one of the fountains in the palace and saw the shade of King Gervase."

Jon-Landon squeezed Ransom's hand hard. "His . . . shade?"

"Truly. He told me of that other world. He told me it is different than this one. Kinder. Gentler. I think . . . I think they *weep* for us, my lord. At what we do to each other here."

"Will my . . . father be there?"

"I think he's there now. And Devon, Goff, and Bennett. And your mother."

The king writhed in pain. "I'd be too ashamed to see them. After all I've done. How I've been persuaded to do . . . the unthinkable. What I've lost now."

"I think they would understand the dilemmas you've faced," Ransom said.

The king grunted. "A favor, Lord Ransom. A final one. Please."

"Anything, my lord," Ransom said, leaning forward.

"Don't . . . don't tell my wife."

Ransom frowned. "Tell her what?"

"Don't tell her what a wretched man I am. What I did . . . to your sister. To others. Especially the boy. His death haunts me the most. Men like Bodkin . . . encouraged me to do what I wanted. They told me the Deep Fathoms was only a myth for children, and there would be no price to pay for breaking the oaths of my office. I did awful things, Ransom. I was . . . horrible. I tried to . . . to break you." His grip began to slacken. "But you were . . . made of stronger stuff. You were iron. I couldn't . . . bend you. If she finds out . . . don't lie. But please . . . don't ruin her belief in me. I . . . oh, by the Lady . . . I . . . I . . . I'm dying . . . I'm dying. Can't . . . breathe . . . don't let me go . . . don't let me die yet! Léa . . ."

Pain squeezed Ransom's heart as he heard the final breath wheeze out. Tears trickled down Ransom's cheeks. He grieved for the king, for the man he could have been, for the regrets that had tormented him at the end. Jon-Landon had longed for the comfort of his wife's touch, her voice, in his final moment, but that wish hadn't been granted to him. And Ransom doubted he would have that comfort either.

A prick of light stabbed him in the eye, coming from a chink in the storm clouds and shutters. Dawn had come with the king's dying breath. Ransom sat in the stillness, hearing the gentle sigh of a little boy fast asleep. His own breath came in choking sobs as he mourned the death of yet another king. A king whose only friend, in the end, had been Ransom. The burden was too heavy. He felt it breaking him.

One of the knights standing guard stepped into the room.

"He's gone, then?"

Ransom couldn't speak, but he nodded.

"Then that's the end of this," the knight said darkly. "Foul and salty as the sea is, it will be made fouler still by Jon-Landon Argentine."

"What of the boy?" asked another knight. "Do we stand guard still?"

"No," Ransom said, rising from the bed. "I'll take him to my room."

Walking around the bedside, Ransom carefully cradled Devon Argentine in his arms and held him close as he walked away from the awful scene of death.

They were gathered in the great hall of Glosstyr's majestic fortress. A final council of war. Ransom led the meeting, which consisted of Simon of Holmberg, Dearley, Dawson, James Wigant, Lord Faulkes, and three lesser lords who had come after receiving word of the treaty and Estian's attack. The look of rivalry between James and Faulkes showed the bitterness between the two men. They were done with fighting each other, but their mutual antipathy hung in the air like smoke.

"Any word from Kiskaddon?" James asked after Ransom had explained the situation and the lopsided balance of power between the kingdoms.

"None," Simon answered flatly.

James looked haggard and worried. He had a bruise on his cheek and scratches on his brow.

"Why not go to Kingfountain, combine our forces, then return to break the siege against Thorngate?" Faulkes suggested.

Dawson leaned forward. "Because Thorngate cannot last that long. It's not a powerful fortress. According to our sources, Estian's army has already broken past the outer walls—"

"How did they manage that so quickly?" Faulkes countered angrily.

"He brought siege engines," Dawson said, glaring at Faulkes. "He's planning to use them on Kingfountain itself."

"And you know this how?"

Ransom held up his hand to stop Dawson, who looked ready to punch Faulkes in the mouth. The man had feelings for Cecily, and she was there in the castle to protect the queen, Lady Deborah, and the princess. Estian had the Wizr board, so he knew exactly where they were. Slipping out of the castle would be too risky. No, they had to wait for help to come to them.

"Estian has the interior of the town," Ransom said. "The last message arrived during breakfast. They'll try to break through the keep. We don't have much time."

"We have the hollow crown," James said. "Why not name our own king? Forget the charter."

"I knew you'd say that," Faulkes growled.

James gave his enemy a withering look.

"That's not possible," Ransom said.

"It is, actually," James countered. "Hear me out. Ransom . . . it could be you—"

"No!" Ransom shouted, loudly enough that the room fell silent.

"You alone command enough respect," James persisted. "Not a boy, not *that* boy."

Ransom shook his head. "You don't understand."

"I understand the situation pretty well, I think," James said angrily. "Estian has come with his full force. We do not have enough men to counter him. If we go to Kingfountain, we'd at least stand a chance. Let Thorngate fall."

"No!" Dawson snarled.

"Why not you, Wigant? Why don't you be king?" Faulkes taunted.

"I am of noble blood, but sadly I lack the resources and don't command the respect. Give it to Kiskaddon, then! But breaking the siege at Thorngate will accomplish nothing."

"If it were your wife and child there, would you feel differently?" Dearley asked pointedly.

James frowned and shot an angry look instead of a reply. Then he threw up his hands. "If only this abominable rain would end! Some of the roads have already washed out, and there are rivers of water coming from the hills. It must end eventually."

"It won't end until this conflict ends," Ransom said. "Our kingdom will be flooded. The rain will not stop. Winter will not come. We will be trapped in perpetual autumn until there is no way to grow food, no way to live, and no way to escape."

Faulkes looked at him with incredulity, James with confusion.

"But it's only a storm," the duke of the North said.

Ransom shook his head. "No, it is a punishment. An ancient curse. It destroyed King Andrew's court and shattered his kingdom. And it will befall us next if we do not band together and confront this threat to our realm."

Faulkes shifted uneasily. "You sound rather certain of this."

"Once the lad is crowned at Kingfountain, I believe the storm will end."

"Then why not crown him now and see?" Simon said. Turning to the others, he said, "Look, gentlemen, I know this is difficult to understand, but there are forces at work here that you do not know about. But I can assure you they are very real. The sea heaved itself beyond its bounds and took the king's treasure. Maybe you've heard about a similar incident that happened on the bridge outside the sanctuary of Our Lady—"

"We don't have time for a coronation ceremony," Ransom said, breaking in. "We don't have time to summon the deconeus of the sanctuary of Our Lady or even St. Penryn. If we don't break Estian's army here and now, we may be securing our own doom. We cannot abandon the defenders of Thorngate. I know Estian. I know what he's capable of."

"That's what worries me," Faulkes said. "He'll want revenge."

"So we must stop him," Ransom said. "We must go . . . today . . . now! I know you're both weary of fighting, but you are needed. Devon needs you."

"What if we lose?" James said.

"With that attitude, how can we not?" Dawson quipped.

James glared at him. "Will someone shut this upstart up?"

Ransom appreciated Dawson's exuberance, but a knight railing against a duke was disrespectful. He gave Dawson a subtle shake of his head, and the knight sat back angrily.

He faced the others in the council with a stern gaze. "If we fall, if everyone abandons the boy but me, do you know what I will do? I will carry him on my back. And as long as I can hold him up, I will hop from island to island, from kingdom to kingdom, even if I have to beg for my bread. That is what *I* am willing to do to see this kingdom saved. What of you?"

He was willing to do more. He was willing to give up his own life. But he felt a nudge of warning not to say so.

The passion in his voice affected them.

"I'll go with you," Dearley said.

Dawson grunted and nodded in affirmation.

Simon nodded as well. "To the end, my lord."

Ransom turned to Faulkes next.

The lord had been loyal to Jon-Landon while he was alive. But he hadn't wanted to watch the king die. His allegiance could not be counted on.

"Aye," Faulkes said. "I'll do it for the princess and the prince. None of this is their fault."

They turned as one to look at Lord James.

He sat unflinching. His teeth were clenched with anger, and his fingers gripped the armrests of his chair.

"I left my wife and child at Ploemeur," he said finally and firmly. "And that is where I am going next. You can have the realm. I'm done with it."

Ransom dispatched a letter to me, despite the storms raging over Glosstyr. The king is dead, and his body is being sent to Kingfountain for the final rites. But Ransom is not going there. He is determined to face Estian alone and drive him out of Ceredigion or perish. These unnatural storms will only subside if the boy Devon becomes king. That is what the Fountain told him, he said. He said it might be his last letter to me and that he goes willingly to face his foes. He asked me not to mourn if the worst happens, but how can I not? How can I face the rest of my life without him? Fate is cruel, but she has claimed Ransom as her own. Little Sibyl asked why I was weeping. I cannot tell the children. Not yet.

For I fear these may indeed be the last words I get from him.

—Claire de Murrow
Connaught Castle
(news from the storm)

CHAPTER THIRTY

Thorngate Castle

It was a miserable trek through mud and rain. They traveled with no wagons, which would have been bogged down by the driving rain, but instead bore their rations themselves, trudging eastward on their horses through an endless drizzle. There was no sun during the day, no moon at night. Only the ever-present pall of the storm and damp and the rust smell of their armor.

There were some Espion still afoot, and Ransom put Simon in charge of them once again, to spy out the road ahead and discern information about the enemy. They would approach Thorngate from the west, whereas Estian's legions had come from the south.

Ransom had never been to Thorngate himself. He knew from Lady Deborah that she had gone there as a lass of sixteen, her husband twice her age. She had become mistress of the castle upon his death and, despite many offers, chose never to remarry. She'd won her place on the Elder King's council through her own shrewd wisdom. Lady Deborah had been a staunch ally of Ransom and a friend for years. His worry for her, the queen, and the others trapped in the castle lent him the courage and determination to get there before the castle fell.

Dearley rode next to him. Faulkes was farther back, leading the foot-bound troops who were cursing the rain and mud. Ransom had sent Dawson up ahead with some valiant knights to secure the way. And James—well, he had abandoned Glosstyr for Brythonica the previous evening. The defection saddened Ransom, but it did not surprise him. In the end, James Wigant had done what was in his own best interest, the same way he always did. Ransom thought on his sister, Maeg, his nephew, and his mother, wishing he could embrace them one last time.

"Did you hear me, Ransom?" Dearley asked, rousing him from his reverie.

"Forgive me, I didn't. Say on."

"I said the boy's fallen asleep against your back."

They'd brought young Devon, the king's heir, with them, for Ransom hadn't felt safe leaving him behind at Glosstyr. The lad's arms were wrapped around his armor, so he hadn't noticed the change in pressure. Glancing back, he saw the boy's head was bouncing in cadence with his destrier's pace.

"He'll be all right," Ransom said. "He'll be with you." He'd assigned Dearley as the boy's protector. If things went bad at Thorngate, he was to rush the prince back to Glosstyr and seek refuge in Legault. That might not stop Estian from winning the Wizr game. But at least the boy's life would be spared.

Dearley shook his head. "I wish I could be sure. I'd rather fight in the battle, you know. You could leave him with other knights to protect him."

Ransom reached and wiped the wetness from his face and beard. "I don't trust anyone else more."

A look of gratitude lit Dearley's eyes, and he knew he'd chosen well. Like him, Dearley would protect the boy to the end, however it came.

They rode at the head of the column, so they were the first to see riders returning. Simon and Dawson were both mud-splattered when they arrived and reined in. Ransom looked from one to the other, but he could not judge the news from their wearied expressions.

"How bad is it?" he asked gravely.

"There are thousands encamped south of Thorngate," Dawson reported, although he did not seem the least bit daunted by the news. He was ready for a fight, eager for one.

"They're not in the town?"

"Yes, they are. But the town isn't big enough for the whole army. I've never seen so many tents and pavilions. There was a massive one with the flag of the Fleur-de-Lis. The king is there; I'm sure of it."

"At least it seems he's there," Simon corrected. "I couldn't get any of my men close enough to be sure."

The knights were already beginning to cluster around them, each man eager to hear information about what lay ahead. The foot soldiers under Faulkes's command would not catch up for a while yet.

"What about the castle? Could you get an Espion inside?" Ransom asked Simon.

His old friend shook his head. "The western gate to the city was blocked with rubble. I think Deborah did that herself to limit possible entrances. But they have the keep surrounded. Hans Dragan had his crossbow, and we fixed a message to it. I think he got the bolt in through a window. There's no way to get a message out."

"That was clever," Dearley said with an approving nod.

Simon shrugged. "We do what we can in war. But I'm certain, Lord Ransom, that Estian knows you're coming." He didn't want to reveal his knowledge of the Wizr board with so many listening in, but his meaningful look said it plainly enough. Yes, Estian knew Ransom was coming. Did that knowledge fill him with fear or eagerness? They'd long been enemies.

"Oh, and there's a river going through the road about a league from here," Dawson said. "I think the Holbrook overswelled its banks. We shouldn't stop for the night until after we've crossed it."

"We're not stopping to rest," Ransom said. "There isn't time."

Simon gave him a worried look. "Estian's men are fresh. He has enough to switch out the siege every day."

"How many trebuchets did he bring?" Ransom asked.

Simon leaned forward in the saddle. "He's using three against Thorngate. I think the rest he's sending on to Kingfountain. He hasn't done much damage to the castle so far, but all it takes is one lucky hit . . ." He shrugged and left the rest unsaid.

"Tell me the lay of the land," Ransom said. "I've not been to Thorngate before."

"There's no way to disguise our approach. There's a small hunting woods to the north, but it's not near the town," Dawson said. "There weren't many of us, and we still encountered a few scouting parties. They rode off, though, and didn't engage us."

"How did you get close enough to shoot a crossbow?" Ransom asked Simon.

"The keep is on the western side of town," Simon said. "By the rubble blocking the gate. We shot it from outside the town and them scampered off before reinforcements came."

"Did they chase you?" Ransom asked.

Dawson grinned. "Aye. We let them for a little while, then turned back, attacked, and drove them off."

Simon smiled at the younger knight's bravado. "There was another hundred not far behind them. They stopped coming for us after we crossed the river blocking the road."

"Did you leave any men behind?" Ransom asked.

"A few Espion. We wanted them to think they'd driven us all away, but Dragan is still back there, along with a few others who will try to find a way for us to get into the city. I'm presuming you don't want to attack the bulk of Estian's army in the plains when we're outnumbered ten to one."

"I had considered it," Ransom said with a wry smile.

Simon took it as a joke. "Fighting from the town itself would be better, of course. It would limit how many men they could send against us. The town is on higher ground than the plains to the south. If we could lay claim to it, they'd be attacking uphill."

"But they control all the gates now," Ransom said.

"Yes," Simon agreed. "My hope is that the Espion will find another way in. If not, we'll be fighting in the plains while they lob boulders at the keep."

"Good work," Ransom said, giving them both encouraging nods. He turned and looked at the knights who had assembled. "No one said this would be easy," he said. "But we fight for a worthy cause. We attack in order to defend our loved ones—our wives and our children. To defend our home." He thought of Claire, Willem, Devon, Sibyl, and Keeva. He thought of Queen Léa and her daughter. He knew Dawson was thinking of Cecily. That Dearley was yearning for his little daughter, who had only just been born.

It made his throat thicken. "Remember who you are, men of Glosstyr. As one—*Dex aie!*" he shouted.

"Dex aie!" resounded the chorus of knights.

Ransom had, by his best estimation, four hundred and eighty-five knights. And thrice that number in foot soldiers and Gaultic archers. If Simon's description of Estian's host were true, then it *was* ten to one, and he needed every advantage to even the odds.

They rode through the night and into the next day and reached the field of Thorngate as the invisible sun sank in the sky. The mud was horrendous. Little Devon ate from a loaf of damp bread and drank from Ransom's own flask.

"Would you like to walk around a little?" Ransom asked him. He'd dismounted the destrier to give the boy some space to eat his meager repast.

Devon shook his head. "It's too muddy."

That was true. The road was a churning mess of filth, and the mud gripped his boots with every step. His men had also dismounted and were caring for their weary horses, feeding them the remainder of the provender they'd brought. Ransom gazed at the tent camp on the south side of the town, which was lower down from their position. It was a gradual slope, but at least it was in their favor. There would be no tents, no pavilions for Ransom and his men to rest in, save what they conquered for themselves. He could see smoke rising from the Occitanian camp as well as from the town chimneys. Where had they found wood dry enough to burn other than by pillaging the townsfolk of their winter stores?

Simon approached him with Hans Dragan in tow. The man's crossbow was slung across his shoulder. Dawson had taken some knights to scout the area. Dearley glanced at the newcomer and then came up to the prince and spoke to him in kindly tones.

"I managed to spear myself a pheasant with a bolt," said Hans Dragan with a smirk as he bowed to Ransom. "Made a little fire to cook it on a spit too. It's been a quiet day. What took you all so long?"

"Enough of the boasting," Simon scolded. "Tell him the news."

Ransom lifted his eyebrows, his weariness deep as his bones. "You caught another one for me?"

Dragan chuckled. "I should have, my lord. I should have. Beg your pardon. But I think I can get your army into the city."

Ransom narrowed his gaze. "The gates are defended."

"All but one," said Dragan.

"Hear him out," Simon urged. "He's been studying it all day."

"Go on," Ransom said.

Other than Dearley and the prince, the others weren't close enough to hear. One weary knight had laid his blanket down on the mud and fallen asleep on it already.

"The western gate's full of rubble," said Dragan. "I think we can clear it. It is right nigh the keep. Estian's men have totally ignored it."

Ransom squinted. "If we march there, they'll see us. They could get men up on the wall and shoot down on us while we moved the stones."

"Aye, I know!" said Dragan excitedly. "That's why we send some brave lads to attack the north gate. Make 'em think that's our goal. We'll leave some lads behind to clear the debris. I don't think it will take as long as all that. Once it's open, you reverse and come in through the west gate and attack the knights laying siege to the keep."

Simon grinned. "Estian will see that we're attacking the north with the bulk of our army, but it'll be a feint. If we get through the gate, we'll send in some foot soldiers with pikes. Draw their forces that way to keep them from guessing our true aim."

Ransom looked from Simon to Hans Dragan. He felt a surge of possibility well up inside him, a rush of confidence and gratitude.

"Do you think Lady Deborah did that on purpose? Made the rubble seem like an obstacle?"

Simon nodded vigorously. "Maybe she was hoping we'd figure it out in time."

If they could lure Estian's forces into defending the north gate, then a few select men could heave away the stones. It would be hard work, and his men were exhausted. But it was the kind of advantage he desperately needed. One that could even the odds a little. The fighting would not be quite so badly stacked against them if they were within the town walls—there would be no bottleneck, and they would be able to use the various buildings strategically. And if Ransom managed to get to Estian, to challenge him, perhaps they could end the battle then and there.

It was a chance. A thin one. But it was better than facing the Black King's army head-on.

Ransom looked to Dearley. "What do you think? If we could get to Estian before he realizes what's really going on . . . we could end the battle more swiftly."

Dearley handed a strip of dried beef to the prince from his own food pouch. His smile revealed his answer faster than his words. "I think it's bloody brilliant."

Devon and Willem dragged their sisters outside for a brief adventure. The boys wanted to see the barrow mounds, but they are too distant. I need to stay at Connaught so I can find out what happens. Another new moon is coming, which means another journey to Atha Kleah. The pumpkins in the garden are as fat as hogs right now, and it reminds me of the young men who will soon use them for sword practice. My sons included. I must distract my thoughts. I must think of anything but what I fear. I've heard nothing. And that is the most dreadful thing of all.

—Claire de Murrow
Connaught Castle
The autumn harvest

CHAPTER
THIRTY-ONE

Into the Breach

After returning from examining the defenses himself, Ransom summoned his leaders together in the rain and dark. There were no stars overhead, just the relentless clouds and constant rain. Flames from the town and enemy camp caused strange ghostlike glows in the low-hanging clouds, offering sufficient ambient light. The young prince sat on his horse, drenched but brave, and listened to the men discuss strategy for the coming battle. Dearley, Dawson, Simon, and Faulkes were gathered around Ransom. They were all weary, but the urgency of the moment had settled on them, and each was willing to brave the hazards ahead.

"There are only a few ways to breach a gate," Ransom said, looking from man to man and then up at the prince. "We can either go over it or through it."

"Making ladders will take too long," said Faulkes.

"Then we need to use battering rams," Dawson said. "There's a stand of ash trees northwest of town."

"Thick ones?" Simon asked.

Dawson affirmed. "We'll need two or three to take them down, and a hundred men to move them."

"They will rain down arrows as soon as you get close to the walls," Faulkes said.

"Armor will protect us," Dawson said, giving him a provoking look.

Ransom held up his hand. "Faulkes is right. Although we're attacking the north gate as a distraction, it is another way into the castle if our first plan fails. They need to believe we're serious."

Dearley spoke up. "Then the Gaultic archers should go with them. They can shoot at anyone peering over the walls."

"Good suggestion," Ransom said. "Simon, I want you to oversee clearing the rubble from the west gate. Use your Espion and hand-pick men who are strong and quiet."

"Of course," Simon said. "We don't have to clear the entire gate. Just enough to get horses through."

"I've a suggestion," Faulkes said. "When we cut down the ash trees, save the larger branches. We can use them to lever the stones."

Simon gave Faulkes a surprised look. "I hadn't thought of that. That will help our men move the bigger ones."

Faulkes's smile showed he was pleased by the compliment.

"You've run many sieges, Faulkes. I'm glad you're here," Ransom told him.

"May I lead the battering rams, my lord?" Dawson volunteered.

"Yes," Ransom said. "You can have two hundred men. Just make them sound like more. Bellow and rage and yell threats at the defenders. Make a ruckus the whole town can hear. The foot soldiers will stand by, watching the walls in a line, as if ready to attack."

"And the rest of the knights?" Dearley asked.

"They'll be with me, farther back. When Simon gives the signal, we'll ride through the west gate and attack from the inside."

"We must hurry," Simon said. "They have men with torches on the walls, watching for us. Once dawn comes, we won't be able to hide what we're doing at the west gate."

"I know," Ransom agreed. "Faulkes—you lead the archers."

"They're Gaultic," he said angrily. "They hate me. My *wife* hates me," he added under his breath.

His attack on Legault had not been forgotten. Or the wife who had chosen to leave him after being forced into the marriage. Ransom looked up at the eerily lit clouds again and then reached out and put a hand on Faulkes's shoulder.

"Then this is the day you begin to redeem yourself in their eyes. And hers. Let her go. Own the mistake. I'm giving you this command to do your duty. If we survive this, make amends."

Faulkes's expression of resentment wavered, and then he nodded in submission.

"I will." From the way he said it, it was clear he didn't just mean in the battle. "I only did what my king bid me do," he said hesitantly, rubbing a hand over his beard. "But I let the power turn my head. I didn't respect them as I should have."

"There is no better day to start than now."

"My lord, what shall I do?" asked the young prince.

"You will watch with me and my knights," Ransom said. "You'll observe the battle. Although you are too young to join this fight, your presence on the battlefield will lend courage to the men. We're vastly outnumbered. Nothing is certain."

The boy looked at him sagely and nodded. "The Fountain is with us, Lord Ransom. Because you are."

His words caused Ransom's magic to awaken. He felt his bond with the boy grow stronger.

"Thank you, lad," Ransom said huskily.

"How will we know when you've broken through?" Dawson asked. "It will be difficult to communicate."

"Then let's save our battle cry for that moment," Ransom said. "If luck is on your side and you break down the north gate, let out that cry, and we'll hear it. We'll do the same if we can breach the west gate first. Understood?"

Faulkes nodded. "The cry of the Elder King. *Dex aie.*"

"Get all in readiness. First, we need those battering rams."

"It'll be done in a trice," Dawson boasted. They gave each other the knightly salute, and Ransom felt a kinship with them that made his heart throb with pride. Yes, they were outnumbered. Yes, the field was a muddy mess. But they were true knights, and he doubted not their courage and resilience.

Both would be needed before the night was over.

Ransom sat astride his impatient destrier and watched their plan unfold. They were a good distance from the walls, but Dawson and the knights were making an unholy racket. Two battering rams took turns, and the grunts and groans of men were followed by the distant thud of the rams striking the gate, one and then another. Arrows clattered off the stone walls, but occasionally a cry of pain announced one had found a victim.

Staring up at the darkened keep, Ransom imagined Lady Deborah and the others huddling in darkness, observing the night siege from the narrow windows.

He was anxious to join the fray. He had one lance at the ready and his scabbard and sword at his waist. The chill of the night hadn't penetrated him even after the hours they'd waited. Each time one of the horses grunted, he worried that the enemy would hear them and know that they were perched outside the town. He had scouts monitoring the encampment. No one was sleeping, and reinforcements were being sent into the town to defend the northern walls. Ransom wondered what the Wizr board looked like, and if Estian had discerned their strategy, or if the pieces were already so close together he could not tell the difference. No word from the Espion and laborers. All was deathly quiet.

"The sky on the horizon is brightening," Dearley whispered. The prince sat astride his own horse next to him, an animal that had been used for baggage on the way.

Ransom knew what he was saying. The sun was rising, and they were still not in, either through the west gate, which was their chosen approach, or the north. The north gate had proven to be sturdy, and no doubt the defenders were barricading it from the inside.

"They can do it," Ransom insisted. He'd lowered his chain cowl so he could hear better, and his helmet hung around his neck by the strap.

The horses were getting restless and hungry. More of them started to grunt, and the knights riding them whispered soothing noises. They had no more provender with them. They had to win the day, or all would be lost.

A shadowed figure came slinking up from the western gate. Ransom recognized the crossbow strapped across his back. It was Hans Dragan. He jogged the rest of the way to them and was breathing heavily when he arrived.

"It's nearly done, my lord," he said. "Sir Simon will have the rest cleared before you get there. Ride on!"

Ransom glanced at Dearley, smiling, and then returned his attention to Dragan. "No one heard you?"

"Nary a one," the Espion replied. "We already have men inside the city, keeping watch for any sentries. The street is empty, my lord."

Ransom felt a surge of relief. Yes, the eastern sky was starting to brighten, but so were his hopes. Not for himself—he'd accepted his fate—but for those he had pledged to protect. "Your plan may work yet."

Turning toward the men, he lifted his voice so the other knights could hear him. "We go to save the queen," he said firmly. "Once this battle starts, it will not end until one side prevails over the other. May the Fountain be on our side. Courage, men. I know you're weary. I know you're spent. But this is the moment you have trained for your entire lives. When we breach the city walls, scream *Dex aie!*"

He looked at Dearley, who stared at him with pride tinged with disappointment. He wanted to ride into battle with his master for this crucial battle.

"I'm counting on you to save the boy," Ransom said to him. His throat thickened. "You will tell Claire what happened here."

Dearley's brow wrinkled with concern. "My lord?"

"We go. Now!" Ransom said, straightening in the saddle. He grabbed his lance and rested it in the crook of his arm.

Dearley said something else to him, but he ignored it. The excitement of battle was spreading through the ranks.

"Lord Ransom!" called the prince. "Your helmet!"

Ransom realized he'd nearly ridden into battle without it on. He grinned at his own mistake and quickly set down the lance. He heard some chuckles around him as he arranged his chain hood and then pulled on the helmet. The moment reminded him of another one, when he'd faced Estian in a tournament with his helmet askew. He'd been half blind, but he'd still won. He'd win this one too, by thunder!

Ready at last, he picked up the lance again and led his knights in a charge across the sodden meadow. Clumps of mud flew everywhere, but the scent of manure faded as they left their camp.

The eastern sky was a sliver of gray. Rain pelted them. Still, they rode on.

As they reached the walls of Thorngate town, he saw Simon and the Espion waving them through the open breach. Spontaneous cries of joy came from the men.

After crossing the gate, he let out the battle cry he'd shouted so many times before. *"Dex aie!"*

His knights' thunderous reply came as they joined in the call to arms. The muddy field was replaced by wet cobblestones. He saw men emerging from the shadows, waving to him and pointing to the nearest street.

"This way, my lord! This way!"

Was it a trap? Even as the thought occurred to him, he dismissed it. His Fountain magic was thrumming through his veins, rejoicing. The enemy was aware of them now as they rode through the street to the keep. After turning the corner, they saw a cluster of Occitanian knights who'd gathered at a distance from the keep wall. Up close, he could see the damage caused by the enemy so far. Parts of the wall were sagging dangerously. But the several trebuchets were at rest, although the men were not asleep.

"*Alarum! Alarum!*" shouted one of the knights, pointing at them. "*Vite! Vite!*" He spoke in Occitanian. *Hurry. Hurry.*

Ransom lowered his lance and charged the startled knights. One was on a horse already, and he turned to face Ransom with his own lance. Fire from pitch-soaked torches illuminated the area. He sensed his opponent's skills—his training, his youth and vigor—but Ransom was much more experienced. He aimed the tip of his lance and unhorsed the knight in the first pass.

The chaos of battle erupted around them, and Ransom drew his bastard sword and charged into the thick of it. He slashed at the knights who came at him—some mounted, some on foot—his Fountain magic pouring into him, wave after wave. He heard the battle cry rise up behind him as more of the men of Glosstyr poured into the city. Perhaps fifty had been guarding the keep, and they were all soon dispatched. None of them surrendered or cried to yield. That didn't surprise him given the way the last Occitanian hostages had been treated.

Ransom whirled in his saddle and saw the foot soldiers jogging through the gate, coming to join the fight. He brandished his sword and cried for his knights to join him.

As they went to the north gate, they saw a stream of soldiers coming from the south to join the fight at the wall. Again the sound of alarm came just before Ransom's knights crushed them. He could see an endless flood of soldiers coming toward them. Looking around, he saw Simon battling a foe on horseback. The other man tumbled from his mount, and Ransom shouted his friend's name.

Simon turned his horse, his eyes fearful as he beheld the mass of men coming toward them.

"Get that north gate open!" Ransom shouted. "We need Dawson and his knights right away."

"What will we do?" Then his eyes widened at something over Ransom's shoulder. "Look out!"

Ransom sensed the danger too late. A wounded knight had risen with a spear and thrust it at him from behind. He felt the tip pierce through a slit in his armor, puncturing his hauberk, but he didn't feel any pain.

Ransom swiveled his horse around sharply, and the spear was yanked out of the knight's hands before the destrier trampled him.

Gritting his teeth, Ransom used his other hand to pull the spear loose. There was still no pain, but the Raven scabbard began to glow. He turned back to Simon.

"We need Dawson's men," he said, breathing fast.

"You're injured," Simon said worriedly. "You've done enough. Come. Others can lead this fight."

Ransom shook his head. More soldiers were rushing toward them, roaring with anger, but they were running up a slant. Ransom and his knights had the higher ground. If they pushed, and pushed hard, they could drive the Occitanians out of the village.

But they couldn't end the battle that way. The Occitanians had men to spare. They were more rested and well fed. The only way they could hope to win—or at least not to lose—was to break the Occitanians' will to fight.

"I will fight . . . as long as I have . . . breath," Ransom said to him. "Get Dawson. I'm going after Estian."

There was a hush in the wind today. It sounded like a sigh.
Please, please, don't let him die.

—*Claire de Murrow*
Connaught Castle

CHAPTER
THIRTY-TWO

Dex Aie

The rain did not cease its relentless aggression. Even the clouds seemed angry, and the thunder that started to the east was soon overhead. They were outside the town now, pressing into the thickest mass of soldiers to reach the center. For there, deep within the throng, he thought he saw the banner of Estian Vertus. Ransom felt nothing beyond wet, aching muscles, and raw determination. He deflected a blade aiming for his neck but kept pressing through the thickest part of the enemy, going deeper into the maelstrom of mud, shooting, and clashing arms. In his heart, he was determined to peel the fruit and expose the seed. He would not stop until the Black King was his.

"Pour le sang!" shouted a knight, charging at his flank. He recognized the battle cry of the royal house of Occitania—*for the blood!* He was too slow to block the strike and felt the blade shear through his armor. A hot, stinging pain stabbed into his chest. The knight pressed harder, and Ransom twisted in his saddle and struck the man's helmet with the pommel of his sword, the blow hard enough that it dented. The knight sagged off his horse into the slick mud, facedown, and didn't move. But his fall had dragged his sword out of Ransom's chest, and the

pain quickly faded as the scabbard's magic continued to heal him. He'd been struck repeatedly, and whether any of the blows were mortal, he didn't know. He couldn't dwell on it.

A foot soldier rushed forward with a halberd to impale his horse, but Ransom urged his destrier forward and got past the man's reach. Mud was smeared on every face. Some of the men and horses were tripping over themselves. Ransom used his mount to press through the fray, although the din of the battle raged around him.

More thunder rippled through the air, followed by a blinding shard of lightning. Some soldiers winced, shielding their eyes. Others were already fleeing, only to be turned back by the rush of advancing men.

Ransom risked a backward glance and found his knights hacking through the mob. They were trying to keep up with him, but it was like riding against a river's current. An axe struck against his back, the blow hard enough to leave bruises but the weapon too dull to cut through his steel. The knight attacking him drew the weapon back again to make another swing, but Ransom stabbed the man with his bastard sword, his stroke finding a gap. He heard a gasp of surprise and pain, and the axe fell from the knight's hands.

Yanking on his horse's reins, Ransom turned the destrier about and knocked over two foot soldiers in the process. They'd been reaching for the bridle. If they'd managed to seize it, he would have been helpless. He whacked the flat of his blade against his destrier's armored rump, and the two surged forward again, forcing others to dive away or be trampled.

"*Dex aie!* To Lord Ransom!" came a shout from behind.

His knights were gaining ground and shoving their way through the press of men. He clenched his teeth with pride. The mettle they'd shown that day went beyond his wildest hopes. They'd been driven past the point of exhaustion, yet still they fought, and still they conquered.

Reaching out with his magic again, Ransom altered his course to intercept Estian. The Black King was in the center of his army, so there was no way he could flee. Ransom's lungs were burning for air, but he continued to slash and block his way to his quarry.

Then suddenly, the Occitanians pulled back. A row of foot soldiers with spears quickly formed into a wall, the tips of their blades pointed out like the spikes of a hedgehog. Behind them, Ransom saw the muddied black tunics of Estian's personal guard, each man mounted and with a lance couched and ready. Estian, with a crown fixed to his helmet, sat astride his great stallion in the middle, holding a lance made of ash wood and a pennant of the Fleur-de-Lis.

Hoisting his sword into the air, Ransom pulled back on the reins of his destrier to make it rise and flail its hooves. He brandished his sword in several sharp circles before pointing it at the wall of spearmen.

"Dex aie!" he shouted at the top of his lungs, his voice hoarse and straining.

There was a cry again, a bellowing of voices to match his own.

A knight near him cried out, "Let's end this! Ride on! For the Fountain! For Lord Ransom!"

Ransom saw that his knights had caught up to him, maybe a score of them—no more. Gazing at the wall facing them, he jabbed his destrier with spurs, and the beast lunged forward. The quickly assembled phalanx charged.

Through the openings in the spearmen's round, shield-like helmets, he could see their fearful eyes. They grimaced with dread as the knights bore down on them. A few even closed their eyes, fixed their spears, and looked away.

Ransom's destrier jumped, smashing through the spearmen, and he swung his sword down when it landed. Several horses screamed in pain, and he worried his mount would crumple from a wound to its chest, but it didn't. He'd made it through the wall.

Estian lowered his lance and began to charge at him.

A knight with a lance had an advantage over one without, for he could strike his enemy from a greater distance. The only chance he had was if he dodged at the last moment, letting the tip of the lance pass by, which would bring his enemy within range of his bastard sword. His magic sensed that Estian's skill was still prodigious. He didn't compete in tournaments anymore, but he'd kept his body fit and strong, and while he was slightly older than Ransom, he was still a fearsome opponent.

They locked eyes on each other, and Ransom resolved to finish his life in a final act of knighthood. He lifted his weary sword arm, preparing to deliver a counterstroke if the king's aim was off.

It wasn't.

Ransom twisted in the saddle, but the lance struck him in the chest and exploded into a shower of splinters. He felt the weight of the blow sending him backward. His arm muscles strained to hold on. His foot left the stirrup as he swayed and bent, farther, farther . . .

And then Ransom came back up again, just as Estian's horse was passing him. He swung his sword and smote Estian's shield arm so hard that his blade cleaved through the shield. The recoil rocked Estian off his horse's rump, and he landed on his back in the field of mud.

The black-garbed knights turned as one, staring at their fallen king. Estian writhed, trying to get up, but the mud gripped him, and he only managed to sink deeper.

Ransom charged back to the king and met two of Estian's knights, who attempted to block him. He knocked one off his horse with a powerful blow, and the other, in sidestepping, nearly trampled the king. Ransom grabbed the enemy knight's bridle and yanked the bit out of his horse's mouth. The beast, in pain, charged away while the knight fruitlessly tried to stop it.

Ransom swung off his horse and stood over Estian, who barely managed to bring up his broken shield. His legs found no purchase as he scrabbled weakly and then collapsed, trapped by the weight of his armor and the mud. They were surrounded by Occitanians, almost on every side. There wasn't much time before the numbers would overwhelm him.

Rain pattered against Ransom's armor and dripped down his blade. For years he had hated the Occitanian king. Estian and his father had destroyed the Younger King, the Elder King, Benedict, and, finally, Jon-Landon. Four kings lay dead because of their influence. The anger in his heart was fierce.

Estian's visor had been knocked open during his fall. He sucked in his breath, his eyes wide with dread. Ransom lifted his visor so his face could be seen too.

"Don't kill my son," Estian breathed out. He didn't plead for his own life. He knew he was a dead man. That he could expect and deserved no pity.

"Do you yield?" Ransom demanded, lowering his sword point to Estian's throat.

Surprise widened the king's eyes.

"You will . . . spare me?" Estian grunted.

"Do you yield?" Ransom repeated, stepping closer. The battle raged on around them still, but no one was near enough to stop him from killing the king. The tide had shifted, even though their numbers had not changed.

"I yield," Estian said, lowering his shield a little.

"Louder," Ransom insisted. "We won't slaughter your men if you surrender. You are my hostage. The rest may go free."

A look of disbelief washed over Estian's face. He would not have offered the same grace, and both of them knew it.

"I yield!" Estian bellowed.

Ransom reached out with his left hand to help Estian rise. It took all their combined strength to free him from the muck.

Ransom still held his bastard sword, though he no longer felt the temptation to slay Estian. His anger had burned away. He wasn't the monster inside him. He was his own man.

"Order your men to disarm. They must leave all of their weapons here in the field."

"And you promise they'll go free? Why should I trust you?"

Ransom gave him a harsh look. "Because you *know* I keep my word."

Because of the confusion and threat to their king, the knights of Occitania hesitated, giving the knights of Glosstyr the opportunity to gather around Estian and Ransom, creating a shield of horses around them.

Estian met Ransom's gaze and then lowered his eyes. "Lay down your arms!" he cried in Occitanian. "It is finished!"

There was grudging obedience. The Occitanians had been defeated by a smaller force, tricked at Thorngate castle, and now their king was being held for ransom by a knight who had been an enemy of their realm for years. Ransom saw the anger in their eyes, the despair, but they complied and threw their weapons into the mud. Jubilant cries rose up from his men as Dawson and his knights arrived on horseback, coming to join a fight that was already over.

Ransom was relieved. His whole body ached, but the scabbard's magic kept him from falling down. He was afraid of his injuries, but as long as he had the scabbard, they would all heal.

"I want the Wizr board," Ransom said. "Where is it?"

Estian bared his teeth. "I sent it away during the battle. One of my knights has it."

"Where were you sending it?"

"Back to Tatton Hall, where Alix is waiting."

Ransom ordered his knights to find Estian's horse and bring it to them. He would take the king to Thorngate, but not before the Wizr board was in his possession. Otherwise, he would be leading Alix straight to them.

When Dawson reached him, he looked relieved to see Ransom still alive.

"You have a piece of lance in you still," he observed. Ransom hadn't even noticed.

"I'll be fine. Take some men and fresh horses and ride toward Tatton Hall. Estian sent one of his knights with a special treasure, a Wizr board. Bring it back, Dawson. Don't fail me."

"I won't," Dawson promised and promptly obeyed.

Estian rode silently at his side, unarmed, spattered with mud. The people of the town cheered them as they came toward the castle, Ransom's soldiers ensuring the orders were obeyed. The muddy field was now scattered with swords, axes, lances, and the like. When they reached the keep, Ransom found Dearley and the prince already outside with a crew of knights as bodyguards.

As they rode up to the drawbridge, he heard a familiar voice call down. It was Lady Deborah.

"Is that you, Lord Ransom? It's difficult to tell!"

He chuckled softly, his body aching from the battle. "We bring a guest, Lady Deborah. The King of Occitania requests your hospitality."

"I think I have just the room for him," she replied. The winches began to groan, and the drawbridge slowly lowered, bridging the gap. As Ransom rode up the wooden plank, Estian on one side and Prince Devon on the other, he saw the group of knights on the other side. In all, there were perhaps fifty defenders left, and they had a look of dizzied relief.

Lady Deborah stood beaming at him, her eyes twinkling at the rescue. The rain, Ransom noticed, had slackened. The sky was still full of clouds, but the storm had finally begun to ebb. It was a hopeful sign.

"Welcome to Thorngate," she said to Estian. "Your Majesty."

From beyond the inner yard, he saw Queen Léa and her daughter emerge from the castle. When the queen first saw Ransom, she didn't recognize him, but after a moment, her eyes widened with hope. She hurried to him, her face eager. The princess was no less enthusiastic.

The queen reached up and touched his gauntlet. "Where is Jonny?"

Ransom's heart ached as much as his body. He shook his head slightly, not wanting to dash the little girl's hopes so quickly.

The queen recognized his gesture, and her mouth drooped in anguish, her brows coming together.

"Come, Léanore," she said to the princess. "Come back inside."

"Where is Papa? I don't see him."

"Come back inside, dearest."

Lady Deborah had discerned the news. Her happy smile had shifted to a thinly pressed line. "So the Fountain wills." She looked at Prince Devon. "Welcome to Thorngate as well, Prince Devon. My liege."

When Simon arrived next, Ransom gave the order for his knights to secure the town and bring the Occitanian provisions from the encampment up to the keep. His men were hungry and weary and deserved to recuperate from the battle. Simon took charge and said the Espion would look for stragglers with evil intentions.

As they spoke, Cecily approached their horses.

"Where is Sir Dawson?" she asked worriedly. She looked like she hadn't slept much the last few days. Her first question was telling.

"I sent him after one of Estian's knights," Ransom said, "who has something we need."

Simon nodded in understanding.

"I hope he returns soon," Cecily said, her face twisting with worry. After a moment, her expression softened, and she glanced at Ransom. "That was an impressive victory, my lord. I don't think a battle such as this has ever been won. Let me fetch a barber for you. I don't know how you're still standing."

Ransom returned with her to the keep and, with the help of one of Lady Deborah's squires, managed to detach his armor, which the lad set about to clean. The room was sparse, but servants brought him a washbowl and towel and a change of clothes. When a barber arrived, Ransom sent him away to attend to the wounded on the battlefield instead. He stripped off his tunic and hauberk and began to scrub away the grime. His wounds were still painful, but the scabbard was glowing. He sat at the edge of a sturdy cot and put his head in his hands, shocked he was still alive.

Then he slumped onto the cot and promptly fell asleep.

He awoke when a soft hand touched his arm. Blinking, he lifted his head and saw Dawson and Cecily standing there. By the flushed looks on their faces, he suspected they'd been kissing, and from the way she leaned into him, one hand on Dawson's chest, he imagined they'd been exchanging promises as well.

"You're back?" Ransom said, grunting with pain as he sat up. His legs and knees throbbed with protest. He was cold, and he realized he hadn't replaced his tunic and had slept in his muddy boots.

"I think you should put on a tunic, my lord. You have visitors."

Ransom arched his eyebrows wonderingly. Could it be Claire? Had she managed somehow to come?

"Who?" he demanded. He rose and grabbed the fresh tunic that had been brought for him, folded on the table by the washbowl, which had been thoroughly muddied.

"Lord Montfort from Brythonica," said Sir Dawson. "And Lord James Wigant. They brought five hundred knights with them." He sighed, his shoulders slumping a little. "I didn't catch Estian's knight before he reached Tatton Hall, my lord." Then he grinned. "They did."

The storm is over. The waters have calmed. I've ordered Captain Grenat to prepare my ship. We're sailing for Glosstyr.

—*Claire de Murrow*
Connaught Castle
(bright skies in the east)

CHAPTER
THIRTY-THREE

Ancient Covenant

Ransom dressed in fresh clothes, then went to the solar to join the others. He was surprised to have survived the battle he'd expected to be his last. But the Ondine's words still nagged at him. Had he truly cheated death, or only delayed it?

Lord Montfort and James were both there, the latter sitting languidly in a stuffed chair, eating a piece of roasted fowl from the table of refreshments. Queen Léa, Cecily, and Simon were all present, sitting on various surfaces, and Lady Deborah stood at the window. Dearley had been dispatched to Glosstyr following the battle to bring the tidings of their victory to Claire, and to bring her and the children to Kingfountain for the coronation of Prince Devon. Faulkes had been sent ahead to the capital to alert Lord Kiskaddon of the victory so preparations might begin for the coronation. The prince and the princess were absent from the room.

Ransom's gaze was drawn to the chest with the Wizr board, which sat atop a rounded table in the center of the room. He recognized the handle instantly. But still, he had to be sure. With their eyes following him, he approached it and undid the latch. He opened it.

The set was unmistakable, and he breathed a sigh of relief. As he examined the board, he saw the Black King piece in the center, surrounded by several powerful pieces. Few black pieces were left. But he spied the Wizr piece, the one representing Alix, a few squares away. He suspected she was at Tatton Hall, as Estian had said.

"Is all in order, Lord Ransom?" asked Montfort with a smile.

"It appears so."

The queen approached, her eyes red-rimmed from crying. "Is this the set that Jonny told me of? The one that was stolen from Benedict?"

"It is, my lady," Ransom said. "Only heirs to the throne can move the pieces. Your son and daughter for our side."

"So few pieces remain," she said sadly.

It was true. The board was badly diminished. During the game, the two sides had nearly destroyed each other. Ransom closed the lid and then looked to Simon.

"How many did we lose?"

"Around four hundred," he replied.

"And the Occitanians?" Lady Deborah asked.

Simon stroked his goatee. "Two thousand, probably. After they abandoned their arms, we compelled a thousand men to bury their dead. The rest began the long walk to Westmarch."

"Where is Estian?" Ransom asked.

"He's in the dungeon," said Lady Deborah.

"Where he belongs," James added in a snide voice.

"How many guard him?"

"Enough, Ransom," Simon said soothingly. "There is but one fountain here in the keep, and it's guarded by six men. The Espion are watching Devon and Léanore."

"We need to discuss Estian's ransom," Ransom said. "I have my own ideas, but I'd like to hear yours."

The queen stiffened, her lips pursing in a look of revenge. "The same that we paid for Benedict is more than fair. Our treasure is lost, so I hear."

Ransom looked to Lady Deborah next.

"You intend to release him?" she asked.

Ransom nodded. "Eventually."

"I say we strap him into a canoe and throw him over the falls," said the queen.

"I promised I would spare him," Ransom said.

The queen huffed. "It wasn't your decision to make alone, Lord Ransom."

"My lady," Simon interjected. "If he had slain the king, none of us would be here right now. The Occitanians would have swarmed us. Capturing him was what ended the battle and saved our lives."

The queen flushed and turned away. "My husband is dead. Why can Estian not suffer for it?"

Lady Deborah went to her and stroked her arm. "I don't think Lord Ransom was suggesting letting him go free for nothing."

"He's not been weakened sufficiently," Ransom said. "We need to buy ourselves some time. We need to buy the prince time."

Simon gave him a quizzical look. "You want to exchange hostages, don't you?"

Ransom nodded. "I'd like to trade him for Lady Alix. She is the one who must be brought to justice."

"I'm glad to hear you say so," Deborah said. "Even though she did Estian's bidding."

"We execute the poisoner?" the queen asked, her eyes glittering.

"I didn't say that," Ransom answered. "She needs to be taken off the board. But there is much we could learn from her. The poison, for example, that she used to kill our kings. Is there a cure?"

Simon's expression was conflicted. "I won't deny that I want that information and more. We could better defend ourselves if we knew what they were capable of. But . . . you know how dangerous she is. How she can travel between fountains. What would prevent her escaping?"

"She is the one who murdered my husband. Who murdered *all* of them," the queen said with anger in her voice.

"We must be very careful about this," Lady Deborah advised. "She cannot be allowed to escape."

"Agreed, and I have no doubt she would try," said Ransom. "But she also is the only living person who knows the location of *The Hidden Vulgate*. It is a dangerous book of great power, and if we can find and bury it, it will be to everyone's benefit." He paused, then added, "Alix is Emiloh's natural daughter. I don't know that she would want her put to death. She also saved my life, so I do feel a debt."

"Her actions since do not make up for that," Deborah said. "We must be careful what we do. A spider cannot injure inside a jar. But if it gets out . . ."

"In addition to giving Prince Devon a chance to grow up, we also need time to train our own poisoner." He glanced at Cecily. "While they do the same."

The queen gave him a heated look. "I want her gone, but I'm not an unreasonable woman. I can see the wisdom in not executing her immediately. What do you intend to do to keep my children safe?"

"I've seen enough blood to last a lifetime," Ransom said. "She would need to be imprisoned. Permanently."

"Where?" asked Simon.

"The dungeon here, for now. Away from any fountain. She must go wherever I go for now. I can sense her presence. I'll know if she escapes. But I'd trust the Espion to watch over her . . . if you were leading them."

Simon grinned. "I would be honored."

"Why is Ransom making all of the decisions?" the queen complained.

"Because he will be the lord protector," said James at last, setting down the chicken bone on a plate and rising from the chair. "No one else could do it. Your son, Highness, is too young to rule in his own right."

"I could rule," said the queen.

James gave her a look of disgust. "You could *try*." He looked back at Ransom. "I'm going back to Ploemeur with Lord Montfort. I'll bring Maeg and our son to the coronation. Do I still get to keep the North? It will take twenty years to recover our losses."

Ransom nodded. "Come to the coronation." Then he looked at Lord Montfort. "Will Constance come?"

Lord Montfort pressed his lips together and shook his head no.

"You may come in her stead," Ransom declared.

"Brythonica will remain an independent duchy," said Montfort. "But you will find us a strong ally, Lord Ransom."

Ransom gave him a knightly salute, which was reciprocated.

"I'll go attend to my children," said the queen hotly. "Seems that is all I'm good for in your eyes." She left in a huff, her eyes burning into James.

"And with that display of annoyance, I'll leave too," he said with a smirk. Lord Montfort nodded and departed with him.

Once they were gone, the door shut behind them, Ransom turned to Simon.

"I'd like to see Estian," he said softly. "Bring him here."

"Alone?"

Ransom shook his head no. "I want all of you here," he said to the others. "We make this decision together."

Simon left to release Estian from his cell. After he left the room, Deborah approached Ransom, holding the leather cylinder that contained the charter.

"Can I request, Lord Ransom, that we keep the charter here at Thorngate? There is another copy at the sanctuary of Our Lady if I understand correctly?"

"And more will be made," Ransom said. "Yes, I think that would be a good thing. Keep it here."

Lady Deborah smiled, pleased. "Thank you. Thank you for everything, Ransom. If you hadn't come, the keep would have fallen today. We were desperate. I'll remind the queen of that. She should be more grateful."

"Maybe in time she will be," Ransom said.

Cecily, who'd sat quietly through the meeting, approached him after Lady Deborah retreated with the charter.

"Pisan, is it?"

Ransom shrugged. "Do you object?"

She shook her head. "I hope I won't be gone for too long. I'm rather partial to one of your knights."

"So it seems," Ransom said with a smile. "You know, I had to wait a long time for the woman I loved."

She gave him an impish smile. "Yes, but that makes me no more eager to suffer through the same. He's a good man."

"He is. He could have an heiress, but he wants you. It's a sign of good judgment."

Cecily offered a pretty smile. "You're kind." Then she turned toward the door. "They're coming."

Ransom folded his arms, his gaze fixed on the door as Simon opened it and allowed Estian to enter first. Several knights had escorted them, but they remained outside. Ransom motioned for Simon to join them.

Estian quickly appraised those in the room, but it was Ransom who held his attention. The king's muddied clothes had been replaced. Some of the king's belongings had been stolen from his tent after the battle, but they'd managed to bring several chests to the keep, which had supplied a change of royal garb.

Ransom walked to the Wizr board in the middle of the room. When Estian's eyes fell on it, he blinked with surprise. He clearly hadn't expected them to retrieve it.

"Tell us what you know about this board," Ransom said. "How long has it been in your family?"

"Since Leoneyis drowned," Estian replied smoothly. "It is both great and terrible."

"What else?" Ransom pressed.

"I don't understand your question."

Ransom gave him a warning look. "Tell us what you know of it."

"Such things should be discussed between kings," said Estian tightly.

"Alas, but you've murdered all of ours," said Ransom.

"'Tis the way of kings," answered Estian with a mocking smile. "We all seek to bring one another down, and have for thousands of years. I will humor you, though. This game was made in the East Kingdoms by the great Wizrs. It is not just a game of strategy, but one of dominion. It is a game of dynasties. This particular conflict began over a century ago between Jessup, the Duke of La Marche, and my great-grandfather, King Chatriyon the Wise."

Ransom furrowed his brow. "Oh?"

"The duke was the bastard son of the king," said Estian. "Of the same blood as King Andrew, but sullied. They invoked the game afresh. They each made a covenant, binding them to the rules of the game. Ambition and pride are powerful motives. So is hatred. The game will go on for generations until one side wins. Or the Dreadful Deadman returns."

Simon's eyebrows creased with confusion.

"You are speaking in riddles," Ransom said.

"The bastard duke was convinced that he and his line would make stronger kings than Chatriyon's pampered sons. In order to play the game, he needed to become a king himself first. He only had the resources of a duke, so he had to conquer a stronger force. He chose Ceredigion over the island nations of Brugia or Legault. And Genevar didn't have a king, just a doge."

"The conquest," Ransom said, nodding. "He defeated King Ethelring and claimed Ceredigion."

"Yes, he took the hollow crown from Ethelring, and that is when this iteration of the game began. A contest between two realms. Claiming a kingdom, however, was easier than keeping it."

"So it seems," Ransom agreed. "There were many fights over succession."

"Yes," Estian said with a smirk. "That happens when all the heirs are unworthy. My father taught me it is easier to weaken an enemy from within than to destroy it from without. As I've learned to my folly. I thought . . . I *believed* that I would win the game and end it."

"By destroying us?"

Estian shook his head. "That was never my intention."

"Your presence here belies those words," Simon said mockingly.

It also went against Alix's threat and the Ondine's warning.

"Only a fool utters things he does not understand," quipped Estian in rebuke.

"Enlighten us, then," Simon responded with a look of distrust.

"I had Alix steal the board back because you do not understand it," Estian said to Ransom. "You risk destroying us all."

"If you didn't seek to ruin us, what *was* your intention?" Ransom asked. He couldn't trust Estian to be truthful, but he had to ask anyway.

"To destroy that hated king, Jon-Landon, yes. But not his children. I wanted to rule Kingfountain, not obliterate it. If either side wins the game, everything ends. But there is a way to *stop* the game. To pause it if you will."

"How?" Ransom asked.

"Only someone who is Fountain-blessed can retrieve it . . . or put it there. Your kind can reach into the Deep Fathoms itself. When the Wizr board is returned to the waters, the game is . . . 'paused,' for lack of a better word. There is less of a press to fight, to conquer. A semblance of peace can be had, so long as there are potential heirs on both sides. So long as there is still an Argentine living when I claim the hollow crown, I could rule all the lands and do what my ancestors could not—bring Andrew's kingdom back in all its glory. One king, one will, one dominion."

"The same can be said in reverse," Ransom surmised. "If Occitania is conquered, one king may rule both realms."

"Yes," said Estian. His eyes narrowed. "What is your intention?"

"First, tell me of the Dreadful Deadman," Ransom said. "I know it is whispered that a scion of King Andrew's line will be born. That he will restore his kingdom."

Estian shrugged. "I thought it possible that Constance's son might be the one. But he is dead."

"Is this prophecy written in *The Hidden Vulgate*?" Ransom asked.

The king looked at him in confusion. "What is that?"

"The book Alix stole from Claire in Legault. A tome copied by the Black Wizr."

The king shook his head. "I know nothing of that."

"She stole it when she tried to abduct my sons," Ransom said.

"I know nothing of it!" Estian said angrily, but his confusion seemed real.

"For your side, there is yourself, your son, and Alix herself. What of your sister?"

"Noemie is barren," Estian said. "She cannot conceive. She was . . . poisoned." Something flickered in his expression, and a very real horror entered his eyes. "Lord Ransom, Alix will try to claim the throne of Occitania herself while I am imprisoned. My son is in danger!"

"There is a way to summon her," Ransom said. "I know you've done it before. If you move her piece, she will be forced to come."

"Through the fountains," Simon said with a nod.

"The fountains are manifestations of an older magic," Estian said. "Their locations were carefully chosen to fall in areas of magical confluence. They're called 'ley lines.' That is how I returned from the East Kingdoms so quickly. And yes, I can summon Alix."

"Does she know you lost?" Ransom asked.

"I have no way to communicate with her except summoning her through the board."

"Then we summon her now," Ransom said, pointing to it. "In addition to your ransom payment, I want Alix in exchange for your freedom. We take your most valuable piece and agree to bury the board in the water and pause the game."

Estian blinked quickly. "I'll do it. My life for hers."

"She can disappear without a fountain, though," Ransom said. "How? When she attacked Claire at Connaught—"

"The ley lines run through Connaught," Estian explained. "Pree too. And Kingfountain. But she needs to be in a fountain to leave."

Ransom shook his head. "Claire saw her disappear."

"She can vanish," Estian said. "She has the ability to turn invisible. When she fled Connaught, she deceived your wife into thinking she was gone. But you, I know, can sense her presence, just as she can sense yours."

Although Ransom didn't trust Estian, his explanation fit. Because if Alix had the ability to appear and disappear at will, she would have used it much more frequently. "Summon her. It serves both of our purposes."

"I will," Estian said. "If you let me go."

"Don't," Lady Deborah warned.

Ransom glanced at her, thoughtful.

"Lord Ransom, she could get back to Pree in an instant!" Estian implored. "If she believes I'm dead, she will kill my son and take the throne herself. None of you would prevail against her."

"Summon her to Thorngate," Ransom said. "That is what she would expect if you won the battle, correct?"

"Yes, but I don't see how—"

"Then we'll bring both of you to Kingfountain. See that Devon is crowned. If all goes well and the board reflects it, then I will submerge it and release you to leave by ship."

"I see. But you will . . . destroy Alix? The only way to kill a Fountain-blessed is to send them over a waterfall."

When we arrived in Glosstyr, we learned the news of Ransom's victory at Thorngate castle from Dearley himself. Ransom sent him to Glosstyr to come fetch us to Kingfountain for the coronation of Prince Devon. He will be Devon Tercer, I believe, the third of that name. I'm so relieved. The awful pangs of worry and grief have come to an end. Estian the Black is captured, and he will be brought to Kingfountain as well. Lady Alix is the final threat on the board. Once she is removed from the game, we can all breathe easily. Willem and Dev asked if the princess would be at the palace. They want to introduce her to Sibyl. I asked Dearley to send a knight to the Heath to fetch Ransom's mother. She is ailing, but she will want to be there to witness her son's triumph. He will be the lord protector of the realm. At last, at long last, we may finally get a season of peace and solace.

Yet none of us are safe while that poisoner is free. I know she saved Ransom when he was a young knight. He will want to spare her life for that and because she is Emiloh's daughter. But can so much guilt be purged with forgiveness?

—Claire de Murrow
Fortress of Glosstyr
(We ride by horseback. The roads are thick with mud.)

CHAPTER
THIRTY-FOUR

Poisoner's Fate

All was in preparedness. Ransom had iron cuffs around his wrists, but they were not secured and could be shrugged off. His knights, including Dawson, wore the livery of the Occitanian king and stood in a semicircle around the fountain within the trampled gardens behind the keep at Thorngate castle. Within the trees perched Hans Dragan with no less than three loaded crossbows. The drawbridge of the keep was up, so there was no way for Alix to get to the queen and her children, who were sheltered with Lady Deborah and guarded by Cecily. There were no fountains within the keep.

The Wizr board was set on a small stool before the fountain, its lid propped open to reveal the set. Estian stood next to Ransom, waiting for the order to move the piece that would summon Alix.

Ransom wore a hauberk beneath his muddied tunic. Although he was posing as a defeated man, he still wore his sword, the scabbard positioned at his back. An Espion, garbed as a servant, held a knife at Estian's back. They had hastily assembled the scene, knowing that every moment increased the odds that a survivor of the battle would return to Tatton Hall with news of the crushing defeat.

Ransom met Dawson's eyes. Would they be able to capture the poisoner? Estian's suggestion of how they might execute her, by plunging her alive over the falls, was tempting.

"What do we wait for?" Estian asked with a nervous edge in his voice.

Dawson nodded. If the knights could subdue her, they'd lock her in chains, which were at the ready in a nearby sack at Dawson's feet. Hans Dragan would send a crossbow bolt through her heart if she tried to escape.

No one knew how she would react to the betrayal. She might try to kill Estian too, which was why Ransom would be at the king's side.

He let out a calming breath.

"Bring her," he announced and dropped to one knee, his whole body tensing and ready for action. His Fountain magic had been depleted during the battle, but he had an ample store remaining. He would fight, and he would prevail against her this time.

A bird dived and flew away. The smell of mud and wet lawn filled the air. The whole moment felt charged with meaning, with anticipation.

Estian reached into the Wizr set and put his fingers on the piece representing Alix. A trickle of sweat went down his cheek as he slowly dragged it to Thorngate castle.

All eyes were fixed on the fountain.

It only took a moment for the waters of the fountain to start rippling. But Ransom saw no poisoner. She was invisible.

So Estian had been honest about that, at least.

"Show yourself, Alix," the Black King said curtly. "And bring our prisoner back to Pree."

His words hung in the stillness for a moment, and then Alix appeared in the fountain's waters. She had a dagger in an underhanded grip. She wore a cloak that swayed where it touched the waters. Her eyes went from Estian's to Ransom's.

Ransom lowered his gaze, trying to look defeated. The chains clinked as his shoulders sagged.

"He's still alive?" Alix said. Her voice was taunting.

"He was not easy to vanquish," Estian said. "Bring him to Pree and then meet us at Kingfountain."

Ransom swallowed, his throat dry.

"I would like to bring him to Kerjean," she said. "May I look after the prisoner?"

"You may have your revenge on him later," Estian said. She still hadn't left the waters. Ransom hoped his knights wouldn't foolishly try to grab her from there. Patience and subtlety were not traits that came easily to men who preferred killing with swords, but if they attempted that now, she would elude them.

"I will have him," Alix said, her voice throbbing with revenge.

"As I promised," Estian replied. "Now take him. We must depart."

Alix turned and looked at the keep. What was she thinking? Ransom risked a slight glance in that direction and saw nothing to give them away.

"As you command, my king," Alix said in a haughty tone. She stepped out of the water and approached Ransom. When the scent of lilac hit Ransom's nostrils, memories pummeled him in a fierce cascade. Of kissing her. Of listening to her lies and deceit. Of all the men and women she had killed. His emotions roiled, but he commanded them. He was the Fountain's creature now.

"Rise, Ransom," she said. "Your suffering is only about to begin."

Ransom rose, and as he did so, he flicked his wrists. The chains dropped to the grass with a rattling noise and heavy thump.

Alix's eyes widened with surprise.

He grabbed her by the wrist of the hand that held the knife, the same one bearing the pearl bracelet, and squeezed hard enough to make her wince and drop it.

"Stand back," he said to the king, but Estian was already withdrawing out of her reach.

Her look of surprise turned to one of betrayal. She gazed at Estian, her eyes widening until the whites could be seen around her irises.

"You lost?" she whispered to Estian.

"Dawson, the chains," Ransom said urgently.

The knights came around quickly and blocked her access to the fountain. They each had a dagger in hand, having set their swords aside to avoid telegraphing their intentions. Ransom had even asked his men to shave before putting the ruse into action, so that they resembled Occitanian knights. It had worked.

Alix looked into his eyes. The sight of her face, so hauntingly like Emiloh's, stabbed him in the heart. He felt her arm muscles tense, and he tightened his grip.

"Don't," he warned her. "I've a crossbowman with orders to kill you. The tables have turned, Alix. You are *my* prisoner now."

"Are you going to kill me?" she asked him, glancing briefly at Dawson as he approached from the left, pulling the chains from the bag. There were four manacles, one for each wrist and ankle.

"You're going into the falls," Estian said with a throb of triumph.

Alix flinched at the word. She gazed at the king with a look of hatred and then lowered her head and held out her other arm.

Ransom kept hold of her until the shackles were in place and the dagger taken away. He removed the pearl bracelet himself and stuffed it into his pocket.

As their horses were prepared for the ride to Kingfountain, Cecily searched and disarmed the poisoner. When she was finished, Ransom was summoned to the solar as Alix was escorted out by Dawson and three other knights to the dungeon. The chains had been designed to restrict a knight, but they'd ensured that the cuffs were narrow enough for her smaller wrists and ankles. Ransom was given the stubby key that would open them. Alix didn't even look at him as she was shuffled past.

Lady Deborah, who had been in the room for the search of Alix's person, gave a sigh of relief.

A small round table contained the different artifacts of the poisoner's trade. Daggers that had smudges of oil on them. Sharp hair pins. Jewelry with hidden compartments. Cecily picked up one of the rings and twisted the crown of it, revealing a small needle. She showed it to Ransom and grinned. Several vials sat on the table too, tiny ones that might only contain a few drops of deadly poison.

"I'll admit I'm curious to know more about these," Cecily said. "She even had a thin dagger—that one—hidden in her corset."

Ransom stared at the arrangement in wonderment. "Put these in a chest and keep them safe," he said. "I wonder if one of those vials contains a cure for the poison she's murdered our kings with."

"I can ask her," Cecily said. "She might, after some confinement, prove more willing to share her secrets. And Estian's."

"We must confirm the truth of her stories before we dare trust her," Lady Deborah said. "And I, for one, feel we've grabbed a snake by the tail. The whole time she was being searched, I feared for my life. She may try to barter those secrets for her freedom."

"I don't intend to set her free," Ransom said. "If she won't cooperate, then I see no reason to let her live."

"Seems a pity to send her over the falls too soon," Cecily said.

"Oh, I'm not going to send her over the falls," Ransom said solemnly. "If it comes to that."

Lady Deborah looked confused. "But the king said that was the only way a Fountain-blessed could be killed?"

"I don't trust him. Who knows how much of what he said is true? Like Alix, he will say and do anything to win his freedom. And hers. I'll honor the vow to release him after we secure a proper price and the prince's realm is more stable. Where to keep her is the challenge."

"What would Lady Claire do with her?" Cecily asked with a cunning smile.

"Probably put her in the burial mounds and seal the door. A dungeon will do. Maybe the queen's tower if she offers help? But we may need to find another place for her. A place she is unable to escape."

"You can't watch her day and night, Ransom," Cecily said.

Ransom sighed. "I cannot. For now, I want you and Hans Dragan to take turns guarding the poisoner. She must not escape."

"I have no intention of letting her go," Cecily said. "The sooner we get back to our stronghold, the better I'll feel. I miss the Espion tunnels."

Ransom retreated from the room while Cecily gathered up the poisoner's tools. The knights had finished their preparations for departure, and they were soon on their way to Kingfountain. Estian rode by Ransom's side the entire journey. Dawson rode with the prince. The storm had finally ended, and the cool air and orange leaves suggested that winter would soon be upon them.

It was a two-day ride to the palace, but they were met by Lord Kiskaddon's men before they arrived. Faulkes had done his duty and related the events, and Kiskaddon had come personally with his knights to escort them back to the city. When he saw Estian, his brow lowered and his lip curled in disgust. He was another man who saw the Occitanian king as his sworn enemy.

When they reached the palace to the fanfare of a jubilant city, the streets were thronged with people who cheered for the young prince. The peoples' cries of adoration were enough to warm Ransom's heart. But it pleased him even more to learn that the fleet Claire had sent had ravaged Estian's ships in the harbor. The flag of Legault flew aboard the ships, its beautiful knot pattern rippling in the pleasant breeze. Only three of Estian's ships had surrendered during the fighting. His defeat was absolute.

As they rode over the bridge, the noise of the falls filled Ransom with a surge of homesickness. There was the palace atop the hill, still standing—forever unbreached. But he could not forget the whispers he'd heard on his last visit.

Part of him feared this was not over, however it might seem.

After disembarking at the palace, he was greeted by the aging Sir Iain, who had come up from Beestone and was preparing accommodations for the upcoming coronation. Ransom carried the chest with the Wizr set into the palace himself, not trusting it to any hands other than his own. He slipped away from the others as soon as he could, retreating to the garden where he used to meet Claire and Emiloh. It provided an entrance to the cistern below the castle. As he paused at the steps, he opened the board once more. All was in order. And there was a new piece coming along the strip of black and white squares from the direction of Glosstyr. Claire. He breathed out a sigh of relief. She was coming.

After closing the lid, he carried the case down the steps to the edge of the water. He felt a ripple of his Fountain magic as he bent low and set the chest into the waters. After straightening, he looked down into the water, but the chest was undetectable. He retreated back to the palace and felt weariness pressing in on him.

As he approached his room, he saw Cecily standing to one side of the door, her back against the wall. Dawson was holding her hands in his, having just lowered her knuckles from his lips. They both turned and smiled when they saw it was him approaching.

"It's dusk already," Ransom observed, noticing the torches were all alight now, and the sunlight was fading outside. "Where is she?"

There was no doubt as to whom he meant.

"The dungeon below the palace," Cecily said. "The Espion all know none of them are to bring her food or speak with her without little dabs of wax in their ears. They know her magic is very persuasive. She's alone, in her chains, behind an iron door."

Ransom could sense Alix in the palace, and although the presence was dimmed by distance, he knew exactly where to find her.

"Good. I will speak to her tonight before going to bed. Where is Estian?"

"He's in the stateroom on the east side of the palace. Six knights guard him."

Ransom nodded and then looked at Dawson. "I think Dearley might return with Claire and the children by tomorrow. Let Sir Iain know and find out if we can be moved to a different set of rooms so we can all be together."

"Of course, my lord," Dawson said. He squeezed Cecily's hand once more and then departed.

Ransom lifted his eyebrows at her playfully, and she smiled with contentment.

"He's agreed to wait for my training to be done," she said. "Not every man is so patient. Shall I join you?"

He nodded. "I don't want to lose my head either. Why don't you put the wax in your ears and take the key to her shackles?" He reached into his pocket, felt past the pearl bracelet, and then gave her the key.

They walked together, discussing the news. Simon had returned with them, resuming his old position as Espion master, and he was already hard at work determining which Espion were loyal and which were not. Those sympathetic to Bodkin and his manner of doing things would be let go.

They descended the steps to the cells, and Alix's presence became more intense. There were two knights at the outer door of the dungeon and an Espion posted just inside.

A different guard unlocked the door. Cecily waited at the opening, wax in her ears, while Ransom walked inside.

Alix sat on a small cot, her cloak off now and covering her knees for warmth. The chains rattled as she moved her arms. Her head was bowed, her golden hair blocking her face.

"Are you going to put me to death, Ransom? Send me over the falls to punish me for my crimes?" she asked him in a weary voice. Again, he smelled the scent of lilac, although it was faded. One of the vials they'd taken from her had obviously contained her perfume.

"No," Ransom said.

She looked up at him in surprise. "After all of the people I've killed?"

He folded his arms. "You did that under Estian's orders."

"Did I? Can you be sure?"

"I'm fairly sure. You didn't tell him about the book. The one you stole from Claire. Why?"

She gazed at him, her expression inscrutable. "Because of what he would have made me do if he knew what I could *really* do," she answered softly.

He didn't trust her words. Not in the least. But she wasn't using her power against him. What had she become over the years since she'd tended his injury? There was a dark look in her eyes, an absence of goodness.

"Where is the book now, Alix? I'm going to make it a term of his release. Part of his ransom."

She shook her head. "He can't get it. I sent it to Pisan. They have other ancient tomes there, ones only the Fountain-blessed can read."

"So it is already gone?"

"I felt its influence on me the moment I saw it," she said. "I don't like to be . . . manipulated."

"A wise decision. It would have destroyed you."

"Maybe it already has, Ransom. If you're not going to kill me, then what? I'll never go free again. And that would be a fate worse than death."

"It might teach you patience," Ransom said.

"Where is the bracelet?" she asked him as he turned to go.

He looked at her. "Safe. What is it?"

"It was the only thing I had that belonged to my mother," she said. "It has no magic. May I have it back?"

He felt a throb of Fountain magic push at him. It came from her.

"I don't think so," he answered. "I'll have the guard bring you some moldy bread later. And some broth."

Hatred and anger gleamed in her eyes. Unnerved by the look, he left the room, and it was locked up behind him.

"Will you have some dinner?" Cecily asked as they mounted the steps.

"I'm too weary," Ransom answered. "I'm going to get some rest. Tell Dawson that I'll meet him in the training yard at first light." He needed to replenish his magic. Practicing in the yard had always done that for him because, he suspected, his devotion to practicing, to becoming the best swordsman possible, extended from loyalty to the crown.

"Very well. I need to check on Devon and Léanore. They were so glad to be back in their room again. They've always shared one."

"I can't wait for my sons to see them again." He let a sigh escape him. "This will all be a memory soon."

She put a hand on his arm. "You did it, Lord Ransom. No one else could have. I look forward to serving you when I return from Pisan. I assume you want me to find that book you mentioned?"

He gave her a grateful smile, and then they parted. Back in his room, he pulled off his boots and set them down. He was about to unbuckle his scabbard but decided not to. His body was still healing from the wounds he'd earned at the battle. One more night with the scabbard would completely restore him.

He blew out the candle and lay back, relishing the quiet and the darkness. Clasping his hands over his chest, he fell asleep in moments.

And awakened—groggily—to the warning pulse of his Fountain magic.

Lady Alix was coming down the corridor.

It is after midnight, and my hand trembles. We stopped for the night at Greton Lodge on the way to Kingfountain. A nightmare awakened me. It's one I've had before. A warning that Ransom's life was in danger. My heart is racing. The only news we've had is good news, of the coming coronation. Yet I cannot control my fear. I will awaken Dearley. We will rouse the children and ride to Kingfountain in the night. I pray that my fears are unfounded. But the Aos Sí do not always hear our prayers.

—Claire de Murrow
Greton Lodge
Midnight

CHAPTER
THIRTY-FIVE

When Courage Fails

Ransom threw off his blanket. The scabbard and blade were still snug around his hips. He groped in the dark for his boots and quickly tugged them on as he felt the presence of the poisoner coming toward him. He strode to the door.

"Who is on guard?" he called through the wood. How had she gotten away so quickly? She was in chains, behind a locked door, watched by guards with wax in their ears. It infuriated and confused him.

"It is I, Sir Galt," came the muffled voice on the other side.

"Call for the night watch," Ransom ordered. "The poisoner is—"

He heard a startled grunt and felt the shock of a body falling against the door. Then the sound of Sir Galt sliding down onto the floor, gurgling, followed by stillness.

Sweat beaded on Ransom's forehead. The bar was still nested in place, so his door was locked. The room was pitch black, and when he turned and searched for his hauberk, he tripped over something on the floor. He sensed Alix's presence arriving at his door. His fingers found the chain mail, and he began to pull it on quickly, knowing any protection was better than none.

"Anoichto."

He recognized the word as the old speech, but he didn't remember what it meant. The bar locking the door slid open, revealing torchlight from the hall beyond but no poisoner. With one arm through the hauberk sleeve already, he drew his bastard sword. He was about to lunge into the doorframe when he smelled the sweet odor of lilac. Before he could react, a puff of dust stung his eyes.

He blinked, trying to clear his vision, and then swung his blade in a wide arc, hoping to catch her by surprise with the sudden movement. His muscles constricted, and he felt his heart begin to race. The blade dropped from his suddenly numb fingers. A strange taste came from the back of his throat, almost like corn but harsher. He started to gag, and Alix shoved him backward onto the bed.

A strange euphoria began to fill his thoughts, like a suppressive cloud that made thinking difficult.

Sir Galt's body was dragged into his room and dumped unceremoniously in the corner. Then Alix appeared suddenly at his bedside, her image just a blur to his fogged senses, and used a dagger and flint to light the candle he'd extinguished earlier. He sensed her going to the door and shutting it, then heard the bolt slide back into place.

The fear he'd felt earlier was gone. It was a pleasant feeling, like he was floating down a river. His wild imaginings wondered what it would feel like to go over the falls.

"I don't have much time to interrogate you," she said, coming to the bedside again. "You've ingested a strong dose of nightshade. Any stronger, and it would have killed you." He felt her magic slip over him, coaxing and gentle. "Where did you hide the Wizr board?"

He wouldn't tell her. She was his enemy.

But his lips betrayed him.

"In the waters of the cistern beneath the castle."

"Interesting," Alix said, bemused. "I wouldn't have thought to look there. Does anyone else know where it is? Did you tell anyone?"

Again he spoke truthfully, unable to resist her question. "No."

"Oh good, then no one will stop me when I come back for it. I've been to this castle many times already, you know, always while you were away. I hid weapons and poisons in various fountains for just such a situation. Oh, Ransom. You should have killed me back at Thorngate. A costly mistake."

"How did you escape?" he asked, though it felt wrong asking for some strange reason.

"I have many tricks you don't know about. There are books in Pisan that teach words of power to the astute, to the sensitive. Your chains couldn't hold me. Neither could an iron door. Now I must go and finish my task. The last Argentines have to die. This game has gone on long enough. Let fate have its due. Let it be revenge for my mother joining the wrong side. And for my husband's untimely death. The hostages your king killed were all helpless, Ransom. It seems only right that your people should pay in blood. When I draw the Wizr board from the cistern, the flood will come. And I don't even care that Estian drowns too. As long as there is a Vertus left to win the game, it will all be worth it. It was a close game, Ransom. I'll give you that. You played it well."

She was still a blur to him. He felt peaceful, though.

Lowering herself down by his head, she leaned close enough that her hair tickled his cheek, but he couldn't move his arms. "A little sip. You've no reason to fear it. It's not the same poison that killed your kings. That, I'm saving for *his* children. Fitting they should die the same way. But this will hamper you considerably. I want you to see the end come to Ceredigion, Ransom. I want you to see what failure looks like."

He discerned a little movement as she removed what he imagined was a vial. Then she pressed her lips against his.

"We could have been so much more together," she whispered. "But you would not forsake your honor. In the end, your honor forsook you."

She brought the vial to his lips. He tasted the bitter fluid on his tongue and reflexively swallowed. He couldn't resist her, not while everything was in a fog.

Her fingers stroked his cheek gently. "I'll grant you no more mercies," she said in a whisper. "The game will end, and your children will perish in the flood. Your wife will drown in despair and water. But not you. Moving water cannot kill a Fountain-blessed. When you are ready to die, go to the North and freeze to death. This is my last revenge." She put away the vial and drew her dagger.

His eyes were starting to clear again. A strange halo seemed to surround her face, her golden hair. Holding the dagger tightly, she drove it into the meat of his leg, the one that had been injured before.

A gasp sighed from his lips. He didn't feel the pain, but he knew it was a serious blow. One that had penetrated to the bone.

A satisfied smirk showed she'd done what she came to do. She yanked the dagger free.

"Farewell, Ransom. You won't remember this conversation for long. But I will. And I will savor the memory of your failure."

She blew out the candle with a puff of breath, plunging the room into darkness again.

He didn't know how long he lay there, but he clenched his hands as his leg throbbed dully with pain. Even though the candle had been snuffed, he wasn't entirely in the dark. The scabbard glowed, showing its magic was healing him. But it would not heal him of the poison he'd ingested. The bitter flavor was still on his tongue. He breathed and sighed and tried to move his body. He had to remember. He had to tell someone. Summoning his Fountain magic, he found enough strength to sit up. It was an effort, but he succeeded.

The sound of boots came tramping down the hall, loud enough that he knew it was more than one person. They stopped at his door, and a fist pounded on the wood.

"Lord Ransom?" It was Dawson's voice.

He strained against the power of the dust and tried to swing his legs to the edge of the bed.

"Lord Ransom?" Then he heard Dawson mutter, "Where is Galt?"

"I haven't seen him," said another knight from the watch.

The door handle jiggled, and the door suddenly opened, splashing torchlight into the room.

"Lord Ransom, the poisoner has escaped the dungeon. She killed—" Suddenly his words stopped as he saw Ransom sitting on the edge of the bed, breathing fast, and then noticed the body crumpled on the floor.

"Water," Ransom pleaded.

Dawson hurried to the pitcher on the far side of the room and filled a goblet. As he handed it to Ransom, he snarled to the others, "She's already been here!"

Ransom took a soothing sip, and the cool water washed away the bitter taste. His magic churned inside him, lending him strength, but not enough. He felt weak all over.

"The prince and princess," Ransom wheezed. "She's going . . . to kill them. Poisoned me. Not fatal, but I'm weak."

"Cecily!" Dawson gasped. "You two, stay with him. The rest, come with me!"

He charged from the room, and the two knights entered. One sighed upon seeing Galt's corpse.

"The night watch," Ransom said, his voice a raspy whisper.

"They've been summoned. Sir Simon has been awakened as well. The Espion are searching the castle."

"She can make herself invisible," Ransom said. But he could sense her. He alone could sense her. "Help me stand."

"We can do this, my lord."

"Obey me," Ransom said, struggling to rise. The two knights helped him stand. "My . . . armor . . ." he panted.

They helped him finish putting on the hauberk, then one grabbed the sword he'd dropped and put it in the sheath. His leg burned with pain, but the scabbard kept it from bleeding. He had to stop Alix from killing Devon and Léanore. Otherwise, his own children would die as well. Hundreds of thousands would.

"Where should we take you, my lord?"

Ransom's memory began to fog. Alix—she had been in his room. What had she asked him?

The Wizr board. She knew where it was being kept, which meant it needed to be moved. How long would he be able to remember? Part of him was tempted to tell them, but he didn't recognize either man and thought it wise to practice caution. He put one foot ahead of the other, with the two knights assisting him, and they left the corridor. The torchlight gave off strange colors that made him dizzy. It was the poison working on him. Slowing him down. His very bones began to ache.

He closed his eyes, trying to sense Alix's location. She was moving swiftly. But he knew the castle better than she.

"The queen's tower," he said. "Take me there."

"Yes, my lord."

As they walked, Ransom's strength increased. Soon he didn't need their support. He could walk on his own despite the injury to his leg. Thank the Fountain Alix didn't know about his scabbard.

Confusion struck him as he realized he suddenly couldn't remember where they were going or why.

"What's happening?" he asked the knights, confused. "Where are we going?"

"The queen's tower, as you said," answered one of them. He looked at the other knight as if Ransom were going mad.

"The tower, yes," Ransom said. That was right. His memory flared awake again. He could sense Alix. How had she escaped the dungeon? "The poisoner has escaped."

"Yes . . . we know," said the other knight, baffled.

They went down the stairs and started across the corridor. There were no other knights visible, but he heard voices echoing down the halls. The night watch was going from room to room.

When they reached the door leading to the tower, he motioned for them to open it. He knew Alix was above him, for he'd sensed her going up the stairs. Why would she go to the tower, though? There was no way out from there.

The knight opened the door, a sword in his free hand, and then backed away.

A torch bracketed to the wall revealed Cecily sprawled on the first steps, a dagger still in her ribs. He recognized the hilt on the blade—it bore the symbol of the Elder King. All the knights of the castle had one. He'd seen it a hundred times. Blood had soaked her dress.

No! Ransom hurried to her side, seeing her eyes still partly open. Had she died already?

"Ransom?" she whispered, her brow twitching.

"Get the night watch here! Now!" Ransom ordered, and one of the knights rushed away and began to shout the alarm.

Alix was nearly to the top. He grabbed the arm of the other knight. "She's up there."

"I'll go," said the knight with determination.

"She'll kill you," Ransom said. "But the prince . . . the princess . . . Cecily, are they here?"

He looked at her face and saw her nod once.

"Ran from her . . . needed . . . keep them safe."

The knight began to run up the steps, sword in hand.

Ransom just gazed at her for a moment. She'd lost so much blood already. The wound was fatal. His heart panged. No—he couldn't let her die. The Ondine had suggested he would have to forfeit his life. When he hadn't fallen in battle, he'd thought there was a reprieve, but he'd only let himself believe that because he had so badly wanted it to be true. Drawing his sword, Ransom leaned it against the wall and unbuckled the scabbard.

"Tell . . . Dawson . . ." she whispered.

He would need the scabbard facing Alix. But Cecily needed it more. "You will live!" he said firmly. "You will go to the poisoner school, and you will protect the Argentines from such treachery in the future. And you and Dawson will be married. I swear it." He left the belt attached and pressed the scabbard against her bosom. He placed her hand atop it to hold it there, and the raven sigil sparked to life once again.

Pain flared from his leg, and blood began to seep from his pants. He tugged his belt loose and wrapped it around his leg, tightening it to the point of it aching. He cinched the leather strap and then rose, pressing his hand against the wall.

Cecily's head lolled to the side, but he saw her chest rise and fall, the scabbard going up and down with it. He pulled the dagger from her ribs, and no surge of blood came. He grabbed his bastard sword with the other hand and started up the stairs.

Why was he in the tower? How had Alix escaped the dungeon? He couldn't comprehend how anyone could have been so careless as to set her free. Or maybe one of the Espion was secretly loyal to Occitania? His mind was a jumble, but he knew his path. With his leg screaming in pain, he lurched up the steps, taking them two at a time.

A shout of surprise came from above, and the knight who'd ran ahead came plummeting down the shaft of the tower. Ransom saw his body go rushing by, something that happened too quickly for him to intervene, and then there was a sickening noise as the knight landed on the paving stones at the base of the tower.

Ransom looked up into the darkness. "Alix!" he shouted.

He grunted as he continued up the stairs, his chest heaving with the exertion. A bitter taste came into his mouth again. He gritted his teeth, stumbling into the wall of the tower. One wrong step, and it might all end now, before he even reached them. Slow. He was too slow.

Sweat streaking down his back, he found himself thinking of the previous occasions he'd climbed this tower. He'd come to this very tower to visit Claire. Claire and Emiloh. Now the former queen's daughter was out to destroy the last of the Argentines.

He couldn't let her. Whatever it cost.

When he reached the upper landing, the door at the top of the tower was already open. He sensed Alix in the chamber beyond it and charged forward. His leg spasmed, and he nearly collapsed, but through sheer strength of will he kept himself up.

Alix stood at the far side of the room, facing Emiloh's old bed. The curtains of the bed had been yanked aside, and the only light came from the balcony window. The moon was a silent witness to the scene.

The poisoner turned to face him, her mouth a snarl of frustration.

"You will not stop me," she said threateningly.

"I must," he said, shaking his head. He feinted with the sword and lunged at her with the dagger.

She dodged the blow and kicked his injured leg, making him hiss in pain as he dropped to one knee. Wrenching his arm, she forced him to drop the dagger and jabbed her fingers into his throat. He couldn't breathe.

Ransom grabbed her by the fabric of her dress and yanked her down to the floor. He lifted his sword to finish her off, but she landed a kick to his groin that made him double over in pain.

She swept free of him, kicking him in the temple to knock him down to the floor.

Then she yanked up the bedcover and dropped low, looking in the darkness beneath the bed. He was gasping, struggling to breathe, but from his position, he saw the underside of the bed as well as she did. The space was empty.

Alix shrieked in frustration. She went to the curtains and shoved them aside, one by one, revealing nothing. The children were not there.

Then Ransom heard the creak of the roof. He looked up, and so did Alix.

The children had gone outside and climbed up on the roof. If they'd held still for a moment longer, the trick might have worked.

A smile of triumph came to Alix's lips as she drew another dagger and walked to the balcony window. The sound of shouting came from the bottom of the stairwell. Men were running up the steps in hastened fury, but it would not be soon enough.

He watched as Alix opened the latch of the balcony door and stepped into the night. What fragile moon was left glowed in her hair. Ransom saw a pair of legs dangling there, the prince's. He no doubt had helped his sister up first. The boy was honorable, nothing like his father.

Ransom grunted, his loins throbbing with pain still, but he rose and charged Alix.

She'd pulled back her arm to stab the boy in the leg. One cut was all it would take for the poison to destroy him. But she didn't finish the stroke. Ransom grabbed for her wrist, thinking of nothing but saving the boy, the young king, and was nicked by the blade as he deflected it. He felt a sting of pain shoot up his arm as his body collided with hers. He had time for one thought—*it's over*—and they both tumbled into the stone barrier of the balcony. When she lifted her leg to kick him, she fell backward, and the momentum carried them both over the edge. In a panic, Ransom grabbed at the stone ledge, and his fingers found a firm grip.

Alix grabbed his foot.

He hung at the edge of the balcony, his fingers straining from the weight of holding them both.

"Don't! Don't!" Alix screamed with real fear throbbing in her voice.

Ransom twisted slightly, his muscles and tendons strained beyond endurance. He tried to reach up with his other hand but missed.

Alix's fingers dug into his pants and then the fringe of his chain mail as she attempted to climb him. The added strain of the swaying made him moan with despair. They were both going to fall.

He looked down at Alix's upturned face, at the desperation and terror in her eyes. She'd dropped the poisoned dagger to cling to him with both hands.

"Hold!" she pleaded.

Her strength failed before his did. As she reached to grab him higher, to pull herself up more, she lost her grip and went plunging down into the darkness. He heard her body strike the stones an instant later.

Without her weight, he sighed in relief. He still sensed her, down at the base of the tower, still alive—still breathing. That surprised him. The fall should have killed her.

And then it did.

The sense of her Fountain magic guttered out.

His wrist screamed in pain. He knew he couldn't hold on any longer. In a moment, he'd join Alix on the stones, a strange embrace of two enemies at the end.

He thought of Claire calling him an eejit. It made him smile as his grip finally failed.

Two young hands grabbed at his hauberk, and another two grabbed his wrist.

"Pull, Léanore! Pull!" said the prince, his teeth chattering with cold.

"I am! He's . . . too . . . heavy!" moaned the princess.

"We can do it. Pull your hardest!"

Ransom dangled from the tower, twisting slowly, his strength gone. He had no dregs of Fountain magic left. No scabbard to heal his injuries. What remained of his life was literally in the hands of two young children.

"We have to pull him up," Devon said. "We have to! Come now! Pull!"

The two children strained. Ransom reached out with his other hand and caught the lip of the railing. With his own power assisting them, they got him on his chest on the edge of the ledge. Dawson and his knights found them then and helped haul him the rest of the way over.

He lay panting on the balcony floor, gazing into the eyes of the prince and the princess.

Alix had come to kill them, and if he hadn't been there to stop it, she would have. His life had been spared, for a little while, by the strength of an eight-year-old boy and his sister, who had refused to let him go.

I will save my tears for later. They can do me no good today.

—Claire de Murrow
Palace at Kingfountain

CHAPTER
THIRTY-SIX

Beloved

The deconeus of the sanctuary of Our Lady finished the rite and bowed his head in solemnity as the commotion of the river rushed past. It was time to lift the canoe with the pallid body stretched inside. The barber who'd prepared it had meticulously wiped away the scabs of dried blood around the eyes and nose. The lifeless hands were crossed over the corpse's chest.

Ransom breathed out, preparing for the pain as he grabbed the staff and helped hoist the body. He couldn't conceal the grunt caused by a jolt of pain in his leg where Alix had stabbed him, and the small yet soon-to-be fatal wound on his wrist. He felt a trickle of blood go down his leg, but he performed his duty. Faulkes held the other end of the staff and gave Ransom a worried look, prepared to shoulder the front of the canoe himself if Ransom faltered.

He would not falter.

With a limp, he marched in step with the others and carried Jon-Landon's body down the planks to the edge of the platform. Simon and his Espion had said that a large crowd had gathered on the bridge to witness the rites. The sun was directly overhead, but it was a cool autumn day, and the gentle breeze was soothing to his soul. His insides were on fire, though, a series of cramps and burning sensations that rode his every step. The same poison that had killed Jon-Landon. And Benedict. And both Devons.

When they reached the end of the docks, he squinted and prepared to lower the staff, which he and the other knights did with practiced grace. The men in the rear, including Sir Dawson and Lord DeVaux, lifted their end a little higher. The canoe plunged down and splashed into the river. It bobbed a moment before the current dragged it away, sending it on its one-way journey to the Deep Fathoms.

As Ransom watched it go, he thought about the king's final moments of grief and guilt. Four kings he had failed to save. But the fifth, named after his predecessors, would be crowned this day. The boy would have a clean slate, a fresh chance.

He released his grip on the staff and turned to the crowd assembled at the docks, mostly nobles and knights. The queen dowager—so strange to think of Léa with that title now, for she was still so young—dabbed her eyes with a kerchief. The look of misery on her face moved him. The prince stood at her side, silent and resolute. The young princess approached Ransom, squeezed his hand, and told him that he'd done his duty well.

He smiled at her and thanked her before limping back toward the castle. Dawson walked behind him, providing distance but also ready to lend aid if it was needed. He appreciated the concern. Before either of them reached the door, they heard a collective gasp as the boat carrying Jon-Landon's body arrived at the falls.

"It is over," Dawson said.

Ransom nodded, grateful to be alive but grief-stricken that his own death would so quickly follow that of the king.

"Can I help you climb the stairs?" Dawson asked.

"I was going to the queen's garden," Ransom said. "I'd like to be alone."

"I'll check on Cecily, then. I never knew about your scabbard, Lord Ransom. I cannot thank you enough for saving her life. She's weak, but the wound is nearly healed. We're lucky the blade wasn't poisoned."

Ransom turned and gave Dawson an affectionate smile. "It has served me well these many years. Please keep its secret. I haven't even told Dearley."

Dawson gave him a knightly salute, his pledge to honor the request.

After they separated, Ransom moved his way gently through the interior of the palace, watching as the servants prepared a luncheon for those who had attended the rites. The cramps were becoming more severe. Sweat trickled down his back. A seizure of sudden pain came so startlingly fast that he had to stop and lean against the wall to keep from crumpling to the ground. So this was the agony the others had endured. He would bear it too.

Once the searing pain had ebbed slightly, he continued through the corridor and exited into the garden. He forced himself, step by step, to go to the nearest fountain and sat at the edge, grateful to relieve the pain in his leg. Lowering his head, he breathed out slowly, trying to master the anguish ravaging his innards. A blob of sweat dripped from the tip of his nose. The sound of the fountain waters was soothing.

He looked up at the trees. Their leaves had turned into a dazzling array of autumn colors. Some yellow, some as orange as pumpkins, and others the same crimson as the streaks in Claire's hair. A stab of pain dug into his heart. He would miss running his fingers through her hair. Miss waking with her at his side, their bodies generating warmth and feelings of safety. For many months of their marriage, she had wakened alone because of his calls of duty to the king and because of the malice of others who had brought war to their land. Peace. That was all that he wanted now. Estian could endure his confinement a little longer. Bennett had in Brugia. It was time for a change of seasons. An end of war, an ushering in of peace.

He didn't know how long he'd sat there, breathing through the stabs of pain and tormenting thoughts, but he heard voices, and he recognized them. He tried to stand to greet his family, but the needles were too strong.

Willem and Dev rounded the corner at a run, followed by little Sibyl, who brightened when she saw his face. Tears stung his eyes at the sight of his family, Claire coming next with Keeva in her arms, escorted by Dearley himself.

"Papa! Papa!" the children cried in a tumult of arms, hugs, kisses that nearly knocked him back into the fountain water.

Claire's eyes were full of worry when she saw his face, but she strode up and knelt in front of him, her hair windblown, and her cheeks a little pink.

"You're still alive," she murmured. "Dawson told us what happened. My beloved. Oh, my dearest!"

She clung to him, sobbing into his shoulder, squishing their youngest between them. Ransom's heart was breaking, but he was so grateful to see them again. If they hadn't started their journey sooner, he might have been dead before they arrived. His tears wet her hair. Looking up, he saw Dearley choking back his own emotions.

Claire pulled back and kissed Ransom on the mouth. He could taste her tears. "There is time to grieve later," she whispered. "You're alive, and we love you, and we want to be with you every moment."

"We do, Papa!" said Sibyl. "Are you really going to die?"

He looked at his daughter and nodded truthfully. "But I will always be your father," he told her, pulling her in with one arm to hug her. The boys' eyes were wet, but they tried to be brave, even though their breathing was ragged, their emotions a heavy load to bear.

"I'll be a knight like you," said Willem proudly.

"So will I," said the younger Devon with equal conviction.

"You must serve the king since I cannot," Ransom said. "He'll need you both to be loyal and true."

"We will, Papa. Just like you," Willem said.

Ransom saw Dearley turn and begin to walk away, his head bowed.

"John," Ransom called, stopping him. He took Claire's hand and grunted as she helped pull him to his feet.

Dearley turned, his eyes streaked with tears, and the two men embraced each other like brothers and wept.

The pain was unendurable.

Ransom tossed and turned on the bed, one moment overwhelmed by fire and the next trembling with shivers. Claire never left his side, and she did all she could to comfort him, bringing water to his fevered lips and sponging the sweat from his brow. His children were there as well, in the room Sir Iain had prepared for them. The boys slept on the couches and sometimes slunk off with Léanore to explore the Espion tunnels. They'd brought Sibyl into their conspiracy and had begun teaching her the inner pathways on the first day. To everyone's surprise, she enjoyed navigating them. Word had been sent to James and Maeg in Brythonica, but he doubted he'd last long enough for them to return.

"Your eyes are bleeding again," Claire said sadly, dabbing the corners with a wet towel. "How I hate seeing you suffer. Are you hungry?"

"I wish it were winter, and you could bring me some ice," Ransom said, touching her hand and squeezing it. "I vomited everything last night. I'm empty but not hungry."

"It will be winter soon enough," she said. They'd talked and talked for hours since her return. "I think we'll spend it in Glosstyr, though. With your mother."

He began to shiver again, and she pulled up another blanket. He gazed at her, feeling comforted by her presence.

"Is it dawn yet?" he asked.

Claire rose and went to the curtain and drew it aside. "Soon," she said. "I know you hoped you'd last the night. You're a stubborn man, Ransom Barton. You fight it still."

"I wish I could conquer this foe," he said with a gasp. He writhed beneath the sheets, trying not to show his agony. "But it will prevail . . . in the end."

She came back and sat at his bedside. "You have been a faithful husband to me," she said, laying a hand on his chest. "I doubted you when I never should have. Forgive me."

"We've been over it before," Ransom said. "There is nothing to forgive. I . . . I don't think I can last much longer, Claire. I'm so weary . . . so weary of fighting death."

"Let me wake the children, then," she said, rising swiftly. She jostled them and then went to the chair by the door and roused Dearley. He'd not left Ransom's confinement either. They'd spent many hours talking, and Dearley had pledged to protect Ransom's family and ensure they prospered.

As his bleary-eyed children rubbed their faces, they gathered around his bedside. Dearley opened the door and whispered something to the knight standing guard.

Ransom looked at the faces of those he loved. He tried to smile at them, but he was afraid it looked like a frightening grimace. Then suddenly Dawson and Cecily were at his bedside too, hand in hand. Cecily looked at Ransom with gratitude and compassion and bent down and kissed his brow.

"Thank you, Lord Ransom. I owe you my life."

Dawson wiped his eyes. "We'll be married today," he said, holding her hand. "We won't wait."

Ransom gave them an approving nod. "I'm glad of it. May the Fountain bless you."

"May you be blessed as well," Dawson said. He held the scabbard and belt in his hands, as if ready to offer them back to him. Ransom noticed the bastard sword inside looked like his. It *was* his.

"I want Willem to have it," Ransom said. "When he's old enough. Until then—you safeguard it."

Dawson looked startled and then grateful. "I'll give it to your eldest son," he promised. "When he is ready."

Claire looked to Dawson, recognizing the scabbard, and smiled through her tears in agreement.

They withdrew so that Simon and his wife could approach. Ransom did not know Simon's wife very well, for she was a quiet and shy woman who rarely spoke and did so with a stutter.

Simon reached down and clasped Ransom's hand. "You will be sorely missed," he said. "Your bravery and courage will always be remembered."

"T-thank you," stuttered the Lady of Holmberg. She backed away and started to cry.

Ransom's eyes were getting heavier. Each breath was a struggle.

Lady Deborah came next. "Your mother just arrived at Kingfountain," she said. "We're bringing her now. Please . . . stay with us a little longer!"

"Thank you, L-lady Deborah," Ransom said. "You've always . . . been . . ." His words slurred and trailed off. He went wild with panic, not wanting to perish before his mother came.

"Ransom," Claire pleaded, pressing her hip against him and squeezing his hand. "Please . . . tarry longer. You can do it."

He blinked rapidly, the pain easing. He couldn't feel his toes. He couldn't feel the ache in his leg anymore.

"It's the prince . . . make way!"

Ransom turned his head and saw Prince Devon and Princess Léanore coming to the bed with their mother. They looked frightened by his condition, but both faced their fears bravely.

"You saved our lives," said the prince.

"You saved mine," Ransom panted. "I wish I could have served you, my prince . . . my king."

"When I wear the hollow crown, it will be because you put it on my head," the prince said. "The Lady bless and keep thee. The Lady make her face to shine upon thee."

"I love you, Lord Ransom," said the princess with a squeak in her voice. She patted his arm. "Be at peace."

The queen dowager nudged her children to depart, but she stayed. Her eyes were a mix of compassion and distaste.

"Lady Deborah has suggested that Claire rule as protector of Ceredigion," she said with a strained tone. "Better her than Kiskaddon, I say. I know the pain of losing a husband." She looked to Claire with a mollifying smile before turning back to Ransom. "Did Jonny tell you anything . . . anything he didn't want me to know?"

Ransom could hardly believe she was asking such a thing at such a time. But she'd always been selfish.

"Ransom kept many secrets," Claire answered for him. "And he would never break his honor by divulging them. Not even to me."

The queen dowager sniffed, nodded, and then left.

Ransom looked at his wife tenderly and mouthed the words *thank you*.

She brought his knuckles to her lips and kissed them. Another round of pain came, and he groaned in anguish, writhing again, hating to be a spectacle.

"She's here! She's here! Ransom's mother is here!"

Lady Sibyl of the Heath came into the room, one arm clinging to Dearley, who had sent a knight to fetch her when the news had come. Her hair was streaked with gray and fading. Her grief-stricken face registered some relief.

"Mother," Ransom whispered.

She knelt by his bedside, and her wrinkled hands cupped his fingers. "My boy. My dear boy," she said, then bowed her head and wept.

"I love you, Mother," Ransom said, trying to find the strength to squeeze her hand. But even that was too difficult. The pain was receding. He felt a blanket of peace settle on him.

"Ransom?" Claire asked pleadingly.

"I love you, Claire de Murrow," he whispered next. It was his last breath.

"*Is breá liom an iomarca duit*, Ransom," she whispered thickly, pressing a kiss to his lips as he died.

I love you too much.

Ransom looked down and saw his own bleeding face. He saw Claire sobbing against his chest, her groans and tears showing the depth of her loss. His children held hands, standing resolutely next to the bed. His daughter Sibyl's lip trembled, and she swiped her little hand across her eyes. Dawson and Cecily also wiped away tears. Dearley helped Ransom's mother to a chair to save her strength.

A tug pulled at Ransom's spirit-self, like the coaxing of a stream. The room was full of the people he loved most. All of the kings he had served had died with only Ransom at their side. How different this was—to be so loved and cared for that they had all wanted to be with him despite the gruesome affliction caused by the deadly poison.

Gently, peacefully, the otherworldly current pulled him away. It swept him through the castle corridors, where he heard tinkling chimes coming from the various fountains. It sped him down the dock where he had, the day before, levered Jon-Landon's body into the waters. Then he was flying over the river, the rush and noise of the falls growing louder and louder until the roar consumed everything, and he felt himself gliding beyond the falls—not plummeting into the water but soaring like a raven. He felt a freedom unlike anything he'd experienced before. It was freedom and love and contentment and bliss—all merged into one.

And then his consciousness, his spirit-self, plunged into the ocean, and he saw the burned and sunken ships of the Occitanian fleet. Deeper and deeper he went, witnessing marvels of the sea, of creatures he'd never known existed.

There was a city in the farthest depths, one that glowed like stars and the moon, and strangely, the waters parted, and he found himself, his spirit-self, walking up a beach toward a massive set of jutting, block-shaped cliffs rising from the ocean floor. A gap between the cliffs revealed the ancient city. He didn't know if it was the ruins of Leoneyis or something even grander, but he marched up the shore, where he found a crowd had gathered to welcome him. He recognized the water sprite, the Ondine, that he'd seen along the shores near Glosstyr. She bowed her head to him and smiled in welcome.

Joy struck his soul like a bell when he saw the Elder King and Emiloh, hand in hand, smiling at him in pleasure, beckoning him to join them. He saw Bennett and Goff, their grins wide and handsome. Goff's hand was resting on the shoulder of a young man, Drew, his son, who'd been murdered by Jon-Landon Argentine. Drew smiled and waved at Ransom in recognition. The feelings of joy swelled past the point of endurance. He didn't understand how that was possible, when moments before he had departed his living family and borne witness to their grief and sadness. But this feeling, this reuniting with others, caused such an enormous swell of compassion and tenderness that it subsumed the other emotions for the moment. He heard cheers and clapping and recognized William Chappell, the knight he'd so admired as a young man, who'd died in that long-ago standoff with Lord DeVaux. And Bryon Kinghorn stood next to Ransom's brother, Marcus, both greeting him with wide smiles. Gervase was there, beaming with pride and gesturing for him to come.

Ransom stood in the surf, seeing a strange glow around his body, a glow that matched all of theirs.

And then one of them strode toward him, Devon the Younger King, handsome as he had been in life, and the two embraced as the surf crashed around them but did not touch their beings.

"Welcome to the Deep Fathoms!" said his friend and king. "Come . . . join the feast! We've saved a place for you, Ransom!"

There is a legend that the Aos Sí have the power to raise the dead for one night a year. In the darkest night of midwinter, I tramped through the snow to a barrow mound I'd built outside of Glosstyr. I sang the song of the dead. I sang of my love for Ransom and my desire to see him, for just one night. I wept, and my tears burned the snow.

He did not come. Some legends are the withered hopes of the living.

When the spring arrived, things became new once more. The trees, which had appeared dead, came to life once again. We looked forward to returning to Connaught for a visit. I will want Sibyl to be queen there someday, and she will need to know her people and the ways of our land. She has an old soul inside her and a fondness for Lord Toole. She doesn't believe in the Aos Sí. To be honest, I'm not sure I do anymore either. Sometimes legends are just that.

The boys could not be kept from Ceredigion if I ordered them bound with ropes and hung upside down. In one more year, they will become wards to other nobles, a practice that has gone on since the land was birthed from the sea, I suppose.

I miss Ransom. I miss his silence, the tenderness of his eyes, his gentle hands. I miss the love we made and the wars we fought. We had more feeling in our short years together than some couples have in a lifetime. I felt something powerful at Ransom's funeral rite—a deep sense of rightness, as if the Fountain, if it is real after all, was pleased with him.

My father endured the loneliness after Mother's death. I must learn to do the same.

A letter came today from Constance of Brythonica, inviting me to visit Ploemeur. There are things she feels she should tell me, things that might relieve any suspicions or worry I had about Ransom and her. She would like, if possible, and if the negotiations with Occitania go well, to return Josselin castle to my family as a rightful inheritance. Very gracious of her.

I believe that I shall acquiesce. I didn't know Constance very well. But if she is anything like her name implies, perhaps we shall become friends after all.

—Claire de Murrow, Queen of Legault,
Protector of Ceredigion
Glosstyr Keep

EPILOGUE

The Gradalis

The grove was hauntingly beautiful. Claire felt a strangeness about it, the same kind of feeling she experienced when visiting her ancestors' barrow mounds. The earth was damp and spongy, and the light, which shone overhead from the noonday sun, could barely penetrate the thicket of branches of the massive trees.

Lady Constance and her husband, Lord Montfort, stood hand in hand, looking at her with smiling eyes. There was a massive stone slab on the ground and a little trickle of water by it. Mistletoe hung from the boughs of the trees. But her gaze was instantly drawn to a silver bowl engraved with ancient characters, chained to the slab of rock. Ransom had been the sacred protector of this wood. She knew the truth now, of how the bowl had been taken from the Kerjean castle during the age of King Andrew. Of how its magic provided a bridge to other worlds.

Her heart raced with giddiness. It was nearly time. The sun was almost directly overhead, it was the summer solstice—the longest day of the year.

"And Ransom fought in this grove?" Claire asked, turning to look at Constance.

"Many times," the duchess replied. "He guarded its secret to prevent the Gradalis from being stolen by Alix and her minions. They almost managed it, but he stopped them."

"No one could defeat Ransom," Claire said proudly.

The Aos Sí were just a myth, she'd concluded. An explanation for knowledge whose source had been lost to time. Ransom had begun to convince her before his death, and Constance had continued to help her understand and had shared meaningful revelations with her that had put an end to any lingering doubt. Claire knew about the true purpose of the seering stones now. Constance had seen *Claire* in this very grove, tipping over the silver dish during that one day, each year, when a rift could be opened between the mortal world and the Deep Fathoms.

"It is time," Lord Montfort said, coming forward. He tugged on his finger, and the invisible ring materialized in his palm. It was the guardian's ring, the one Ransom had worn for years. She was amazed she'd never felt it on his finger.

Constance took the ring from her husband and approached Claire. Her throat tightened, too thick for her to speak. Constance put the ring on her finger and uttered a word in the old speech. The ring fit snugly.

"What if I don't want to be summoned back," Claire said with a smile, choking a little on her words as she laughed.

"You won't," said Constance seriously. "After you visit there, you will desire to stay. The longer you stay, the more unbearable returning will be. Even your love of your children won't be strong enough to lure you back."

Claire bit her lips. "That is powerful magic indeed. I love my children."

"After we summon you, the magic here in the grove will dim some of your memory of the Deep Fathoms. So that the longing won't drive you mad. But remember, if you take off the ring while you are there, you will not be able to return at all. The desire to stay will be overwhelming."

Claire nodded, taking Constance's hands in her own and squeezing them. They'd visited several times since Claire had traveled to Ploemeur in answer to the duchess's summons. It was Constance who'd taught her the ways of the Fountain. She believed in it now. The traditional beliefs of her people, in Legault, were not wholly wrong. There were just some pieces missing.

"You are a treasure to me for doing this," Claire said. "It hasn't even been a year since Ransom died. I'm . . . nervous seeing him again. There's so much I want to tell him. Only one day a year. But I can accept that. Until it is my turn to join him."

Constance smiled with tenderness and warmth. "Fill the Gradalis and pour it out on the slab. Normally there is a storm that comes when the magic is invoked, but that won't happen this time, because of the solstice. We will summon you back at this time tomorrow."

"Give Ransom my highest regard," said Lord Montfort.

Claire looked at Constance. "And I will tell your son, when I see him, how much you love him still."

Tears welled in her eyes. "Tell him of his little brother too. I hope they will meet someday."

"You have been so good to me," Claire said, kissing Constance's hand.

Then she went to the silver dish—the Gradalis—and carried it awkwardly to the little stream flowing from the boulders. She filled it to the brim and then carefully brought it back to the plinth and let out a sigh as she poured it over the stone. The water splashed her feet, the hem of her dress.

And a lightning shaft of magic swept her away.

She found herself standing on a beach, the dish no longer in her hands. Huge jutting rocks emerged from the waters, their square tops forming a wall that was open in the middle. A vast ocean crashed against the wall of rocks, but only a portion could get through and come gliding up the wet sand to touch her feet.

"Claire." It was Ransom's voice, thick with love.

She turned around and beheld a city brighter and larger than anything she'd ever imagined. She cupped her hands over her mouth when she saw Ransom striding across the sand to her, his arm outstretched to take her hand.

It had all been worth it.

AUTHOR'S NOTE

I first learned about the knight William Marshal in a book by one of my favorite authors, Sharon Kay Penman (the book is *When Christ and His Saints Slept*), that tells the story of King Stephen I of England (whom I based King Gervase off of). Sharon passed away while I was editing this book. I'll miss her very much and especially her books. While I knew about William Marshal through Sharon's work, this series wasn't inspired until I came across *The Greatest Knight* by Thomas Asbridge in a Kindle daily deal. I pick up many books that I never actually read, but I'm so glad I eventually found my way to this one. As I read Asbridge's biography of William Marshal (whom I nicknamed Ransom because of his early experience as a hostage to the king), I was amazed by how much his life reminded me of Owen Kiskaddon's. By the time I finished the book, I was in tears—especially as he lay on his deathbed, bidding farewell to his beloved wife, Isabel de Clare, his children, and his trusted knights.

When I cry writing certain scenes, I have a feeling that many of my readers will as well. And as my wife finished reading this book, she left the room, and I could hear her sniffling around the corner. She came back, wiping her eyes, and said she loved the ending. I hope you did as well. It's not a happily-ever-after-type ending. After the year we've all had (I'm writing this author's note on New Year's Day 2021), we've managed to survive some not-so-happily-ever-after moments. I went to the gravesite of a thirteen-year-old boy I mentored, who'd died in a tragic farming accident. My niece lost another baby. A teenager I know got cancer. And my own wife had brain surgery before Christmas, and we have more trips to a research hospital planned in the future. There are a lot of "feels" crammed into this series. Life is a miracle and a gift, but not all heroes have a Tolkien-length story: Joan of Arc, Tony Stark, William Tyndale, Abraham Lincoln, Joseph Smith. All of these examples show that a sacrifice can result in great good for many. As the greatest example of a life cut short said, "Greater love hath no man than this, that a man lay down his life for his friends" (John 15:13 King James Version).

I took many liberties in telling Ransom's story compared to actual history, but so many of the major points of this series are true to William Marshal's life. His injury while fighting off knights trying to kidnap the queen. Like Ransom, he was saved by a mysterious woman, but Marshal never found out who it was who'd saved him. His service to four Plantagenet kings (Henry the Young King, Henry II, Richard the Lionheart, and King John) was not an invention, and I believe the Plantagenet dynasty—which lasted to 1485, and perhaps longer if you count the Tudors—would not have survived for centuries were it not for Marshal's direct efforts to preserve it against all odds. There was also a sizable age gap between him and Isabel de Clare, which I adjusted for this series. The poisoner, Alix, was inspired from history as well. One of Eleanor of Aquitaine's daughters was named Alix, although she was not illegitimate, as she was born during Eleanor's marriage to the King of France. As I studied the era of these four kings, it seemed quite possible that all four of them had been poisoned.

While I was doing research for this series, my wife and I had a date night at our favorite frozen dessert shop (this was before Covid). A song came on while we ate there, and the words and the melody were just haunting to me. I pulled out my phone and asked Siri to identify it. It was Calum Scott's "You are the Reason." I'd never heard it before (sadly,

I don't watch *Britain's Got Talent* very often), but I ended up listening to it over and over again. It became Ransom and Claire's love song. After the virus struck the United States, a father-daughter duo began singing songs on Facebook and became an internet sensation. When Mat and Savanna Shaw recorded their cover of "You Are the Reason," I loved it so much. It captured all the feelings that I wanted to express in this story. If you haven't heard either version, please look it up. Mat and Savanna are amazing singers, and their music is one of the truly beautiful things to have emerged during this global pandemic.

One of the things I really enjoyed about Ransom's story is that it gives us a peek at what might have happened if Owen and Evie had ended up together. So many readers have expressed to me how much they wished those two had gotten together. Pairing Ransom and Claire also gave me a welcome opportunity to explore family life and the drama associated with it. Children were used as hostages back then, and it must have been impossibly hard for William Marshal and Isabel de Clare to give up their sons as hostages to a king they knew had murdered his own nephew. Especially since William had been a hostage himself, nearly hung from a rope in front of his father's castle.

It is also interesting to me how much Arthurian legends peek out from medieval history. The great King Andrew is, of course, my Arthur prototype. During the era of history upon which these books are based, stories of the knights of the round table became more and more common, although different versions existed. In my research, I watched Professor Dorsey Armstrong's lectures about Arthurian legends and thoroughly enjoyed the feeling of being back in grad school again.

Now that this series is done, perhaps you're wondering what's next?

Ideas come to me in many ways. One idea, in particular, came during a concert with the Piano Guys. While they played their awesome music, there was a screen behind them showing different images. One image of a small castle in Scotland amid a vast lake resonated with me.

Ideas began to bubble and stew. I've been thinking on that image and the story idea that came with it for almost two years now.

It's a story that goes back to Muirwood. Back to the *beginning* of Muirwood Abbey.

I think you're going to like it.

ACKNOWLEDGMENTS

I enjoyed writing this series so much, and so many people helped out along the way. I've had the same team for a long time, and I'm grateful for that long history. Thanks to Adrienne, Angela, Wanda, Dan, and all the others who make my books readable despite the occasional confusion I may cause. I'm grateful to my first readers (Shannon, Robin, Sandi, Travis, and Sunil) who give me early feedback on the books to make them better.

I'm also grateful for friends made along my writing journey, like all the great people at Teen Author Boot Camp, Storymakers, *Deep Magic* (which just celebrated another five years since its resurrection), and to fans all over the world, including Bonnie Scotland. (This is a nod to you, Rosie!) I've also enjoyed mentoring new friends, as well as being part of their first million words. Yes, Alli, I'm talking about you.

And now for another adventure!

ABOUT THE AUTHOR

Photo © 2016 Mica Sloan

Jeff Wheeler is the *Wall Street Journal* bestselling author of the First Argentines series, the Grave Kingdom series, the Harbinger series, the Kingfountain series, the Legends of Muirwood trilogy, the Covenant of Muirwood trilogy, the Whispers from Mirrowen trilogy, and the Landmoor series. His next book is *The Druid*, the first in the Dawning of Muirwood series. He left his career at Intel in 2014 to write full-time. Jeff is a husband, father of five, and devout member of his church. He lives in the Rocky Mountains.

Visit the Worlds of Jeff Wheeler at https://jeff-wheeler.com.